Philip Peereboom was born in Rotterdam in 1949. He studied English and Gaelic Language and Literature at the universities of Amsterdam and Utrecht. He co-wrote several English language and literature courses for secondary schools and, in cooperation with Thames Television in London, he produced a variety of educational audio-visual language programmes, like *J'aime Paris*. A few years ago he brought out a music CD, *I Wish*, under the pseudonym of Philip MacLochlainn. After living in Ireland for a while, he now lives in Wiltshire, England.

Ecuador, at Last

PHILIP PEEREBOOM
_____

Ecuador, at Last

Vanguard Press

VANGUARD PAPERBACK

© Copyright 2016
Philip Peereboom

The right of Philip Peereboom to be identified as author of
this work has been asserted by him in accordance with the
Copyright, Designs and Patents Act 1988.

All Rights Reserved

No reproduction, copy or transmission of this publication
may be made without written permission.
No paragraph of this publication may be reproduced,
copied or transmitted save with the written permission of the publisher,
or in accordance with the provisions
of the Copyright Act 1956 (as amended).
Any person who commits any unauthorised act in relation to
this publication may be liable to criminal
prosecution and civil claims for damages.

Dans Le Monde Entier
Words & Music by Françoise Hardy
© Copyright 1964 Editions Musicales Alpha Sarl.
BMG Rights Management (UK) Limited.
All Rights Reserved. International Copyright Secured.
Used by permission of Music Sales Limited.

A CIP catalogue record for this title is
available from the British Library.

ISBN 978 178465 086 5

Vanguard Press is an imprint of
Pegasus Elliot Mackenzie Publishers Ltd.

www.pegasuspublishers.com

First Published in 2016

Vanguard Press
Sheraton House Castle Park
Cambridge England

Printed & Bound in Great Britain

Acknowledgements

Many thanks to Diarra, Jorrin and Laura for checking my French and Spanish, and Melanie for checking everything.

To Melanie, with love

Introduction

Due to the never-ending tensions in the Middle East and the involvement of the main world powers, people had been waiting with bated breath for the outbreak of another world war for decades. Ever since the end of the Second World War the Middle East had been the scene of fights, short wars, attacks and reprisals – moderate Islamic administrations being overturned by extreme right-wing ones – culminating in the rise of Islamic State and the attempts of the U.S. and Britain, supported by some allies in Europe and the Middle East, to eradicate them.

The killing of U.S. soldiers in the Levant, the problems in Ukraine, the deadly attacks in Paris, the sudden spate of refugees and migrants from the Middle East and Africa and the destabilisation of Greece, to mention just a few, were all false flags, according to a fast growing number of people in the 2010s. They believed that the U.S. and some of its allies, backed by arms dealers and secret organisations, had actually created IS themselves in order to create havoc, to destabilise the world by luring Russia into a global conflict. This would give them an excuse to start a new war and gain global control. Unexpectedly though, it was not this part of the world where the war started.

The initial conflict that led to the Third World War was the direct result of disagreement on the division of the North Pole, that is, which country was allotted to explore which oilfields. Canada and Denmark laid claim to the largest parts, Norway to a smaller one, while the U.S. and Russia were, traditionally, bickering about whatever they could bicker about. They were all completely taken by surprise when China appeared on the scene, claiming vast areas of ice and sea mass. The other world powers, and many countries with them, were too stupefied to respond, since the eyes of the world had been upon the U.S. and Russia, as people generally thought the stability of the planet depended on the balance of power between these two arch rivals. This gave China the opportunity to secretly expand its naval fleet with ultramodern aircraft carriers, small, stealth-like warships, and build the most sophisticated jet fighters. More importantly perhaps, they had also invented a new weapon that emitted shock-waves and EMPs (electromagnetic pulses), which had the effect of an 'HLSI' (high-powered lethal shock impact) and enabled soldiers to kill and mutilate the enemy without having to aim at them, while electronic equipment and installations could be deactivated from a safe distance at the same time.

The Chinese had timed their attack very carefully, for it coincided with a geomagnetic solar storm. This contributed to the destabilisation and, sometimes, deactivation of the Internet in many parts of the world and, as most mobile phones and the latest generation of 'ports' (post android phones) were manufactured and programmed in China, it was fairly easy for them to deactivate these too, so that global communication practically came to a halt.

Almost every country in the world wanted to do business with China and most multinationals had stripped their 'home countries' naked, economically and financially, by transferring the production of goods to China. This led to an unprecedented number of job losses and, consequently, social unrest, while at the same time becoming more and more dependent on China, having to buy goods they could have manufactured themselves. The whole world was regularly inundated with cheap, fancy goods, tables, chairs, Christmas decorations, garlic, or any other product they wanted to dump.

Because of its financial influence, China could manipulate any currency in the world, put governments under pressure, or ignore them. With its meticulously planned economic strategy it had been busy buying raw materials, and even complete mines, in Africa and South America for decades, so it was never going to allow a handful of nations to divide the extensive oilfields under the North Pole.

For about fifty years the North Pole had gradually been shrinking due to melting icebergs and glaciers, and it had become easier than ever before to explore for natural resources. Large environmental organizations could only stand by and witness how oil companies, with their vast amounts of money and political influence, didn't give a damn about the well-being of yet another unique nature reserve.

Numerous countries were suffering from rising sea levels. The European Union, or what was left of it after falling victim to its own drive for expansion, had instructed several countries, like The Netherlands, to evacuate hundreds of thousands of people to other parts of Europe and to sacrifice large areas of land to the water. Holland, which had won respect from countries all over the world for its courageous, never-ending battle against the sea for hundreds of years to hold its head above water, was no longer allowed to spend any more money on sea defences.

Most oil companies and their political straw figures had been trying to suppress new forms of energy by blackmailing or murdering researchers and inventors (and, in some cases, their families too), and by destroying their laboratories. To the majority of people in the Western world these stories sounded like exaggerated, implausible rumours, conspiracy theories, incited by extreme left or right-wing 'terrorists', as they were called by politicians and the media.

In spite of this, most ordinary citizens believed, against all odds, in the sincerity and honesty of their politicians and heads of state. Examples of this were the attacks of 9/11, the outbreak of Ebola in Africa, the spread of the Zika virus, the wheeling and dealing of GMO food giant Monsanto (whose board of directors counted many key U.S. politicians and who were accused of attempting to blackmail governments all over the world) and the deaths of Princess Diana and Dr Kelly, the British scientist who stated that there were no weapons of mass destruction in Iraq when Saddam Hussein was president and indicated that, therefore, an invasion of that country by American and British forces was not justified. By discussing this in secret with a BBC reporter he signed, as it were, his own death warrant. Dr Kelly probably knew he was going to be sacrificed and feared an attempt on his life. In an interview he stated that if Iraq was attacked, he would be found dead somewhere in the woods. That scenario couldn't have been more precise.

Shortly after the invasion of Iraq and the chaos in Afghanistan (both strategic oil countries), strange civil wars in Libya and Syria (more oil producing countries), the continuing tensions between Israel and its 'old enemies', and the systematic vilification of Iran (another oil country) by the Western world, a global bank crisis followed, causing even more chaos.

In the meantime the oil companies kept pushing governments to become less dependent on the Middle East and exploit the resources of not only the North Pole, but of other nature reserves, such as the Amazon Forest. In the 2010s, for example, by promising health care and vast amounts of money, they had deluded and bribed politicians in Ecuador to get permission to search for oil and gas. With the aid of Chinese capital and a company from Spain (the old colonialist country), they polluted rivers and the soil, thus destroying the habitat of both indigenous people and wildlife, driving out tribes that had lived there for millenniums and killing off these people's own, natural healing methods, before these companies were eventually sued and kicked out of the country.

The pharmaceutical industry too, with its enormous influence and scaremongering practices (epidemics and pandemics), drove governments to spend billions on buying their drugs, to push alternative treatments and natural healing out of the healthcare system, and to license, after dubious tests, their own drugs. Employees and directors of one of these pharmaceutical companies tried to bribe doctors in China to get rid of centuries old, proven Chinese cures and to drive out ancient healing practices in the Amazon forest.

Due to transatlantic agreements and further globalisation, the uncontrollable power of big multinationals, certain banks and rich countries, began to pay dividends, while the issues of poverty, hunger, child labour and the plight of millions of people living in appalling conditions in the rest of the world weren't addressed.

The war lasted for only a few months, but it left the world in greater chaos and turmoil than any other world war had done before. There were no winners, only losers. People who were able to escape from the traumatic savagery of internecine warfare or waves of mass suicide in an increasingly dystopic world, left for other, less complicated, degenerated and screwed-up parts of the planet, in search of peace, space, nature and, more importantly, themselves.

1

At the plain beach bar, where the late night was shading into the early morning, some silentlystaringcustomers were sitting on their wooden stools. Roonah O'Shea, a young, slender woman from L.A., was one of them. She just sat there, thinking, listening, observing the scene around her. A few metres away, churning thoughts in his muddled mind, Erasmus Hopper, a student of Greek from the University of Iowa, sat gazing hazily at the opposite wall, stroking his greasy, dishevelled hair. On a rickety stool, very close to him, the slightly portly Bernard Chambers, a former colonel of the Canadian Army, was peering through a nearly empty wineglass at a distorted, alien world and, beyond it, almost invisible, the huge mass of the dark Pacific.

In the clear, cool air of another approaching dawn, insects with see-through, silver, sunlit wings and puny hairs on the outer reaches of their tiny black bodies were buzzing and humming through the first, cautiously peeping light shafts of the morning sun.

After polishing the glasses for the third or fourth time the barman sat down; he was exhausted and wanted to go to bed. Why didn't everybody just go home? He was so tired, too tired to open his mouth and tell them to piss off.

2

Further away on an old bed in a wooden bungalow, lay Desmond Carter – Roonah's sixty-five-year-old boyfriend. His big white hair on a thick pillow, he was in a semi-conscious state; turning from his belly to his back, from one side to the other, because of the pain in his shoulder and an earlymorningormiddleofthenight erection. The former was the result of a bungled parachute jump when he was about sixteen. It hadn't troubled him for years, but because of more intensive surfing and swimming in the past few months, it had come back.

In his misty head he wondered where he was, stretching out his hand to the place where Roonah should be lying, but it was still cool. So she's not back yet, he thought, my sweet, warm Roonah. The pressure in his bladder was building up, but he didn't feel like getting up and going to the bathroom. The very thought of it, sitting or standing there and all the light coming in; it would only wake him up, prevent him from falling asleep again, so he didn't open his eyes.

In spite of the fact that he was only half awake, his thoughts were already trying hard to come to the surface, pushing like an impatient river full of driftwood against the lock gates of his mind. Some had already managed to seep through some cracks in the thick old gates, trickling into a growing lake of deep thoughts. He didn't want the floodgates to be wide open; he'd be inundated then and they'd activate his inner unrest, the dark urge that always goaded him into action, that pushed him to move on. He could never stay in the same place for a long time; it made him restless. But Ecuador was different; the people were easy-going, life was easy and the consequences of the Third World War were hardly noticeable. For the first time in his life he felt a kind of peace and quiet had come over him. It was strange, almost eerie.

'Don't carry the world on your shoulders,' his mother always used to say, and 'Get some peace in your restless bum.' Had he found that, at last? he wondered.

His half-closed eyes were slowly waking up, looking at the low coffee table in the middle of the room, spotting traces of what he and Roonah had done in the early evening, the two fingerprinted glasses, the bottle of Cuarenta Y Tres, 43, how symbolic, their difference in age.

Why isn't she back yet? he wondered. What time is it? He wasn't too worried, for she knew what she was doing, but he was also thinking of the dark thoughts she sometimes had and he knew that Roonah still found it hard to deal with the things she'd seen during the war, like last night, when she suddenly said, 'I sometimes feel, how shall I put it, so worthless, useless. What have I achieved?' A question Desmond couldn't answer. 'It never seems to stop, Desmond; it keeps coming back, the shit, screaming kids, crying mothers. I did what I could, but I often felt so powerless, so utterly shite. Mutilated bodies, faces, that boy, I will never forget him,' she said, with tears streaming down her face.

There must be hundreds of other images that she doesn't even talk about, he thought, just like himself, actually. He also had a lot of unspoken words in his head, things he never talked about, like the stories his dad had told him about his family. He could feel them pushing themselves into his consciousness even now, but he couldn't express them; they kept on milling around in his head and sometimes, for no reason at all, old feelings of pain entered his heart. The strange thing was, they weren't even his own feelings of pain. It seemed he had somehow inherited them.

As to Roonah, it wasn't as bad now as it was a month ago, he thought, but perhaps that wasn't true; maybe she was just fed up talking about it. He thought of the long spells of silence, the quiet, pensive moments she appeared to have more and more often.

'Are you in your thinking mode again?' he had jokingly asked her a couple of times, when she reminded him of that sculpture by Rodin and he had called her *La Penseuse*. Without saying anything, she had only smiled at him, but her eyes and the lines on her forehead had told him enough.

'Your little head's so full, so full of everything.'

'Just as full as yours, darling,' was all she'd said.

3

Sitting at the bar, she was thinking about the school she'd been to, and her friends, Chris, Eileen and Aoife, the girls she'd always had such great fun with. First she wanted to be a doctor, but her life had taken a different turn. Not that it had made her unhappy, oh no, for the university, and also L.A.,– the city her family had moved to from Ireland– had been fantastic, but the words 'doctor' and 'medicine' had settled in her head like a dormant virus. When the war had started and she heard that the authorities were desperately looking for volunteers to work in hospitals on the north west coast of the U.S., where the situation was very serious, she signed up.

After five months of arduous work she came home with a testimonial, but the chaos was still in her head, like an addictive drug. She knew there was no cold turkey for this; she would have to get off it slowly.

She remembered the incredulous look in Desmond's eyes when she came back home and told him, 'I'm going away for two more months, to an island in the Caribbean, probably Haiti, to work in an *ordinary* hospital, as a kind of detox. I need to get rid of the stress, the war, the things in my head. Didn't I tell you I always wanted to work as a volunteer outside the U.S., in a third world country?'

The expression that appeared on his face made her smile, even now. He probably thought she was going crazy. She wasn't even going to a 'real' third world country, but she knew she also did it to get back to 'normal'. However, when she came back from the Caribbean, the fatigue and the chaos were still there; her head was overflowing. She needed to clear it and wanted to think only of ordinary things, like her family, Desmond, and being happy together, having a normal life with kids maybe; a sweet little boy that would look like Desmond, while Desmond would sometimes say he could see a little Roonah before him; a smart girl with big blue eyes and curly blond hair, just like her pretty mum.

He was so sweet, always worrying about her, trying to help her, but she needed her own quiet moments, time to think about everything; it was so much. Maybe she should seek help from a professional. Desmond was a great person to talk to, but she didn't want to trouble him all the time; he had plenty of worries of his own, and although he loved her, he sometimes found it hard to express his own thoughts and feelings, to throw his inhibitions overboard. He didn't have to tell her everything he was thinking, because his face was mostly like an open book and she loved the way he was, like the other day, when she'd only just come back from the Caribbean and he had surprised her.

'Shall we go to Ecuador?'

'Ecuador? Why Ecuador?'

'To get away from all the misery here, to do something else. We can start a new life there. I mean, we've talked about being completely self-sufficient before and I feel there are new and more opportunities in that country. Besides, I think we both need a break, relax, do other things; we really can't go on like this, or…'

'Ecuador, sounds really cool,' she interrupted him enthusiastically. 'I think you're right and it's a great place to go surfing.'

She could already imagine herself walking on a lovely, warm, sandy beach, looking at the woods, the mountains and the ocean.

These images made her think of Ireland again and her thoughts hovered to the part of the country where she used to live with her parents and sisters. The lush green grass, the clouds and rain that were nearly always there. Well, leave out 'nearly', she thought, laughing to herself. The smell of burnt peat rising from the chimneys, a smell she could pick out from a thousand others, the sounds of traditional music flowing outside through pub doors when she was playing outside with her friends. The hubbub and the sensitive, sometimes sad, voices, the special, violin-like sound of the melancholic uilleann pipes and she thought of the peculiar shapes of the hills and that strange mountain, Mullaghmore, which could be seen in the distance from the end of the village, near the campsite. Although they were really there, they also existed in her young head as mountains from a fairy-tale, looking so mysterious and desolate. And of course there was Lahinch, the small town on Liscannor Bay, where it was great to go surfing.

Their cottage, just round the corner of the main street, with the noisy, squeaking, old sash windows and the red curtains. The wooden dinner table with the linen tablecloth, the brass lamp hanging over it and the creaky chairs grandmother had given them, around it. The ever-burning candles, the reassuring, red glow of the sacred heart lamp, the straw St. Bridget's cross over the door, the delicate blue image of Maria, with her peaceful, fine, white, innocent face. She could see it all before her, her mother putting the food on the table and the windows misting over immediately. Irish stew, fish and chips from the chippy, potatoes, cabbage.

It did look a bit shabby now that she thought back to it, but it was so pleasant there. She'd felt so happy. She didn't have a bedroom of her own; she had to share one with two younger sisters, but that didn't matter. If it was cold upstairs, they would sometimes sleep together in her younger sister's double bed. It was so cosy, the three of them under the eiderdown. Usually they didn't go back to their own beds after that. The winter was generally very wet too, but once in a while there was frost with beautiful, thick icy flowers on the small panes, where she could always feel a draught.

More and more often she received signals of her father's growing dissatisfaction, like when she heard him say, 'T is impossible to find a good job here. I was at the job agency in Ennis this morning, but there was nothing, nothing at all and I still haven't heard anything from the recruitment agency in Limerick either. I've sent out a lot of letters and emails too, but you don't even get a reply these days. It's driving me crazy, love.'

Maybe it wasn't so difficult in Dublin or Belfast, but in the rest of the country it seemed impossible to find a job. Her dad had changed jobs a couple of times and there had been weeks when he was at home every day, for weeks at a stretch, despondently waiting for the phone-call that never came. It was an age-old story; hundreds of thousands of Irish people had emigrated in the course of time for that reason, especially to the U.S., but she hoped it wouldn't get that far. How could she live without this funny, little village, the music, the dancing, the old Irish tales, her friends and relatives, the mountains, the moonscape of the Burren, the ocean?

One evening, when she came home from a friend, she saw her dad sitting at the old pine table.

'I've got some good news. I've been hired for the job. At last!'

His face was beaming and the yellowish light of the lamp accentuated his happy smile, but apart from her mother, nobody knew what the job was about. So the rumours she'd heard were true, she thought.

'What kind of job is it, Dad?' she asked, wanting to share his excitement. 'And where is it? Here in Clare, in Limerick, in Cork?'

'Los Angeles.'

She would never forget how the name of that city came out of his mouth, the way he said it, two magic words, four dancing syllables.

'Wow! Very cool, Dad,' she exclaimed, but she wasn't sure if she meant it; she could hear the hesitation in her own voice.

Her dad had probably spotted the panic in her eyes, sensed her feelings, seen she had turned pale.

'Don't you like it then?' he went on.

'It's all right, Dad, I know you want the best for all of us, but it's quite something, moving to the U.S., leaving all my friends behind, our house, this village, Clare, Ireland.'

'I know what you mean, sweetheart; I've been haunted by those thoughts myself. I wasn't sure if I would ever get this job, so your mother and I decided not to say anything about it until it was certain I'd got it.'

She was quiet for a moment. So many things, her whole little life and world, were buzzing through her head.

'I'd hoped the very letters, L.A., would make you enthusiastic, but I was wrong,' her dad continued, with tiny tears in his eyes.

She felt sorry for him; he was such a wonderful dad.

'It's really OK, Dad. Don't worry. I am happy.'

While her father went on talking about L.A. to her sisters and mum, Roonah was thinking of her boyfriend, Mick. She would have to leave him behind too, but it was as if she had already had a sign, a premonition, that this was going to happen when they were in Galway the other day. The weather was atrocious. Standing in the pouring rain, gazing at the fast flowing River Corrib, she saw the head of a seal emerge from the water.

'It was looking at me, Mick!'

'What?'

'That seal, over there. Look! There were tears in its eyes.'

Mick looked at the fast-flowing river, but saw nothing.

But she knew the seal was there for her, and that it wanted to tell her something, say goodbye to her before it disappeared again. She turned round and looked at Mick, with his short, ginger hair, standing under his lame umbrella a couple of metres away from her and felt his utter loneliness, knowing he thought he didn't belong there, that he couldn't get into her world. It made her feel sad and she got this feeling that there was always some kind of fate lurking somewhere, in a dark alley, round the next corner, behind her, and that it was ready to pounce on her, like an invisible enemy. She wanted to go against it, but knew it was no use.

'I don't know what to say, Mick,' she said softly through the rain, wet strands of hair sticking to her face.

'There's a strange look in your eyes, Roonah, an eerie, cool, absent-minded, frosted glass glance,' he said. 'I've seen it before and it scares me. Like now; I'm talking to you, but you're not really looking at me; it's as if you're staring back into your own soul, very deep, faraway, into another dimension almost. What's up with you?'

'But that seal was really looking at me.'

'OK, so what? Why d…'

What followed never reached her; she had shut herself off. She was aware of it and wondered why she always did that. Did it have anything to do with that seal, was it Mick's fault, or was it something else? She remembered how earlier that year, on a Sunday afternoon in July, when she saw a squirrel get under a car, she had let out a scream and the cutting, petrifying sound that came out of her mouth had struck the bone marrow of Mick's mind like an axe, completely paralysing him and she remembered the terrified, bewildered look in his eyes when she cried, howled and cursed the cruel world.

The eyes of the seal; they kept looking at her while Mick was slowly dissolving in the background. On that bleak afternoon in Galway it had become clear that they belonged to two different worlds, forever.

In spite of the sad feeling that had come over her, when her dad said they were going to emigrate, she knew there was something in America that attracted her, that told her she had to go there. Later that night her father talked to her again, trying to explain everything, doing his best to reassure her.

'You're sweet, Daddy,' she said, and kissed him on the cheek, smiling.

The following days she started packing the things she wanted to take with her.

Most of the girls at school envied her, while the next-door neighbours, Mick Nestor, the flute player, and Mr Hynes, who was so good at telling Irish stories and tales, full of rhyme and rhythm, told them one evening, with sorrowful eyes, how sad it was that another Irish family was leaving the village and Ireland, for good. 'For good', it sounded pretty awful.

After her initial fears had subsided, Roonah began to look forward to their departure. A few months later they lived in L.A., in a wonderful house with a large garden and an enormous drive. She loved it, like the rest of the family.

At first she still wanted to study medicine but, inspired by her English teacher, a young woman in her thirties, who taught English literature with a lot of passion, she decided to enrol for American and English Literature. Unfortunately, the teachers at university didn't always have the passion this teacher had, but nevertheless the programme was very interesting and she graduated hands down. Well, yes, literature and Ireland, she thought, rain, fog and sunshine, sometimes all of them at the same time, on the same day. She would love to go back there one day, maybe for a longer time, she thought.

4

'I bet you're not here to improve your Greek,' she suddenly said to Erasmus, smiling.

He didn't respond right away, for it was already late and he had been drinking. Besides, he was thinking about something else and therefore couldn't quite follow what she was on about. He looked into her direction; she was quite good-looking and although it seemed odd, her voice with that Irish American accent somehow sounded familiar to him.

'Can I have a another rum and coke, please?' he asked the barman.

He took a sip from his glass, while his other hand tried to stop his tired, heavy head from falling to one side. He muttered something, but it was barely audible.

'You're very pretty, but it's a waste of your life, an old guy like him.'

She chuckled. She had become used to men making remarks about the age gap between Desmond and herself. She had often heard people saying offensive things about lesbians and gay men. First it offended her, but she no longer cared what people said; it was their problem, not hers. It was difficult enough to stay in command of her own life and she thought of her time at university, where other students always pressurised her to binge with them. She didn't see the need to drink alcohol, but it was very hard, for sometimes it was the only way to meet people and make friends, but at the same time she didn't want to be dragged into boozing, or 'surrender' to these guys, who were obviously only trying to get her into bed.

She remembered that handsome, curly-headed guy at a university party, the macho boy who was hanging around in the basement where the toilets were. Chatting her up, saying he liked her dress, her lovely hair, her eyes, he asked her would she give him a kiss. Stupidly enough, she did, although everything inside her told her not to, but she always found it so hard to say 'no' to people who were friendly to her and she didn't want to hurt anybody. The guy took hold of her hand and kissed her right back and, to her own surprise, she even let him. Was she secretly longing for it? she asked herself, and did it really have anything to do with not wanting to hurt anybody? Is that what this guy instinctively felt? He was so charming. She wanted to run away, but she couldn't. That wouldn't be friendly at all, would it?

After that, with his luring voice and seductive, cloudy eyes, he had asked her to come into the toilet. There was nobody inside, he said, and he could give her a good time, an orgasm like she'd never had before and he immediately started caressing her shoulders with his fingers.

'Don't!' she said, but maybe not convincingly enough.

'Don't worry, I won't hurt you,' he said. 'You look real pretty. What's your name? You sound Irish.'

Again those fingers on her shoulders.

'Just give me a hand job then. We can both have a good time. You're really gorgeous. Come on,' he almost whispered, while his sensitive fingers touched her breasts. 'No, no sex,' he hastened to add, when he saw she recoiled. 'Let's just be nice to each other.'

'Run!' a voice cried out in her head, but she couldn't move and another voice told her to be nice. It was so confusing. She was almost in the toilet, when she felt his hand softly caressing her back, holding her, and it felt so good.

Suddenly she flicked a switch in her head, broke from his grip and ran away.

'Don't run off like this,' he said, almost menacingly, grabbing her hand again and putting it on his fly, moving it over his stiff dick. He started groaning and she quickly withdrew her hand, but almost, yes almost, so hard and he was so charming.

Not that this guy here at the bar had to be like them, she thought, but she wanted to keep her own life under control.

Because of the remark Erasmus had made, Bernard's glazy eyes looked at Roonah. Isn't she beautiful? he thought. He wanted to say something to her, but changed his mind.

'No more wine for me, thanks. A Scotch, please.'
'I'm closing.'
'Don't make my life difficult.'
'Time to go, Señorita, Señoras,' the barman said, looking irritated at Bernard.

'Yes, you do look pretty, Cutey.' Erasmus said again, slurring the words. How he said this, with a fake coolness, which didn't go with his unexciting clothes and appearance, she knew that if he had been sober, he would never have said it to her. She couldn't help laughing.

Erasmus was thinking of all the loves he'd had till now and how tiresome those relationships usually were. Everything had to come from him; it was always one-way traffic. He was getting fed up; all those bloody girls and women. There were always issues. Even now, when he said to this girl she was pretty, she just laughed at him. Why? He never had any issues with his computer, playing games, all by himself.

He was happy the rum and coke brought down a few barriers, made it easier for him to say to this girl what he wanted and he remembered how he'd been able to have a good look at her yesterday, or was it the day before? He wasn't sure, but it didn't matter. Enjoying the scene, the waves, the heat, a soda in his hand, mirror shades on his nose, he could watch her inconspicuously from the beach pavilion when she came out of the water with her surfboard, the glistening grains of sand on her arms and face. So cool, so sexy. Her sensual, tight little arse, the wet, blond hair, the pretty blue eyes.

He'd also seen her friend, that old jerk, floating on his surfboard. Apparently his name was Desmond, and sometimes she gave him surf lessons. Where the hell had that old sucker found such a good-looking young chick? he wondered. He wouldn't mind getting a few surf lessons from her, or any other lessons, for that matter.

All the way from his overloaded brain the sentence, 'I would love to kiss you,' was trying to find its way through his throat and mouth but, once more, it didn't go well. Slurring the words, they came out like a slow stream of mud.

5

'Time to go now. Please. I'm closing,' the barman called again, quite unfriendly this time.

Nobody paid any attention to what he said; they just went on talking. He had already switched off the music, but now and then, when it was quiet for a moment, Roonah could still hear some music. It probably came from one of the wooden beach huts, or villas, as they were officially called, she supposed. Apart from some locals it was mainly people from Europe and the U.S. who lived in them.

She couldn't quite place the fragments of the music, as they came from far beyond her earliest memories. It sounded rather nostalgic, but, then again, isn't all music pure nostalgia? Like a soulmate, it accompanies you, takes you back to personal experiences, schooldays, love, misery, friends and the feelings you had at a particular moment.

Now that it was quiet at the bar, she could hear the lyrics quite well. She liked the song, and the fine, French, female voice that sang it. The words came drifting towards her, on erotic waves of warm silence from a no-man's-land of time, somewhere between the hours of darkness and the rising of the sun:

Dans le monde entier, cette nuit est pareille
A tant d'autres nuits quand disparaît le soleil
Où tant de bonheur côtoie tant de détresse
Tant de choses meurent pendant que d'autres naissent.
Mais ce soir tu n'es pas là
Ce soir tu ne viendras pas
Et tu es si loin de moi
J'ai peur que tu m'oublies déjà

6

The music from the old-fashioned turntable softly slipped through the open window and flew as far as its wings would carry it. Beside the window was a very stylish, old leather sofa, but despite the music it was as if there was no life in the room, and it was still dark, so it was hard to make him out, the slender young man. He'd had just a little too much wine and sat there, thinking of the past with tears in his eyes.

He was not the only one to do so, because however pleasant it was in Ecuador, there were many people who thought back to Europe with a certain sadness. As to the lives of these new, '(self-)displaced persons', they had changed so dramatically as a result of all the recent events. They drank a lot more alcohol during their ruminations now than they used to and more and more of them started taking drugs. There was always an excuse for having a party and a drink, for living life to the full, while there were also people who went into 'retreat', in the darkness of the Amazon forest to 'work with Ayahuasca, a drink that took them to their deepest, inner selves, their unconscious 'I', and gave them insight into the spirits of the earth, so that they could get closer to themselves, and become more spiritual, or self-confident. Some people claimed that, during the sessions, they could look into the minds of acquaintances, friends or family and knew what those people, who were far away, maybe even asleep, in the U.S. or Europe, were thinking. In this way, by looking through the minds of these people, they were better able to look at themselves. How bizarre.

The young man on the couch, Albert du Châtenier, was in his twenties and a great grandchild, but probably not in a direct line, of a well-known French writer from the nineteenth century. Some of his relatives maintained it was Emile Zola, whereas others claimed it was Gustave Flaubert. They never seemed to agree, so maybe the truth lay somewhere in the middle or perhaps it wasn't true at all. In his room, shrouded in a semi-darkness that was gradually dissolving in the indirect light of the rising sun, which crept warily inside through a small window pane, one could distinguish an easel and a canvas with some soft, red strokes on it. Next to the easel, on a narrow table, lay a palette with the finest shades of paint, a painting in itself; around it a dozen or so half-squeezed out tubes of oil paint were patiently waiting to be used again, together with turpentine, some other grimy, slightly caked bottles and a heap of old rags with mainly red, blue and black patches. There was also a delicate, stylish, French armchair with a cherry red cushion and an equally elegant white table with fine, thin legs. When the first real rays of the sun had climbed over the windowsill, it seemed as if the cherry red cushion was on fire.

Tiny white figures, reminiscent of Degas' ballet dancers, resting in separate, small paintings on the wall, appeared to be slowly waking from a spell and danced together until the sun went down, which was the moment when they stood still once more. Caught in a shaft of bright sunlight, myriads of little particles of dust twirled through the edge of light and darkness, downward, back into an anonymous invisibility, sometimes together, but mostly stubbornly solitary. At the bottom of a cut crystal wineglass, with greasy fingerprints on the curvature and soft lines of lips near the rim, lay grains of sediment, a dried up ring of red wine.

Although he was a young man, he often thought of what he called *'les bons vieux jours'*, like the moment his parents bought him his first motorbike. He was only twelve when he started racing it. He appeared to be a *wunderkind*; everything went perfect, right from the start. The track, the speed, the wind, freedom, the whole ball of wax was going through his head. There, in front of him, his brother's bike; it was flying. It was going too fast for him to catch at that moment, but it only took a couple of races before he became the faster of the two.

On Saturday afternoons, if the sun was shining, it was always busy in the garden, with frames and other bike parts lying all over the place. His dad would be working on the bikes to make them go faster and better and the special atmosphere attracted some friends as well. His mum was there with them; she was just as enthusiastic as everybody else. Sometimes he had the idea she was even more fanatical than his dad, and she was always busy looking after them, making sandwiches, getting lemonade for him, his brother and his friends, making coffee for herself and pouring wine for his hard-working dad, who didn't usually drink coffee. Unfortunately, his dad was a heavy smoker and saw to it that his wife was never without a fag either. Would it have made any difference if he hadn't done this, or if his mother hadn't smoked?

Albert wasn't always happy. As he grew older he began to hate all those race weekends more and more and wanted to spend more time at home, indulging in his real passion, painting. One day he told his father this, but the look on the latter's face said enough.

He even laughed at his son when he said,

'You're not a real bloke; you're just a *mauviette*.'

The last word cut him deep. Albert felt sick and sad and resolved never to say anything about his thoughts and feelings again.

'Calls himself a dad, the *con*,' he whispered to the velvet curtain in his bedroom, somehow afraid his short-tempered father could still hear him.

Of course Albert's father noticed his son tried to evade him and shut himself off from him, but it didn't worry him; his son just needed toughening up a bit and sometimes he looked at his son in a provoking way or said things like, 'Don't you speak to your father any more?'

Albert didn't take the bait; he'd had enough, although he was burning to shout at his father, call him names. A few weeks later, when his father was goading him again, he could no longer restrain himself.

'Just leave me alone, you fucking bastard. Don't keep pestering me. Can't you see I've had enough? I want to paint, paint, paint, big canvases, bright colours, so please fuck off with your offensive talk and your bloody motorbikes,' he shouted, left the house and spent the night at Jean Paul's, a mate of his.

That fateful Tuesday. He had just come home from school. His father and mother, in the hall with the stone floor, their voices faltered, the air was so thick, it could be cut with a knife, an icy silence interrupted by a draught, the rustling bitter wind pulling at the door behind him, sucking it open and almost shutting it again with a bang.

'What's going on here? What's wrong, Mum?' he asked, his eyes going from his mum to his dad, and back again, but there was no answer. His dad looked glum and there were tears of tragedy and silent sorrow in his mum's hollow eyes.

The words 'throat cancer' reverberated somewhere in the air, high up in the hall, very far away, near the ceiling, in another dimension it seemed, and then slowly died away with a lonely echo. The door behind him was sucked slightly open and then shut again, with one big bang. A small, pitiful heap on the floor of the passage, in an empty world. His mother's pale hand on his hair, his father sobbing in a corner. He took her hand, but she was so... he didn't know, so different, volatile almost, and it was as if she wanted to withdraw her hand, and walk away from him. He clutched her dress, searching for a hold, a tuft of grass on a bare mountain. He stood up, buried his face, crying useless tears that sank into a sad, soaked dress. He wanted to keep her with him, forever.

A soft, almost inaudible voice spoke.

'Keep up your spirits, sweetheart. It's not the end of the world. Use your feelings to paint. Follow your heart, travel the world,' she said.

He went to his room and didn't want to come out any more. Every day, for hours on end, he would sit there, all by himself, crying, and there was nobody to help him; his brother didn't live at home any more and his dad was much too distressed himself, too full of feelings of guilt. Maybe rightly so, he thought.

Sitting on the couch in his cottage on the beach, the ghastly images of his helpless, dazed parents came back to him. How consumed by grief they were, looking almost like ghosts. In spite of his mother's words he couldn't paint; the canvases remained vacant, like the expression on his mother's face. Whenever he looked at her, she seemed to be light-years away, staring into an unknown universe. After only eleven weeks she passed away. If the cancer had been diagnosed earlier, or if she'd gone to the doctor the moment she felt something was wrong, she might still have lived. Although he'd seen it coming, he fell into a vacuum and lost interest in everything. It was also the end of his racing career. Sadly, it felt as if he had finally found a good excuse to give up racing.

His dad, stricken with inconsolable grief, deeply disillusioned, drowned his sorrow in the silent, dark desert that once was the garden. At first it was hardly noticeable, but then, bit by bit, the plants that were no longer looked after and trimmed by his mum, took over the garden, encroached upon the house and the shed. The poison ivy, twisting and turning, choked the bike frames; nature was claiming them back. The brown, carbolineum impregnated planks of the fence between the garden and street started rotting and crumbled. Some came loose and fell off after a while, making the garden into a place where drunk men urinated, dogs defecated and dirt accumulated. The echoes of the last peal of laughter on a Saturday afternoon had long died away.

Albert realised he badly needed to get away from the house and his father. Why he had lingered at home for such a long time, he still couldn't understand. Looking back at it; all those empty days, the boredom, his listlessness. Even the art academy he went to was nothing but a waste of time. Although he loved it, he hardly ever attended classes and didn't achieve anything. The outside world, from which he was isolated by a huge, heavy, closed, non-transparent curtain, which was never drawn open, became a stifling place, saturated with negative energy.

He made up his mind to go to Paris, where an unattached aunt of his, his mother's only sister, lived. She'd always been the only relative who came to see them regularly, and especially during the past few months she had been very supportive. He remembered how, long before all the misery began, he would sometimes go to Paris and stay with her. She was such a lovely woman and he knew he was always welcome at her place in the old, stately building in the *deuxième*.

He would never forget that day when he arrived at the huge front door, the *court* behind it and him climbing the dark, endless, stone spiral staircase to her *appartement* and her opening the door, taking him in her arms, cuddling and kissing him.

She was so happy to see him. He'd always been such a lovely, tender boy, and she often wondered why his father kept pressurising him. Why did this sensitive boy have to race bikes? If she could see his love-hate relationship with racing, why couldn't his father, or her own sister, for that matter?

She vowed to be there for him, always, although she was deeply worried about his state of mind, Albert being such a loner and having so little self-esteem.

Albert loved Paris. Almost every night, for hours at a stretch, he wandered along the big boulevards and avenues, looking at the beautifully illuminated shop windows with the mannequins that would sometimes stare back at him, as if they wanted to tell him something. They had the same, tight, void, infinite expressions in their faces as his mother had had, just before she died, he thought.

Coming back, standing in the quiet, dark, deserted street where his aunt lived, looking up at her window, he saw her shadow on the ceiling. How relieved she was when he returned home from his nocturnal walks.

'Oh, Albert, *je suis très heureux de voir que tu es de retour,*' were the first words she always said when he came in.

He recalled how, sometimes, for no apparent reason, he fell into a seemingly bottomless pit of sadness, while at other moments he felt he had the strength to fight his negative thoughts and emotions and wouldn't allow himself to be dragged down, and although he loved looking at the romantic lights of Pont Neuf and the Île de la Cité, and was captivated by the watery reflections in the River Seine and the puddles on the road, the magic of the mighty buildings, upside down, the distorted lights of the bridges, and the myriads of red and yellow lights, which didn't only remind him of his red bike, or his mother and her passion for motorcycle racing, but also of movement and love, he nearly always dreaded the approaching, suicidal darkness of the long evenings and nights in autumnal Paris.

One evening he found himself in Quartier Latin, enjoying the buzz of the small, intimate streets, the impressive, old Sorbonne building and the many restaurants and bars. It was an Indian summer night, late in September, and a warm wind was blowing through the narrow Rue de Baune. It was busy; everybody was trying to find a vacant seat at one of the cafés.

There he was, at a *terrasse* in the Rue Mazarine, a street just off the Boulevard Saint Germain, a misty glass of cold white wine in his hand, a figure who had materialised from a dream. The moment Albert saw him he was mesmerised and felt a swarm of butterflies in his belly; he didn't know what was happening to him and, enchanted by the smile that came to him, he could not but smile back.

Sitting at a round table with a red tablecloth, the guy pointed at a chair next to him. The white lattice chair beckoned, called him. He sat down and a glass of cool, sweet white wine was put in front of him. His eyes went from the glass to the young man beside him. They started nattering about the things around them and the weather, when, out of the blue, the young man asked him,

'Are you interested in philosophy? Have you seen any work of Amelie Chabannes, the artist?'

'The name rings a bell,' Albert replied. 'I've heard it mention at the academy. Why?' he asked, surprised at the turn their conversation had taken.

'She's very good, I think; in her work she explores the limitless notion of Identity, its various derivations and representations within philosophy, psychology and art history. Identity, a concept that keeps my mind busy. You should really see her drawings and portraits.'

Here was someone who was kicking his lazy butt, stirring him up, challenging him, and that in his own field, art, he thought. The conversation proceeded in the same vein and he thought of his aunt, who was very sweet and understanding, but they hardly ever had any conversations like this.

This evening and the unexpected meeting with this young person, Sylvain, who looked so gorgeous with his dark, curly hair and white linen suit, appeared to put a permanent end to his everlasting solitude. He worked for one of the major fashion houses in Paris and told Albert all sorts of funny things he had experienced. Albert laughed; he hadn't laughed like this for a long time. They didn't only talk about art and fashion, but also about the world and their mutual dislike of politics.

'What do you do with yourself all day?' Sylvain asked.

'I paint; I'm at the École des Beaux Arts.'

'In Rue Bonaparte?'

'Yes, only a few streets away from here, as you probably know. A fine building. I'm thinking of becoming a painter or an art historian.'

'Mm, interesting. I wouldn't mind having a look at your paintings, if that's all right,' Sylvain said.

'Sure,' Albert replied.

He was thrilled, for apart from his mother and aunt, nobody, not even his father, had ever asked him that.

Sylvain was rather tired and wanted to go to bed in time; for weeks he had been spending many long hours at the fashion studio, so they arranged to meet at the same place the next Friday. Sylvain suggested meeting earlier, so that they could have dinner together.

Albert remembered that when he came home that night he had this wonderful sensation; his whole body was tingling with happiness and the smile on his aunt's face made him even happier. The next morning, having breakfast with her on the balcony, it was as if he could see himself, sitting on his chair, radiating happiness, with the sun shining through the French windows into the apartment.

'What's happened?' she asked.

He blushed and all he could give was a big smile.

She got the message.

'I'm so happy for you,' she said.

How different he looked, how happy. She hadn't seen him like that for years. Actually, she didn't even know him like that. Maybe he didn't want to talk about it now, she thought, so she didn't ask any further questions, but she couldn't help feeling a transparent wave of intense joy coming over her; his quiet happiness was contagious. She stood up, made some coffee and put some fresh croissants in the basket.

His eyes followed her. Shouldn't he tell her everything?

That week flew past, as if he had been dreaming everything and all of a sudden it was Friday again and he found himself back at the café. It wasn't a dream, for Sylvain was there too, with that very same engaging smile on his face and the beautiful, fathomless, dark, adoring eyes looking deep into him. The butterflies were back in droves.

They started dating regularly and had a great time together, visiting Musée d'Orsay, Centre Pompidou, galleries, theatres and making long walks through the city. One afternoon Sylvain took him to the studio where he worked. Everybody was very friendly, apart from a young guy who cast a contemptuous glance at him and made a derogatory remark. .

'Who is he?' Albert asked.

'Just a friend,' Sylvain answered.

'Just a friend?'

'Yes, why?'

For the first time in his life he had been jealous and now, sitting in his armchair in Ecuador, thinking back to Sylvain's body-language, he still asked himself what was going on that afternoon.

'What's your problem?' Sylvain asked, with a dark, uncanny look. 'I explained, didn't I? Come on, let's go to my place,' he added and walked on, not waiting for a reply.

Albert was overpowered. It reminded him of how his father often spoke to him, but an argument with Sylvain was the last thing he wanted, so he didn't push it any further.

But why doesn't Sylvain just tell me what's going on? he wondered. It gave him an uncomfortable feeling; it was as if a barrier of coolness had arisen between him and Sylvain, but he pushed the thought away; he didn't want to know. After a couple of minutes Sylvain calmed down and spoke to him as if nothing had happened, and when they were walking down Rue Saint Honoré, he took Albert's hand in his and squeezed it, softly, lovingly. Albert blushed, his pulse fluttering in his throat.

Sylvain's apartment was in Rue Saint Martin, not far from where the once famous Jean Paul Gaultier used to live. Albert thought of the many walks he had made through Paris and remembered walking through this street as well, past that rather unusual building of the Musée des Arts et Métiers, but he was no longer alone now. He couldn't help looking at the people around them, wondering what they were thinking, but the hand in his hand; it felt so good.

The flat wasn't particularly big, but it exuded a special atmosphere, an air of creativity, art. Wow! Just look at that, he thought, when he saw the wonderful, big modernist paintings on the wall, the beautiful oriental objects d'art on a dainty table by the window, while another room hung full of old black and white photographs of famous couturiers. Even the kitchen radiated something refreshing with its colourful jars and the large, abstract, African country scene painted on the wall.

'Sylvain, this is really beautiful. I have never seen anything like this before.'
'Thanks.'

Observing Albert, how he stood looking at the paintings with his bright eyes and tender face, the long eye lashes and tight line of his chin, his beautiful straight nose, Sylvain wondered how he could best tell him about Richard without hurting him.

As he started talking about Richard, Albert went to have a look at the black and white photographs in the other room. Looking at the photos, listening to Sylvain, Albert put every word, the intonation of every sentence Sylvain said, on a scale of tenderness and emotion. Was Sylvain telling him the truth?

he wondered. But what was the point? He knew he had to take Sylvain's word for it and he didn't want this silly incident to spoil their evening together.

The beautiful photos invaded his thinking, while Sylvain was still talking to him; imagesandsoundsweremixedtogether.

It was quiet for a couple of minutes; Albert was thinking, while Sylvain stood waiting for some form of reaction.

'I'll start doing the cooking,' he then said to relieve the silence of its tension.
'Is there anything I can do to help?'
'No, I'm fine. They're good, are they?
'Yes, I love black and white photographs.'
'Can I pour you a glass of red wine?'
'Thanks. Cheers. This really smells delicious. What is it?'
'A secret, for you.'
'Sorry I was so suspicious,' Albert said.
'It's all right and I'm sorry I didn't explain everything right away earlier,' Sylvain said, kissing Albert on his forehead.

Albert closed his eyes and felt Sylvain's fingers moving gently through his hair, down to his neck and back up again, softly touching his temples. They just stood there, holding each other's hands, smiling, looking at each other, until the first few words of love emerged from their mouths, and while the low hanging sun shone over their faces from a side-window, more and more words followed, evolving into sentences about their love relationship, the future, and sex.

Albert was yearning for Sylvain; he wanted to hold his naked body against his own, caress him, ruffle his beautiful hair, feel his warm tenderness, touch his softness, but he also longed to be touched, stroked and loved himself.

Through the gap between the dark blue curtains the sun of the next Parisian morning let its new light fall over two semi-naked bodies, the creased, white sheet, covering their legs and loins.

The late summer weather couldn't be any better. If they had a moment to spare in the evening, they could be seen in the atmospheric light of the old-fashioned street lanterns, under the big, brown-yellowing chestnut trees of the Champs Elysées, in Jardin du Luxembourg or at their favourite *terrasse* on the Boulevard des Italiens.

After about two months Albert finally took Sylvain home, to introduce him to his aunt. He was quite nervous and wondered how she would react, look at Sylvain, in spite of the fact that he knew she was open-minded.

'This is Sylvain,' he said, looking anxiously at her eyes, her face, perhaps trying to discover something that would betray her feelings for him and Sylvain, their relationship, but there was no sign of disapproval whatsoever. All he could see was tenderness and some tears she was trying to suppress.

'I'm so happy to meet you, Sylvain.'

She wasn't really surprised at what she saw; it was rather a confirmation of what she had known all along and it didn't worry her, as long as 'her' Albert was happy, and then again, who was she to judge? She looked at Albert and Sylvain again. How beautiful and happy they were.

Trying to imagine what was going through his aunt's head, for Albert these tense minutes felt like hours, while his aunt just didn't know what to say; she was so deeply moved by the intense love she saw.

'To be honest, I never thought anything like this could exist, real love between two men, or that it could be as beautiful as yours,' she finally said.

How does one say things like these, she wondered, and although it hadn't come as a complete surprise, she still needed time to let it sink in.

'I don't know what to say, Albert. Sorry about the tears, but it's so special, so romantic, so beautiful and I'm really happy for you, for both of you.'

She embraced Albert and Sylvain and kissed them.

'You're wonderful; all these sweet words,' Albert said, a bit overwhelmed, wiping her tears away, kissing her eyes.

'I think it runs in the family,' Sylvain commented. 'Your aunt is just as lovely as you.'

Even her apartment seemed to reflect the happiness of the two, she thought, with the sun sending its low shafts of early autumn light far into the room, brightening the vase and flowers on the table, making it look like a painting by Van Gogh, bringing back to life the dull, old, dusty brown-beige canapé, adding gloss and depth to its modest colourfulness, while the sombre faces in the ancient paintings on the far wall looked into the room with a new freshness.

Having said what she felt, she was relieved, happy, and while she first seemed to almost trudge through the house, Albert now heard firm footsteps on the kitchen floor and he was proud of her, although he realised how difficult it must have been for her to have had someone as sad as him about the house, when she was overcome with grief herself, after losing her only sister, his mother.

He went to the kitchen, where she was arranging the roses Sylvain had given her, embraced and thanked her.

'I love you and I'm really sorry for having been so miserable sometimes.'

She didn't know whether she wanted to cry or laugh, but it made no difference; more tears of joy and sadness ran over her cheeks into Albert's hair.

'Don't think about it. I'm glad you're happy now.'

During the weeks that followed Sylvain was working overtime for a big international fashion show that was coming up, while Albert was very busy at the academy of art, as there was so much he wanted to catch up with and although they kept in touch, they didn't see each other. At the end of the third week Sylvain asked Albert to come to his apartment, so that they could go out for dinner that night.

It was a beautiful day and, before going to Sylvain's place, Albert wanted to enjoy the last fits of the fine weather, to get some fresh air. He decided to go for a long morning walk through the Bois de Boulogne and have a coffee at the Chalet des Îles.

It was very quiet in the park; apart from a few cyclists and two or three young mothers with prams, he had the whole place to himself. Albert loved the sound of his shoes shuffling through the falling leaves. In the distance he could already see the lovely old Chalet des Îles, one of his favourite restaurants. He realised he hadn't been there for a long time, but nothing seemed to have changed. It was quite reassuring. After a coffee and a wonderful *tarte aux fruits*, he got up again, put on his coat and left. He decided to walk along the water and follow the Route de Suresnes to Avenue Foch, where he took the RER to Invalides, got out and crossed the beautiful Pont Alexandre III. He loved the sculpted lanterns, the gilded sculptures, the extensive views of the Seine; even the arches underneath the bridge were gorgeous, he thought. He walked past the magnificent Petit Palais, which lay there, bathing in the light of the autumn sun, to the Place de la Concorde and got on the metro to Palais Royal, where a peculiar old lady was anxiously feeding the birds in the gardens of the peaceful inner courtyard with its stylish *terrasses* and delicate lines of trees with iron-cast benches underneath. He left through the archway at the back and found himself in the narrow Rue de Beaujolais. After that came Rue Vivienne and some less interesting streets, until he came to the Boulevard Poissonnière, a name which somehow always reminded him of Émile Zola. He studied the Porte Saint Denis from top to toe and enjoyed the finely shaped facades of the elegant buildings.

A clock, high up a building not far from the street where Sylvain lived, told him it was still early, so he decided to sit down on a bench in Square Emile Chautemps, a small park on the Rue Saint Martin, and read his book, *En Attendant Godot*. When he looked up from his book because some dark clouds were moving between him and the sun, he saw Richard walking down the street. Richard? What was his business here? It was obvious he had come from Sylvain's apartment. He waited for about ten minutes, getting more and more angry, deliberating whether he should go home or not, but in the end he resolved to go to Sylvain's apartment.

His heart was pounding, when his nervous finger pressed the large, round, brass doorbell. Sylvain opened the door and wanted to embrace him, but Albert's cool attitude told him something was wrong. Albert stepped into the hall and smelled a familiar scent, Richard's, the one he had smelled at the fashion studio some time ago.

'Is that why I couldn't come earlier, because you had a date with that bastard?' he burst out. 'You're cheating on me, using me!'

He wanted to run away, but still asked Sylvain why Richard had come.

'He never came in here,' Sylvain replied, 'and he just turned up.'

It didn't sound very convincing, although he had told the truth, because he had left Richard standing at the door, but Albert felt he was being deceived.

'I'm going home. You do as you please.'

Sylvain looked at him and saw the angry, sad expression in his eyes. It hurt him.

'Please, Albert, let me explain. There's nothing wrong,' he said, taking Albert by his arm. He wanted to kiss him.

'Piss off!' Albert said, tore himself loose and left.

Powerless and speechless, Sylvain looked at Albert disappearing down the stairways.

When Albert came outside the sun was gone and a light rain was falling. He couldn't and wouldn't go straight back to his aunt's and wandered around in the drizzle for hours.

Why has the fucker cheated on me? What's wrong with me? Why do I always have to be miserable?

While the tears were running down his face, he was thinking of the beautiful Sylvain and already missed him, but he couldn't go back now, could he? That would be so stupid.

Sylvain tried to call him, but Albert had switched off his phone and was walking despondently along Boulevard Sébastopol. When he came to Voie Georges Pompidou, he angrily hurled his book into the cold water of the Seine and saw how it desperately tried to stay above the water, spreading out its pages while it was being carried along, until it was too heavy with water, exhausted, and finally gave up, disappearing below the surface for good. No more waiting for Godot, he thought, *jamais*.

Coming home in the evening, drenched and miserable, it wasn't difficult for his aunt to guess what had happened. He told her about the fight he had had with Sylvain.

'Why don't you ring him up? You can't just throw away what you've got, the beauty of your love. I think you're jumping to conclusions.'

'I don't know what to do any more. I feel so terribly alone in this rotten world. There's no point in going on. I don't care what happens and I don't want him back.'

His words hurt her a lot and she tried to argue with him, but it was useless and there had to be something else that was troubling him, she thought. She was sure he still missed his mother, who had been so cruelly plucked from his life, while his father was nothing but a pool of misery, a man who, if they had any contact at all, was only dragging him down into his own bottomless pit of sorrow and loneliness. Every time after he had seen his father or spoken to him on the phone, it was almost impossible for her to reach him. But sometimes it seemed to her as if he desired to be unhappy, to be alone with his misery, withdrawing to his room, or going out into the street, whatever time of the day or night it was.

That night, in the privacy of his room, he thought about everything that had happened that day, but he couldn't see things in their true perspective.

'Sylvain, Sylvain' went through his head like a pulsing fever. He wanted so much to go back to him, hear his voice, touch him and be touched, but somehow he was unable to break through his own brick wall of *tristesse*.

The day before spring set in his father died. The funeral was a rather straightforward affair, sombre, but not sad. When the coffin was lowered into the family grave, Albert looked at his mother's tombstone. He struggled hard to suppress his tears, but it didn't work. His brother saw it and put his hand on Albert's shoulder.

'You can't hang on to your grief, Albert. You've got to get on with your life. Don't keep looking back. Why don't you try your luck elsewhere, somewhere new?'

'What do you mean?'

'Maybe you should go abroad for a while, be in a different environment. Your English is very good, so why don't you go to London for a year or so, just to get away from it all.'

'I don't know,' he said timidly, although the idea immediately struck a chord with him and he thought of what his mother had said.

'But what about Aunt Sophie; I can't just leave her, can I?'

'Don't worry about her. You've got your own life to live. Just look at her standing there. She'll be fine and it won't be forever, maybe only for a couple of months and you know you don't have to worry about the money; Mum and Dad have left us more than enough.'

The thought of moving away from Paris and Sylvain for a while began to grow on Albert, to excite him. He thought about it every day and discussed it with his aunt.

'I think your brother's right. I'm sure it'll do you good. And don't you worry about me, I'm happy as long as you're happy too.'

Three weeks later, when the sweet showers of April had pierced the drought of March to the root, and the Third World War had reached its zenith, he left Paris for London and rented an apartment in Camberwell, Southwark. Nearly every Saturday he could be seen in Charing Cross Road, looking for books by Beckett, Joyce, Balzac, Yourcenar, Levé, poetry by Baudelaire or the works of Nietzsche, Russell, Kierkegaard and Sartre, which he devoured once he had found them. He was thinking of giving up painting and becoming a writer. There were also times when he struggled with his homosexuality and during some longer spells of dejection he wondered what the point of life was and if he would ever find real happiness. Reading became more than just a distraction for him; he also hoped to find answers to some very important questions. It made him feel better and he realised he had to stay in control of his own spirit and that he shouldn't allow himself to be watered down to someone who doesn't know what to do with his life any more, that he would only drive himself crazy.

He bought some blank canvasses and sat down to paint, but his turbulent mind prevented him from getting anything done and the grim atmosphere in London didn't help either. Because of the war many young people believed they had no future; all their plans and ideas were going up in smoke. Like other generations before them they began to realise they were part of a lost generation.

But not everybody suffered from bouts of depression; there were right-wing, chauvinistic, young people who believed this war wasn't any different from previous ones and thought it was a challenge they had to take up. After all, weren't they the nation that had more experience with foreign missions all over the world, in the Middle East, Asia, South America and many other places, than any other country and, if Napoleon and Hitler couldn't get Britain on her knees, who could? The Chinese? Not very likely.

Albert, however, knew very well it wasn't a conventional war and saw the media were totally unreliable. People were being brainwashed by a constant stream of conflicting, ever-changing news reports from the front, wherever that was. Who could you trust? Why would anyone join the army and sacrifice his budding life for question marks? he wondered. Only if you were suicidal, he thought.

He believed the human world was very close to the brink of self-destruction, at the end of its natural cycle. There were people dying of starvation in the streets and parks of London, while there were also young guys of his own age who were loaded and could do what they liked. Racing through the chaotic, crazy city in their Ferraris, Porsches, Teslas and other supercars, all they could think of was making even more money, partying was their motto and binge drinking one of their favourite pastimes.

One night he went with some friends to a club called The Shining Oval. The venue turned out to be the former Oval Underground Station, one of about a dozen London Underground stations that had been bought up by a young Chinese business tycoon, who had transformed them into bars and clubs. It looked incredibly cool, and the old escalators were used to take people to bars and dance floors on different levels, but, unfortunately, the place was swarming with drug pushers and users, so he went home early.

On another occasion, in a bar close to Monmouth Street, he couldn't believe his eyes when he went to the toilets in the basement and saw some naked guys in the loos. Their clothes were lying on the floor and they were showing off their naked bodies to each other. Apparently, they wanted to go to the Ladies in their starkers, while another guy, about his own age, with pupils the size of one penny pieces, was refreshing himself with water from a toilet.

'Have you ever tried to piss a turd through the toilet? the guy shouted to a friend. 'It's great fun. The solid, splattering sound; it's so cool.'

In another toilet, whose door had been left wide open, he saw a man having sex with a girl, but apart from what was probably a mate of his, who was egging on his friend, and masturbating himself, no one took any notice of them. This is the end of the world, Albert thought and got out as quickly as he could; it was truly sickening.

How, in spite of all this, he had allowed himself to be persuaded to go to another party, he couldn't understand. It was a sort of rave which was held in a former Royal Mail sorting office near Elephant and Castle, but it wasn't one of those parties like in the old days when partygoers only heard at the very last minute where the illegal party was to be held, in an old factory or under a railway bridge. This venue was regularly used for parties by an anti-squat team, who had been hired to look after the premises and lived there for free.

It was incredibly big and there were offices, rooms and a large canteen, where memorabilia, such as posters and signs from the time when people still received mail, which was sorted in buildings like these, in their letter-boxes at home, were hanging on the wall. Here too, party-goers, heteros and gays, behaved as if it was the last day of their lives, shouting, screaming, binging, dancing naked and, of course, screwing.

Halfway through the night, he'd only had two or three glasses of wine, while his 'friends' had already drunk a few bottles. He thought he was going insane. Looking at the chaos of the battlefield of human degradation around him; the floor being strewn with cans, condoms, broken glass, bottles and paper, everything, this whole fucking life, was getting to him. He could no longer restrain himself; he shouted and cursed, but the people around him, and even his friends, only thought he was raising the roof. Overwhelmed by the deep drone and shrill sound of the mad music, the thousands of voices, he freaked out, grabbed a chair and started banging it against a metal window gate. The world was spinning in his head; he was in a merry-go-round of madness. The gate sprung open, but he didn't stop and lashed out with the chair, smashed the window pane and climbed onto the windowsill. Feeling sick, giddy, and utterly confused, he looked at the ground six metres below him.

7

'Can I have a bitter lemon, please?' Roonah asked.
'No, sorry, I'm closing; time to go home. The sun's already coming up. Look.'

8

Albert was about to jump, when someone grabbed him by his shirt.

'Are you tripping, mate? What have you been taking?'

'I want to get out! Let me go!' he shouted, trying to pull himself loose. 'This whole fucking mess, the noise, the fucking music and all these fucking people are driving me mad!'

Some minutes later he stood outside and only when he could breathe in some fresh air, did he begin to feel better. Never again, he thought. He looked back at the building and saw how dilapidated it was and, slowly coming back to his senses, he thought of all the men and women who used to work in shifts there and in his already overloaded head he thought how every day many thousands of letters and postcards went through their hands, all the addresses they had to read, in a time without postcodes and computers, how they had to know what destination bins they had to be thrown into, the jokes they told, how they were eating proper food, not from plastic or paper containers, but from real plates, with metal knives and forks, how they must have gone crazy during the Christmas season with all the Christmas cards and parcels, how they laughed, swore, went on strike for better working conditions, got relationships, fell ill and took their pensions, until the new god, or the Antichrist, called *Ordinateur* Computer, arrived and screwed up the world and brought about the chaos it was in now.

Was it really better in the 'good old days', as the old folks always said? No, it couldn't be, he thought, but people are always kidding themselves, because what about the Second World War, the dubious role the French Government played then, Hiroshima, the ethnic cleansings in the Balkan and Africa, the use of poison gas during the First World War and all the other inventions that were aimed at wiping out people on the largest possible scale? He remembered the countless allied war graves he had so often seen in several places in northern France. It all filled him with horror. Was the world a better place before the First World War then? he wondered. No, because there had always been wars and he thought of the fate of black people who were transported to America to work as slaves on plantations, where, completely humiliated by white people, they lost their essence and dignity as human beings and died, usually in dire circumstances, far away from their native land. And what about the millions of refugees who have to leave everything behind and risk their lives to find a better world in countries that are better off? Very often they don't even get there and, if they haven't drowned or been killed first, they will be sent back. It wasn't hard to understand the adage of young people: 'Fuck the world. We're going partying.' But surely, there must be more than that? he asked himself.

Sometimes he went to a party at a friend's house, as it was usually the only chance to meet like-minded people and forget his own misery, but it didn't make him any happier, and after another month or so he realised he had to quit; all this emptiness was dragging him down more and more. Hadn't he better go back to France, maybe to his brother's? But his brother was married now with a young kid and Albert hardly knew his sister-in-law. To Sylvain perhaps? No, Sylvain wouldn't be waiting for him any more; they hadn't been in touch since that fateful day a year ago. He had sent Sylvain a message, but there had been no answer. No, there was no way back to Paris, or France.

Albert looked up at the clear blue sky, the vast space between the white, silent, moving cumuli. I wish I could fly through that infinite sky, that beautiful, unspoilt, free, no-man's-space. How insane they are, all those countries that are set on claiming and destroying the North Pole, or what's left of it, one of the last unspoilt parts of the world, only for some bloody oil and the South Pole will come next. It seems the world has to be turned inside out, plundered and stripped of everything that grows on it until life on earth has become impossible for humans. Isn't that what happened on Easter Island, where the inhabitants must have known they were cutting down the very last tree on the island? The trees, their life, their only possibility to build boats with, so that they could sustain themselves and get off the island. How myopic mankind is.

One morning he happened to cycle past a gallery just off New Bond Street and saw a few paintings of an Ecuadorian painter, Luis Burgos Flor, in the window. He got off his bike, looked at them and was struck by the colour pattern and structure of the abstract paintings. He realised it had never occurred to him that South America could have any great artists; as if they could only come from Europe and the U.S., while he also knew that for quite some time several African painters had made it in the international world of art.

Beside the paintings hung a portrait of the artist, who, so he read, had also lived in Los Angeles for several years. The big, bushy eyebrows, the long hair, the eyes that expressed confidence. What a flamboyant head, he thought.

He put his bike against the window and went inside, where he saw many more works of this deceased painter. Somehow he was fascinated by Flor, his paintings, his background, perhaps also because the country, Ecuador, called up some magical images of beaches, surfing, warmth, Quito, Inca culture, Spanish, the Galápagos Islands.

As there were a lot of problems with the Internet he had to rely on the large library of the Victoria and Albert Museum in Cromwell Road to try and find more information about the artist, but what he found was rather disappointing, so he cycled to the bookshops in Charing Cross Road, where he managed to get some books on South American art and Ecuador as well. Like a beast dragging its prey to a safe spot, he took the valuable collection to his apartment and started devouring the books. A whole new world opened up for him and, enthralled by the incredibly beautiful pictures, he became more and more excited. It was clear. He knew what he had to do; get out of Europe and go to Ecuador.

How he was going to get there was another matter. Due to the war virtually all air-traffic had come to a halt, so he could probably only get there by ship. It sounded simple, but it wasn't, for all traffic, including modern vessels, depended on satellites for their navigation, and most of them had been put out of use by the Chinese, while China's own fleet of satellites could only be used if there was a signed contract with the Chinese authorities. After searching for a couple of days he found a Chilean company that had traded with China for decades. Some of their ships appeared to sail from Tenerife, which meant he would have to travel to Palos de la Frontera on the south west coast of Spain and catch a ferry to Tenerife from there. It sounded very exciting.

At last, a goal in my life, he thought, something to go for. The next morning he jumped on his bike and, whistling, he rode to the estate agent to discontinue the rent. What a great feeling this was; it gave him wings. He told them he wanted to be out of his apartment in two weeks. That was no problem, but he still had to pay the rent for a full month. It didn't matter; at least he was free!

He first went back to Paris to see his aunt, who was overjoyed to see him again and asked him what he had been doing with his life. He told her about his adventures in London and his plan to go to Ecuador.

'Are you sure you want to go there, especially in these difficult days? Is it really safe?' she asked him, although her belief in him was as firm as a rock, which was probably also one of the reasons why he was so fond of her.

'I hope you don't mind my asking, but have you heard anything from Sylvain when you were in London?'

He felt the blood rush to his face and lower body.

'No, erm, nothing. I often thought about ringing him up, but I didn't. Supposing I look him up now, how will he respond? I don't know what to do. If he really wanted me, why did he never contact me? He could have obtained my address from you,' he added.

'Yes, but *you* were the one to ditch him,' she replied.

'Well, yes.'

That night, as he was lying in bed, he thought of the fresh joy he had felt that afternoon. Watching the wind and the moving curtains playing with the light of the street lanterns on the ceiling of his bedroom, he fell into a deep sleep, a happy smile on his face.

'It's so good to be back with you, and in Paris,' he said to his aunt the following morning, embracing her, 'and although I still think a lot about Sylvain and sometimes miss him too, the deep hurt has gone and Paris is no longer a cloud of painful, negative thoughts and feelings for me.'

'I'm so glad to hear this. I thought you'd never want to come back again.'

'Shall I go and get a baguette or some petits pains?' he asked her and before she could reply he added, 'By the way, I'm going to Sylvain's this afternoon. If he doesn't want to see me again, so be it.'

Off he was. She could hear him singing on his way down the stone stairs and smiled.

Maybe it was due to some unpleasant experiences he'd had in London, but he seemed to enjoy his delightful, unchanged Paris more than ever before. On his way to Rue Saint Martin he saw the small park, the Square Emile Chautemps, and remembered the last time he was sitting there, anxiously waiting to see Sylvain, and what had happened afterwards. Once again he was standing at the big, wooden door. He pressed the brass button of Sylvain's apartment, feeling quite nervous. Not a single sound came through the small holes of the mesh-covered loudspeaker, no voice, not even a crackle, nothing. He pressed the bell once more. Silence. Only when he looked at the nameplates, did he notice there was no plate at all. An empty, rectangular space with two rusty holes was all that was left. Sylvain must have moved, he thought, and nobody else is living there now. He decided to go to the fashion studio where Sylvain worked, but he didn't see any familiar faces there, not even Richard's and when he asked where Sylvain lived, the receptionist said she wasn't allowed to tell him that. He knew he could have expected this.

He realised he had been stupid that strange day in autumn, childishly stupid, to run away so precipitately, out of sheer jealousy, driven by pure emotion, instead of thinking about it and giving Sylvain the chance to tell his side of the story and work it out together. What little confidence he had had in Sylvain. You've been such a terrible fool, went through his head, again and again. Maybe he is living with Richard now, he thought, and shuddered.

From the studio he walked back to Rue Saint Martin, looked up at the windows and little balcony of Sylvain's apartment, into the street and back up again, as if Sylvain would suddenly turn up, if he looked away for a sec, but it was an illusion of time, just like the day he had gone back to his parental home, thinking that if he got his key out, opened the door and went inside, he would find his mum and dad sitting there, watching TV, as if nothing had ever happened.

Somehow this neighbourhood with its fine houses and squares reminded him of the area near the British Museum in London, and while the scent of Parisian trees pervaded his nostrils, he thought there was something about Paris that no other city had, but it was a *je ne sais quoi* feeling, which was probably based on a combination or composition of many different things, architecture, design, like the ever-beautiful Métro signs, he thought, Parisian people, how they were dressed and walked, colour, smell, light. He walked on with a smile, even though he knew he couldn't stay in Paris, not even because of Sylvain. It was time to leave.

But there were also unpleasant scenes he hadn't noticed before, of drunk people hanging in the street, not merely older people, but quite a few young men and women as well. Have I been blind all the time, or has the world changed overnight? he wondered. It made him think of London again and the excesses he'd seen there, the contrasts. So Paris wasn't any different, he thought, while images from the book *L'Éducation Sentimentale* presented themselves in his mind; coaches with ostentatiously rich people, driving up and down the avenues during the crazy days of the late 1840s, the run-up to the next French revolution and the chaos that came with it, a new Napoleon Bonaparte, wealth, but dire poverty as well. Paris will be Paris, he thought. Nothing much has changed.

Maybe he had romanticised Paris all along. Wasn't that also the reason why it looked as if his time in London had been useless, whereas it had given him a new direction in his life and the push to make a trip to Ecuador? He had to be honest with himself. Maybe it was just an escape, as the loneliness of Paris, the new *clochards*, the feeling of isolation, desertion in himself, was coming back to him.

Standing by the Seine, he thought of Sylvain.

'Where have you gone? You gave meaning to my life. I can smell your perfume, your studio, the cloth, the sewing machines. I miss you, I love you,' he called from Pont Neuf to the Seine below, but, indifferently, she drowned his words and just flowed on, steadily, forever dividing this old city, *à gauche*, Musée d'Orsay, *à droite*, Jardin des Tuileries; quietly waving goodbye, whispering '*Adieu, Paris,*' winding its way to the salty sea. *Il faut que je te quitte, tant pis. Paris change! mais rien dans ma mélancolie n'a bougé!*

Sylvain had disappeared and maybe that was for the best, he thought, otherwise he might have lingered here. There must be a reason for all this, he suspected. Not that he really believed in fate, but sometimes things just happen in your life.

He went back to his aunt's and told her Sylvain had disappeared from the surface of the earth, from the surface of Paris anyway, and that he had made up his mind to leave for South America that week. He spent the next couple of days looking for things he needed for the trip and took his aunt out for dinner. He knew he'd have to say goodbye to her the following day. It weighed very heavily on his conscience, as he knew how much she'd miss him.

On the morning of his departure, when they were having breakfast together, she smiled at him, gave him a cuddle and said,

'Wherever you settle down one day, I'll come and see you. I mean it. Take care, Albert, I'll miss you.'

'You're the loveliest person in the world. Look after yourself. I'll be in touch,' he replied, looked into her dark brown eyes, kissed her, and left.

He got on an old coach at Gare Montparnasse and left for the village where his brother lived, a place not far from Chartres. He was looking forward to staying with him and his young family for a few days, or maybe even a week, but once he got there, it was quite different, as if he was visiting an acquaintance instead of his own brother. The children looked at him as if he was an alien and there was no love lost between Albert and his sister-in-law. He felt he was an unwanted guest who was expected to bugger off first thing in the morning.

In the evening he and his brother went to a café and talked about Albert's experiences in London and the political situation in Britain and France, but as far as the war was concerned from a French point of view, his brother couldn't give him much information.

'All I know is things are getting worse here. We no longer live in a democracy, if ever we did. Like the British Government, ours has also taken advantage of the situation to push through new legislation that restricts the freedom of its citizens. Hundreds of people who were too critical of the government have been arrested. They've been put in jail, without any trial, at an unknown location, isolated from their family and friends. It's terrible.'

'It sounds as if the country has gone back to the eighteenth century, to *La Terreur*, the terror of fear and power, the days of Robespierre,' Albert said.

'You're right. Many people have protested against the measures, but they have to be very careful not to be locked up themselves.'

Was this the freedom of the Western world? Albert asked himself. He was quite convinced now he had to turn his back to this foolish Europe.

Not until he had left his brother's house behind him, did his adventure really begin; he could feel and smell his freedom. He first travelled to the south of France at an easy pace. It took him a few weeks to get to the Spanish border. He loved this part of the journey, seeing parts of France he'd never seen before and chatting to all kinds of people. After that the imposing heights of the Pyrenees followed and, the further south he went, the more relaxed the people seemed to become. The countryside surprised him and at times it looked as if he was in the middle of a desert; for decades vast areas had been hit by long spells of drought. Sometimes he travelled by bus and when he was walking along the road people would offer him a lift, even in ox carts. He wasn't in a hurry and when the scenery was beautiful or the people very hospitable, he just stayed a bit longer. There were moments when he didn't feel like moving on at all.

After four weeks he reached Palos. A man who'd given him a lift, told him Palos was the port Columbus had set sail from for his discovery trip. Albert didn't know this, but it could hardly be coincidence, for wasn't he also on a discovery trip? The only difference was, he thought with a smile, that he knew he was going to America and Columbus didn't.

He had a few days to see the town before getting on a ferry to Tenerife, from where he would cross the Atlantic on a Chilean ship. Palos was a lovely, old, historic place where he found a pleasant hostel in the Calle de Juan de la Cosa. He booked in and went straight to the harbour to smell the sea and feel the excitement of the coming leg of the journey, to get into the mood, as it were. In the evening he went to a bar not far from the hostel to have a glass of wine. He was sitting there quietly by himself, looking at the interior, when his eye caught some fine pictures on the wall. The moment he stood up to have a closer look at the them, a strange feeling came over him, which reminded him of a similar sensation he had had in London, a few months earlier.

'What's your business here, foreigner?' a big, tough-looking guy said to him. 'Looking for a nice man? Well, you won't find any in this place. We make sure they don't last very long.'

While this guy was speaking to him, Albert looked sideways and saw the shadows of two more guys who were standing behind him. He began to tremble; knowing he'd better not say anything.

'Look at me when I speak to you, *maricón*,' the guy who was speaking to him said, while one of the others elbowed him in the back.

Some other customers saw what was going on, but looked away. They didn't want to be involved and, like in London, he could sense the deep hatred of these guys, the threat of danger.

'Why don't you just leave me alone?' he asked them.

'Because we don't want your sort in here.'

'OK, I'm already on my way out,' he said.

Before he could turn round, the guy hit him in his face. Albert felt a sharp pain, heard a crack and tasted the blood that was trickling down his upper lip. He couldn't get away because the two others wouldn't let him. Before he could even think, he felt a second blow, this time in his stomach, and collapsed. Fucking bastards, he thought, lying on the floor. Maybe this was his fate, he thought, wherever he went.

Only when the guys had left and he sat up, did some people come over to help him. The barkeeper apologised, but, like the others, he had been too cowardly to throw the guys out right away. With pain in his stomach, a bleeding nose and a swollen eye he was taken back to his hostel. He lay down on his bed, knackered and disillusioned. During that night out in London he'd been able to escape by the skin of his teeth and in Paris they had called him names, but thinking of the mental pain and hell some boys and girls have to go through when they are bullied at school, in the street or in clubs, year after year, because of their sexual orientation, the pain he felt didn't mean much, he realised. The good thing was that he would leave for Tenerife the following day, a trip of about thirty-five hours.

The next morning, when he looked in the mirror, he saw the colourful palette round his eye and although his nose and stomach were still painful, it wasn't too bad. But fate struck again, for when he arrived at the port he learned that, due to the war, the ferry was not in service. Had he travelled all those hundreds of miles for nothing?

'What a bloody mess!' he shouted at the ship that had been laid up indefinitely. It pissed him off more than anything else. He bought a bottle of rum and went back to the hostel; he'd had enough. But when a girl at the hostel told him that he might try and get a lift on a sailing yacht, his mood changed and he made up his mind to go to the harbour to try his luck.

The weather was perfect, so a prolonged stay in Palos wouldn't be a punishment. On the contrary, there were some beautiful sandy beaches nearby and it was probably a nice place, as long as he avoided the obscure bars.

He met the owner of a French yacht, who was looking for an extra hand on board.
'Where did you get that black eye?'
'Somebody just hit me, for no reason at all, at a local bar.'
'Oh, OK.'
A long silence followed.
'I'm sorry, but I don't want any troublemakers on board,' the Frenchman said.
'But it wasn't my fault, I was just sitting there, quietly.'
'That's what they all say. Sorry.'
The next day he had more luck, when he spoke to the owner of an English yacht, who was on his way to the Canary Islands. It was a man in his sixties, with dark eyes, black-grey hair and a beard, who said he wanted to escape from the unpleasant atmosphere and tension in north west Europe. As he was able to sail without GPS, using an old-fashioned sextant, he could get wherever he wanted. The moment Albert saw the man, he knew everything was going to be all right. They would leave in a week, the man, Jack Weekley, said. He first needed to stock up on food, water and fuel.
'Why don't you get your things and come on board right now?' he asked. 'You're very welcome.'
Albert was back in fifteen minutes. They sat on deck for a long time and talked about the war, the situation in England and France. As Jack had been nearly all over the world, there was no end to his stories. But he had never been to South America and was interested in what Albert could tell him about that part of the world.
'That sounds really fascinating. I would love to go there one day,' he said to Albert. 'It's quite a trip, but then again, I've always liked a challenge.'
'Why not go there together?' Albert suggested.
'Not now, but who knows? Maybe one day.'

On the last Sunday in September they left for the south.

'Look at that, Jack,' Albert said, pointing at the coastline of Morocco. 'Isn't it beautiful? I could never have imagined this would happen to me. It's really great. Thanks ever so much.'

'It's OK, Albert, glad to have you on board.'

'And I'm happy I'm not on one of those bloody ferries or on board of that shitty Frenchman's yacht.'

'What Frenchman?'

Albert told him what that man had said and what had happened at the bar the night before.

'I'm very sorry to hear this. I already wondered why you had a black eye. Is it still painful? Are you all right now?'

'Yes, I'm fine, thanks. It looks worse than it is.'

'Unfortunately, there are lots of loonies about. When you're different in whatever way, there's always narrow-minded hypocrites who will try to make life difficult for you, but it's their own problem and their own shortcomings they have to deal with, but they don't see that; they're too stupid, too limited up here,' he said, pointing at his head.

'Maybe you're right.'

'Yeah, so don't you ever question yourself or you will get depressed.'

After a few more days the Canary Islands appeared on the horizon. Jack recognised them at once; the ever impressive, beautiful shapes of the rocks rising from the water. They were already nearing the end of the sailing trip, Albert realised. What a pity; it had gone so quickly and what a great guy Jack was, he thought.

They arrived at the port of Santa Cruz, where Albert went ashore to find the Chilean ship. The harbour was full of yachts, English, French, German and Dutch ones; they all wanted to get away from crazy Europe and had all managed to get here without GPS, which, they said, gave them a feeling of ultimate freedom. The effects of the war seemed to have bypassed this part of the world; bars and restaurants were overcrowded and there was a buzz all over the place.

He enquired where the Chilean ship was, but heard that it hadn't moored in Santa Cruz, but in Las Palmas.

'No problem,' Jack said straightaway. 'Let's go to Las Palmas.'

He was probably happy to move on, Albert thought, and, hopefully, they could still sail to America together.

When they got to Las Palmas, they found the ship. It was a strange moment for Jack and Albert; they had only just got to know each other and already the time had come for Albert to travel on to South America, while Jack said he would stay in Las Palmas or go to one of the other Canary Islands, for the winter anyway. The night before the Chilean ship left, they went out for a drink together and talked about the uncertain future.

'You're a brave person, Albert. You could have tried to find Sylvain, but you decided to go it all alone. I'm sure I will miss your company on board. Take care.'

Standing outside again, in the warm evening breeze, they embraced each other. Walking back to Jack's yacht, they didn't say much, but both of them knew they would meet again one day.

The next day Albert went on board the Chilean vessel, which would first sail to Cuba and from there to Ecuador through the Panama Canal, with Chile as its final destination. Albert might have tried to get another lift across the Atlantic Ocean, but he was happy to travel on a freight ship, which would certainly be quicker, he thought.

It turned out he wasn't the only paying passenger on board; there were about ten others. The cabin was nothing to write home about, but it didn't worry him at all. He had a terrific view of the sea and in the evening, if there was no live music by the crew, he could read his books. Of course he had plenty of time to think about himself, his time in Paris and London. He also wondered where Sylvain was hanging out. He couldn't just have quit his job, could he? Maybe he had moved to another fashion house and that's why the receptionist at his old studio didn't want to tell him anything. But it was so strange that his nameplate had gone as well, he thought. If only Sylvain were standing here next to me, to gaze at the blue ocean together, he sighed.

The Atlantic Ocean was reasonably calm and after about a week the coast of Cuba came in sight. Unreal, he thought, such a large island that he knew so little about. In fact, he had only seen this part of the world in the pirate films he used to watch with his granddad many years ago, but what he did know, was that Cuba had always had good ties with communist countries, because of the diplomatic missions and influence of Che Guevara in the previous century, and the former communist regime of Fidel Castro. Isn't it amazing, he thought, that so many young people all over the world, even so long after Che's death, still see Che Guevara as a hero, a kind of liberator? He also remembered reading that the Americans had, unsuccessfully, tried to topple Castro and his administration several times.

One of the crew members said Cuba was flourishing as a result of the Third World War; quite a few people had moved there as the atmosphere was very relaxed.

'Alberto, if you can get off the ship, there are many bars in Havana with *música*, good *comida*, and beautiful *mujeres*. You will love Havana. Most *mujeres* are very *atractivas* and special; it's easy to get your rocks off.'

The man smiled while he was talking and there was a randy glint in his eyes. When he laughed, it sounded more like a whinny or, rather, the braying of a donkey, Albert thought and it made him laugh too. Although it wasn't the sort of entertainment he was interested in, it was kind of the little man, with his too short jeans and big, black moustache, to think of him. Looking at the man's face, Albert saw the man had stepped into his own daydream; his eyes beamed with happiness, and even his white teeth were shining. He could probably hear and feel the music, because he started swaying on his feet, as if he was already in a bar, dancing with an attractive, hot, oversexed, provoking Cuban woman. Albert patted him on the shoulder and laughed.

They sailed for hours along the coast; it seemed never-ending.

'Doesn't that look fantastic; all those palm trees and sandy beaches?' he said to another passenger, a girl in her late twenties, who was standing next to him..

At last, there it was, Havana, the capital. What an impressive place, he thought, when they sailed into the harbour. There were quite a few high-rise flats, but the streets in the old city centre were also dotted with elegant houses, old churches with towers and big cupolas, which reminded him of Madrid and Paris. The harbour, however, was quite the opposite; it was old and derelict.

The ship was to pick up a cargo of nickel. Although nobody was allowed to disembark, more and more passengers disappeared in the course of the morning. They must have bribed somebody to let them go ashore, Albert thought and he remembered what the little man had said. But if he couldn't go ashore, why should the man have mentioned the bars and women? So he was the person to talk to, he assumed.

His 'friend' with the big moustache was busy cleaning the toilets. Albert asked him if he knew how he could get ashore.

'Your story about the bars, the music, the women; I have to see them for myself.'

The man began to snigger.

'Yes, *no te preocupes*, *Señor Alberto*, I will help you, but I must talk to somebody else first. Wait a minute, he said.

Off he was. Some minutes later he came back, not only with another crew member, but also with two men in uniform, probably Cuban policemen. Albert got a bit nervous when he saw them. He had thought that one, or maybe two members of the crew would be bribable, but not a couple of policemen as well, and where had they suddenly come from?

One of the cops came up to him and said, softly and secretively,

'Good morning, Señor Alberto. Can I help you?'

'I would love to see the city. One of the crew members, that man over there, has told me some very interesting things about it.'

The policeman began to smile, but Albert wasn't sure what that meant, or if it was a genuine smile.

'Yes,' the cop said, 'he knows all the bars in Havana and all the *mujeres*, the women, there know him,' and laughed.

Albert couldn't help laughing too and the little man probably understood what was said in English, for he put up his hands and arms, as if he wanted to say, 'I was right, wasn't I, for it *is* a great place.'

'I can help you; no worries, for only forty dollars,' said the copper.

Albert felt he needed to bargain with the man for a better price.

'I don't know,' he said, 'that's quite a sum; I don't even have the money to go to those bars he was talking about; I only want to see your beautiful city.'

The policeman smiled again when Albert said this, for he was proud of his Havana.

'You're a good man. Let's make it thirty, OK?'

'I'm not sure,' Albert said.

'Make up your mind, *amigo*, for without us there's no Havana,' the man said, almost arrogantly.

'OK, thirty dollars.'

He was a lousy negotiator, and of course the policeman knew it too. He shook hands with the policeman, who winked at him, or so he thought, for the wink was actually meant for the other three men.

'How can I get back on board? Will I have to pay again then?' he asked when he gave the money to the policeman.

'*No hay problema*,' answered the other, still unknown crew member. 'It's all inclusive. We'll be here when you come back, but everything you do is at your own *riesgo*. Make sure you're back in time; the ship won't wait for you.'

'Here's an address of someone in Havana, just in case,' added one of the cops, whose English wasn't too bad, and handed him a piece of paper.

'Thanks.'

It gave him a better feeling, although he wondered what the man meant by 'just in case'.

'Listen, if someone asks you how you got ashore, you know nothing and you talk to no one about us, or you'll be in big trouble.'

Albert didn't want to leave anything on board, so before going ashore he went back to his cabin to get his rucksack. That's how it works, he thought, with money you can buy everything, even freedom.

9

Still sitting at the bar, Roonah looked at Erasmus once more and said, somewhat condescendingly, 'Don't be so dozy, go home, to bed.'

Erasmus didn't answer. Why did she speak to him like that, as if she was his mother? he wondered.

But she wasn't aware of it, as her thoughts had turned back to the secondary school in L.A. and how cruel some of the students there were. They just shelved anybody who didn't fit into their lives and even seemed to gloat at the misfortune of others. All that crap all the time, she thought. She was sick of it and no, nobody needed to tell her that she wasn't perfect; she was quite aware of that and she knew that some of the things she did and the way she behaved would trigger negativity in her classmates and that it might boomerang on her. Everything was so predictable. The only way to avoid these things, she thought, was to say nothing and keep yourself to yourself as much as you could, although that was very hard sometimes. Yes, she knew she was a bit different and yes, it was true, she wanted to get good grades, because she wanted to go to a good university, but what was wrong with that?

She was thinking about the girls and wondered what was left of the relationships that some of them had with each other and she remembered that bizarre love-triangle of three other girls in her class. She could still see them before her. Because she became interested in one or two other girls at school, she had even begun to seriously doubt her own sexual orientation, she remembered, followed by a deep sigh. The boys were different; most of them were easy-going and nice to her, although some allowed themselves to be dragged along by the bitches. Of course, these cunts, and some of the boys too, liked to make derisive remarks about her, saying and whispering things like, 'Isn't she small, that Irish girl?' One of the boys, however, who was in love with her, had told her that she looked really beautiful, that she was different from the other girls.

'Those bitches are only jealous, because of your good looks and your accent.'

It was very kind of him, but she didn't like him much; in fact, she never much liked boys her own age anyway, but at least his words had made her feel good.

Although she was aware of the fact that her short shirts and the blond curls on her tanned body made men look or whistle at her, she hated it, as she didn't want to be seen as a sex object.

She remembered telling a couple of scaffolders in Santa Monica, 'You're a bunch of sick, pathetic pricks. Shut up and mind your own fucking business.'

'You're just a lezzie, but I like your tits and temper,' one of them called back. The others just laughed at her.

Sometimes she wondered if she looked flirty, if she had some sort of naïve, voluptuous look that attracted men and sort of invited them to look at her and make remarks. She didn't know. It was always so hard to do the right thing, she thought. She only wanted to be a loving, caring, young person who was conscious of the world she lived in, and she cared about every living thing, animals, nature, people; and perhaps in that order.

Bernard Chambers laughed at what Roonah had just said to Erasmus; she definitely had something enigmatic and it attracted him. He had only seen her here a few times, but she knew a lot and could talk about almost anything. Besides, she looked good in her shorts and red shirt that so beautifully accentuated her body and she had a lovely, little nose, which moved a little when she laughed or smiled; how cute. And what about those big, blue eyes and beautiful blond curls? Yes, she definitely was a gorgeous girl with her open, innocent face, he thought. That pretty mouth, her nice arse, he wouldn't mind…, but she was also a bit too pushy, he thought, especially when she thought she was right. Wouldn't it be fun to see her tipsy or drunk? Maybe it would loosen her up a bit, he thought, make her sexier, hotter.

He had been to quite a few army parties and seen how easy it was for officers, or uniformed men in general, for that matter, to make a pass at women. It was as if it didn't matter what was inside the uniform; sometimes a fine black or blond lock of hair and a smile were enough to get a woman into bed and the more decorations one had, the easier it was to impress the girls and women, however young or old they were. In the end he had married one of those beautiful, lively ladies.

Roonah couldn't help looking at Erasmus once more; he was a handsome guy, with his full lips and delicate nose and he had beautiful, deep blue eyes with a soft expression. There was something vulnerable about him in his silly, old-fashioned trousers and shirt, she thought and she could already see how she would draw or paint him; that was how she always looked at people. She wasn't sure, but in spite of his drink talk he seemed to lack self-confidence. Perhaps it was the way he moved, or spoke and she wondered what had made him study Greek and why he had come to Ecuador. With his narrow shoulders he definitely wasn't one of those macho men. He had the beginnings of a paunch, she noticed. He probably spent a lot of time indoors or maybe he drank too much beer, she thought. But she shouldn't judge him like that, she admonished herself, because she disliked being judged herself and he was probably very nice, but the words of the French chanson came floating back again and diverted the stream of her thoughts away from the people at the bar once more.

Et tu es si loin de moi
J'ai peur que tu m'oublies déjà

The rivulet of soft sounds and plosive-less consonants, the rhythm and the warm, sensual rhyme of the lip-rounding vowels blurred the image of Erasmus and mingled with her silent thoughts. The voice, it sounded so pleasant and she could understand the words quite well; she had been taught French at school for some years and because Desmond loved the language, he regularly spoke French to her.

The song was played over and over again. Apparently, someone in one of the cottages on the beach was feeling miserable, she thought. She didn't know anyone here who spoke French, so what lonely soul was playing this chanson, again and again? Maybe it was rather cliché, but in her imagination she saw averyhandsomeblackhairedsadlookingmanofaboutforty, hanging in a chair, with watery eyes and tears running down his face, a glass of tequila in his hand and a cigarette in his mouth.

10

Albert got up from his chair and looked at the candlelit photo on the wall. There he was, in his racing suit, with his bright red motorbike and he vividly remembered the day it had been taken. It was a Saturday and he had been testing his bike in the neighbourhood of his home, close to Jargeau, on the fast, twisting road along the Loire. Coming back, his mother was waiting for him, a cigarette in her mouth. His dad, with black, Brylcreem hair combed backwards and grease and oil on his bare arms, was sitting beside her. It was '*Moto Samedi*' and a neighbour had taken the photo.

He looked at it again and saw that someone was missing; the newspaper boy. He would be sitting on a low stool behind the open gate and Albert could hear how his mother always used to say, 'Hello, come on in; you don't have to wait there. Here's a stool, sit down. Would you like some lemonade?'

The boy, he was about twelve, was impressed by the bikes, and he always had this look of admiration in his eyes for Albert's mother when he saw her long, black, curly hair. In summer he turned up in his shorts and Albert remembered the big scar he had on his left leg, which had the shape of a hockey stick. A quiet boy he was, from a large family of twelve children, a loner, Albert supposed, just like himself. The boy looked up to him, Albert had noticed, when he was standing by his bike, in his tight, red and black racing suit.

Studying the picture and his father's face, he could, as it were, see the questions he would ask: 'How did it go? Did it sound all right? Valves OK now, do you think? Brakes better with these new pads?' On a stand, next to his dad, was his brother's bike; a very fast, dark blue one. His brother was standing next to it. Albert remembered how he loved the bikes, their design, the colours, the sound, the tight leather suits, but he loathed the macho world that came with it, however kind some people were, and he thought of the weekends when the whole family went to the *24 Heures du Mans*. What a spectacle it always was and how much he liked the special smell of the circuit, the tarmac, the tyres, the exhaust fumes, the rubber, the fuel. What fantastic weekends they were.

He looked at his mother, bless her, and his thoughts wandered to Paris, to his aunt, who, he now saw, looked more like his mother than he had thought. His mother and aunt, two emblems of love. The room with the breakfast table, the wrought iron balcony, love, Paris, Quartier Latin, the café, the white wine, the warm evening, the museums, the paintings, Sylvain, Luxembourg, the chestnut trees, Square Emile Chautemps, Richard. The last name brought his flight to an abrupt end.

While he was sitting there in his chair, ruminating, the pixels of the sun were touching, feelingly reading the miniscule holes in the wooden wall of the cottage, a *camera obscura*, letting in the light, like in his mind; projections of the past on now, of love on sadness, of the unconscious on the conscious; upside down, through a glass with a dried-up circle of red wine.

11

Roonah slipped off the stool; she was tired and wanted to go home. The barkeeper heaved a sigh of relief when he saw the others followed her example.

'Thanks! Goodnight!' they said, one by one.
'Morning, you mean,' the barman said, grumpily.

'Tough,' Bernard Chambers said to Erasmus, mockingly. 'That's life. Next time better, young man.'
What an asshole, Erasmus thought, but said nothing.

12

Strolling through the streets of Havana, Albert couldn't believe his eyes; what a fine city it was. In the distance he saw the sun fall over the bald, grey cupola of the Iglesia de Jésus de Miramar and the stately, bare ribs of the white-grey Cupola del Capitolio. Wasn't it *magnifique*? It was good to be delivered from the ship and he was happy to hear Spanish again, although it sounded different from the Spanish people spoke in Spain. In spite of the heat and dust it all felt so new, fresh and exciting, the buzz perhaps of the feeling that he was in a new world, and this was only the entrance hall of all the Hispanic American countries. How must Columbus have felt when he arrived here? Albert wondered. He had never read much about Havana or Cuba; what he knew was from what he had seen on TV or heard from other people. Apparently, there were still lots of American cars from the 1950s driving around, there was a high standard of healthcare and the people there were crazy about art and music. If it was true, he didn't know, but he intended to sample it all. Walking past a taxi-stand he asked one of the cabdrivers if he could show him some interesting places.

'Of course,' the driver answered, 'Get in; there's plenty to see.'

On their way to Havana Cathedral they drove past a street called O'Reilly and Albert couldn't figure out why there would be a street in Havana with a name that sounded so typically Irish. The driver told him O'Reilly was one of many Irishmen, called 'wild geese', or 'goose', he wasn't sure what the right word was, who had fought for the Spanish Army against pirates and men from other colonial powers.

'But did you know, Señor, that the most famous South American, Che Guevara, was also of Irish descent, that his *antepasados*, erm, ancestors, were called Lynch?'

'No, I didn't. All I know is he's still a cult hero in the Western World. By the way, are there many art galleries in Havana?'

'There are some 'arty' streets with galleries, if that's what you mean. Shall I take you there?'

'Yes, please.'

They drove to a district not far from the cathedral, called the Taller Experimental de Grafica. He got out and paid the driver.

'Would you like to join me for lunch?' he asked the man.

'Sorry, I have no time for that, but thanks very much. How long are you here for? Maybe we'll meet again.'

'I'm not so sure. I'm only here for today. Thanks again.'

Albert sauntered through the area, visited several galleries and spoke to a couple of artists. Being in this very inspirational environment, the urge to take up painting started itching. One day I will, he said to himself, when I'm in Ecuador.

As he liked the atmosphere of Havana, and the Chilean ship was to stay there for a few days anyway, Albert decided to find a cheap hotel in the city. Apart from the fact that it would be more pleasant than the cabin on the ship, he also hoped to be able to mix with the locals in this relaxed city.

When he came back to the place where the taxi had dropped him off, he saw it was still there and asked the man if he knew a nice hotel or hostel.

'No problem,' the man said and took him there in his cab.

The place was ridiculously cheap, so he checked in for two nights, put his bag in his room, and went back to the city centre to enjoy a bit of *craic*, as an Irish guy he knew in London called it, and spent the night in a great little bar with some terrific Latin music.

At around three o'clock in the morning there was an agitated knock on his door. It was probably the landlady, he thought. She was obviously in a panic, shouting *'ataque'* or something like that, he couldn't hear it very well. Albert thought that this part of the world, and especially Cuba, wouldn't be much affected by the Third World War; certainly not in this final phase. He went to the door and opened it, but there was nobody there. He closed the door again and sat down on his bed. What should he do? He didn't know, but when he heard the banging of doors and people shouting in panic everywhere around him, he leapt to his feet, ran to the door, pulled it open, but couldn't see anybody. He grabbed some clothes and ran into the street as fast as he could, afraid the old hotel would collapse any moment. It was chaos all around; people, many of them only half-dressed, were screaming, women and children were running about, crying with fear. Because of the noise he'd heard earlier that night, he had expected to see planes, complete squadrons of them, like in those horrible war films he had sometimes seen because his father and brother liked watching them, but they weren't there. He stood nailed to the ground, was at a loss what to do or where to go. He couldn't think clearly; he was terrified and felt utterly deserted and alone in this strange city. Should he perhaps try and get back to the ship?

His thoughts were interrupted by the sound of sirens that broke loose everywhere, causing even more panic. He stood trembling on his legs, his heart was beating like mad, he got enormous cramps in his stomach and felt a diarrhoea coming up. He ran back into the hotel, into his room and the safety of the toilet as fast as he could.

Sitting on the toilet it was as if it wouldn't stop; it flowed, bubbled, gassed and still the pain in his bowels didn't go away. Fear and nerves, he thought, for he remembered the diarrhoea attacks he had when he saw his brother slide with his bike over the tarmac of the Dijon circuit and the morning he had to go to school for the first time. He tried to relieve the pain by massaging his belly. It always helped, but not this time. He could see himself sitting, alone in the dark room, with his trousers down, belly and legs bare, an open curtain, the door to the room ajar. How long he sat there, he didn't know and he didn't care what would happen next. At last the pain eased off. He stood up and lay down on the bed to recover. So many thoughts passed through his head. How could he get back to the ship? Where had everybody gone? He couldn't hear a single human voice; it was so unreal.

After an hour he got up from the bed, dressed, took his rucksack and went out into the street again. Wandering around for a long time, he saw or heard nothing that indicated there had been an air-raid. Lights went off and back on again and there were still people running and shouting in the street, disoriented. In the distance he heard the sound of anti-aircraft guns; they were firing, but there was nothing to be seen, no fires, smoke or any collapsed buildings. Was he in a movie? Was all this really happening? Maybe someone had heard a rumour and driven other people crazy, which had caused the panic, he thought.

The city had been ruthlessly roused from a sleepy, silky slumber and slipped into a state of chaos. Perhaps it was a hoax and he'd better go back to his hotel, he thought, but when he got back, there was still nobody there. He shut the windows to keep most of the noise out and lay down on his bed, waiting.

His head was like a city, with streets of chaotic thoughts, criss-crossing in an illogical pattern; endless avenues of chimaeras, suffused with confusion; squares full of cars, maniacally hooting unintelligible words; a port of irrational ideas without an exit.

He shouldn't have left the hotel; not a single bomb had fallen on the city. It seemed Havana had been the target of a U.S. bio-warfare attack. He didn't know why, but the word 'chemtrails' entered his thoughts. U.S. Coastguard planes that were normally used for tracking down drug traffickers appeared to have dropped an unknown substance over the city that night. It hadn't come as a complete surprise, as Cuba and its foreign policy had been a thorn in the side of the U.S. for many a decade. It was a recalcitrant country they couldn't get a grip on.

Albert later heard that in the second half of the previous century Cuba had protested several times at the UN against other bio-warfare attacks, during which not only plants and crops, such as coffee, cane sugar and tobacco had been targeted, but also animals, such as pigs, young cows, bullocks, rabbits and even sea tortoises. Humans, too, had fallen victim to substances that caused haemorrhagic dengue, haemorrhagic conjunctivitis and dysentery. Were those Americans completely crazy? he asked himself and he also remembered the rumours about the involvement of the U.S. in the Ebola outbreak in Africa in the 2010s.

Some eye-witnesses of the attack claimed they had seen a purple glow hanging over the city when the planes were gone. Government officials stated these were the clouds that contained the contagious virus. Once again it was a variant of the enterovirus. It wasn't taken very seriously at first, because the symptoms would normally only manifest themselves after three to four days, but this time it was different. Of course the U.S. denied their involvement.

The very next morning, when Albert woke up, he felt nauseous, had a terrible headache and pain behind his eyes and in his joints. He was not the only one though; thousands of habitants of Havana had been infected, whereas there were also people who had no problems at all. Maybe they had remained indoors, or perhaps some parts of the city had not been affected.

There were long queues at all the surgeries and hospitals were prepared for the worst, as this variant of the virus was not known, although the first symptoms resembled those of the Dengue Fever, but this was a much more aggressive form.

Albert grew weaker and weaker and didn't even think of his journey to Ecuador any more; all he wanted to do was stay in bed, but his mind was so restless.

'Get back to the ship. Get back to the ship,' went through his head like a fever, 'if you don't go to the ship, it might sail away without you.'

He tried to get up, but he felt so feeble and fell back onto his bed. He made another attempt. This time he was more successful. Fortunately the harbour wasn't too far away, but it seemed to take hours and the houses looked funny; as if they were moving. When he finally got to the harbour, he saw the Chilean ship had disappeared. Dejected, he went back to the hotel and lay down again. How could he get away from here? he wondered. Later that day he felt so bad that he knew he had to go to the hospital a few streets away.

Although not everyone in Havana had been infected with the virus, it was a mess. Public transport had come to a standstill, there were hardly any taxis available and people avoided each other for fear of infection. Police cars and other vehicles were driving through the city with big loudspeakers, telling people to contact a doctor immediately, even if they weren't sure if they had been infected.

All those sounds and impressions; they were driving him crazy. In the overcrowded waiting-room, surrounded by groaning men and women, crying children and panicky voices, he felt terrible; his eyes were trying to close themselves and his head wanted to go to sleep. More faces, more crying, it was hot, he couldn't breathe and slowly sank away into the lower regions of reality, his rucksack still on his back. In a mist he saw himself dying, in a strange city, in a country far from home, among unfamiliar faces, without a relative or a friend near him. Nobody even knew he was in Havana. He just wanted to die. Cloudy images appeared; of his mother on her deathbed, the Brylcreemed head of his father in the garden, of his brother and Sylvain. He sank into a sea of unintelligible voices and sounds.

13

Desmond was sitting on his bed, half-awake, thinking of Roonah and her warm body and how she sometimes kept on turning and turning if she couldn't sleep. And if that didn't work, she got out of bed and went outside to get some fresh air.

With her feet kicking against the friable sand, she walked past the wooden cottage where, she thought, the music had come from. It was dead quiet now. She was trying to peep inside, but couldn't see anything. Suddenly she saw someone standing very close to her, next to the cottage. It gave her a fright, and a feeling of guilt and shame as if she was a voyeur.

Albert saw her feminine contours, her face and hair catching the first sunlight.

'*Bonjour, Mademoiselle.*'

Because of the dazzling, early morning sun that was shining in her face, she couldn't distinguish his features.

'Oh, hello, sorry, good morning. How are you?' she replied and laughed, slightly nervous and maybe a little embarrassed, like someone who's just been found out.

That accent of hers, it sounded Irish, he thought. He knew he had heard it in London, and somewhere else too, but he couldn't recall where. The thin, warm tone of her voice, the sounds of those few words evoked images of beauty, mist and sensuality, an abstract watercolour that could speak. The fresh rays of the sun fell on her body, exploring her red shirt, her breasts, her skirt, her curls, against the scintillating background of the blue water. She had something familiar, he thought, but she was already gone again. Only the wishshshshshsh and washshshshsh of the waves remained, back and forth, but apart from that, silence reigned.

14

The people in the waiting-room who saw Albert collapse, panicked, called for help and went to find a nurse.

'There's blood coming from his eyes,' a little girl whispered to her mother.

He passed out and a little later he was lying in a bed, on a ward full of fellow-victims, the needle of a drip-feed in his arm. In a bed next to him lay the likeable cabdriver, the one who had driven him through Havana the day before and on another ward lay one of the sturdy policemen who had helped get him off the ship; the man had turned into a wreck.

The atmosphere in Havana changed dramatically. Although there had been no military invasion and no buildings had been destroyed, shops, restaurants and public buildings remained closed, there was no music to be heard and there were hardly any people in the street. Those who did venture outside, covered their mouths with cloths, tissues or whatever else was available, while on the radio one news bulletin followed the other, sometimes with completely contradictory information. Apart from these news bulletins only nationalistic songs were played, but very often only crackling and whining sounds emerged from the old-fashioned devices.

Nobody really knew what was going on, although, overnight, placards appeared on official notice boards, telling people what to do. Here and there dogs and cats, with funny patches on their bodies, were lying dead in the street, and in alleys and parks lifeless bundles of homeless people could be seen lying on the ground or leaning against walls or gates, waiting to be cleared away. Havana had become a ghost-town, with squeaking metal signboards, closed shutters and doors, empty streets, pieces of paper swirling past locked up shops, street noises without children's voices and the whistling of birds; a deserted warmth.

The inhabitants of Havana weren't allowed to leave the city and people from outside couldn't get in for fear of infection and to keep the virus from spreading. Of course, it was virtually impossible to prevent the rules from being violated, but the inhabitants of the city realised it was more sensible to stay in Havana and people from outside knew that it wasn't very clever to look for misery in the city and run the risk of being infected themselves. It was all very annoying for people who'd left the city for a few days and couldn't come back, even though they weren't infected, and also for visitors to Havana who had suddenly got stuck there.

The situation in most hospitals soon became unsustainable; doctors, nurses and ambulance staff didn't turn up for work, because they had been infected themselves and were either at home or in hospital. The emergency situation was declared and Havana was designated a national disaster area. The army was brought into action and some hospitals had to be evacuated, whereby patients were taken to other places and hospitals on the island.

In the meantime a UN team investigating the bio-warfare attack said there were indications it hadn't been carried out by the U.S. at all, but by Russian planes with American markings. The Russians, once staunch allies of the Cubans, were probably very much disgruntled by the success of the Americans in bringing Cuba under their sphere of influence.

An international appeal was made to get nurses and doctors to come to Cuba. Volunteers needed to have guts to do that, for, of course, no one wanted to be infected by an unknown virus, but also scientists from the U.S. offered their assistance to try and identify the virus. Apart from the familiar symptoms mentioned earlier, people who were infected also appeared to suffer from amnesia. This was an unknown symptom and in various laboratories in the world scientists were anxiously looking for the cause, even in China, as it feared they might be the next target. The Chinese had been affected anyway, because in the port of Havana were several Chinese naval vessels and other ships, whose crews had been infected with the virus. Some of them had already passed away, as they failed to seek help from a doctor, while others, who did go to hospital, were unable to communicate, as they could only speak and understand Chinese.

This bio-warfare attack, the worldwide panic ensuing from it and a leadership change in China, as a result of which the country dropped its claim to the North Pole, heralded the end of the Third World War. Many political cards had been reshuffled, but for the umpteenth time it had resulted in a human and ecological drama.

Albert and the taxi-driver were transferred to another hospital, in Santiago de Cuba, on the other side of the island, more than five hundred miles from Havana. They were flown to an airport near Santiago in a military aircraft, from where they were transported in special vehicles to the hospital, which had been prepared in great haste to cater for infected and sick people from Havana. Other patients there were either discharged or taken to other hospitals. Very slowly Albert began to feel better, but the doctors didn't know if it would take weeks or perhaps months for him to recover fully, as his symptoms were very serious. Due to amnesia Albert didn't even know how he had landed in hospital and, when he was informed, he thought he was still in Havana. After about ten days he had a serious relapse and needed to be drip-fed again. Even when his head was clear for a brief spell, he thought he was living somewhere in a sea. Everything was hazy, feelings of warmth and extreme cold alternated, as if he was tossed from a tropical sea into a polar sea and back again, while voices around him sounded muffled, bubbly and watery. His arms, one of which appeared to be attached to a hook or fishing-rod, were dangling around him, while his legs felt like a tail or went completely numb at times. The cabdriver was in the same plight. In a bright moment Albert had recognised him, but the driver had a blank look in his eyes.

Cuban nurses and foreign volunteers worked extremely hard, mostly round the clock, but it still took more than six weeks before the worst was over. There were no new cases of infection and a laboratory in Australia had successfully identified the virus. It appeared to be a laboratory cultivated mutation and was a lot more dangerous than existing viruses.

Sometimes Albert slept for days on end; he had completely weakened, was still dizzy, nauseous and his eyes and joints were very painful. At night he was delirious, saying things in French and the nurses often wondered whether he would live to see the next day.

There was a nurse who only did nightshifts and every time she looked at Albert, lying there in his bed, she delighted in his beautifully shaped face. If he had a sudden relapse and seemed to stop breathing, she would take her rosary and start to pray for him without delay; there wasn't much else she could do for him. If it really helped or not, she didn't know, but he slowly got better.

Because his infected eyes hurt so much and she was there only at night, he could never see her very well. He only knew that she had a lithe body and long hair, which she mostly wore in a tail or knot. Occasionally he woke up and, smelling her perfume, which he somehow thought was Trésor, he knew she was on the ward. He often wondered if she really existed, because she only appeared at night, while all the other nurses also worked in the daytime. He dreamt a lot, which made him think that she, in her white uniform, was someone from one of his dreams, or an angel who'd come to comfort him before the man with the scythe would come and get him. He didn't care, as long as she came back. When he was finally getting better, she was still very busy looking after other patients who were quite poorly, so she could never talk to him for more than five minutes, but what she said helped him a lot.

It took another couple of weeks before he could stand on his legs again, albeit with the help of crutches. Due to the deterioration of muscular mass they had become almost half as thin as they used to be. Fortunately, his eyes were no longer as red and bloodshot as before. Sometimes he would sit on his bed for a long time, watching the sun rise, looking at Santiago, listening to the church bells and the sounds of life outside. How terrible it was to be confined to this place, he thought, and he hated the fact that he was dependent on others and couldn't go for a walk on his own. He felt useless and never saw anyone he knew. The only things that had remained loyal to him were his sombre thoughts.

However, one of the male nurses, a blond-haired guy, called Gabriel, was incredibly kind to him and did everything he could to help Albert get better. He took him for short walks on his crutches along the corridors, made sure that Albert ate well; in short, nothing was too much for him. Albert was so beautiful, he thought, so special, and because of this long beard he called him Alberto Jésus. It didn't take long before every member of the nursing staff called him by that name.

Albert no longer had any plans for the immediate future. It was no use making them anyway, he thought and, moreover, he didn't have the strength for it. He had lost more than fifteen kilos and all his clothes were too big for him. Once more Gabriel came to the rescue by buying Albert some better fitting ones and, full of adoration, Gabriel sat down at Albert's bed one day and asked him,

'What is it you're thinking of?'

'Too many things.'

'I am so happy to just sit here, on this iron stool, this plastic *cojín*, at this plastic table, and look at you.'

It made Albert laugh and every day Gabriel came back to sit at Albert's bed and talk to him for at least fifteen minutes.

'Please tell me a bit more about Paris, about its atmosphere, the fashion shops, the clubs,' Gabriel would ask him, like a child who never tires of hearing the same fairy-tale over and over again, and he also loved to hear Alberto talk about art and painting.

Albert knew so much; if only he knew half of what Albert knew, he thought, and sighed.

Sometimes Albert was very depressed, which, apparently, was one of the symptoms of the disease, and talked to Gabriel about the purpose or, rather, the total uselessness of life and the books he had read about it. It scared Gabriel and he was afraid Albert might take his own life.

'Alberto, please don't give up. You're so good-looking, so wise, so special. Hang on to your *sueño*, your dream. Go to Ecuador,' was all he could sometimes say. 'I feel so powerless. Tell me what I have to do. Why don't you listen? Am I too stupid for you?'

Although Albert didn't say it directly, he drew a lot of strength from Gabriel's words. He would look at poor Gabriel and was afraid of giving him too much hope. Just asking Gabriel to come back the next day might give him the idea they could be lovers. Why he couldn't say this to Gabriel, he didn't know.

When the danger of infection was over, he was allowed to walk in the garden of the hospital. In the beginning he had to use crutches, but very soon he needed only a walking-stick to support him. The nurses and doctors had done a fantastic job; without them he wouldn't have survived this ordeal, he thought.

He realised he hadn't seen the night nurse for a while. Maybe she'd been transferred to another department or hospital, he thought. What a shame, especially now that I'm feeling better; we could finally have talked a bit more.

At last the news came that he was going to be discharged. It would be days rather than weeks before he could go home, but there was no home to go to, so what could he do? It made him feel even more depressed. He wished he could fly to Ecuador, to Paris, or wherever, he thought. He was a prisoner on this island, surrounded by friendly people, but a prisoner all the same.

Standing in front of the mirror in his white pyjamas, he saw a pale, old man with a stick, an apparition, with thin arms, a hollow, wrinkly face, bags under some strange, bleary eyes, thin, wan lips, temples tinged with grey, someone who looked like a prisoner in a concentration camp or a patient in a psychiatric institution.

'Wouldn't it be better if you, yes you, decrepit old guy, shaved off your beard? You're not me. You're somebody else, a broken image, an effigy, the result of a bodged attempt to resurrect the young man who has died. I don't like you. You scare me.'

Sometimes, in the darkness of the night, shrouded in a cloud of sheer depression, he was swallowed up by a swamp of sullen sadness, a mire of misery, attacked by invisible, unknown agents of self-destruction, throttled, garrotted and dumped like dirt by feelings of dire desperation.

'Why can't anybody give me some pills or an injection? I'm fed up. Just let me die.'

Nobody heard or understood what he said.

One afternoon, when he was walking in the garden again, he saw the taxi-driver who had shown him Havana the day he arrived there. How awfully sad and fragile the man looked, sitting in his wheelchair, his dull eyes staring into a void. Albert realised Raoul, that's what Gabriel called the taxi-driver, was much worse off than himself, and it helped him look at his own situation from a different perspective. He went up to Raoul to talk to him and saw a tiny glitter in the man's eyes. Had Raoul recognised him, or was he just happy somebody talked to him?

'Let me push your wheelchair,' Albert said, 'so that you don't have to stay in the same place all the time.'

'*Gracias*,' the man's lips seemed to say.

The tables had turned; Albert had become the driver and Raoul the passenger. The mere attention Raoul got from Albert made him feel better, which, in return, reflected on Albert. The next day he was even more surprised when he came across yet another person he had met previously, even though he had never been to Cuba before. It was one of the two policemen who were standing on deck of the Chilean ship when he arrived at the port. A real cop, the man recognised Albert at once, in spite of the latter's beard and sickly appearance.

'No more sight-seeing in Havana?' he asked Albert and laughed at his own joke. 'What ward are you on?'

'Thirty-three. Why?'

'A few weeks ago I overheard a male and female nurse talking about you. They were scared Alberto Jésus, the young Frenchman with the rucksack, wouldn't make it. I also heard them say how beautiful this Alberto was.'

It made them both laugh.

A week later he learned that a large group of patients, including himself, Raoul and Eduardo, the policeman, would be flown back to Havana. Both men offered Alberto, because that's what everybody called him now, to stay with them as long as he wanted. Since Eduardo would be very busy once he was back in Havana, Albert decided to move in with Raoul's family.

'I know where to find you,' he said to Eduardo, who got the joke and laughed.

In spite of his busy schedule at the hospital Gabriel also tried to be with Alberto as much as he could and, if Alberto liked, he could also move into Gabriel's apartment in Santiago or stay a bit longer at the hospital.

Why, for God's sake, should I want to stay here? Albert asked himself and what to do with Gabriel? How can I tell him there's no place for him in my life, that I don't love him now and never will? Somewhere, deep in his head, only one name resounded, Sylvain.

When he was allowed to leave hospital, Gabriel stood looking at him, tears in his eyes. Albert felt sorry for him. They embraced each other and promised to stay in touch. Albert wanted to say goodbye to the other nurse, the one of the nightshift whom he would always remember as 'the sweet young light in the darkness of the night', if his memory didn't let him down. But she wasn't there.

Like Lazarus he had risen from the dead and he would soon be going back to Havana. On Thursday morning they got on a military plane to Havana, where some coaches stood waiting to take them back home. Albert was happy to see life there was gradually getting back to normal; there was music coming from most bars again and happy faces had returned to the streets, in spite of the enormous tragedy that had taken place and the realisation that death had taken a heavy toll. He was walking past a flower shop, just when the florist came out of her shop to empty a bucket of water in the gutter. He heard the fresh water splatter on the cobbles and realised how much he had missed street life and how glad he was to be back in Havana, out of confinement.

When Raoul saw his loyal, old 1950s Chevrolet waiting for him patiently, he cheered up, stroked the car, gave her a loving kiss and smiled. His son came running outside and flew round his dad's neck, while his wife stood looking at him with a worried look on her face.

But when Eduardo came home, there was nobody waiting for him. His wife was one of the many casualties who hadn't survived the attack. Eduardo had heard the tragic news when he was in hospital himself, but, because of his own illness, it didn't really get through to him and after that he had pushed it away and never talked about it.

His situation was not an isolated case. The same thing had happened in tens, maybe hundreds, or possibly thousands of other families, Albert thought, and, of course, it had a gigantic impact on everyday life in the city and its surroundings. It would take many years before everything would get back to normal.

For the time being he moved in with Raoul and got his son's bedroom, who went to sleep in his parents' bedroom. At first Albert didn't want this, but he couldn't refuse. He contributed to the food and other household expenses, which was quite a boon for the family, as Raoul hadn't been able to earn any money for some time. Albert gradually got his strength back and put on a bit more weight, but Raoul's health was a different story. He was being troubled by amnesia again, only this time it was worse, and his eyes looked strange. Later that week, when they both had to go to hospital for a check-up, it turned out Raoul's blood count was not in order and his immune-system wasn't working properly; he had too many white blood cells. Albert heard a doctor say to a colleague that it was better to admit Raoul to hospital for close observation, but things didn't improve and the symptoms indicated that the illness was coming back. Once more he was isolated from his family and friends, because the authorities were afraid of a new wave of contamination. Raoul had been so close to a full recovery, a return to normal life with his wife and son, but now he was back to square one.

Albert supported the family as well as he could and couldn't bear to think of deserting these lovely people in this time of misery, and flee to Ecuador, but the heavy, thick depression in the family could be cut with a knife.

'I don't know what to do any more, Albert,' Raoul's wife said. 'What if he dies?' she sobbed.

Albert didn't know what to do. All he could say was,

'I'll help you. Don't worry about the money; I'll take care of that.'

Since his mother was very sad and his father not at home, the little boy had the feeling he was losing both his parents, Albert noticed, so he tried to divert the boy from all the troubles as much as possible by taking him out. A good thing was that the boy knew the way in Havana quite well, having regularly accompanied his father in the taxi, so that Albert got to know the city better than the average tourist. He also became the mainstay of the family, although Raoul's brother and sister, who didn't live in Havana, also sent some money now and then.

After three weeks Raoul's condition had deteriorated so much that the doctors gave up all hope. He went into a coma and a couple of days later he passed away. It was an enormous blow to the family and Albert was devastated. Every day he was confronted with the pain of Raoul's family, and since he hadn't fully recovered himself yet, he became more and more exhausted and depressed. What else could he do for Raoul's wife and son? he wondered. He gave her money, as there wasn't much else he could do, but, in order to get better himself, he had to take a decision. It was time to move on, but he didn't know how, for shipping traffic had almost come to a complete standstill as a result of the epidemic; foreign yachts and other vessels, which might have helped him to get away from the island, could only enter the harbour with permission from the authorities.

Would he ever be able to escape from this place? he asked himself. He thought of Robinson Crusoe, and although that man was on an uninhabited island and he wasn't, it still felt the same; being cut off from everything and everybody, his illness, the hopelessness, the waiting, more waiting. Maybe one day a ship would turn up to rescue him. Even a 'Man Friday' would be welcome, as long as it was Sylvain. The thought made him laugh at himself.

He often went to see Eduardo and tried to support him as much as he could. He'd been very lucky, he realised, for Eduardo didn't look too good either, although he was making some progress. Sometimes they went out for a coffee together and once in a while they had a drink at a bar. On Sunday afternoons, often for hours at a stretch, they would sit together, in total silence, on a bench at the Malecon, a busy boulevard along the shore, watching the sun go down over the Gulf of Mexico, each with his own thoughts and memories from the past, although there were many things they couldn't recall yet.

In his pocket Albert found the scrap of paper that Eduardo had given him when he went ashore.

'Who was that mysterious person on the piece of paper that you gave me on the ship?'

'Funny you should still have that paper. He's a cousin of mine and he knows lots of people in Havana. Some of them are quite influential guys too.'

Eduardo noticed that Albert was restless and getting impatient. It was time for him to move on, Eduardo thought, but there was no ready-made solution to help him.

15

Roonah came into the bedroom and Desmond started kissing her right away, however sleepy he was.

'Come here, darling, lie down. Empty your busy head and take a rest. I love you,' he whispered sleepily. 'How was Pepito's?'

She kissed him back with her ever warm lips.

'Love you too. It wasn't too bad, but I'm so tired. By the way, You really look like Father Christmas now with your long white hair. If you had a beard, kids would really be confused,' she said, with a smile. 'Only joking. Come here,' she whispered in his ear, kissed him and pulled him towards her, letting her sweet hands slide through his hair.

When she turned round, her curls fell over her face and shoulders. It didn't take a minute before she was asleep. Looking at her, in the thin darkness of this naked day, lying under the sheet, soft and sweet, Desmond realised he dared to think he was really happy for the first time in his life. He closed his eyes to get used to the new light.

After only a few hours of sleep her smile greeted the warm efforts of the morning sun. Desmond's broad thumb travelled over her lips and the corners of her mouth that went slightly upwards in such a funny, happy way; then proceeded over her warm cheeks, the breeding ground of her smiles. Her breasts were pressing against him, and when he embraced her, he felt an erection coming up. The obelisk in Central Park, skyscrapers, and many other images of Manhattan popped up in his mind's eye.

New York, the city where they had met, in the almost yellow, fairy-tale like light at the twenty-three metre high marble-white arch in Washington Square Park, an American 'Arc de Triomphe'. He remembered the time he was there for his great passion and work, photography. Every day he would walk through the never sleeping city, from early in the morning till late at night, his eyes scanning, looking for the most wonderful compositions of light and disfigured objects on the numerous Art Deco and Postmodernist buildings, faithfully following his weary feet, his heart, arteries and blood vessels pulsing with the rhythm of his excitement. He never took time for himself to eat something, have a coffee or a much needed pee; it didn't even cross his mind. The camera, the different lenses, that was him, the knowledge of the left cerebral hemisphere at the service of the right half of his brains, where the limitless powers of creation and intuition dwelt. Together, one. In December and January he had been there too, to avail himself of the ultra-sharp, stark winter light. It was freezing and a polar wind was blowing, but the photos spoke for themselves.

When he met Roonah, however, it was mid-July, the temperature was in the high twenties and the light from the sun hit the city at another angle of inclination. It was still quite hot that evening and the warm light round Washington Square Arch, combined with the bustle of all the people who were making music, dancing, hanging, kissing each other, watching, or just standing there, had attracted him like a moth to a candle.

There he was, sitting on a bench, the camera still around his neck like a flexible, add-on limb, watching the spectacle, imbibing the atmosphere. Close to the arch he saw a young woman, looking up and down the arch. He could see she was thinking about what she saw. Engrossed by her presence, he couldn't keep his eyes off her, with her short, brown skirt and sky-blue top that left a large part of her shoulders uncovered and when she was looking up, her long, blond curls fell down, reaching almost the bottom of her scapulae. This is a goddess, an angel who has just come to earth and who is now looking up to see the gate, the arch of heaven closing, he thought, and the light of the arch, half a halo, is there especially for her.

'Excuse me, can you tell me the way to Union Square?' a beautiful, black lady asked him, interrupting his thoughts. He only half-heard the question and looked confused.

Turning towards her, he said, 'I beg your pardon, Madam?'

'Could you tell me the way to Union Square, please?' she asked again.

He happened to know where it was and told her the way. She looked at him with her big lookers, thanked him and walked into the direction he had told her.

He turned back, but the blond, curly-headed girl was no longer there. Where's my angel gone? he wondered, while his eyes were feverishly searching for her. She had vanished. A light attack of panic seized him, as if he'd lost something valuable.

There were a lot of people standing near and under the arch, but still the square felt deserted. Had she really been there? he asked himself, or had it been a hallucination? He suddenly saw her again and almost blushed. She smiled at him and pointed at the empty space on the stone bench beside him.

'Can I sit next to you?'

He was taken aback for a moment.

'Could I refuse?' he said, almost clumsily, wiping away some leaves.

Sitting beside him, she told him about the mathematical lines of the arch, pointing at it with her delicate fingers. These fingers were more beautiful than the arch, he thought and wondered if he'd landed in a fairy tale, or if he'd fallen asleep, because of the long walks, or if he was dreaming.

'I like the way you speak, with your Irish accent, the fine, tender 't's and 'l's, if I may say so.'

She blushed a little.

Although he didn't know what she said, he did know how she said it; the other vowels and consonants which were formed with a curved tongue at the front, against her palate, her 'arch'. Moreover, her appearance was overwhelming, with her big, blue eyes. The last time he had had this feeling was so far away in the past, but in a split second it had come back to him, and very violently too; he was falling in love.

'What kind of photos do you take? Can I see them?'

'Sure. Here you are. Press that little button.'

'I know. Wow! They're really cool. Have you ever been to the Museum of Modern Art?'

'I'm afraid I haven't.'

'You've got to go there; they have the finest collections of modern art. I'm saying this because your photos would fit in perfectly. By the way, do you do nudes as well?'

'No, I don't, I haven't really tried, to be honest,' he said, once more overwhelmed by her outspokenness.

And so their conversation went on, about art, New York, life. She told him she liked drawing and painting and said she would like to make a sketch or do a nude of him. She looked at his head and thought how she would paint it and she wondered what he looked like naked, being so different, so attractive.

'Would you like to come with me to the American Natural History Museum tomorrow? We could first go for a walk through Central Park, if you like,' she proposed.

He was still thinking about what she had just said. She would like to see the dinosaur skeletons, she said, and asked him had he ever seen the film *A Night At The Museum* which was filmed there ages ago.

Thousands of small lights around them, the park, the arch and the attention he suddenly got, he couldn't believe it; he was overwhelmed and felt severed from his 'I-thinking'. Never before had he experienced anything like this. It was as if they were standing in the middle of a shower of shooting stars. He didn't even realise he hadn't given an answer. She woke him from his evening dream and asked him once more if he'd like to come with her the following day.

'Yes, I believe I have some time for that,' he said, and immediately realised how stupid it sounded.

'But why don't we have a drink somewhere now?' he asked her. 'I know a pleasant little place, close to Gramercy Park.'

He sounded disoriented and she thought how different he was from all those young guys she'd met. She chuckled. Maybe he was a bit clumsy, she thought, but very sweet, like a child, a boy. That she would ever think this of someone who was so much older than herself she could never have imagined, and without any hesitation she took him by the hand. Taking someone by the arm was so old-fashioned, she thought.

'What a fine, soft hand you have, so warm.'

'Thanks.'

Tingles in his chest, butterflies in his belly; he was definitely dreaming. He looked at her, into her eyes and saw all the romantic lights of Manhattan reflected in them. He smiled, for there were no words for what went through him.

In a pleasant-looking street, with brick-built houses, shops and bars, they entered a cosy café with old, leather seats and an open fire. They sat down and had some wine. In the background there was music from the previous century, *'She's like a rainbow'*, *'We love you'*, and *'Sympathy for the Devil'*, all songs by the Rolling Stones, a famous band, apparently, for a bygone era.

If this is the coming of the Anti-Christ, Desmond thought, let it be, and laughed to himself.

The next day they met at the American Museum of Natural History and in the afternoon, strolling through Central Park, they made plans for the rest of the week.

After struggling with life for so many years, Desmond was convinced he had finally found the Holy Grail, love, in a strong, invisible breeze of energy. They took their time enjoying museums, having a pizza in Little Italy, sitting in a park in Chinatown, where they were the only white people among eating, dancing and running Chinese families, seeing and feeling the tear-jerking Irish memorial garden with the 'speaking' tunnel (where Desmond saw Roonah's happy face change into a sad, pale Irish bog-scape of waterlogged soil and centuries of suffering), drinking tea at a café by the Hudson, walking through Harlem in the heat, with water spouting from fireplugs, lying on a colony of ants in Central Park, going to the 1950s style seaside resort off Coney Island, visiting the Museum of Jewish Heritage, where Desmond fell silent, the power of his speech being blocked by old sores and emotions, his eyes full of tears, standing on the Empire State Building late at night, getting goose pimples in Strawberry Fields, in front of the Dakota building, where John Lennon had lived and was murdered, walking among thousands of pairs of shoes in Macy's, sailing on a ferry on the East River, kissing each other at Times Square and oversleeping and missing the bus to Bear Mountain State Park. At night they lay close together, so as not to miss a second of the bubbling brisk breeze blowing through their heads and hearts. When the darkness of the night enveloped New York, everything around them ceased to exist, right until the first rays of the sun illuminated their naked bodies, lying unwittingly entangled on ruffled starch white sheets, and woke up, with searching eyes and four, speechless lips.

Desmond was staying at an expensive bedsit near Columbus Circle, only seconds away from the huge, silvery globe that never failed to mesmerise him when he got on the subway there, while Roonah stayed at a hostel on the north side of Central Park, but within a week her things were moved to Desmond's bedsit. Sometimes they had breakfast in the whole foods supermarket in the basement of the shopping centre or at Angela's on the Avenue of the Americas.

He would have loved to move to another, cheaper bedsit, preferably in Greenwich, East Village, Tribeca or Chelsea, but, unfortunately, those parts of Manhattan had become unaffordable, for in the past famous people had invested their money in real estate there and they didn't buy just one house, but two or three at the same time to guarantee their privacy. The trend had been set and prices went through the roof accordingly.

Desmond was thinking of his first time in New York, when he was staying at a hotel near Amsterdam Avenue. During one of his long photo-walks he had come to what looked like a Belgian beer bar in the older district of Tribeca and now that Roonah was with him, he wanted to go back there to let her taste the atmosphere and the beer, but first they planned to go to a music bar in Ludlow Street for a wine and listen to a live band. Unfortunately because of her age, Roonah, couldn't get any alcoholic drinks and even got a stamp on her arm, which looked more like the tattoo of a German concentration camp than the stamp of a club, while the bouncer also warned bar staff with a very loud voice that she wasn't allowed to drink any alcohol. That was the last straw; they were furious and left *The Living Room* to find the other bar, the one with the Belgian beer, which, funnily enough (as they discovered the next day), was called *Anotheroom*. It was definitely near Canal Street subway station, he remembered, but there were several other subway stations in Canal Street with the same name and, unfortunately, very far away from each other. They kept trying, but never found the bar that night. They looked until two in the morning and landed at a bar in Church Street, which looked more like an Irish pub. Later that night they laughed their way home.

They resumed their search the following evening and did find the place then, on West Broadway, which turned out to be very close to the pub in Church Street. It was very busy, but some local people said they could come and sit at their table. One of them, a very friendly, self-confessed Jewish man called Max, who was slightly intoxicated, asked Desmond if he was Jewish as well. They got talking and in the end Max said Desmond could always count on him if he needed help to find an apartment. They were Jewish brothers, weren't they? Desmond accepted Max's offer and Max very soon fulfilled his promise.

Shortly after that, when Roonah had gone back to L.A., Desmond moved into a quaint, older apartment in Chelsea, where the street was paved with cobbles, people had front gardens and there were trees at almost every house.

Small shops, bars, restaurants and coffee houses completed the cheerful atmosphere of the neighbourhood, a village in a megacity.

They tried to stay in touch as much as they could, sending text messages, or phoning each other, for they wanted to get together again and see something of the world.

Not much later they went on holiday to England. Desmond knew it very well and wanted to show Roonah some special areas, like Wiltshire and Somerset, where there were ley-lines, he said, high energy lines connecting places and ancient monuments, such as Stonehenge, Avebury and Glastonbury in England with, for example, the Greek island of Patmos and the pyramids in Egypt.

Roonah remembered how excited they were when they were standing at Stonehenge and spotted some crop circles in the distance, towards Salisbury and she thought of the countless tumuli spread out all over the Salisbury Plain, a vast area where the hills were less steep and the countryside more undulating. It was a shame that a large part of this plain, where there were so many interesting things to be seen, was not accessible, as nearly all the land was owned by the Ministry of Defence and used for army training purposes. When they came back Roonah went to her parents in L.A. again.

Some months later the Third World War broke out. It was quite bizarre, actually, but in spite of the fear and panic, caused by the war, there was a sense of optimism in New York. Of course Manhattan, the Achilles heel of the U.S. economy, was extremely well protected, while the West Coast of the U.S. suffered a great deal more, which was another reason why people in New York thought there was nothing much going on and were convinced no one could touch the U.S. and bring it to its knees and they felt safe behind the huge flood barrier.

After four weeks Roonah let Desmond know she was going to drive back to New York, in an old 1950s Buick. That was really cool, he thought, and he was proud of her. The moment he saw her drive into the street, his heart started palpitating and what a sight it was, the slender young woman behind the wheel of this huge automobile. Until she sold it, this piece of nostalgia attracted a lot of admiring eyes.

She moved in with him, and although he noticed there was something unusual about her, he couldn't put his finger on it. Maybe she had to get used to him again or perhaps she wanted to tell him in person that their relationship was over, he thought. He hardly dared to ask her, for fear of hearing something he didn't want to know. He could live on his own, without her, if he had to, he bravely said to himself, while he realised that the impact she had made on his life was probably far greater than he could ever begin to imagine.

It kept his mind busy almost every hour of the day, while she was thinking of her sweet Desmond, the man she wanted to stay with despite the arguments and fights she'd had with her parents about her unusual relationship. She hadn't told him anything about that yet. She thought of her mother who was no longer able to go to work, her father who was listless, sad and sometimes even depressed, of her sisters who'd laughed at her, of her own feelings of guilt, that she had forsaken and disappointed her parents, given them so much pain, while they thought the world of her and loved her unconditionally. Maybe as a result of all this she had thought very hard about her own life, her own development, for she knew that she was still very young to throw herself into a fulltime relationship. In spite of all this she was determined to carry on with Desmond and she knew the fights at home had only made her stronger, more independent, more determined.

How can I tell Desmond? she asked herself. He loves me so much and he doesn't want to spend a minute without me. Well, not more than a couple of weeks anyway, she thought, and smiled. Of course, I want to be with him too, but I really have to do this and I won't be away forever. If we can both hold on, it may even strengthen and invigorate our relationship. I know *I* can do it, but I'm not sure if Desmond can. It would hurt me terribly, if he couldn't, but in the end it's my life and I mustn't let my happiness depend on somebody else.

'What's up with you, my darling?' he asked her, as he didn't want to put off the question any longer.

'I'm going to be a nurse. I want to volunteer.'

Utter silence. She got tears in her eyes.

'I want to help women and children, victims of the war. I just have to do it.'

He took her wet hand, moved it away from her eyes and kissed her fingers.

'I have thought about this for a long time, darling,' she said, 'but since I wanted to be a doctor in the first place and am still fascinated by medical science, I decided to volunteer. It was a very difficult decision and there's still so much going on in my head. I'm not leaving you, don't worry. I want to be with you, live with you, but I've got to do this.'

Still loosely holding her moist hand, Desmond tried to assess the consequences, but he was confused. Of course she had to follow her passion, her dreams, he thought, she had no choice and that's what he had to accept, however hard it would be, not only on him, but on both of them.

Roonah looked at him, anxiously, saw him thinking and could understand it if, in the end, he didn't want to, or couldn't carry on with their relationship.

'I understand your decision; you've got to do it,' he said. 'It's going to be hard, but we'll be all right.'

The gigantic thumb that had been pressing on her throat for weeks seemed to have gone.

'I was so much hoping you'd say that, so that we could make further plans. You're grand! I'm so relieved.'

It took a lot of guts to say something like this, she knew, and that was exactly what Desmond had, guts. She loved him for it and was happy that she had defended their relationship at home with so much fervour. If her parents could have seen this, they would have understood her, she thought. She wasn't crazy, she knew exactly what she was doing and the words which Desmond had just said proved she was right. She held his head with both hands and kissed his lips.

'Thank you, sweetest,' she whispered in his ear.

During the days, and sometimes even nights that followed, they went on talking about her decision. There were moments, especially at night, when Desmond was haunted by negative thoughts. Was she flying away again, this angel, this beautiful butterfly that had settled in Washington Square Park? Maybe she would meet somebody else, a young doctor. He knew it was sheer jealousy, but he couldn't help it and it made him feel sad.

When Roonah saw the recurring gloomy, contemplative look on Desmond's face, she wondered if she had made the right decision. But these were different days. As a woman, she also needed to think of herself, but maybe he didn't see it like that. After all, he had grown up in another culture, time and society, in another world, with different views. Although she found his world and background very fascinating, she shouldn't forget her own life and world either.

Before she could start her job, she had to follow a short training course. Fortunately it wasn't far from New York, so that they could be together quite often. After her training she would go to Washington State, which lay under heavy attack.

He wished she could have spent more time with him, in his happy, new apartment in Chelsea, but they did as much as they could; they went out for dinner and a dance, listened to music, saw a Broadway show and talked for many hours. The whole situation made him think of a story from *Dubliners* by James Joyce, where girls went out to have fun, before they went into retreat.

As she didn't have a contract, she planned to come back to New York after a few months. After that they would decide what to do next. In the meantime Desmond was busy preparing an exhibition of his photographs and he had signed a very lucrative contract with an important fashion house on Fifth Avenue for a series of photos. He wasn't going to be bored, he knew, and moreover, he could do everything on foot, which gave him the opportunity to shoot other pictures in the street.

The day of Roonah's departure was drawing near and the tension was becoming increasingly tangible, as if fate was coming to get them. The night before she left they were very restless and neither of them could sleep. They just lay in bed, looking up, following the random routes of the cracks in the old plaster ceiling, or tossing and turning, sometimes whispering things like 'I'll miss you' and 'I love you', or just softly and sadly squeezing each other's hands with tears in their eyes, but the earth just kept on revolving and when the morning came they were exhausted. They went to Penn Station and said goodbye to each other, knowing that if they could pull through this situation, they would emerge from the battlefield stronger than before.

Only occasionally did the sirens sound in New York. Everybody would flee into the subway then, but apart from that it was as if nothing had changed in the daily lives of most people. Of course they were inundated with tragic news bulletins stating the number of casualties and wounded people of that day, but they grew immune to them and didn't know if those reports were reliable. The authorities in the U.S. were working very hard to restore everything that was electronically operated, and the Internet was slowly getting back to normal, albeit with delays and interruptions. It became easier for Desmond to contact Roonah, although she was usually too busy to talk to him. If he didn't hear from her for some days he would start worrying and he wondered if she was all right.

She had a very hard time; the work was extremely exhausting and very gruesome. All the terrible things she saw during the day came back to her at night, whether she was awake or asleep. She was constantly haunted by horrifying images that drained her energy. She desperately needed a break, and thought working in a 'normal' hospital would be much better for her and she remembered how she'd always thought of going to Africa as a volunteer, while deep in her heart she was longing for peace and the soft grass of Ireland, County Clare, the village, her roots.

After five months she resolved to volunteer with an organisation that not only provided medical care to poorer countries, but also assisted other countries in cases of emergency. She didn't know in advance where she was going; it could be Africa, South or Central America. It didn't make much difference to her, as long as she could help other people and calm down.

When she told Desmond what her thoughts were, he became even more anxious and didn't know what to do or think; it could only lead to the end of their relationship with her going even further away. He felt terrible and the whole situation made him feel insecure, something he had never experienced before. Time and again he had to try to be flexible, he thought, but it was so confusing. For how long would he be able to cope with this? he asked himself. Wouldn't he rather go back to his old, less exciting, but clear-cut and quiet life? All these questions kept milling in his head. He did his best to bolster his confidence, to harden himself, although he didn't really want that, as their love might ooze away. Sometimes he felt so bad that he went into the street at night and roamed around the city for hours, thinking about life and how, when you are born and grow up, you are looked after and surrounded by love, but little by little that life becomes more complex and complicated. He ate irregularly, wandered around in the rain and didn't care if he got wet through or started coughing.

He could often be seen following the same route, along West 25th Street via 7th Avenue to West Houston Street; from there to East Houston Street and Brooklyn Bridge, where people lay sleeping behind gates under the South Street Viaduct and one of them, a shadow, was watching him. He walked past the City Hall to West Street and back home again. He would also walk to Washington Square Park, the place where they had first met and to get close to his old sense of happiness, the thought that everything was possible, every day again.

One night, just before daybreak, he was attacked by the unknown shadow. He wrestled with him and got free, but he was struck on the hip and walked with a limp for a couple of days.

He didn't need a drink; his brothers had been proof of what alcohol could do to a man. His eldest brother boozed so much at weekends that his body needed a week to recover. Another brother, an artist who was two years older than Desmond and lived in San Francisco, had been addicted to alcohol for years. He'd lost his wife, followed by a girlfriend, another girlfriend and, after that, the world, and he remembered how that brother had once knocked on his door in the middle of the night and begged him to let him in. He looked like a tramp, with his torn, filthy, stinking clothes and sores in his face. He talked to his brother for hours, but it was a useless exercise. Fortunately though, after a last warning from the doctor, his brother had woken up. The only one who didn't have an alcohol problem was his youngest brother, but his life was complicated enough without alcohol, he thought.

Only once in a while did he go to a bar to have a few glasses of wine, which led him to the deepest, most vulnerable, spot of his emotion and made him cry desperate tears that fell onto the naked wood of the table, where they fused and submerged.

'Pull yourself your together, or you'll end up in the gutter or in a loony bin. It's going to be all right,' he had to tell himself, but there were moments when he didn't have the strength to do so; all his resources were running dry and he was getting tired of life.

When he came home again he started writing, stories, poems, e-mails to keep himself on the right track and express his feelings.

The butterfly in New York

*When she came to me,
I was stupefied;
A butterfly,
Fantastic colours,
Settling softly
On the flower of my soul.*

*I could watch her,
Nay, let her rest,
For a sec,
On the thin blank canvas
Of my emotions.*

*Behind her trees
And grass;
The perfect décor
For the searchlight
Of her radiating aura.*

*I could only watch,
Looking for the contrast
In the composition for my inner image;
Like finding the right words
In a haystack of outdated platitudes.*

*A face,
A smile,
Scents,
In splendid colours,
Monet, Manet, Van Gogh, Renoir, Pisarro,
Together, a vivid tableau,*

*Blond hair,
Falling down,*

Along the open, red coat
Curls on the banks
Of her soft skin.

She was so great,
I felt so small,
So very small,
That I could
Almost feel
The basic truth of life
In the living world
Of all creatures,
Great and small.

An image,
Peace,
A solemn sigh, serenity,
In a sacred sea of silence;
My voice
That couldn't touch anything
But the framework of a ritual,
Lost in confusion and,
In nothing.
I could only watch
And breathe in the airy freedom
Of this butterfly,
This belle, Inachis io,
Before she would take off
And fly,
In the face of the thoughts
That were making their way
To my lips.

But I was silent,
Fell on my knees;
Only then did I see

What's lacking in
Our lives and time.

Take a rest
My butterfly,
Let me watch and learn,
Learn to watch and see,
Then let me die in your serenity.

On a Thursday, late in the afternoon, she remembered it exactly, she was called up and within a couple of days she was on an old, military plane, with four propellers and a big red cross on it, and flew non-stop from Seattle to an island in the Caribbean. In spite of her fatigue she felt great; she was longing for the sun, the sea, swimming, white beaches, a less hectic, more peaceful life.

In the darkness of the night her plane landed on an island with huge palm trees. Not until that moment did she realise how much she actually missed Desmond and she reproached herself for being a selfish, egocentric person and she remembered what the girls at school had said. Were they right after all? But she couldn't go back to the U.S., not at this moment anyway. The fact that communication with the U.S. was still virtually impossible made her feel even more miserable and Desmond was further away from her than ever before. When she arrived at the hospital, she resolved to take the nightshift, so that she wouldn't be alone in the darkness of the night, when people grow sad and most suicides are committed.

Desmond was getting used to the thought that it was all over between them. He tried to push it away, but in his dreams these thoughts came back to him. He would sometimes pretend Roonah was lying next to him in bed, so that he could fall asleep more easily, but there were also nights when he could be heard shouting things at the plates and mugs in the kitchen, like 'Roonah, why did you do this?' or 'Why the hell am I doing this to myself?' Once or twice some saucers followed his words against the white, callous wall. It was as if the meeting in Washington Square park had never taken place and the beautiful lights of the arch had become one big, dark spot of anti-light, he often thought.

One evening there was a knock on the door. He opened it, but saw nothing. Around the corner a dark shadow was lurking.

16

Albert was in the kitchen, talking to Eduardo.

'You probably think I'm OK,' he said, 'but I'm not. I feel shit in my head and it still feels as if I'm a kind of hostage. It's all so bloody pointless, but what can I do? How can I get to Ecuador?'

Despite his own situation Eduardo was quite positive.

'I can ask my cousin,' he said. 'I'm pretty sure he can help you out; he knows so many people.'

'Are you sure? You know I like this city and you're all so good to me, but please, help me. I need to get out now, or I'll go crazy.'

'I know, Albert. I'll go and see him right now.'

That same afternoon the three of them were sitting in a café, discussing the possibilities there were. Eduardo's cousin had made some inquiries and told Albert the harbour master regularly received requests from yachts that wanted to moor in the port of Havana, but due to the current situation and the Chinese keeping an eye on all the shipping traffic, they hardly ever got permission to do so.

'But I was thinking that if another request is made, we could ask the captain, or owner of the yacht, if he's willing to take someone who got stuck here because of the crisis with him, and if he is prepared to do so, I can see to it that his yacht gets permission to moor here, but it all needs to be done with the utmost secrecy, as our backs are being watched from all sides,' he said, 'especially by China, as I said before. That country regularly wants to inspect all our shipping documents, but, with a little bit of luck, I should be able to arrange something.'

'That would be really, really great,' Albert said. 'Thanks ever so much. I can't remember, but did I tell you I also hitch-hiked from Spain to the Canary Islands, because all the ferry services were cancelled and that I got a lift from an Englishman then, Jack Weekley?'

'Yes, I think you told me that story at the hospital, but I'm not sure, though. Bloody amnesia.'

'Well, whatever, he was a wonderful guy and even took the trouble to sail to another island to get me on that Chilean ship, the ship that suddenly disappeared just before or right after the attack. Remember?'

He looked at Eduardo and thought how the latter had changed since he first met him on the Chilean ship. He was such a macho man then, big, square and sturdy, but it was as if he had grown smaller; even his already thin moustache had dwindled, and he was a lot milder now, it seemed; maybe because he had lost his wife or perhaps because he had been quite ill himself. Eduardo, the hospital, he thought, and Gabriel, who had already written to him a couple of times and who was happy to hear 'his' Alberto was getting better and better. 'Alberto,' he chuckled, when he said the name aloud. He had become quite used to it and it sounded cute, he thought. And everybody was so friendly here; Eduardo's cousin too. The man had been able to sell Raoul's taxi at a reasonable price to a foreigner. It was shipped to Germany via Venezuela, the only country in the area that Cuba had good ties with. It was an illegal transaction, but it made life for Raoul's wife and son a little easier.

Every day after their meeting Albert was hoping to hear some good news from Eduardo's cousin, but nothing happened. Many weeks passed by and he was beginning to lose heart, until, quite unexpectedly, Eduardo stood at his door, saying he had some good news.

'If you believe in coincidence, this is it,' he said. 'My cousin saw a form at the harbour office with the name 'Weekley' on it. He remembered the name, because when you mentioned it some weeks ago, he thought it meant "weekly, every week". Funny, isn't it? Anyway, this Weekley, who is on his way to the Panama Canal, said he needed to carry out some repairs to his yacht. He got permission to enter the harbour and my cousin has arranged he can stay there for a week.'

'*Fantastique, incroyable!*' Albert called and gave Eduardo a hug. He thought of Jack, hoping it was him. Perhaps he would be his redeemer once more. After being discharged from hospital some months ago, Albert could finally be discharged from Cuba as well, he hoped. Ecuador, the unknown country, was calling him, but, strangely enough, it also felt as if he was going home.

17

On the beach, not far from Pepito's, Bernard Chambers shuffled through the sand that had cooled down, but it wouldn't be long before the sun was going to heat it up again. The elusive horizon was playing tricks with his eyes; one moment the sea appeared to be close to him, while the next moment it seemed a lot further away. His thinking followed the same wave-like pattern, had a similar rhythm; one minute he could think clearly, while the next minute his brain was like a thick, creamy soup.

The bar was closed now and the barman was in bed, at last, far away from the world and his customers.

Isabelle was probably asleep, he thought, her dark hair on the white pillow. That party, a very long time ago. Didn't she look gorgeous, with her long hair, the yellow dress? And how she stood there, outside on the veranda, looking at the lights in the distance. So beautiful. She could dance very well, and all the men were looking at her. Standing there, in his black uniform with four golden stripes, he was one of them. She was interesting and he wanted to hear every word she said. She played squash and went for a swim every other day, she told him, with an engaging smile and dimples in her cheeks. And how she said her name, Isabelle Franklin, with her sensual lips, when they were introduced to each other. He just had to have her.

But where have they gone, those fine and funny stories? And why did she always drink so much, wine, whisky, rum or whatever else was available? If she couldn't sleep, she just took some sleeping pills. What's happened to her? he wondered while he stumbled on a big, dark, crumbling chunk of wood.

'Damn it!'

As far as their sex life was concerned, the thermometer had been below zero for a long time; he couldn't even remember how long. And the good talks they used to have, or thought they had, were long gone as well.

'You always take things for granted,' she had told him some time ago, 'because you always think you're perfect. Your expectations of me and other people are far too high, but what's the point of telling you? It's your own problem and you're your own barrier.'

Nag, nag, nag, nag, he thought. What, for God's sake, was she on about? he wondered.

Not long ago, on their way to Ecuador, she had regained some of her old spirit, but when it was about to bloom, it faltered and started withering almost instantly. Why? Why, for god's sake?

Emptiness, emptiness, one vast emptiness.

So many questions milling in his head, and so many images; the radiant Isabelle, Plateau Mont Royal in Montreal, what a lovely city, nightlife, the French atmosphere, Vancouver, the arguments, the wonderful apartment, the sea.

Breathing in the fresh sea air, he tried to think clearly and not to fall over, but it was hard and sometimes he just muttered some hollow phrases to himself. He thought of the past, his mother.

'Mum, you were so sweet and you were always there for me. How beautifully you sang,' he said aloud.

Nearly all the songs she sang she'd made herself, he remembered. He was three, he thought, when he sat on her lap by the window, waiting for his father to come home. He could still remember sitting there, peering into the darkness of the early night, looking out for the lights of his father's car and his mum teaching him a ditty she'd made for his father. Even now he could remember how, one ear pressed against his mother's chest, he could hear her voice there when they sang the song,

Daddy, Daddy, come home soon, we are waiting here for you. Daddy, Daddy, great big man, please come back to us again. When the lights in town go on...

The rest of the song wouldn't come to him now. Always, when his mum was singing a song, with her fine voice, he would look at her soft, warm face, the dark, brown eyes and the long, waving, maroon hair that smelled so nice. If she noticed it, she would kiss him on his cheek and give him a cuddle.

It was probably due to her that he had become interested in literature, he thought, for she was also good at acting and knew so many lines from plays, often complete poems, by heart. Sometimes she suddenly started talking to him like a little girl and acted like one too, he remembered, with a smile on his wan face.

One day his mum took him to kindergarten, a few streets from their home, he recalled.

'I want to go back home with you, Mummy,' he cried when they got there. 'Don't leave me alone!' he called, begging her, knowing his mum was feeling unhappy too.

When she turned round to go back home, with tears in her eyes, he wanted to go with her, be with her, comfort her, but that bitch, the school-mistress, he remembered her vividly, held him tight. He tried to break free, but it was no use. He screamed and kicked as hard as he could, with his short, helpless legs, but it was no use. That evening his father was very angry with him. In December, he wasn't four yet, he spoiled the Christmas party out of sheer revenge and anger. Together with his friend James, whom he had set up, they had made a mess of the chocolate figurines and the cakes, bitten big chunks off them, while the school-mistress was standing at the door, welcoming the parents. She was fuming, his mother was burning with shame and in the evening, when his father came home, he was punished. There was something else, but he couldn't remember what it was. Did he have to stand in his bare bottom as well?

At primary school he liked bullying the other kids, he remembered, and wanted to be the tough guy. He had good grades, but he was always baiting the weaker teachers. He smiled. How glad they must have been when I left school, he thought. Secondary school wasn't too bad either, and he wasn't only good at maths, but at literature and visual arts too. Maybe literature was his favourite subject, but he didn't want anybody to find this out, as they would have thought he was a wimp. He loved poetry; he always read one or two poems before going to bed and learned some by heart.

He was the only one to go to the Royal Military College of Saint-Jean, about thirty miles south of Montreal and after that, for additional education and training, to the Royal Military College of Canada in Kingston, Ontario. He was a cool guy, passed with honours, joined the army and rose through the ranks to become a colonel.

He shuffled on. Before him lay a big beam, like a railway sleeper, a piece of driftwood that had been washed ashore. He sat down on it and although he was very tired, his mind was still clear. Around him numberless, small ridges of sand, shaped by the sea and wind; billions of grains, always on the move, carried by that big, invisible drive, the wind, the anonymous leader they sometimes betray by making him visible. Though travelling without a destination, they get everywhere, stick to wet feet and sandwiches, between hairs and buttocks, in babies' mouths, noses and ears, they settle in eyes, swoop low over their kin on the ground, sneak in secret silence through a crack under a window, creep into bed or wait patiently at a door until bare feet or shoes take them inside. They've seen so much, in light and darkness and, although they used to be a lot bigger, they are much lighter now, floating on the wind, faster, freer.

Nothing matters when you're free and when you can be who you really are, wherever you are, no, nothing matters when you can let love come into your heart and feel it, cry for it, love on wings, giving love, but that's so much more easily said than done, giving love and when the world is turning, in your head, in your head; tanks, bombs, guns, around you, sensible love, cold sex, to give or not to give, drown or live, Joe, drink, drink, drink, drunk, drunk, drunk, drown, drown, drown, turn, turn, turn, the big wheel, *Under the Volcano*, turn the earth, turn round, round ground around.

He looked up and there, high above him, he saw, or thought he could see them, only just, more and more, too many. In a few minutes they would be gone. He knew them, but his head was spinning. They were gone. Oh no, here they were again, in his head, Mercury, Venus, Mars, Jupiter, Saturn, Neptune, Pluto. Shape-shifting, they were no longer planets, but thousands of beautiful butterflies, flying to the water, skimming over the ocean, uncouth and pure; the long, rolling waves, turning, tripping over each other, ellipses eclipsing, thundering, hissing, below a hurricane of myriads of wonderful butterflies, metamorphosing into trillions of fireflies, exploding, up, down, to the left, to the right, gliding on as zillions of white, foamy drops, swallowed by the scintillating morning sun. Gone they were. Forever?

One big heap of broken images, fragments. They are so hard to comprehend and to connect, these polished, solitary bits of wood, hard plastic, sharpened, bones on the ground; future fossils of now. Bones crack, but is it true that dry bones can harm no one?

Dear Richelieu, flow softly, till I am at the end of my song. Flow softly, for so fast or long I cannot speak in this Chapel of Emptiness. Those who died now live. We, who live, shall die. The rites of sepulture, or was it sepulchre? I cannot remember anything. New beginnings. Did he say his eyes were pearls? I can't see anything. Fear death by water, it said, but I'm no longer sure. T.S. Eliot, on the river, Saint Jean, literature, Joe, love. Drunk, drowned, drowning the past.

A wood under water, brown trunks, green leaves, moving like algae in the cool currents of the sea. A face, a body, a corpse, lifeless. The water is receding now. Trees, trunks, branches, leaves, dripping. A watery sun is shining warily, almost fearfully, through the steaming forest. A man, a boy, together on a path. He wants to touch the boy, feel him; the boy shudders with horror, panic in his head, angst. His mother, where is his mother, so honest, so soft, so open and sweet? At the window? He's shouting at the top of his voice, her voice, his voice, when the lights go out.

The young woman at the bar, her genuineness, frankness, openness. Why are there all these ever-changing images? When the lights go… the Pole Star, home, the guiding star, the maze, World of Warcraft, item level 232, one hand; broken images. Home, he wanted to go home, to Isabelle, to the young woman. He tried to stand up, but slowly sank to the ground, lay down and fell asleep, where he was submerged in the waiting morass of his unveiled past, the man, the boy.

18

An early bird, or maybe a late one, saw someone collapse on the beach and walked up to him to try and put him back on his legs, but it was no use; the man was more like a big bag of sand than a human being. The 'sandbag' mumbled something and spat a little, allowing some fresh sea air to flow inside through his nostrils, which invigorated him slightly. The shadow on the beach of the early morning, a slender young man, made another attempt; he wanted to prevent the man from falling face downward into the sand or the water, when the tide came in so that he wouldn't suffocate or drown. The good Samaritan had problems of his own, but he realised this man was in greater need of help than himself, so he stayed with him and spoke to him, first in Spanish, then in English and finally in French, not knowing where this man came from. He tried to wake him up and keep him awake, but the stranger was exhausted. Only when he heard someone speak to him in French, the language of Québec, did he open his eyes a little. He raised his head and looked into the direction where the voice was coming from and distinguished the vague silhouette of a thin man against the backdrop of the increasing brightness of the rising sun. He said a few words back in French and did his best to cooperate when the young man hoisted him up and once more tried to make him stand on his feet.

Supporting each other the two tottered to the cottage where the young man lived. They entered the living-room, where they fell and crashed out on the pillows of the settee. What a sad creature, the young man thought, as he loosened the collar of the man's shirt and belt. He put a pillow under his head, after which he sat down on the settee beside Bernard. Words from the song he had played that night crawled through his exhausted head: *dans le monde entier cette nuit est pareille a tant d'autres nuits quand disparait le soleil tant de détresse tant de choses meurent et tu es si loin de moi j'ai peur que tu m'oublies déjà tu m'oublies déjà tu m'oublies si loin de moi tu m'oublies déjà.* He put down his weary head and within seconds he was fast asleep.

19

Roonah had come to rest in Desmond's arms. She sometimes needed to be alone and do her own things, like going to Pepito's. Not that she thought it was an exciting place to go to, or that she was desperate to go out without Desmond, but she liked to look around, observe people and listen to what they had to say. Especially during the last few months all kinds of obtrusive images from a large hospital where she had worked imposed themselves on her: operating theatres, corridors, wards, beds, patients, syringes, nurses, aids, pulses, trolleys and, on top of that, when she was almost asleep, fragments from pieces of English literature rose to the surface from the cellars of her mind, images from the novels of Virginia Woolf, a woman who inspired her so much, and someone she seemed to look like as well, at least, according to Desmond; D.H. Lawrence and his analysis of love and sex, the triangular love relationship between men, women and nature; sayings by Oscar Wilde; beautiful lines of poetry by another compatriot of hers, Seamus Heaney, and she regularly had the same crazy dreams, in which the hospital became a maze, an asylum, where empty beds were moving around automatically, nurses got drip-feeds, syringes protruded from mattresses, pillows and food, where trolleys had become unmanageable, pulses exploded and patients were looking at her in an eerie, penetrating way. And that's how it went on. Sometimes, her head resembled a lunatic asylum. But now, thank God, her head was empty for a moment. She removed and kissed Desmond's heavy hand, which was lying on her tummy. He kissed her and away she was, fast asleep.

20

Erasmus was on his way to the hostel, which lay a bit further away from the beach than the villas. He didn't mind the walk; it was refreshing and he loved being alone with the sound of the breakers. He didn't care too much for people, but as Pepito's was generally quiet, it was okay. Most punters were lonely foreigners looking for some company, hoping to find people who were in the same plight. When they had come to Ecuador it all seemed so beautiful, the weather, the beach, the ocean, life, but as a result of the impact of the war some were suffering from an *Entfremdungs* effect. Phrases like 'What would it be like in Berlin now'? and 'The last time I was in Amsterdam, I…' could be heard regularly. They expressed nostalgia, homesickness and some people just sat at the bar, lost in thought, staring outside.

He had some difficulty walking, not just because he had been drinking, but a while ago he had had a motorcycle accident and, in spite of what that mysterious Mrs Hopper had done, one leg could still be painful at times. He was a passenger on the bike of a cool guy at university. Although they weren't going that fast, the guy lost control and Erasmus was thrown off the bike, flew over the road, chased by the bike that hit his right leg and pushed it aside; it felt as if it was being torn off. There he was, lying in the road, with a fractured leg and a terrible pain in his groin, having done an involuntary split. Some ligaments were ruptured and, as his left leg had been in contact with the flaming hot exhaust pipe, he had some serious burns, but all the scars had healed in a miraculous way.

Wearing protective clothing, he had been more fortunate than the guy in front, who was in his shorts and T-shirt when he was launched from the bike. During his flight and successive landing he narrowly missed a concrete pole that stood along the road, but apparently he had still hit something else, for there was a huge cut on top of his head, while the bones of both his legs were shattered and he had a collapsed lung. In the end he was in hospital for almost three months and from the window he had seen how the seasons had succeeded each other, while Erasmus was out of hospital in a few weeks. Although he wasn't very keen on sport and therefore didn't have the six-pack so many other guys prided themselves on, he exercised very hard to get his legs back to normal. Unfortunately, due to the accident, he had also lost almost a whole year at university.

Erasmus, who would want to give his son such a name? His father, because he had once read a book about Desiderius Erasmus, a Dutch scholar, and he had got a lot of respect and appreciation for him, as he was one of the first humanists. Even long before his father married, he had decided to name his first son after this learned man. His mother didn't have any objections. She'd never heard of the name, but thought it sounded interesting enough, and the second child could always get an ordinary, American name, like Faith if it was a girl, or John, if it was another boy, but those kids were never born.

Erasmus quite liked his own name, as it was rather unusual. Besides, he had discovered that Desiderius Erasmus hadn't only become famous for his writings in Latin, but also in Greek, a language that had somehow always fascinated him, ever since he was a boy. It started when he saw some strange words on food packaging; all those different, mysterious signs, some of which he'd seen before, such as α, β, Ω, μ. When he was twelve he knew the whole Greek alphabet (another Greek word) by heart and discovered that innumerable words from Greek had found their way into English.

Apart from when he was studying, which he did in the living room, he would retire to his bedroom for hours to play games on the Internet. Those were the moments he felt good; when he was all by himself and there was nobody around to bother him.

He remembered a teacher asking his mother carefully if her son was perhaps – how could he ask her without stammering or offending her – a tiny bit autistic (another Greek word). Erasmus wasn't meant to hear this probably, but even if he was, perhaps, a little autistic, it didn't worry him in the least, he thought. It was a very nice word and it sounded good.

The black era of his childhood. He was between schools, when he heard his parents were getting divorced. He wasn't sure what to think, because he didn't even know what the word meant.

When she was young and still at home with her parents, his mother hadn't seen much love going around, at least, that's what he'd sometimes heard her tell his dad. This didn't only make it difficult for her to accept cuddles, but also to give them, something his dad thought was quite important.

'Everybody needs love', he would often say, but Erasmus too had to forgo his mum's cuddles; he couldn't recall she gave any at all. But he had got used to it.

He remembered his mum's dad was a peculiar, unfriendly, grumpy man, who always looked angry, while his grandmother was very sweet and caring. She always cuddled him, so he didn't quite understand his mother's words. Much later, it was on his aunt's birthday, he happened to overhear his aunt telling an uncle that, when his mother was a ten-year-old girl, a man from the choir she was at, had fondled her and asked her to take off her knickers, and that maybe that was also a reason why she took her distance from people, and men in particular. There were more things that had happened but he couldn't hear what they were, for when his aunt noticed he was looking at her, she started whispering.

Why his mother also took more distance from his father and even himself, he couldn't quite figure out and nobody talked about it either; they were all taboos. What he did notice though, was that his mother, before his parents split up, had started smoking funny things and drinking. At first she only smoked cigarettes, but more and more often there hung a sweet, sometimes nauseating smell in the house. He remembered coming home from school and the dreadful smell meeting him in the hall.

'Mum, what's that funny smell?' he'd often asked her.

'I can't smell anything.'

He began to hate the smell; it was so revolting and she always smoked in the living room, until his dad sent her into the garden. When she was watching TV she occasionally smoked ordinary cigarettes, using one of those wretched cigarette pipes, or old-fashioned, electronic ones and she also had one or two glasses of wine. In the morning when he had breakfast in the kitchen, he could smell the ashtrays, full of bent cigarette buds, he remembered, and the box for glass recycling was getting fuller by the day.

More and more often his dad retreated to his study in the evening and never said much about it. Maybe he did when they were in bed, he thought, although his mother generally kept watching TV until late at night, or early in the morning when his father had already gone to bed and she didn't get up till late in the morning, when his dad had already left for work. He remembered waking up one night, because his dad was swearing at his mother.

'Why do I always have to go to bed alone? Why can't you just switch off that bloody box and come to bed? You know you will wake me up when you are searching for the bed in the dark, smelling like smoke and wine.'

'You don't have to shout. You're waking up Erasmus and the neighbours. Just go to bed. I'll come up in a minute. The programme's almost finished.'

'What do you mean, "almost finished"? You've recorded all those bloody programmes and you can watch them whenever you like. But suit yourself. Go on drinking your wine. I'm off to bed now.'

When she was watching TV in the afternoon, sitting in her own cloud, and he was off from school, he found it difficult to talk to his mother or ask her any questions. His dad had the same problem and called them 'pause button talks'.

Not until he went to university did he begin to recall and really understand all these things, but when he was a young boy, he didn't have a clue what it was all about. Of course there were more kids at school whose parents were divorced, but they said it wasn't a problem; they were actually always spoiled. So maybe it was an attractive prospect that his parents were going to get divorced.

What he didn't know at the time was that, for almost a year, his dad had had a girlfriend. He'd only heard that much later, for his mum didn't want his dad to tell him that; he was much too young to understand, she said, and she also kept hoping that it was a whim of his father's and that he'd come back to her.

Always those taboos, Erasmus thought, feelings of false shame and embarrassment, like 'What would the neighbours say or the family think?' He remembered the secretive, suddenly aborted conversations between his parents when he entered the room; he wasn't allowed to hear anything, but kids aren't crazy and he had his suspicions that something was terribly wrong. Bit by bit his parents' talks became more acrimonious and one day he heard his father say she shouldn't smoke and drink so much, that she looked terrible. More and more often he heard his mother cry, in the kitchen and on the toilet.

'What have I done wrong?' he heard her ask herself. 'I can't understand it. I never expected it, not from him.'

She kept reproaching herself, sometimes for days on end.

'Mum, what's wrong? Why are you crying?'

'It's nothing. I'm not crying.'

At night, when it was quiet in the house and his dad was not at home, he woke up when she was sobbing.

All this made him feel miserable and he remembered thinking his dad was a very nasty person to hurt his mum like that, but he didn't say anything. His ever-tough dad, however, was also in pain; he could tell that by his red eyes. Why did they cause each other so much pain? he asked himself. It drained him; it was so terrible, much worse than he had first thought after all the positive stories from other children. He felt like a bucket that was continually being filled with sad drops of water, until they reached the brim and the bucket started overflowing.

'What's the matter, Erasmus?' the schoolmistress asked him one morning, 'Your eyes are all red and you look tired.'

He started crying and couldn't stop any more. The woman took him back home and asked his mother what was going on, but his mother didn't want to talk to her at first; she was too embarrassed, but the schoolmistress insisted and his mum had to let her in. He couldn't hear what they were talking about.

The following morning was even worse when he saw the kitchen table was unlaid. He ran upstairs, where he found his mother in bed, alone, sobbing.

'Your father has left us,' she finally managed to say, her eyes and nose full of tears, strands of wet hair all over her face.

The deep hatred he felt for his dad then, the total desolation, the utter emptiness of the house, the terrible, suffocating atmosphere and how he thought he could never be unhappier than at that moment.

Apart from the fact that his father sent his mum some money, they never heard anything from him again. It made no sense. His dad gone, for good, without even talking to him or saying goodbye? Only much later did he hear his mum had forbidden his dad to do that. There were so many moments when he was very angry and sad and at school things were so bad his mother got a letter, saying that if things didn't improve, both at home and at school, he would be placed at a state boarding school. That was how the state dealt with situations like these, which caused even more tears and misery at home.

But one day, when he was at home, because he wasn't feeling well, he found a letter from his dad on the doormat. In the letter his dad explained he had new life and was living with somebody else, very far away from him and his mum. He also wrote he had always been very proud of his dear son and that he was convinced he'd get very far if he worked really hard at school. He would be so proud of him then. He also hoped Erasmus would look after his mum and he promised to write again.

Erasmus was deeply impressed by his dad's words and he made up his mind to work very hard at school. He wrote a letter to his dad, but it came back; apparently, there was no one called Jacob Hopper living at the address he'd sent it to. His results at school were getting better and better. He went to secondary school, finished it and was admitted to the State University of Iowa. However, in all those years he never received another letter from his dad; the first letter had also been the last. He did write some letters to his dad though and gave them to his mother to despatch them, as he had the feeling she knew where he lived, but there never was an answer. He was deeply disappointed.

He thought of the photo in his rucksack, the only one he had of his dad. His mother had thrown all the other photos they had into the open fire, out of sheer anger. This was probably the only photo to have escaped the fate of being burnt at the stake. His dad was twenty-three when the photo was taken, long before he got married to his mum. He must have changed quite a bit now, he thought, when he looked at the photo. Already then did his dad have a beard and glasses. They'd got married when his dad was forty and his mum only twenty-five. He was born when his mum was thirty-three and his dad was forty-eight then, so his dad had to be in his sixties now, he thought.

Fortunately, his mother had found a new friend and remarried. This new guy was all right and he was only two or three years older than her, but Erasmus often longed for his real dad, whom he had known for only such a short time and he wanted so much to tell his dad what had become of him.

But who knows, he thought, maybe one day he would meet him here, in Ecuador.

Years later, he was in his second year at university, his mum told him his dad had written more letters, but she had thrown them away the moment they arrived. He realised how lucky he had been to have found that one letter on the doormat that day. He lost his temper and called her names. He would never forget that moment; he was heartbroken and felt like giving up altogether.

Why did she do this? he kept asking himself. Was it only because she felt deserted, angry or very sad, or didn't she want him to be in touch with his wicked dad? It was very likely a combination of the two, he thought.

'Please let me explain everything,' she said.

'No, you're just a liar. I don't trust you. I want my dad.'

She'd found an office job and because of that she was no longer entitled to an allowance from his dad. As a result all ties were severed.

He wanted to find his dad, but didn't know where to start. He tried the local council, but it didn't get him any further. He also searched the Internet for people who were called Hopper, but it was in vain. His mum tried to help him, but the information she had was no good either. All she could remember was that his dad's last letters had come from a place in California and that was years and years ago now. What he did know, however, was his dad had a younger brother, who lived in New York, but he had never met him, that is, not consciously, for he was only two or three years old when his uncle came to see them.

His mother remembered there was a rumour that his father was originally related to an artist, called Hopper. She'd never heard of the guy herself, but Erasmus found some articles about the actor/photographer, Dennis Hopper, and the painter, Edward Hopper. Both of them were dead, but Erasmus started fantasizing that the two famous men were relatives. Although he didn't really believe there was a link with either of the two, the idea was very exciting. He discovered that both the actor, who'd acted in several cult films in the twentieth century, and the painter, who'd lived a bit earlier, had had a lot of influence on the pop culture of the last century. If either of the two was related to him, he hoped it would be Dennis Hopper, because the guy was such a fascinating, versatile person, having been an actor, a photographer and a painter. It showed him what you could achieve if you put your mind to it, which reminded him of one of the slogans of his university, 'one day you will wake up in your dream'.

His curiosity had been sufficiently aroused to do some more research, a sort of investigation that, however ridiculous and impossible it seemed, would hopefully lead him to his dad. At the same time he intended to visit as many exhibitions and museums, where works of the two Hoppers could be seen. That's why he also decided to give up his studies. That was a good idea anyway, as the war had already started and he wanted to fully recover from the motorbike accident. Moreover, he was fed up with home, and it was high time to exchange the boring scenery of Iowa, with its vast cornfields, prairies and tens of tornadoes every year, for different, more challenging parts of the States. The long-distance buses would come in handy. He bought a big rucksack, put the photograph of his dad in first, then the rest of his stuff, asked his mum for money and left. He thought of another slogan of his university: 'Who decides your adventure?' His leaving home was the answer to that question.

Images of the long journey he had made appeared before his unreliable eyes; he was so tired and badly needed a pee. He finally reached the hostel, peed over the toilet bowl, staggered to his room, climbed into bed and fell into a deep sleep, his clothes still on.

In a tangle of memories he dreamt about New York and a slender, handsome, young man and then, after a long range of unrecognizable images, there was the beautiful girl he'd seen at Pepito's. She was wearing her tight, black wetsuit and her long blond hair and curls fell over her shoulders. She was smiling and beckoned him with her finger. She wanted something, but the beautiful image gradually dissolved, chaos returned and crazy, blurry images of something that looked like a funfair, with merry-go-rounds, lots of colours and sounds took her place. Finally all this disappeared and there was nothing; it was quiet and his head came to rest in the hazy tranquillity of a new morning.

21

'You've lost quite a bit of weight,' was the first thing Jack said to Albert, when he embraced him. 'You're as thin as a rake. I can feel your bones. I know you're a vegetarian, but you could do with a bit of bacon,' he added, laughing. 'But it's so great to see you again, here, in Havana of all places!'

Albert was speechless for a second and had tears in his still slightly sunken eyes when Jack said this.

'It's almost too good to be true. I so much hoped this 'Weekley' would be you.'

A feeling of freedom and deliverance came over him.

'But what's happened, Albert? What have you been doing with yourself? Gosh, you really look emaciated. When I heard from the harbour master a stranded Frenchman wanted to get a lift through the Panama Canal, I was almost sure it could be only one person,' he said with a laugh.

Albert smiled and gave him a brief version of what had happened, the Chilean ship, the epidemic and told about the wonderful people he'd met and lost, that he'd been very well looked after in the hospital and what a great country Cuba was, but that he was so desperate to get away now.

'But you, Jack, how did you fare?'

'I'm fine, but have a look at the yacht.'

Jack showed him the damage to the front of his yacht, caused by pieces of driftwood and that he would very much like to repair it. Albert told him about Eduardo's cousin.

'He's a great guy and he knows a lot of people. I'm sure he can help you.'

'Sounds very good, Albert. Thanks. But you've been here for quite a while now, haven't you?'

'Yeah, much too long.'

'I'm sorry. I stayed on the Canary Islands and you know I didn't have any plans to go to America, but you were so enthusiastic about South America, and Ecuador in particular, that I started thinking about it and changed my mind.'

'That's funny,' Albert said, 'for already back then did I know you'd be coming this way. I felt it. Maybe I even told you; I can't remember.'

'No, you didn't, but as you know, I had never crossed the Atlantic Ocean before. I always thought the shortest route was via Newfoundland, but I was told it was a very difficult and perilous crossing, so I took the route from the Canary Islands. It was perfect, also because it was the best time of the year for it.'

'And you did that on your own?'

'Of course not. I found two new crewmembers in Las Palmas, Steve and Rosalie, two young people from Holland. They're on board. Still asleep, I suppose. You'll meet them later.'

'Cool.'

'Two other yachts came with me. They are lying off the harbour, waiting to hear if my yacht can be repaired.'

'OK. I'll go and speak to Eduardo and his cousin, to see what they can do for you.'

'Great stuff. Thanks.'

Looking at Albert again, Jack noticed the latter's former flexibility and vitality were gone; there was a sombre and desperate expression in his face.

'Stop worrying, Albert, I can understand you feel cooped up, but everything's going to be fine, I'm sure.'

Albert didn't reply.

'Do you know a good bar or a restaurant where we can have a drink and something to eat?' Jack asked.

'No problem. Maybe Eduardo would like to join us too, if that's all right with you.'

'Of course it is.'

Two sleepy faces appeared on deck, looking around them, a bit disoriented, as if they'd fallen from one dream into the next. They came ashore and Jack introduced them to Albert.

Albert contacted Eduardo and together they went to the office of the harbour master, where they met up with Eduardo's cousin. A repair team was found and an hour later they were at Jack's yacht.

'Eduardo, would you like to come with us for a coffee?'

'Thanks very much, Albert. Very kind of you.'

Looking at Steve and Rosalie, Jack said,

'Wouldn't it be better if they stayed with the yacht to keep an eye on things?'

'Don't worry,' Eduardo said. 'My cousin's got everything under control. Let them come with us. There's a nice place not far from here, where they also do light meals, if you want to eat something.'

They sat down at a large, communal table. Albert was sitting next to Steve and Rosalie and they were soon talking about Paris, Amsterdam, Europe and lots of other things. On the walls of the restaurant were several paintings, made by local artists. Rosalie couldn't keep her eyes off them; while the others were talking boats, classic cars, the weather and food, she stood up to have a closer look at the paintings. One painting in particular captivated her; its bright, yellow colours thrilled her and she wondered what the small, black objects on the canvas were meant to convey.

Albert, who had just told Jack, Steve and Eduardo what had happened from the moment he'd disembarked in Havana, noticed Rosalie was intrigued by the yellow painting. He wanted to go and talk to her about it, when Jack began to tell his story of the crossing, so he couldn't leave their table, but at the same time he couldn't take his eyes off Rosalie, who had changed her clothes before she went ashore, and he noticed that the tall, svelte, somewhat tinged, young woman with half-long, wavy, dark hair, looked very elegant. Around her neck hung a white gold necklace with a locket and in her ears were matching earrings with a flower on them, he noticed. She was wearing a red dress that looked rather short and red and black canvas shoes. How unusual for a boat hitch-hiker to have brought these clothes with her, he thought. With his attention focused on Rosalie, he missed some bits of Jack's account. Standing there, in her red dress in front of the painting with the bright yellow colours, she looked so beautiful, a composition in itself, he thought. He wished he could paint her.

He didn't know why, but she reminded him of a passage from the bible: *whatever is pure, whatever is lovely, whatever is commendable, if there is any excellence, if there is anything worthy of praise, think about these things.*

Feeling Albert was watching her, she suddenly turned round and looked straight into his eyes. He blushed a little and she smiled at him. She didn't mind his looking at her at all, her eyes reassured him. He had felt uneasy for a split second, but that feeling was now replaced by a sense of admiration, no, it was more than that; it was adoration. She was a very special woman, he thought, who had taste and there was something very special about her, which she wasn't aware of in her seemingly naïve innocence and spontaneity; there was a power in her with which she transcended the down-to-earth Steve. The words *femme fatale* flashed through his head.

He was so fascinated by what he saw that he hadn't even noticed Jack had paused to see what his eyes were focused on. Jack just smiled and continued his story, while Albert only saw red, yellow and some black, and how the diffuse light that fell through the glass of the kitchen door, over Rosalie and the painting, made the scene look like a painting by Vermeer. Art, he thought, this young, slim woman is pure Art; all he needed to do was look at her and the picture would fix itself on his retina without his interference. In the background of this dream scene sounded voices, the metallic clatter of knives and forks, scratching on plates and in bowls, while through the open windows and doors music came flowing inside and flies were buzzing in circles; separately, they conjoined to create the ultimate fourdimensionaltotalcomposition.

From a corner in the restaurant somebody else was also admiring Rosalie and her attractive, sensual beauty. He looked distinguished in his black suit and shoes. He had a finely trimmed moustache, a straight, Greek or Italian, authoritarian nose, piercing Salvador Dali eyes and lush, exuberant eyebrows, which were jet black, just like his hair, where the first grey hairs had been neatly smothered with black dye.

She's got class, he thought, when he saw her pose, and how she swayed, so elegantly, on her fine hips, while she was watching the yellow painting. The short dress was slightly provocative and her nicely shaped legs lent her a lascivious look, while at the same time, there was an innocence and a *ternura*, tenderness, about her. He couldn't keep his eyes off her. Who was this young lady? She looked absolutely stunning. He had never seen her before. He didn't live in Havana himself, about twenty miles away from it, but he came here regularly for his work, nearly every week.

'Who's that beautiful lady over there?' he asked the waiter.

'I don't know, Señor Odini. I've never seen her before. She's with that group of people at the long table.'

He looked their way, but didn't recognise any of them. They looked foreign, he thought, apart from one man, who looked more local. They didn't interest him, so his eyes went back to the image of the woman in her red dress, a hind, a young antelope that had strayed from the herd, a beautiful, easy prey for any predator.

Lunch was served and Rosalie sat down on the chair between Steve and Albert, with whom she almost immediately had an interesting conversation about the paintings. Jack had ordered wine for everyone and, as they raised their glasses, he toasted to the next part of their trip to the Panama Canal and his fantastic crew.

The large, gold watch was ticking on his wrist. He looked at it. It was still early. Outside he heard the clock of a church strike twelve and somewhere a cock crowed. That cock was out of his mind, he thought. She doesn't come home till about four o'clock this afternoon; there's plenty of time. The cock crowed again. That red dress, her full lips. More crowing. How she, this red rose of damask, had been looking at the painting with her searching eyes that yielded nothing to the sun; her coral lips, the tender tissue, touched by her breath and the music of her voice, while she was lying next to him, her perfume invading his nostrils, and he was overwhelmed by her warmth in an adventure of art, culminating in an explosion of pure surrealsensualsexualism. Beads of sweat appeared on his forehead and nose.

'Another tequila, please.'
'Here you are.'
'Thank you.'

All the scraps of paper in his diary. It was driving him crazy. Where the hell was that address, that telephone number? How else could he get to her in time?

'Another tequila.'

'Here you are.'

More perspiration, less concentration.
Ah, here it is. That last digit, is it an eight or a zero?

'Can I make a private phone call, please?'
'No problem, please follow me.'

'Ola. Partagas Cigars. How can I hel…' Fuck, wrong number. So it must be a zero then.'
'Ola. Farmacia Centra. Good afternoon. What can I do for you?'
'Can you put me through to Syreeta Cartega?'
'One moment, please.'
'Syreeta.'
'Hi, I'm with a customer and I can't make it at four. It will probably be a few hours later; it's an important deal.'
'Shit! It's always the same with you. What about tonight then, the dinner we were going to have?'
'I'm sorry, baby.'
It was quiet for a few seconds. Enjoy yourself, asshole, she wanted to say, but instead she said,
'What time are you coming home?'
'No idea. Not too late, I hope. But you know how these things go.'
His standard answer, she thought, the prick!
'OK, see you. Take care,' she added, and hung up.
'No worries. Adios,' he said into the linear emptiness of a long beep. But he didn't care. Done, he said to himself.

'When is that tequila coming?'
'You have already drunk it, Señor.'
'I want another one.'

He made up his mind not to get up from his chair before the others, together with the 'Red Rose', would be leaving, so that he could find out what their plans were. It wouldn't be long now, he thought, for he saw one of the men was getting restless.

'Can you find out what they're going to do?' he asked the waiter, putting some money in his hand.

The man nodded at least three times and did what he had to do. A few minutes later he was back, a triumphant smile on his face.

'They're going to the yacht of the Englishman, that older guy at the table, the one who's standing up now, but they're coming back here later and…'

'*Gracias*.' He'd heard enough; he was going to leave the restaurant at the same time as them, so that he could get closer to the Red Rose, maybe touch her.

They were all standing at the open door, ready to leave. He got up and walked towards them. Near the door Rosalie dropped a paper with information about the artist of the yellow painting and, because she, the stray antelope, was the last person of the group to leave the restaurant, none of them saw it fall. Odini picked it up as quickly as he could and patted her on the shoulder.

'Excuse me. I think this yours,' he said with an engaging smile, 'information about one of the artists, by the look of it.'

While he looked deep into her eyes, she blushed and smiled at him. The piercing, dark eyes, the eyebrows, the straight nose, his seductive smile, the warm, gruff voice, she just had to listen.

'He's very good, Ramirez is. He has made many more brilliant pictures.'

'Really? Is there a gallery where I can see them?'

'No, I'm afraid not. This is one of the few places where he exhibits his work, if he displays any at all, for he hardly ever does. He's a very introvert person, difficult to make contact with. I met him a couple of times and I have some paintings of his in my apartment. If you like, you can have a look at them. When are you coming back here with your family?'

'They're not my family,' she said, and laughed. 'That's my friend over there and that man in front of him is an Englishman. We came here on his yacht. That other young man is from Paris; he's been here for a while. I don't know the other guy. I've been told he's from this city. He helped the Englishman with his yacht; there was some damage. But we're back here around seven, I believe. I would really love to see those paintings.'

She blushed again. The words had come out before she'd even thought about what she was going to say, but she couldn't help it; he was so good-looking and charming.

He took her hand.

'No problem. Why don't you come and have a look at them when you are back here tonight, or maybe some other day?' he replied. 'Here's my telephone number. Just give me a bell. I hope it's not a problem; I mean for your friend or the others,' he added.

'No, it should be fine. My friend is not interested in art anyway and I don't know about the others.'

She could feel the blood rushing through her body.

'All right then, see you later. Oh, before I forget, here's your paper. I'll write my number on it. Give me a ring when you want to come, so that I can give you some instructions.'

'Thanks.'

He gave the paper back and touched her fingers. She quivered; his touch aroused her.

'Thanks again, Mr erm…'

'Odini. But don't thank me; *el gusto is mio*.'

'Sorry, but I really have to go now,' she said, a bit impatiently. 'The others have already walked on. By the way, my name's Rosalie. Bye.'

She walked off hurriedly to catch up with the others.

'Beautiful name, beautiful flower.'

She looked back once more, a bit nervously, and walked on. There was a lot of noise in the street and the others were nattering away, so no one noticed she had been talking with Odini. When she caught up with Albert, who was walking alone at the back, she told him enthusiastically about the paintings. He looked back to see where this Mr Odini was, but the bird had already flown.

'You look quite excited.'

'He was a real gentleman,' she said, blushing again, 'but I don't think I'll go to his apartment, not alone anyway.'

'Why don't you ask Steve to come with you?'

'He's not that interested in art; the only true great work of art for him is Rembrandt's *Night Watch*. But let's forget about it. By the way, have you ever been to Musée d'Orsay? I love it.'

He said he knew it quite well and told her about other fabulous museums and galleries in Paris and why he wanted to go to Ecuador.

'In fact, I want to be a painter myself,' he finally told her.

Her eyes looked at him, full of admiration, but her thoughts were miles away. How could she see Odini again?

22

Still lying in bed, Desmond was wide awake. He got up, went to the loo and then sat down on the old couch in the plain living room, rubbing his still weary eyes. He had just disengaged himself from Roonah's warm arms; she sometimes lay coiled around him like a snake. She woke up when he broke away from her grip, kissed and asked him if he was getting up. He was about to reply, wanted to whisper something, but she was already fast asleep again.

All was quiet; everybody was asleep. Bernard and Albert were lying close together, holding each other, on the sofa bed. Erasmus lay knock-out in bed with his pillow propped against his belly. Isabelle was lying alone, on her own, narrow, warm patch of the not too spacious bed. Occasionally she woke up, wondering what time it was. She felt the empty place beside her and thought maybe Bernard had already got up. Whatever. The barman of Pepito's dreamed he was filling glasses; it never ended. He wanted to go home; he was so tired, but his customers wanted to go on drinking. He sank through his knees behind the bar. He woke up, desperate to go for a quick pee, came back and went on dreaming his professional dream.

The light of a lamp in one of the villas was making a fruitless effort to get outside through a window. Earlier that night it had managed to do so, shining on a small, square patch of rippling beachscape, but now the ashen, limpid light from the lamp was slowly dissolved in a cautiously emerging haze of waxing sunlight. It had to flee back inside, but even there it wasn't safe; it was forced to retreat further, until the day came in to overpower, break and dissipate it. After that it would take many hours, usually until the sun sank into the sea before the light from the lamp could come out of hiding and gird itself for the next noiseless battle and another temporary conquest.

In a bedroom behind that window sat a young man on his bed. He didn't need a new day, because his sun had set, forever. He still couldn't understand how it had come so far, how naïve and stupid, so stupid, so unforgivably stupid he had been. An older friend, who lived with him, kept trying to comfort his mate, cheer him up, taking him on trips to places in the neighbourhood to divert him, although he still couldn't understand it either. If only they had been more alert, it mightn't have happened. He had escaped from one problem, only to be caught in the snares of someone else's misery.

What's the point of life? he wondered. Why do people always want to hurt each other? What, for God's sake, is mankind doing to the world, his ancestors, himself and, ultimately, his progeny? A gaping hole, a false emptiness, a void space, an infinite ocean in an insane desert.

In a strained silence he thought back to his schooldays, the beautiful things he wrote down in his little blue notebook, like a hard to fathom, but impressive fragment from the poem *Ash-Wednesday*, planning to read it again one day. Like a faithful companion, the notebook always travelled with him. It was a kind of diary or logbook and was already full of little and big things that fascinated him, proverbs, a conversation he overheard on a bus, an article from a newspaper, or a passage from a novel or poem. Sometimes he wrote them down because they were too difficult to grasp at that moment in time or his life. They were all pieces from a gigantic jigsaw, the big puzzle of life.

How did some people manage to catch the world and all its feelings in a few lines, like in this poem, *Ash-Wednesday*? Why couldn't he think of those things? he wondered.

He thought about the relevance of the words. The rose, broken but still in one piece, alive, as it were; the rose that would always remind him, and make him forget things at the same time. A paradox, wasn't it really, as it would make him think of his eldest daughter. But it also made him realise that life went on, that memories can be life-giving, however exhausting and sorrowful they may be. The one rose, a symbol, a kind of pars pro toto for something much bigger, a whole garden, or a field full of roses, like poppies in a way, insatiable. A rose, love, unrequited, unsatisfied, unattainable. A rose, an object of desire and greed, but once it is severed from its stem, it dies, and the fulfilment of its beauty swiftly withers with it. Here love ends, a field where all loves end. But does it take away the desire? he wondered.

Where are we travelling in this whirling world? Aren't we just walking on the outer perimeter of a merry-go-round, a Ferris wheel? There is no end to our journey; we travel willy-nilly. And to what avail are these unspoken words, these thoughts, in the centre of this silent world? Can I pray? Is there someone, a pure being without sin, a nun, who can pray for me, for her, for us, for all those who do not or cannot believe, who have lost faith, or those do not see the light, but only darkness in this barren, waterless place? But what about our children, the future, the silent stream that trickles underneath the dry soil?

23

It was clammy and oppressive in Havana, where the heat of the day like a damp blanket over the city lay. Sitting at his snug desk, Jack kept wiping the sweat off his face. He was hoping the thunderstorm he could see in the distance would break loose sooner rather than later. It was terrible; his whole body was wet. He was happy his yacht had been repaired. They could leave anytime they liked now, even though he wouldn't mind staying in Havana for a few more days. It was a very nice city, but he knew Albert was desperate to leave.

Rosalie didn't notice the heat; she wiped the glistening beads of perspiration from her forehead and neck without thinking about it. She was restless; her head was full of Odini and she wondered how she could meet him. The sweaty, moist piece of paper in her hand, the telephone number; it was calling her. Steve was lying on his bed; his eyes only wanted to close themselves. The beer, the heat. Her eyes, the wet piece of paper, his elegant handwriting, black and blurry. What shall I do? She went on deck to think about it.

The skyline of Havana; Albert liked the view, especially from where he was standing, on deck of Jack's yacht. It wouldn't be long before he would finally say goodbye to this exotic city. He was so much looking forward to leaving it behind. For a split second he thought he saw Sylvain, but it was a delusion, wishful thinking, for it was Rosalie; she had put up her hair and was making a phone call. Wouldn't it be good if Sylvain was here? Albert thought, watching the sun disappear behind a big, thundery cloud. The next moment Rosalie was gone. She had probably gone back to her cabin, he thought. The colours of the sky, the water, the simmering, sultry heat of the city. How he would love to make a painting of everything he saw.

Rosalie was panting; she wanted to get away from the harbour and the yacht as fast as she could, but it was so stifling hot and there were drops of perspiration streaming down her body. She needed to slow down or she would be completely wet when she arrived at his apartment. She hoped Albert would find the piece of paper she'd slipped under his door. She was sure he'd understand; he was such a lovely man. She had thought of giving it to him when he was standing on deck, watching the sun being swallowed by some huge clouds, but she didn't want to disturb him, and it was too confronting, perhaps; it would certainly have been difficult. She looked at the instructions Odini had given her. She could already smell his eau de toilette; it was probably Egoïste. It wouldn't be long before she could have a look at those paintings by Ramirez. But what was it that really attracted her, that had made her leave Steve and the others so precipitately? She crossed the Maximo Gomez, a somewhat wider street than the others. It was old, and large parts had fallen into decay; there were gaps and also some ruins, like a rotting set of teeth. She didn't like the atmosphere at all; it scared her. Hadn't she better go back? It was such a long street. She looked at the instructions again.

A little later she arrived at a house in what looked like an alley. It was much quieter here than the other streets, and the atmosphere was a lot more agreeable. It wasn't so dark either, but perhaps that was because the thundery clouds had just passed over this part of the city. There was the door to his apartment. She touched it; her fingers began to tremble. When she'd pressed the bell, there was a click and the door opened. But there was no Odini. Should she go in? She wasn't sure now. She could still turn round and walk away.

Another door opened.

'Hello, Rosalie. I'm glad you could make it. Don't just stand there in that dreary hall. Come in,' he said, taking her by the hand and kissing her on the cheek. 'I love your red dress. I forgot to tell you this afternoon.'

'Thank you.'

'Mm. Lovely fragrance too. What is it?'

'Gucci.'

At first she thought it was a bit odd, all these compliments, but according to what she'd heard, it was typical of Latinos and, actually, she didn't mind, because she didn't often get them from Steve. Thinking of him, a smile appeared on her face.

Odini thought it was meant for him and he thought how, in a few minutes, he would be alone with her, and that smile was the most sensual smile he had ever seen.

'Please follow me,' Odini said.

She followed him through a long, narrow passage, which was very brightly lit. There were some paintings on the wall; very beautiful portraits, actually. At the end of the passage was a glass door that led to the sitting-room. It looked rather like the lounge of an airport, that's how big it seemed. On the floor was a large, bright yellow carpet with some black leather seats and two big, beautiful sofas. Against the wall stood a posh cabinet, made from dark wood with cut-glass doors, and a proper bar with a range of bottles and some exotic objects.

'This looks very stylish, Mr Odini. Very smart.'

'Thank you. I love beautiful things,' he said, looking into her eyes. 'Here are some of the paintings I was talking about this afternoon, the Ramirez ones.'

Rosalie stepped forward to have a good look at them.

'Really nice,' she said after a while, and she took a few steps back to look at them from a distance.

'Wow. Really wonderful. I like them even better from here. Those bright, vivid colours. Really, really magnificent.'

'What do you think of that black one over there? Oh, sorry, I beg your pardon. I forgot to ask you, but what would you like to drink?'

'It's all right. What have you got?'

'Whatever you like. There's wine, rum, cognac, Armagnac, Cuarante Y Tres, Bacardi, several liqueurs, and soft drinks, of course.'

'I'll have a Bacardi coke, please.'

He poured out two tall glasses and while he handed one to her, he touched her fingers. It aroused him, although he kept looking straight into her eyes.

This afternoon it had almost put a spell on her, but now his piercing eyes were quite unnerving; she was even a bit scared, although she didn't know why. She wasn't the kind of woman who easily panicked; she'd found herself in a few difficult situations before. She thought of the owner of a sailing-yacht, who'd given them a lift and who tried to persuade her to open the door of the shower she was in. He wouldn't go away and there was that other guy, who had asked her to come into his cabin while Steve was asleep in the cabin right next to his and, of course, she knew very well how some men looked at her. She didn't mind that. On the contrary, it excited her. Maybe it was because she also loved wilder, different sex, with sex toys, but Steve wasn't interested in that sort of thing at all. Some time ago, when they were at a sex store, it was she was who wanted to see and hold everything, while Steve only was desperate to get out of the shop as quickly as possible. It had made her laugh, but these things just didn't interest him; he was happy with sex and everything that came with it in the old-fashioned way. She found it a bit boring, unadventurous. Not that she wanted to go to bed with other men to have a good screw. Oh, no, not at all. It was rather the excitement that attracted her, she thought, andmaybe those men knew that instinctively. She remembered how, about a year ago, she'd tried to arouse Steve by going through Amsterdam with him without her knickers on. When they were standing on one of the rounded bridges over a canal, she said to him, 'I'm not wearing anything underneath my skirt,' and pulled it up right away. She thought no one else was watching, but at that self-same moment one of those fast, noiseless, glass-topped tourist vessels appeared from underneath the bridge, with most passengers looking up to enjoy the view. Steve laughed and said, 'You might have shaved yourself a bit better for all those people down there. You'd better be careful or you'll catch a cold; it looks so bare.' Once, at a party of his family, where there were only lah-di-dah people, she had lifted her shirt and shown him her naked breasts, perhaps only to prove to Steve she was different, but it didn't really excite him, she remembered. He only said, 'Not bad, Rosy, I love them.'

Here, in this room with Odini, she also felt a sexual excitement. Maybe it was the way he behaved and moved, or his eau de toilette, his gestures and other little things. He was tense, she noticed, although he was trying hard to conceal it, pretending to be cool and casual.

'Oh, sorry. Cheers. I was looking at the painting and my mind wandered off. I don't like this black one very much, to be honest. It looks menacing, aggressive, intrusive even.'

'Aha. I love it.'

'Well, there's no accounting for tastes. Yes, it really scares me. But maybe it says something about you.'

He was quiet for a moment. That other girl. Two years ago. Rosalie was different, so outspoken. She had guts. She fascinated him.

She took some sips from the glass.

'Oops, that's quite a strong one,' she said, 'but it's good; I like it,' she added and emptied the glass.

'No, it's not bad, is it? Take it easy,' he said, with a grin on his face.

It felt as if she came under his spell again, a sensation she'd never had until this afternoon when she'd first met him. Her insides were in a flutter; there were sexual tingles and triggers. She had another drink, which she finished as quickly as the first, and asked for another one. He popped something into her glass, but she didn't notice it and slowly she drifted into another dimension.

'This is good,' she said, 'I feel so relaxed.'

She felt the current of his gigantic energy and allowed herself to be swept along by it. She began to yearn for him; she wanted him. Never before had she experienced such a mega excitement, such an irresistible attraction. Of course she wasn't stupid; she knew he didn't know Ramirez, but it didn't worry her.

'Have you got another drink for me? The same, please.'

Full of style and charm he took the glass from her hands, but he didn't touch her fingers this time, deliberately, while she was hoping he would.

Looking at her, this beautiful woman, so close to him, he felt very powerful. He was going to have sex with her, in a big way. It was part of his strategy to make her eager and it was working, for when he had poured out the glass and handed it back to her, she touched his fingers. She quivered a little; the sensation, the excitement, the yearning and she kicked off her shoes. He withdrew his fingers, which made her want to feel them even more. She looked at him; her eyes begging for his glance, his piercing eyes, where the deepest passion of his feelings lived. She was allowed a glimpse inside.

All of a sudden he took her hand and held it firmly; it was slightly moist. His other hand took the glass from her weakening fingers, put it down and went to her head, her hair, stroking it gently, before moving to her back, sliding into her red dress, rubbing her skin, softly, caressing it and coming back up again, while she was wriggling in his arms, with her eyes closed, breathing heavily, almost fainting from excitement, but he kept her on her feet; they weren't there yet; he kissed her while his hand was feeling for her breasts, massaging her skin, the hardening nipples, more and more firmly, harder and harder, so that she started making soft, randy noises and wanted him to pull her onto the sofa, tie her up, screw her; her hand moved to his loins, felt his trousers, searched the zip and pulled it open; they were still standing; his hand moved over her belly and navel, while she could feel his fluid flowing; they were mad with excitement, but he still knew exactly what he wanted; it had to be perfect and he wanted to stay in control, although he was almost coming and wanted nothing else but enter her and have an orgasm with her that would last for hours, while she started pulling at him, dragging him to the sofa, falling onto it and her asking him to tie her up, squeeze her breasts, kiss her all over her body, take her, so that he tore her dress open at the front, pulled her bra and knickers off, tied her feet with a cord, which sent her into ecstasy and made her almost faint again; there was her beautiful nakedness and he kissed her lips, her breasts, her arms, her belly; the panting in his ears, his tongue massaging her skin, searching, her labia, the ultimate wetness, withdrawing, his body struggling to disentangle itself from her desperate arms and hands, fighting the temptation to let her make him come, with her sweet, soft hand around his penis, moving his foreskin up and down, before he was in her, before he had tied her feet and rubbed her body with oil, which he started doing now, standing above her; having to let her go, leaving her for a moment to herself, in her loose, hot, naked, wet passion; then started touching and fondling her again, rubbing her with some special oil, kissing and licking her till she almost shrieked, desperately pulling on his pants, wanting him to drop them, taking his penis again, while he touched her clitoris, carefully rubbing it with two fingers, allowing her, with her nails in his back, to pull him into her, to go in and out with slow, firm movements, to drive her and himself crazy and come to a climax and, in the end, let his soft, savage, eager, living fluid find its way in her quivering, red sheath, to penetrate into the core of existence, an eruption…

VESUVIUS

Fluttering   hearts

She was the apotheosis of all women. Like a goddess, or Jesus Christ herself, she had come to earth, taken on a mortal existence, enabling mankind, that is, him, to reach the level of divinity. In order to reach immortality, the messenger, the medium, the messiah, the 'anointed one', 'the bearer', had to die on the cross, to be sacrificed, buried, breathe her last breath, or the other way round, as a new Pompeii. She was greater than him and only by taking her life, could he transcend her. He, the black king, Vesuvius, the unquenchable, the insatiable, hurling lava, violence.

He stood up, zipped up his pants and stared at her; her heart exhausted and extinguished; her brains, intoxicated by a drug, alcohol and sex; her lungs, still gasping for breath; her body, still hot, ultra naked and defenceless.

His unstoppable, unequalled, crazy urge to achieve grandeur and supremacy, to destroy, kicked in again. Possessed he was, in a trance. He reached out his firm hands and, like clamps, they locked behind her neck, while his strong thumbs went for her soft, hot, sweaty neck, brutally squeezing the life out of the tender body. Struggling in vain, the sweet, begging, powerless hands loosened their grip on his wrists and slipped away, softly. He looked at her. Two years ago. The knife. She bled so much. And the other two. How they had screamed. Yes, Rosalie was different.

A torn, red dress, cold folds, deserted, a chair.
A void of time, silence.
A minute.

He lifted her naked body and carried it to the back entrance of the building, opened the door and, without looking around him, walked into an unlit alley to his black car, opened the boot lid and let the still warm, lifeless body sink into the boot, next to the old spare wheel, closed the lid, which burst open again because of a rubber that had got stuck, closed it again with a bang, got into the car, lit a cigarette, started the engine, adjusted the mirror and drove off. After fifteen minutes he had left Havana and all its lights behind him. There was no moon and there were no other cars on the rocky road along the coast. His right foot was heavy on the pedal; the tyres squealed at every bend in the road, the springs and dampers creaked, the body sighed and groaned, while the big, black mass with two white and two red lights sped over the potholes in the tarmac. Now and then, when there were no trees along the road and the very last rays of light were about to drown in the water and sink into the road, the chrome of the wheel caps, the door handles, the window strips and the bumpers glittered.

He was tired, but he loved pushing the old car to its limits. In the boot of this fast-moving coffin Rosalie's body was tossed from left to right; sometimes it flew up, only to fall down again, gurgling. A sharp curve, a big rock, some branches, a damp surface, braking, wheels skidding. He could have taken it easy, for nobody knew where he was heading, but because of the tension, the high speed and the darkness he lost control of the car, went off the road and crashed over the rocks into the sea. In a reflex he pulled the chrome door handle up to open the door and, as a result of the enormous impact, not only his door, but the boot lid flew open as well.

There she was, the white queen, naked, soulless,

Spermatozoa and ova, drowning, dead.

The car first floated, then half submerged, and finally disappeared, nose down, into the warm sea, gulped by the greedy water, which burst in through the open door. The lifeless flower, now free, rose, turned, moved with the current, her legs still tied with the cord, her arms moving, a mermaid, a cross, naked, with the golden chain and earrings, an offer to Poseidon.

Dazed by the crash when the car hit the water, Odini was hanging in his seat, his head against the windscreen. The freshness of water, however, roused him. Instinctively, he reached for the clasp of his seatbelt, undid it and escaped from the water and imminent death, neatly, in his black suit. Where, or if he went ashore is still not known.

24

Albert found the piece of paper on the floor and looked at it. Apart from info about this painter there was a telephone number on it and in the corner Rosalie had written, '*Don't worry about me. I've gone to see the paintings. I'll be at the restaurant at around eight. Love, Rosalie xxx.*'

He became worried, confused, and read the message again. Was she safe? he wondered. Was he the only one who knew where she'd gone? Why? What about Steve? Shouldn't he tell him? Had he become part of a plot? He went to Steve and told him Rosalie had gone to look at some paintings at a gallery in the city and that he'd agreed to meet her there before going to the restaurant.

Steve was stupefied; his thin lips quivered.

'I'm off now. See you at the restaurant,' Albert called.

Before Steve could ask him a question, Albert was gone, the piece of paper with the name and address of the gallery clutched in his hand. The closer he got to the city centre the more worried he became. Why had she done this? His heart began to palpitate and sometimes he was short of breath. When he had finally found the gallery, he was told they didn't know anyone called Odini. He wondered whether he had remembered the name Rosalie had mentioned correctly. Bloody memory! He started sweating and had difficulty breathing. Fate had dealt him a final blow and he was sure that the direction the life of this beautiful Rosalie had taken was irreversible. The flower had been culled, her petals torn out.

He ran to the restaurant as fast as he could; he had to alert the others, but the effort was too much for him and the black spots he saw became bigger and bigger. He realised he didn't have the strength yet. He had to stop again and again to get his breath back, and when he finally got to the restaurant, he more or less stumbled inside and, stammering and faltering, he related what had happened. Everybody panicked and he felt weak, so terribly weak.

The news of Rosalie's disappearance went through the restaurant like a typhoon. The waiter, who felt he'd been an accessory to the disappearance, told them what he knew of Odini and where they might find him. Eduardo immediately phoned the police station and all four went to the address the waiter had given them. When they got there, the police had already arrived and were knocking at the door. They stepped back to see if there was any movement, but when nobody came to the door, it was bashed down and the police stormed into the house, only to find the deserted room with Rosalie's clothes, her knickers, her bra, the black canvas shoes and the torn red, too short, cold dress. There was no trace of her, or Odini, to be found and although the torn dress hinted at the use of violence, the shoes and other articles of clothing indicated she'd probably taken them off of her own free will.

Steve got into a frenzy of rage, shouted, cried, wanted to murder the man, but later his sadness took over and he broke down completely. Jack was thinking about Rosalie, could see her before him, sitting at the table in the cabin, with her smile and sense of humour, standing on deck in the freshness of the morning, or sitting between him and Steve, watching the breath-taking sunset, talking, philosophising about complicated matters, her future, Steve and their children in a new, post-war world, her funny remarks, her optimism, her pure beauty, her fresh, rosy complexion and blush.

Albert became very depressed. After all the shite he'd experienced, he began to doubt more than ever what the purpose of his life was; feeling fettered to sorrow, the inescapability of fate, loneliness and disease. It reminded him of his mother, her illness and death, and he thought of his sweet aunt, Sylvain, and even of his father. He missed them and realised he had to get out of this country, no matter what. He was drifting towards a dark chasm, its treacherous, obscure edge, beyond which there is no life, but he didn't care.

The next day, after the police had received information from a fisherman whose nets had got stuck in the water, the car was found and hoisted out of the water. As the doors and the boot lid were open and the police diving-team couldn't find any bodies, both Odini and Rosalie were declared dead. The chance of survival was virtually nil anyway, due to the shark-infested waters.

Odini's girlfriend, Syreeta, heard the strange story and contacted the police. They questioned her, but as it was clear she wasn't involved, they let her go.

The waiter was on his way to the police station to tell them what he knew about Odini, when he met a customer who told him about the car that had been found. He turned pale, felt sick and had to hold on to a gate for support. After all, he was an accessory to murder now. He couldn't take another step to the station and went back to the restaurant. Many thoughts and a feeling of guilt scourged his mind. There was nobody at the restaurant yet. He went to the larder, where he sat down on some wooden steps and tried to think, but it didn't work; his head was full of pain. Because of his naiveté and greed the life of a beautiful young woman had abruptly been ended. He took a bottle of rum from the shelf and drank most of it. After that he stood on the steps and put the rope that was hanging from the roof hatch around his neck. He wanted to take another draught of rum, but he lost his balance and fell.

The following days Steve, Jack and Albert spent many hours at the police station, giving further information and to hear if there was any news. The authorities were trying to contact Rosalie's parents in the Netherlands, but were informed that they were abroad with thousands of other Dutch people who were going to be housed in Germany due to severe flooding.

In spite of the fact that her body hadn't been found, Jack suggested they held a service for Rosalie. It was a good way to come to terms with the situation and, hopefully, it would give them some peace of mind, he said. When they were all back on board, Jack took his guitar and played some songs he'd written. Albert didn't feel like being with people and retreated to the privacy of his cabin; he needed some peace and quiet, time to think. It was good to be back; as if he had come home again, in spite of everything that had happened. Later he went back on deck. There was Steve, looking over the water. Albert sat down and apologised to Steve, telling him how rotten and guilty he felt.

'You can't help it either, Albert. I think she was fed up with me; she just didn't want me any more,' Steve said.

That night Jack lay awake for a long time. It was as if, once more, in the warm silence of just one innocent night, the purest and most beautiful feelings had been ruthlessly pulled through a callous shredder. How could he tell Steve and Albert to take heart, when he felt so bloody miserable himself? he wondered.

The following morning Eduardo came along. Like the others he looked confused and exhausted. Too many things had happened in the past few months; his own wasting disease, the deaths of his wife, Raoul and another relative, and now this. It was all becoming too much for him, he said. He shook hands with Jack and Steve, embraced Albert, kissed him on the cheek and pressed him hard against his chest, trembling. Both were deeply moved and saw a deep, sad, mutual history of pain in each other's eyes. They had been through so many things together and now both of them were at the end of their tether.

The engine was started, the ropes were cast off and the first sail was hoisted. Eduardo was standing at the quay, looking at the water, while his thoughts floated to the young woman, whose body was roaming in the swell of the dark sea, her soul in search of afterlife. He crossed himself and murmured a prayer.

A few miles off the coast they halted, cast the anchor and laid a wreath on the water. Albert read a poem, full of red and yellow imagery. Steve just stared. Albert and Jack took his hands and said they were sorry. Three men, joined together in sadness; three pairs of troubled, moist eyes, looking at the sea and the sky, all seeing Rosalie in their own way, with their own palette of thoughts, a composition of colours, love, feelings and sounds.

Blown away by the wind, Steve's letter of farewell, creased and stained, was floating on the water, lonely, unread.

The crying of the birds in the sky turned into singing and the sea splashed with fresh, light, hissing sounds against the stern of the ship, stirring it, urging it to move on. The grey, meagre morning haze with a sad, solicitous sun, shaded into a bright, blue, open, endless, sky.

Far, far away, upon this dark-blue mirror of a tired sky, the small yacht sailed out of sight into the fading light of yet another night.

25

Desmond was already up and moving about, Roonah noticed, but he was later than usual, she thought. Since they had been living together, he could finally give in to what he had denied himself for many years, rest. A busy bee, that's what he was and always had been. He wanted to make use of every hour of the day to 'do things', as he would call it. She was quite active herself, but she had been able to quieten him down. He loved it and, although she was slumbering, he saw she was aware of everything that was going on around her. From under the sheet she saw Desmond putting on his white, linen trousers and a Nepalese shirt. If he put that on, it was as if he began to change gradually. He'd told her himself that he felt different in that garment, more enlightened, more at peace, maybe a little like a Buddhist monk. She had laughed at it, but there was definitely some truth in it.

While he was busy making breakfast from some fruits, she stretched herself, rolled over a few more times, quietly got out of bed, sneaked up on Desmond, took him by the waist and pulled him against her body. He couldn't hold her now, she knew, with his wet fingers. She kissed his neck, his arms and back until he was able to turn round and kiss her, keeping his wet, sticky hands out of the way. He had only just kissed her and she was gone again, jumping onto the bed, laughing at him, making a handstand and off she was, quickly sitting down on a chair at the table.

'Shall we sit outside? The weather is really gorgeous,' he said and saw how she threw open the door to the veranda and peered into the distance. There's my rash Roonah, he thought.

'I don't know. I think I'd rather go surfing now, the waves look really great,' she said, dreamily.

'But we could still have something to eat first, couldn't we? I would like to go surfing too, but I also want to do some other things.'

How predictable, she thought.

'Have breakfast yourself then,' she snapped, 'I'm going surfing, so that you can "do your things". Maybe I'll see you in the water later.'

'OK, you have it your way. How nice this,' he said.

These silly squabbles called up a kind of aversion in him; he could feel it in his chest. If she put her mind to something, everything else had to yield and sometimes she just forgot him; he didn't fit into her world then. He was used to it now and he didn't care much, but once in a while he had to put the brakes on it.

'Bye. Enjoy yourself,' he said, and started eating right away.

'OK, you win, I'll have some breakfast now,' she said, picking up her surf gear.

'It's your own doing. I only asked you if you wanted to have breakfast with me. Sorry.'

'Don't say sorry.'

After this it was quiet for a moment. Roonah remained seated on her chair, out of anger, rebellion, or both and Desmond was looking at a magazine, pretending to think of something else. Gradually the situation got back to normal and they both realised what trivial things they would sometimes argue about.

Once more she looked at his shirt and its colours, the vertical stripes, blue and yellow, and his big, white hair above it. He looked a bit like a priest or a shaman. They'd bought it a while ago in a town in England. What was that place called again? It wasn't far from Stonehenge and Avebury, two special places that attracted him like a magnet. And she remembered the cosy pub, The Red Lion, almost in the centre of the circle and the three or four trees, with their fine, intricate pattern of entwined roots, on a hill, barely holding on to it, and their branches and leaves which were hanging so freely over the hill. Gosh, what was the name of this place? She thought of the beautiful book of crystals she had seen in the local shop there and suddenly she remembered the name of the place. It was called Glastonbury. What a quaint little town that was. All the people there looked so different than in other places where they'd been, like hippies from the 1960s, but also as if they were from another part of the world, with their dark skin and raven-black hair, maybe from South America, or maybe they were of Celtic origin. The first man they'd seen there, for example, had a ponytail of more than three feet and the women they had met were wearing dresses that made them look like priestesses. She recalled the numerous shops, where they sold these unusual clothes, but also spiritual books, Tarot cards and special food; they'd seen several yoga and 'healing' centres, and places where you could have your future told. Apparently, Glastonbury was a magical place, where, so the story went, King Arthur and his wife, Queen Guinevere, were buried, the site where Joseph of Arimathea brought the Holy Grail, and there were indications that it could be Avalon.

She remembered the shop where he'd bought the shirt he was wearing now, and what he said to her, 'I can't put it on yet, I'll have to "grow" into it, undergo further transformation.'

It had made her laugh.

'One day I'll know that I can put it on,' he added.

That had happened. What wonderful days they were, she thought, and they'd seen so much. No wonder she couldn't immediately recall the name of the place.

That delicate nose, she thought, the lines of his face, his slightly fiery, but still oh so sweet eyes, and his mouth with the full lips; she could kiss him all day, she thought and with her soft hand she went over his bushy eyebrows, his eyes, lips and chin. She could feel his philosophical, deep thinking, his love and tenderness for her. She got butterflies in her belly, took off her T-shirt, enjoyed her free nakedness and cuddled him once more.

After breakfast she took her surfboard and walked past the cottages on the beach to the water. There was a little girl standing by one of them. It was the cottage, or hut, as they would often call these villas, where she'd heard the French chanson coming from that night. She couldn't hear the exact words the girl said, but it sounded like 'Señor Jésus'. She paused for a minute and tried to remember where she'd heard this name before, but she couldn't recall the place or moment and walked on; she was probably mistaken.

It was quite hot in her black wetsuit and she wanted to be in the water as quickly as she could. She didn't need to put on a wetsuit, but she felt better in it, safer. This was a top surf spot; never before had she had the opportunity to ride such waves, so close to her home. Behind her the girl once more called, 'Señor Jésus, Señor Alberto Jésus,' but Roonah couldn't hear it because of the noise of the breaking waves.

26

Somebody was calling his name, a high-pitched voice, somewhere. Was it in his dream? For a moment he thought he was still in hospital and Gabriel was standing at his bedside. He rolled over and felt the body of a man, not Gabriel's, but of a somewhat heavier man, who automatically put his arm over him, as if he was looking for, or perhaps wanted to give him, warmth or security. He lifted the heavy arm and put it back where it belonged.

'Señor Jésus, Señor Alberto Jésus!'

He was trying to think, but it didn't work. 'Señor Jésus!' It was a child calling him, not an adult, not Gabriel or the angel nurse. He sat up, but didn't feel like getting out of bed; it had been such a short night. It finally got through to him that the man who was lying next to him was the one he had brought home with him early that morning. The man was sleeping very peacefully and he snored quite heavily, as if he was lying comfortably in his own bed. Albert got out of bed and went to the front door, where the sound of the voice was coming from. There was a girl of about six years old, in a flowery dress, standing barefooted in the sand. Although he remembered her face, he couldn't recall her name. Bloody hell, why do I keep forgetting things?

'Hello, Señor Jésus. Can you help my mother move a wardrobe?'

'Is that why you have come to wake me up? Don't you know it's still very early?'

'Sorry, Señor, my mummy asked me,' she said with her dark eyes and innocent smile.

'I understand. It's all right. Sorry. Tell her I'll be with her in a minute.'

'OK.'

'Adios, Margarita,' he said, suddenly remembering her name.

He hadn't lived here long yet, but the people in the neighbourhood knew him as a soft, kind young man, who was always willing to help, an angel from a land far away from here. They thought his name, Alberto Jésus, was exactly right for him. He was a bit different from other men and sometimes he forgot things, your name or your face, but he was very sweet.

In the distance he saw the first surfer on the water; it was the young woman in her wetsuit. She looked familiar, he thought, but he didn't know why; there was still something wrong with his short-term memory, it seemed. Maybe he didn't know her at all. Just look at her; see how she rides the waves, he said to himself, more or less waiting to see if she would dive into the huge waves or be swallowed up by them. Wow, she could swim really well; look at those powerful strokes. '*Superbe!*' he said aloud.

Behind him somebody was groaning; it was Bernard who was waking up. His head felt like concrete, his stomach like a bag of gravel and his eyes were misty, for what he saw didn't look familiar. He rubbed his tired, bloodshot eyes and closed them again, hoping he would recognise the scene when he made another attempt to open them. Unfortunately, it wasn't any different. By a window, or was it a door, he saw the shadow of a man he didn't know. Had he been kidnapped? Was the war still going on? He didn't get it. He then noticed his belt and shirt were undone and began to ask himself what had really happened to him. He was almost inclined to inspect his body with his hand. He quickly zipped up his trousers, fastened his belt and sat up, but his head protested; it was as if all the church bells of Montreal were ringing at the same time. He wanted to say something, but couldn't think of any words that would make sense.

Albert came up to him.

'*Bonjour. Comment allez-vous ce matin?*'

When he heard these French words, a voice from far away, last night, he thought, told him he'd spoken to this man before.

'*Ça va, un peu. J'ai mal à la tête; c'est tout,*' he replied.

Yes, that he had a headache, was clear to Albert.

'*Voulez-vous manger quelque chose?*' he asked Bernard. He then told him what had happened that night.

Bernard didn't feel ashamed. He actually had to laugh, until he realised he hadn't gone back home, to Isabelle.

'*Je suis désolé, c'est très gentil, mais il faut que je parte; il y a quelqu'un qui m'attend, j'espère,*' he said with a wry smile.

It made Albert laugh.

'*Vous venez d'où?*' he asked, '*du Canada?*'

'*Oui, de Montréal, Québec, mais vraiment, vous pouvez me tutoyer.*'

'*OK. Moi, je viens d'un village près de Paris, et j'ai aussi vécu à Paris même,* but we can also speak English, for I lived in London too.'

'OK. I used to live in a part of Montreal where a lot of people spoke English. But I'm sorry, I should really be going now. Somebody's waiting for me, as I said. Thank you so much. What's your name?'

'Albert. Nice to meet you,' he said, stretching out his sweet, soft hand.

'My name's Bernard. I'm sure we'll meet again. I live close by, more or less round the corner. Thanks for everything.'

'*De rien. C'était un plaisir.* Take care.'

Bernard stepped outside, into the hot sun, pointed at Roonah and said, 'Good-looking young woman over there on the surfboard. Something for you? Sorry, I'm only joking. That elderly man, who's with her, he is her friend or husband, isn't he? Big age gap, but they're a special couple.'

'I know. *Oui, elle est très belle, bien sûr, mais je ne m'approche jamais des femmes,*' Albert said.

'Well, what difference does it really make? *Peut-être que tu es plus heureux que moi,*' he chuckled.

Walking home, he thought about what Albert had said about his not fancying women. It didn't surprise him and when he shook hands with him, he was sure the guy was gay, but he wasn't too bad for a poofter.

Albert had intended to ask Bernard what the name of 'that woman' was, but had forgotten to do so and Bernard was too far away now; he only heard the sounds from the beach and the heavy, curling waves Roonah and Desmond were riding on. It was fascinating to see how those two were a match for each other, climbing onto their boards, laughing, battling with the sea on their tiny boards. Now and then the already bright sun was shining on their wetsuits, which made them look like two fast-moving, shining, dazzling stars.

27

With his hands on his abdomen Erasmus lay staring at the ceiling. He was trying to remember what had happened during the last twenty-four hours, but some of his recollections were very vague. He thought about Iowa, home, his mother, the university; it all seemed so far away, not in space, but in time. He remembered how he used to saunter over the lawn of the campus. It was as if he was looking at himself now from a distance, in time. There were some guys he would sometimes talk to, but he usually kept himself to himself. It wasn't too bad really, he thought, for he was there to study and wanted to be good at it, maybe even the best and he didn't care for the unions and all those people who liked to exaggerate everything, especially if they wanted to be friends with you, while nine out of ten times such a 'friendship' was as thin as ice. And then they expected you to take part in everything, the socials, the parties. No, he didn't want that, he preferred to be on his own. The only guy he would sometimes speak to was, funnily enough, his very opposite. It was someone who wanted to experience everything life had to offer and therefore partied as much as possible. One day he had climbed onto the roof of the university, that gigantic roof over the entrance of the building, which looked like a Greek or Roman temple. He had only done it because of a bet, he said. The board wanted to expel him, but as he was supported by so many students, they let him stay. He had a lithe, slender body, black curly hair and Erasmus suddenly remembered he had dreamed about the guy that night. In spite of his bravura this guy was always kind to Erasmus, which Erasmus couldn't understand. Why would anyone want to be nice to him or take an interest in his life?

The smell of fried eggs penetrated his nostrils; somebody at the hostel was probably cooking a very elaborate lunch or late breakfast. It made him feel hungry.

Coincidence had it that, when he arrived in New York, he saw that very same guy, Jim, walking along Vanderbilt Avenue. He didn't even know that Jim was from New York, so it was really great to see him there, among thousands of other people. He called his name, with a loud and excited, almost trembling voice, but because of the traffic noise and the voices of tens of thousands of people, Jim didn't hear him, so he called him a few more times, much louder. Jim was amazed and took him to a bar just off Fifth Avenue for a coffee. Erasmus told Jim he was in New York to try and find some relatives of his and perhaps to have a look at some paintings by both Dennis and Edward Hopper.

'Are you in any way related to these guys then?' he asked.

'I don't think so, but there was a rumour, so I thought I might like to learn a bit more about these two artists, now that I'm in New York. It would be really cool. I've read some things about Dennis Hopper. He was an intriguing person.'

'Yes, I can imagine that, but did you know that there are quite a few works by Edward Hopper at the Whitney Museum of American Art, here in New York? You really got to see them; they're fabulous!'

'How do you know?' said Erasmus.

'Well, my dad works for a company that establishes whether objects of art, especially paintings, are genuine or not, and that's how I sometimes hear things. But I'm very much interested in art myself too. Shall I come with you?'

'Yeah, great. Have you got time for that?'

'Not right now, but tomorrow or the day afters' fine.'

'Awesome. Where shall we meet? You tell me, you're the one who knows this place.'

'I don't know about that, but my dad's office is just round the corner, so shall we meet here tomorrow, at, say, eleven a.m.?'

'Fine. See you tomorrow at eleven.'

Meeting Jim here, in this enormous city, wasn't it incredible? There's something special going on in this bubbling, almost swirling city, especially after this meeting, he thought. He felt free here and something told him to detach himself even more from his earlier life, to try and move on to the next level, like in his games, to have the guts to break free from the negativity of the past and his home.

The following day they went to the museum. Erasmus was deeply impressed. For the first time he learnt that the Hopper name originated from the Netherlands. This adventure was like a jigsaw puzzle of himself; every time he got a new piece.

Jim's father had a list of customers on which some Hoppers happened to appear and so, possibly with the help of Jim, he could try and trace those people. The list went as far back as thirty-odd years, so the question was if those Hoppers lived at the same addresses and if they were still alive. The chances were very small, he realised, but there was always the telephone directory or maybe a library where he could find some information.

Now that he was in Manhattan he intended to make the most of it. He spent a lot of time in Central Park, alone, among the beautiful trees and saw the leaves change colour, the transition of one season to the next, like in himself, he thought. He began to feel at peace with himself and took his time to think about his future, the course he wanted to follow and a plan to find his uncle.

'Why don't you move in with me and my dad?' Jim asked after a week. 'I'm sure it's much better than that awful hostel in Harlem.'

'It isn't such a bad place,' Erasmus said, 'and I don't need a lot of luxury, only a clean bed and a bath,' he replied, laughing. 'But it's very kind of you and I wouldn't mind, to be honest.'

Like Desmond and Roonah he found out that the war didn't affect New York much and he was struck by the optimism of the people in New York. Maybe it was characteristic of this place, he thought.

Now and then, but not very systematically, he went into town with a Hopper address in his pocket, hoping to strike gold and meet his uncle, but it didn't work like that. Usually there was nobody at home, so he had to come back.

In a house in the meatpacking district, a Hopper man asked him to come in and talk about his family in Iowa, saying he had been there too, a long time ago, with a brother of his. He might be my father's brother, Erasmus thought, thinking of the photo of his dad when he was in his early twenties, and he became more inquisitive. The man wanted to know everything. They were sitting in a fairly dark living room, having coffee and eating cookies. The man said he would get some old family photographs from the big closet upstairs the next time Erasmus was around. Erasmus came back three times, but the photos didn't come. He discovered the man lived alone and just loved meeting somebody from the outside world.

Another man, who lived in Bleecker Street, opposite a bar called Wicked Willy's, which Erasmus thought was a queer name anyway, also wanted the young Erasmus to come back, but for a different reason. Erasmus had been there for only about ten minutes when the man said, 'You can always stay here, if you like; family ties are very important, aren't they?'

It made Erasmus feel very uneasy. Moreover, the man was looking at him in a very intrusive way and when he began to say things like, 'I like the colour of your shirt' and 'you've got a lovely face,' this first time also became the last time.

If fate had wanted it, he would have met Roonah and Desmond in New York. On a Wednesday, it was a sunny, but fresh afternoon in late autumn, the chair he was sitting on almost touched theirs. All three were sitting outside, near Rockefeller Centre, in a place that looked more like a garden, where all kinds of small shops, huts or market-stalls, sold home-made jewellery, Swiss chocolate, cakes, decorations, trinkets and gadgets. They were sitting with their backs to each other, on cosy, French-style folding chairs. He heard the two talk about some sort of photo-shoot in the neighbourhood. Her accent was a mix of American and Irish English, whereas the man's was more British than American English, but he didn't say much; he had a bad cough. Erasmus wasn't really interested in their conversation, but he did hear her say that it was a pity a lot of the tall buildings, which were normally open to the public, were now closed, for fear of possible attacks, so a visit to the Empire State Building, the Rockefeller Center or the Freedom tower was out of the question. Useful info, this, he thought.

That same afternoon he found another Hopper at home. This time, however, it was a lady, a Mrs Hopper who invited him up when he said his name. She looked at him, from top to toe, as if she was looking for something. It made him feel a little uneasy, but that was what he could expect if he just rang the doorbell of an unknown person, he realised. He was about to say something else, but just then she said he'd better come in, so that they could continue their conversation inside. He had probably passed the reliability test, for she told him right away that her husband had recently died and that she was living alone in the apartment.

'Let me take your coat. Please come into the living room,' she said, while she hung his coat on the hat-stand.

How is it possible, he thought, when he entered the living room; this room doesn't breathe a whiff of sorrow. The woman, she had to be in her forties, he estimated, and looked really attractive, was very cheerful and seemed to be in a buoyant mood. She appeared relieved, and had an inner happiness, he thought, as if she was glad her husband had gone to heaven.

'Would you like a drink, some coffee, tea, a soda maybe, or would you rather have a wine?' she asked him, while she poured out a glass of red wine for herself.

'A coffee, please.'

It was only eleven o'clock in the morning or so, he thought, and a bit early for wine. She had to be well-off, as the house, a pretty large apartment in the Murray Hill district, had recently been redecorated and refurbished very stylishly and there were some fine oil paintings on the walls.

Without asking her any questions, she told him that she had a lot more freedom now. Her husband had been ill for some time and he was always very suspicious. If she went out to do the shopping, he always wanted her to be back at a pre-arranged time. If she returned home five minutes late, he would start asking questions, but, being very tight-assed, he never went shopping with her. When he was gone, she found out there was a lot more money in the piggy-bank than she had bargained for, so she resolved to get rid of all the old furniture and most other objects which reminded her of the late Mr Hopper.

'I have a lot more space in my head now,' she said to him, 'our marriage never was a very happy one.'

Erasmus had already guessed as much.

It called up images of his own situation at home, many years ago, the silent tension, the unsaid words, the painful glances, the red eyes and tired faces. For the first time he realised it had been for the best that his parents had separated.

On the large balcony he saw cords with nuts strung on them and birds flying on and off. Funny, he thought, when people think of New York, they hardly ever think of birds. They were beautifully marked, blue birds, with a black circle around their heads and a striped tail.

'They're always the same birds that come back,' she said. 'They've all got names, too. That's George over there and the one next to it is Abraham and that smaller one over there is Jimmy. Look, Jimmy is staring at you; how odd, he never does that. Not that they listen to their names, but it's great fun. But tell me, why did you come here in the first place?' she asked him casually.

He told her about his past and that he'd never really known his father, but that he had an uncle who probably lived in New York and that he would like to find him. Maybe his uncle could tell him a bit more about his father.

Although Mrs Hopper looked at him, she didn't appear to be listening to what he was telling her. It was as if she already knew what he wanted to say. She just went on talking about her husband and his sisters, bitches really, who turned up at her doorstep once her husband was very ill and dying, only to get money from him, she supposed, as they never came to see him, or her, earlier. She didn't even know them. She imitated how they talked and it made him laugh.

'What slimeballs they were,' she said with a sour face. 'After his death I never saw them again. Good riddance,' she added, and chuckled. 'But a brother who could be your dad, no, sorry. But then again, my husband never was much of a talker. Let me have a look at your face.'

She came quite close to him, as if she was going to touch him for some reason. When she spoke the smell of wine invaded his nostrils; it reminded him of his mother. He felt strange and wanted to leave, but he still had a spark of hope that the woman's late husband was his uncle after all. Not that it would be of any use to him now.

Apparently, she enjoyed his company, for she kept on talking, pouring cups of coffee and was having another wine herself, maybe her third or fourth glass. What does this woman do all day? he wondered. The paintings on the wall, the furniture, she did have taste. He had to give her that.

By pushing some buttons on a remote, some wonderful music pervaded the room. He couldn't see any loudspeakers, though, and it wasn't really music, but rather sounds of nature, birds, water, rain, animals running, ice cracking, rustling leaves, supported by soft, music-like, wavy sounds of some kind. It was very peaceful and he wanted to close his eyes, get into the waves. From air ducts at the bottom of the walls came scents of silt sea air, fir trees, oaks, poplars, the smells of a stable, flowers and fresh grass, all clearer and lighter than incense. There was no need for him to say anything.

Together they were enjoying themselves, listening, inhaling, smelling, while the paintings changed colour, became black and white, to the rhythm of the sounds, which affected their very composition.

This was so weird, he thought. He didn't even know anything like this existed. He wouldn't have been surprised if the comfortable armchair he was sitting in was going to massage him to the same rhythm.

'What do you think?' she asked, almost inaudibly, 'lovely, isn't it?'

He only nodded, anxious no human sound should disturb this experience.

She smiled. How long they were sitting like this, he didn't know and didn't care. He would never have wanted to miss this, he thought, sitting, enjoying himself, with his eyes closed.

The spectacle grew dim and gradually faded away. She stood up quietly, came to him and asked him softly if he wanted to eat something. He couldn't refuse. It was one of those moments when you just undergo something, he thought. Anything may happen once you open your mind, he thought, and he remembered the inner voice that had told him he should free himself of all his inhibitions.

He felt so relaxed that there was no reason for him to stand up. He needed nothing else now; this was terrific, he thought, while she was looking at his young body and noticed his sweet, but deeply worried face, and she knew how he was yearning for affection, having gone without it at home, and that he was looking for something or somebody.

When he finally said 'Yes, please', she'd already gone to the kitchen. A little later she returned with two large glasses of sweet, white wine and some food. Once again he surrendered. This was another world, he thought, this could never be New York.

'Would you like to come to the relaxation room?' she asked him.

'I gathered we were there already,' he said, for what could be more relaxing than what there was in this room? he wondered.

She didn't ask him any questions about his life, as if she didn't want to know anything about him, he thought. But the woman knew exactly what she was doing and she was well aware of the fact she shouldn't ruin the special atmosphere, disturb Erasmus' inner balance and field of unmagnetic peace. She went to the other room, with the glass of white wine in her hand. He followed her example, his eyes scanning the room, while the beautiful music followed them and he could still smell the wonderful scents.

There was a reasonably big bed in the room, with satin sheets, embroidered with the golden letters 'I. Hopper'. She lay down on it; he followed. Lying next to each other, in silence, listening to the sounds, she took his hand. He didn't withdraw it, but allowed her to give him energy; an energy that was like the sound and scent, synchronic with them. He felt her hand go over his abdomen, her fingers following the lines of his body, and her only saying, 'how good'.

He found it confusing, because he had always been ashamed of his body. He was too fat, he always thought, and during P.T. lessons at school he never dared to take his shirt off. With the energy she instilled came security and confidence. Her hand slipped to his loins; it confused him, made him restless. This was really enough, but still he let her, as if he had no choice and desired it. She touched his leg, the troublesome one of the accident, his hip joint and it was just as if energy and strength were radiated into it.

'It'll be all right,' she said, 'don't worry, you're a fine young man. Your leg and belly only make you more beautiful,' while she put her hand into his pants and very carefully moved her warm, slender fingers over his big scar, which first started to glow and after that it disappeared, as if it had never been there.

'You should take more magnesium and zinc,' she said.

Who is this woman? What does she want? he asked himself, when her hand went over his other leg, back into his pants and out again, while the fragrances and sounds in the room were caressing his nose and ears; he was in heaven. An erection was coming up, but the hand had already moved on, out of his pants, into his shirt and back again, slipping along his neck and face, finally reaching his head, staying there, massaging his forehead and temples with her fingers.

She sat up and looked at him.

'Did you want to have sex with me?' she asked.

He was too embarrassed to look back at her.

'No need to be ashamed,' she said.

'Erm, yes,' he replied, hesitating, with a scarlet face.

She raised her glass, gesturing to him to do the same. They toasted, took a sip and lay down again. Occasionally they looked at each other in silence, while his feelings were in a vacuum, he thought, not in a void, but in everything, an invisible, firm, but flexible soap bubble, into which nothing could penetrate.

'I knew you wanted it, and I would've liked it too, for you have a beautiful body, but it's good we didn't. Hold on to the energy that I have passed on to you; you will need it. Don't allow yourself to be dragged into negativity. I know everything about your past; you don't have to tell me anything,' she said. 'Your mother is happy now; she doesn't feel the need to get everything out of life; for her, little is enough. She wanted to protect you, without any more disturbances of her new life; the past was too much for her. Only in her next life will she be able to carry on,' she added.

Erasmus couldn't believe his ears.

'You have come a long way; you have started your search, not only for your father, but especially for yourself. You're in the right place here, in New York. It's a very spiritual place and it will give you an insight into the past. You have already experienced what New York, or Manhattan for all that, does to you.'

Erasmus was speechless.

'The Department of Defense think the Chinese haven't attacked Manhattan, because it's so well protected, but that's downright nonsense, for if they want to, they can bring chaos to the whole city, annihilate it, but because of their age-old spiritual background, the Chinese respect Manhattan's spirituality.'

'Is that also the reason why so many Chinese people live here?'

'Well, what do you think? This spiritual history of Manhattan goes back to the time when the Native Americans settled here and brought their ancient knowledge with them. The Chinese just know they shouldn't touch such a sacred place. Don't think they're scared of America,' she said, mockingly. 'Manhattan, Manatus, Manna Hatta. Just look up the word *mana* one day, or what this clever Swiss guy, Carl Jung, said about it. Even all the explanations given on the Internet never mentioned it.'

'Wouldn't there be any people in the U.S. Administration who know this?'

'Maybe one or two, although I'm not sure they're that clever. But if they do know this, they're not telling us about it. That's the way these things go. 9/11, a plane flying into the Pentagon. Nobody ever saw it. An unmarked plane flying into the W.T.C. building. And how come one of the towers came down vertically?'

'Well. Yes.'

'But to come back to you,' she continued, 'besides being better able to deal with the past, you will also be able to better cope with the future. Don't be afraid of yourself. Your friend will come with you,' she said. 'Your father is very close to you, always, and you will meet his brother, your uncle, very soon.'

It didn't stop there.

'The sun and moon are calling you, the woman from the Land of the Rising Sun will lead you to the moon, take you inside, show you lots of things, although your eyes won't believe it. You will go south, to Mexico and South America, to Ecuador, to be precise. There you will find what you're looking for, as soon as you know what it is you're looking for. Beyond it are clouds, love in a city under the breath of the big ocean.'

There she stopped abruptly. She swallowed, raised her eyes and then turned them away from him, he noticed. Strange, he thought, but didn't dare ask any questions. Why should he? The oracle had spoken. It remained quiet for a while. It all sounded so weird, he thought and he wasn't sure if he should believe her. It was so overwhelming, so much, but he could feel a lot of energy. He rose, got off the bed and went to the living room. Mrs Hopper was already there, staring a bit absent-mindedly. Her eyes were moist, he noticed. Maybe she was thinking of her late husband.

He knew it was time to leave; he even felt a bit awkward. She came towards him, looked deep into his eyes, kissed him on his cheek and forehead.

'It was so good of you to come. I knew you'd come here one day, but I didn't know when. If you need me, you will find me again, somewhere, in the last minutes before the rays of the sun will bless you. Thanks for everything, hold on to your energy; it's very important.'

He didn't know what to say. She kept surprising him, time and again and he wanted to embrace, hug and kiss her, but he felt that he had to take all those beautiful feelings with him. He was still thinking about it all when she had already gone to the hall, and stood there, waiting for him, his coat in her hands. She opened the door for him. He gave her a kiss on her cheek and felt a tear roll over her smile. She took his hand and held it for a moment; then let it slip away. He put his coat over his arms and went to the staircase.

'Take care, Erasmus, and mind your coat,' she said.

He came outside. The sun was shining shyly over the tall trees; there was a strong wind blowing, but his head was in the clouds. The music, the scents, the birds, his scars, Mrs Hopper, South America, the land of the rising sun, the moon, Ecuador.

He was about to put on his coat when a gust of wind snatched it from his unsuspecting hand and blew it against the stem of a bare, young tree, where it fell to the ground. He picked it up and put it on. In spite of the cold wind, it felt a bit like spring, he thought. How odd.

28

After their departure from Havana some gloomy days followed. Although Jack did his best to cheer Albert and Steve up, it was far from easy. But after a few days Albert's mood changed. He became more positive when it got through to him that he was no longer chained to Cuba. It didn't matter where they were going now, he thought, he was free! The Atlantic Ocean, the Pacific, they'd be going straight through America, and after that they would sail south, to Ecuador; at last. He had been really lucky to have met Jack again when he was heading for a big depression. The guy had saved his sanity, maybe even his life, he thought. Thinking about the past week, he realised Jack must have had a terrible time too, in spite of the fact that he was a strong man, who seemed to be able to take everything in his stride. He felt ashamed of himself and said,

'I'm sorry, Jack, for having been such a miserable bastard.'

Jack gave Albert a smile and patted him on his shoulder.

'No worries. I understand, but I'm glad you're feeling better.'

Together they tried to help Steve, but he didn't say much; he just wanted to be left alone for the time being.

For a long time Jack had wanted to go to the Bahamas and since they weren't too far away from them, they decided to sail north, in the direction of Florida. The Bahamas were the islands where Columbus had first set foot on American soil, Albert thought and, like Columbus, he had sailed from Palos, via the Canary Islands to the Bahamas. The islands looked enticing with their wonderful white beaches, exactly as they had always thought and seen in films. Arriving at the harbour, it felt as if they were going on holiday. In the evening they went to one of the harbour clubs and met some friendly people.

'Did you know that the Bahamas used to be a safe haven for pirates, like the notorious Blackbeard, until the British Government, or, actually, the governor of these islands, Woodes Rogers, put an end to piracy?' an elderly man asked them. He came from England, but had lived on the Bahamas for most of his life.

'By the way, we've hardly had any problems during the war here; only seen a couple of Chinese vessels, but they disappeared the moment they spotted some American warships. Maybe they realised it was too expensive for them,' he said, laughing at his own words.

Thinking of the yachts they'd seen in the harbour, they understood what the man meant. They intended to stay for a week, if they could afford the port charges. They wanted to relax, swim with the dolphins and do other things that would take their minds off the recent events. In the end the week became weeks.

Steve even wondered why they should want to move on; this spot was just perfect. It had been very difficult to leave Havana, since it still made him feel guilty; it was as if he had deserted Rosalie, but on the other hand, wasn't she the one who had left *him*?

At the marina they met a young black guy, Jonathan, who came from South Africa. He was eager to join them on their trip through the Panama Canal. He told them the yacht he was on had crossed the Atlantic via the northern route, to Canada and the U.S. It had been quite an adventure with big storms and heavy seas. He had seen some huge icebergs; signs that the last icecaps and glaciers of the Arctic region were disappearing fast. Although he found the Bahamas very cool, he wanted to get to Peru, to explore this old Inca land and visit Machu Picchu. Apparently, there were a lot of people of African descent in Peru, he said.

'Why don't you come with us to South America then?' Jack asked him.

After a couple of weeks Albert became more and more restless. The claustrophobic feeling of being stuck on an island was coming back to him. It was time to move on.

29

The next day, at ten in the morning, Erasmus was on his way to the address of the next Hopper on his list, in Hudson Street, West Village. Shabby looking houses, in unpleasant rows, alternated with posh buildings and cosier parts of the street. It was an incredibly long street, but he loved to stroll around the streets of Manhattan, gain new impressions, see people and get a more complete picture of New York. More and more he realised he would rather live here than in Iowa. What a difference it was. Of course there was more space in Iowa than in this bustling city, but somehow New York gave more space in his head and, of course, there were the cultural challenges, museums, exhibitions and people with lots of different backgrounds.

After some fifteen minutes he found himself at the address, a two-storeyed house with a tiny garden, a big tree in the middle and an iron gate around it. It looked really attractive. He pressed the black button of the doorbell and waited, with a certain uneasiness. He heard footsteps in the hall and once more it was a woman who opened the door.

'Hello, good morning. What can I do for you?'

'Erm, I'm Erasmus Hopper and I'm looking for a Mr Hopper, an uncle of mine.'

He had already seen the initials P.J. on the nameplate; the same as his uncle's.

'Really? How wonderful, an uncle. Yes, you do need to speak to P.J. then,' she said with a smile on her deep, dark face. 'I'm not his wife, by the way, if that's what you think. I'm only his 'aide', assistant, nurse, or whatever you'd like to call it. Come on in, don't stand there, outside. I'll call him. I am Mrs Schwartzkopf, Klara Schwartzkopf.'

'P.J., there's someone at the door for you!'

Nothing happened.

'Erasmus. What a nice name, rather out of the ordinary, isn't it? By the way, P.J. is always a little reserved, or should I say, reluctant, when it comes to meeting people he doesn't know. Please come into the living room; he'll be here in a sec. He was reading. Why don't you sit in that big, comfortable armchair?'

Erasmus didn't have to say anything; he only had to follow her directions, which was fine by him. He looked around the room and was struck by the weird range of chairs, the vast table, the large bookshelves, the beautiful pictures on the wall. It looked like a museum. What kind of man is this P.J.? he wondered. The woman had said he was a bit different. There was something odd about the room, but he couldn't put his finger on it, and although it was written all over the place, he didn't see what it was, until it began to dawn upon him that everything, the furniture, the pictures, were all perfectly aligned; nothing, not a book, nor any other object, lay askew.

The sun that was shining through the stained-glass windows, projecting beautiful colours and shapes on the wall, the table and the floor reminded him of a church. How intriguing. But in spite of the sunlight the room was rather dark and there hung a musty smell. The room was probably never properly aired. On the large table lay a big, thick, history book, perfectly aligned, symmetrically in the centre, a pencil beside it, perfectly parallel to the book. Nothing is left to coincidence, he thought. Next to a big old-fashioned chair he saw some toys lying on the floor, while nothing else indicated the presence of children in the house. If there were children, he would have some cousins. How odd. He had never thought about that. Even the toys lay perfectly straight and well-aligned. He picked up the book, looked at it, leafed through it and put it back again. Cousins, funny he should never have thought of that earlier. If they existed, they could be of his age. How strange.

He heard feet shuffling in the passage; the door stood half open and it seemed somebody had to come from far away. He looked at the woman, who was standing with one foot in the living room.

'Come in, P.J.,' she said. 'He's in here.'

The way she said it, was like she was talking to a child, he thought. Slowly, a man in his late fifties appeared in the doorway.

'This is Erasmus Hopper,' she said to him.

'Good morning,' Erasmus said.

P.J. only half looked at him.

'Hello,' he said, and 'hum', keeping a close watch on what the woman was doing. He rolled his head a little, but he didn't show any emotion of surprise or happiness that someone had come to see him. He looked at the table and the book.

'No, no,' he said, with an anxious look in his eyes, went to the table and put the book, which Erasmus had put back without thinking about it, perfectly straight, picked up the pencil and put it down again, exactly parallel to the book. After that he looked round the room, wondering if there were any more imperfections.

'This is P.J.,' the woman said to Erasmus.

Once more the man rolled his head a little, gave Erasmus a very weak hand, but said nothing, and it was clear he didn't want to make eye-contact.

'Erasmus was a famous writer,' he suddenly said, in a reflex. 'He lived from 1466 till 1536.'

Erasmus looked at the woman with bulging eyes. He didn't even know himself when his namesake lived.

The woman smiled again.

'I'm here to help P.J.; I cook for him and talk to him. He is a bit different. I live here; it's all right, it's not all that serious.'

'Erasmus Hopper,' she said, with the stress on the surname, 'is looking for his uncle, who happens to be called P.J. as well, just like you.'

'Oh.'

'You got a brother, don't you?' she asked him.

No response.

Erasmus was even more surprised when P.J. began to sum up a whole list of U.S. presidents, stopped at Bill Clinton and started all over again; this time in reverse order, including the dates of their presidencies. After that came a shorter list, beginning with Gerald Ford and ending with Ronald Reagan, followed by some U.S. states, Nebraska, Georgia, Illinois, and the word 'peanuts'.

That man's a nutter, Erasmus thought. I'm quite sure now I haven't got any cousins.

P.J. paused, looked at the history book on the table, took it and put it back again, very precisely, rolling his head.

'Peanuts and Iran, yes.'

Erasmus and Mrs Schwartzkopf looked at each other with raised eyebrows, but the show wasn't over yet.

'Erasmus Hopper, Charlie Hopper, Crazy Hopper, Edward Hopper, Hopper & Hopper, the Netherlands,' and continued 'President George Washington, Washington Square Park, Hoppers, upside down, in time. So many people were buried there. Hostages.'

'Huh?' Erasmus uttered. He could feel a certain excitement coming up. All those Hoppers.

'What's the connection?' he asked. 'Why did you sum them up and why did you mention those dead people in Washington Square Park?'

No response.

On the wall hung what looked like a genuine Hopper and beside it a print of another Hopper painting, showing a view of the sea as seen from the room of a house. It was as if the house stood in the sea. P.J. saw Erasmus looking at the picture.

'The answer is on the canvas.'

Erasmus heard it, but he didn't understand its relevance; to him all the information he got was cryptic, unrelated stuff.

'South America, Ecuador', were the next words that suddenly came out of P.J.'s mouth.

Erasmus could hardly believe his ears. Only yesterday Mrs Hopper told me I wasn't only going to meet my uncle, but that I would go to South America as well. So is P.J., this autistic man, really my uncle? And why did he, this uncommunicative man, mention South America?

He studied P.J. to see if he could detect anything familiar, a trait that would remind him of his father, or of something else in his own unconscious mind; that would confirm P.J. was his uncle. He mentioned his mother's name to see how P.J. would react, but the latter was far away again, somewhere deep in the oceans of his own thoughts, gazing with a seemingly empty look at the opposite wall where the Hopper print hung, automatically repeating or, rather, 're-mumbling' the words he had said in connection with the U.S. presidents.

This is utterly useless, he thought. Apart from a few cryptic hints it was also as if there was something this man didn't want to talk about, as if he was hiding something.

P.J. took some books from a bookshelf and made a neat pile of them; he was back in his own world.

'Would you like to have lunch with us?' Mrs Schwartzkopf asked.
'Thanks very much. I'd like that.'
P.J. is a lucky man to have such a fine woman to look after him, he thought. He really wanted to stay, because that was the only way to find out a bit more, he thought. During lunch, too, he noticed that P.J. was programmed, as it were; everything had to stay in the same place and he even ate with a certain pattern. As to Mrs Schwartzkopf, nothing was too much for her and she was infinitely patient.

Erasmus kept looking around him and listened to every word that came from P.J., searching for any clue that could be hidden in the sentences the man said, hoping to hear, see or find something that sounded familiar. In his daydreams he'd sometimes gone back into the past to see if he could go back even further in time than he had first thought, trying, for example, to call up his uncle's voice as he had heard it years ago, or feel his hands as he must have felt them when he was a boy; making an attempt to bring back lost images and here he was, at last; the man who could be, or probably was, his uncle, but who lacked the warmth he would so very much have liked to feel; who didn't have the recognisability, or even a little piece that could be reminiscent of, or connect with his own identity, he thought. Yes, there was the very kind woman, but, unfortunately, she wasn't his aunt. His uncle's face was like a map of some kind, where he was hoping to come upon the sources of a rivulet he knew, or other vestiges of a hidden past; his uncle's mind, with a locked-up secret inside, a neat tangle of pent-up thoughts and feelings he perhaps so much willed to express. Maybe both of them desperately needed affection or wanted to share their thoughts and feelings with a close relation, he thought, but there was still so much he would like to know.

'Have you seen my dad recently?'
'Yes and no.'
'What do you mean?'
'I have seen him as my brother, but not as a Hopper,' was the next, useless answer.
'Sorry, I don't understand.'
It took a minute before he got an answer.

'Your father was unhappy at home; he loved you, but he had to go. He came here a lot. He loved action and went to South America, but I don't know this.'

So this man really is my uncle, he realised, but he was so disappointed; there was nothing between them and what he said was so vague.

'What can you tell me about your parents and how was it at home, when you and my dad were children?'

'We often played together. I went to a special school. I slept there, too. I didn't see him for a long time. When you were a little boy I saw you,' he said, with an expressionless face.

'I can remember that, vaguely. Have you got any photos?'

'Cabinet thirteen, shelf six.'

That sounded very promising; some photos, at last. P.J. fetched them and for the very first time Erasmus saw some pictures of the whole family, his granddad, grandmother and four children. He recognised P.J. and his father, although they were only four, five or six years old. This was good fun. Why didn't we have any pictures at home? he wondered, although, hang on, there were some on the mantelpiece, he remembered, but it was more than likely his mother had disposed of them. He'd never known his grandparents, but he saw his father resembled both of them. Maybe his father now looked like his granddad. How funny. There were two other boys, one with a little spade in his hand, or was that a girl in the corner? Uncles, an aunt? No, he had never seen them before; they lived somewhere on the west coast. The rest of the photos only featured P.J. What a shame.

Although this was his uncle, he had come to a dead end, while there still were so many unanswered questions. But he didn't know how to go about it. Maybe his expectations had been too high. He felt sad and empty. Everything, this whole life, it seemed, was one big show. Today's experiences had been a show too, a charade, and a very disappointing one at that, but he had to move on. He said goodbye and left.

It was quite dark when he got back 'home', where Jim was waiting for him.

'How was your day? Did you find your uncle?'

'I did, but it was very disappointing. The guy's autistic, I think.'

'Sorry to hear this. But could he tell you anything about your dad?'

Erasmus told him about the U.S. presidents and the photos he'd seen.

'By the way, I won't be around for a few days,' Jim said, 'I'm going to see some relations of mine in Philadelphia. Why don't you come with me?'

'No, I'm fine, thanks. I want to see some more museums. There's so many of them; it's amazing.'

What he was looking for, he didn't know exactly, although he noticed he was looking more and more for things related to South America. Not only the words of the strange, clairvoyant Mrs Hopper, but also what his uncle had said about his father and South America had made him curious and seemed to point him into that direction. Who was his father? Where had he been? Who was he with? Why South America? And how had he travelled there?

Erasmus' own interest and commitment, his hankering after knowledge, his desire to tackle things on his own, like the famous scholar he'd been named after, gave him a push. He wanted to learn about the cultures of Central and South America, the Toltec, Aztecs, Incas, Mayas, their language and mythology, just like the Greek language and mythology had always fascinated him.

He spent hours in the huge American Natural History Museum, but also searched for small-scale exhibitions. In second-hand bookshops and libraries he discovered some very exciting books with information on the various cultures he was interested in, so that he gradually fell under the spell of his mission and began to compare the mythology of the Greek gods and goddesses to that of, amongst others, the Aztecs. He studied the parallels and contrasts between the Greek god of the sun, Apollo, his sister Artemis, goddess of the moon, and the Aztec god of the sun, Huitzilopochtli; he read how Coyolxauhqui's, Huitzilopochtli's sister, chopped off head became the moon. He was so captivated by everything he read that he began to look for more data and also started looking at Maya mythology.

When, in a relatively unknown museum, he saw a fragment of a Greek text that referred to several symbols and drawings of the Toltec, Aztecs and Mayas, his blood really began to flow. There was information on the civilization of Atzlan, an area 'somewhere in the north', where the Aztec had originally come from and that their gods were, sometimes very consciously, brought face-to-face with those of the Greek, as if these cultures were in direct contact with each other.

The Greek had Gaia, or Gaea, the great mother of all, the Mother Goddess, creator, giver of birth to the earth and the universe, whereas the Aztec goddess of earth Coatlicue, whose name meant 'The One with the Serpent Skirt'. She wasn't only the goddess of life (the womb), positive, but also of death (the grave), negative. She looked dreadful, wearing a skirt of serpents and a necklace made of human hands, skulls, and the hearts that had been ripped from the bodies of her victims. Both her hands and feet were sharp talons, and she had a deadly desire for human sacrifice.

The Greek started looking for peace, so chaos disappeared and Gaia came. The Aztecs, however, were still dealing with chaos then, not only in life, but in death as well, with fear playing the main role. It reminded Erasmus of some recent world leaders and their divide and rule policy.

Erasmus read on and found that Gaia had a son. He was called Python, and was depicted on Greek vases and sculptures as a snake. His name came from Pytho, the centre, the heart of the earth, which was represented by a stone, the 'Omphalos' or 'Navel', the remnant of physical and symbolic connectivity between man and creation, the bond with new life, the womb, the Mother, the universal unconscious. Wasn't it incredible, he thought, that the place where the Aztecs settled was also regarded as an 'Omphalos'? That was why they called it 'Mexico', which meant 'In the Navel of the Moon' or 'Navel of the Rabbit' and, like the earth, the moon was female. Apparently, the Aztecs thought the surface of the moon resembled the landscape of Mexico, with its lakes, and also saw an association with the rabbit, the symbol of fertility.

This was unbelievable, Erasmus thought, and while he was digesting the information he had read, a feeling, an urge began to stir inside him, and it was getting stronger and stronger. He had to go to the south-west of the U.S., where Atzlan probably lay, and after that he would travel further south, to Mexico, like an Aztec.

Later that week Jim was back again.

'What have you been doing with yourself?' he asked Erasmus. 'Seen or done anything interesting? I bet you didn't just sit down on a bench somewhere to look at the water,' he said, with a smile on his face.

'No, you're right. I've done quite a lot, actually.' He also laughed. 'I've been to the A.N.H.M. What a huge place that is. But two days ago I was in a relatively small museum and read some incredible things.'

He wanted to tell Jim everything as fast as he could, but he was so excited that he sometimes stumbled over his words.

'Take it easy, Erasmus. Sit down. Have a coffee. Relax.'

Erasmus laughed a bit nervously, and went on telling Jim what he had read and said,

'There's only one conclusion, Jim. I just have to go to Mexico. Nothing can stop me. Are you coming with me?'

'Hold on. You're going way too fast for me.'

But Erasmus' excitement was contagious, and as he was always in for a new adventure, a trip to Mexico sounded like music to his ears.

'Sounds really cool, but I have to think about it and talk to my dad, but yeah, wow, what a challenge.'

Later that evening, after thinking it over and talking to his father, Jim said he would come with Erasmus.

30

Jack was busy checking everything for the long trip to the Panama Canal. It was about a thousand miles from the Bahamas via Jamaica. He was looking forward to it and was sure it was going to be a fine journey. There were moments when he thought it would be better for Steve to stay on the Bahamas, or go to the former Dutch Antilles, so that he could get his life back on track and perhaps get in touch with Rosalie's parents. As far as his own life was concerned, he wondered when, or if, he would ever return to England; he no longer had a home there; his yacht was all he had now. Sometimes his thoughts went to the past, the place where he came from, his Jordanian wife, whom he had met when he was roaming around in her country many years ago, his two daughters, the blond Djamila and dark-haired Django, his eldest daughter, who had died of breast cancer at a young age; she was in her mid-twenties.

Although he liked the Bahamas a lot, Albert was desperate to leave and travel on. He was looking forward to the trip through the Panama Canal and wondered how it would feel to enter another part of the world, the Pacific Ocean, that enormous water mass, surrounded by so many impressive countries. The Panama Canal was a gateway to a new kind of magic, he believed, and it made him think of Columbus, who thought that he was going to the East Indies if he sailed west. If there had been an open connection from the Atlantic Ocean to the Pacific in his days, he still wouldn't have been able to reach the Indies, for Albert had read somewhere that Columbus hadn't only made a mistake in calculating the distance, but also that they could never have covered that distance without stocking up on fresh food, fruits and drinks. They would simply have perished.

After a few more days the moment was there; the ropes were cast off and they sailed away. The weather couldn't be better, with the sun high in the sky and a fine breeze; the sea was calm and once they were under way, they saw more wonderful islands with long, white beaches. It was as if they were watching a film loop.

One morning, sitting on deck, they started talking about dreams and their possible meanings. Albert didn't say much at first; he was thinking and listening to the others, before he told them about a very unusual dream he had had when he was in hospital. In the dream it seemed as if he was accompanied by a guide, someone who answered his questions. The dream went as follows:

The earth and form

I saw the earth. It was far away and it was enveloped in an aura, a cloud of haze and fog. And there were shapeless forms. They looked like skyscrapers, attempting to pierce through the clouds, striving to be seen. But they had to stay in the fog, for they were abstract, absent, actually. I know it sounds crazy, but they were only seemingly present, like an illusion or a mirage.

Mankind was there as well, not in their usual, human form, but rather as a cloud of consciousness, a diffuse nebula. I was told by my guide humans are always trying hard to see forms, shapes, in order to make things visible, to make the abstract concrete, so that they are better able to comprehend them in their worldly existence. It is a bit like looking at somebody who is inside a balloon, pressed against its latex wall. You can see bulging forms, but not the clear shape of a human being. Humans have difficulty in understanding the abstract, and in adapting to it, because they do not always realise that in this shroud of the omni-conscious, or 'overall conscious', comprising both the unconscious and the conscious, the particles in the dark recesses of the unconscious are constantly stimulated and challenged to reach consciousness, to see things as they really are, without form or shape.

My guide explained that our life, the conscious, is placed in a haze, a nebula, of both absence and presence, comparable to a mist hanging over the land. The contours of things or animals are distinguishable. As humans we cannot even understand semi-abstractions. Therefore we try to give them presence and clarity by means of a recognisable shape or form.

We like calling things 'mine' or 'ours', and saying 'I, or we, think that', but we cannot possess anything and we lack an understanding of things. But by giving it form, or presence, we think we can grasp it. We put the different concepts from the haze into our psychical pocket, so to speak, ponder over them, sometimes discuss them with others before acknowledging them as a universal truth and forcing them upon others. This behaviour arises from the fact that we are dominated by fear and are always looking for security in this formless, abstract world. As a matter of fact, we are fighting an almost hopeless struggle to become conscious.

> 'But why then do we want security?' I asked.
> 'Out of fear, the mainspring of human thinking,' the guide told me.
> 'When did that yearning for security get into us?'
> 'When man slowly became conscious; when data from his unconscious began to surface in his consciousness, which he tried to understand, but could not.'

I asked if the male of the human species is more belligerent and less close to nature than his female counterpart. That was only partly true, he said, for both are part of a collective unconscious, which both males and females want to develop. In general a male has less aversion to violence, but there have also been women, such as Queen Boadicea, Gudit, the Trung Sisters, Artemisa I of Caria, Zenobia, Joan of Arc, the Amazons, who did battle, but because a woman cbrings forth life herself, and wants to preserve that instinctively, she detests the destruction of life and abhors violence.

At the same time women give men some scope to use violence, possibly to get closer to 'presence' themselves more quickly, for by waging war mankind does not only hope to conquer land, which is really of less importance and shows the yearning for the material presence, but mainly to 'invade' and 'conquer' the minds of a large group of people, enter their consciousness, their abstraction, in order to get closer to the concept of the conscious.

This explains the 'Big Brother' concept, for in the end it is all about mind control, not about gaining material supremacy. Conquering a piece of land is relatively easy; invading a mind and manipulating it is an entirely different matter, although the ultimate goal is not solely to manipulate, but rather to add, without being aware of it, more individual fragments from the collective conscious of a number of individuals to one's own consciousness.

Great, independent, individual minds

Some minds, like Newton and Einstein, detach themselves from society to become more conscious, and use their own individuality as a starting point. Because of their clearer insight and greater purity of mind, uncorrupted by common beliefs, they are better able, in the solitude of their minds, to give depth to everything there is. Besides, they are not usually confined to one field of science. Due to their greater brainpower and analytical skills, they are more proficient at making abstract matters present. However, when they too reach the limits of their brainpower and individual region of the conscious, they will have to pass on their findings to the next generation of great, conscious minds, who will continue the job of giving the abstract more form and making it more concrete, so that other people are better able to understand it.

Nevertheless, in spite of all the efforts of mankind, there is no such thing as the ultimate concrete, or unique form. The concept of the greater conscious will always remain abstract.

There will always be a 'fog', or clouds of vagueness, in which matters take place that cannot be understood. This elusive, ever-present 'fog', an abstract form of 'Sein', 'to be', a supercluster of gas/chaos, will lift one day, and a new presence of consciousness will come into being, only to reveal more and bigger clouds.

Man will always have to evolve, for perfection does not exist in itself, but only as a neutral result of the balance between opposites: heart and mind, the two hemispheres of the brain, matter and antimatter. Progress, or striving for perfection, is nothing but growing towards a greater consciousness, and, ultimately, another, higher, life form than man.

The omni-conscious is so immense that it exists everywhere and does not know (linear) time, so that the future can be seen in the past and present and the other way round. Leonardo Da Vinci was able to use his insight into the omni-conscious and draw a helicopter, a thing of the future which was already there. Many humans cannot comprehend this. That is why some clear, (super)conscious, minds, are often said to be crazy, like seers, prophets and clairvoyants.

Nature, the environment, the earth

It is all a process that started when Life began. Maybe some psycho-analysts are right that man will be more conscious in (many thousands of)years to come. That's how we can explain the gross mistakes people make: pollution, environmental disasters and, as a grand finale, the gradual, but total destruction of their habitat, Planet Earth, a kind of Endlösung for the whole of mankind. They may not really want this, but it is part of their evolutionary process to understand matters in their struggle for presence.

This process may be 'erring', but there is a meaning behind all this. In his struggle for consciousness, man has to detach himself from nature and go against it and analyse it to understand things. Reversely, the greater conscious has to give mankind, as a thinking organism, scope to err, only to live in harmony, in balance, with the greater nature, the universe, later on.

Nature, as the essence of purity, is timeless; she just exists. She does not know man and is not interested in what he is and what he does. Man has made an impact on the world, on nature, but so have other organisms, for a much longer time. What man does, are, in fact, relatively minor skirmishes within a much more complex, untouchable 'Being' or 'Presence'.

This part-destruction of (local) nature, the world, is comparable to a hatching chick that destroys its shell, the very thing which protects it in its earlier development and life, in order to be free. Like in a womb, all essential nutrients are present in the egg, until the chick has consumed them all, like mankind is doing with the resources of the world.

In my dream I was told that nature, earth, the superclusters, the universe, and perhaps something that is even bigger than the universe, all are part of an omniconscious that needs to develop and of which man is only a tiny, mostly unconscious, fragment, struggling, like a force within a force, a search within a search, a phase within a phase, a gas in a chaos, to go from anti-presence to presence .

Relationships

'What are relationships for?' I asked.

'Apart from love for a material body, relationships are also part of a process to help each other develop a greater consciousness, provided that both parties are aware of that. But, even if they are not, they will still be searching to enrich their own unconscious minds. If this mutual enrichment is frustrated by one or them, it is better to terminate the process.'

Nobody knew what to say; there was so much to think about and how was it possible that someone could get so much information in a dream? they wondered. Jack came with the proposition that something like this wasn't as strange as they thought.

'When people come close to the limit of their stamina, their existence, the edge of life, due to exposure to extreme temperatures or exhaustion by swimming in a heavy sea, for example, they can reach a state of consciousness by experiencing the unconscious. With Albert it was probably the attrition of his illness and, consequently, his mental emptiness and despair and his unconscious struggle for survival, which helped him reach consciousness in a dream.'

'The unconscious is primeval, pure, timeless and formless. It's a haze, immeasurable, a databank of knowledge, of 'to be and not to be'. Forgive me for saying so, but what happened to Rosalie in Havana is compatible with what you have dreamt, Albert, someone killing another person, unconsciously thinking they have gone one more rung up the ladder of consciousness.'

The last part of the dream made Steve think about his relationship with Rosalie, how each probably had to go their own way.

Without being able to add anything to it, they didn't only talk about the meaning of the dream, but about the meaning of life as well. Was the bit about nature only there to be used as an excuse for what mankind is doing to the environment, Gaia, earth, the North Pole? they wondered.

Dolphins came swimming round the boat; it seemed as if they wanted to accompany the people on board to their next destination. Jonathan dived into the water to swim with them, be one with them; he wasn't scared of anything and the dolphins loved it.

They were sailing in a south eastern direction, between Cuba and Haiti to Jamaica, the last stop before the Panama Canal. Far away in the distance they could see some other sailing-yachts, but apart from that, they had the sea and the sky to themselves.

Jack stood enjoying the view. There was only one cloud to be seen; it was hanging above the water, far away on the starboard side. It was probably a fog patch. What a great life this is, he thought, the gentle breeze, the birds, the clear blue water, the dolphins.

'How odd,' Albert said to Jack, 'it looks as if it's getting foggy. A moment ago it was still as clear as a bell. Just look, over there, on your right.'

The small cloud of fog that was so far away a minute ago, had suddenly come very close and was much bigger than he had thought.

'I can hardly see you,' Jonathan's voice sounded from the forward deck, where he stood looking at the dolphins.

Albert held on to the railing next to him. It was getting cold and damp.

'What's going on?' Jack said, as he gripped the helm. 'I've never seen anything like this before. I can hear noises, humming or zooming sounds, but I can't place them. This is very strange.'

Breathing nervously, Steve was standing behind him now and took his arm. 'Jack, what's all this about?'

The next thing they heard was a muffled, metallic sound and through the mist came soft, unintelligible voices, a buzz, a foreign language. Jonathan thought it was all a bit eerie and joined the others on the rear deck. There was one, big, white darkness. Jack caught his breath, his heart thumped, his mouth ran dry. Angst. It was as if they were near the eye of a hurricane without having noticed anything at all; none of them had felt a change in air pressure, temperature or humidity, only the mist. He just knew there was no getting away from it.

A matt black vessel loomed out of the fog, on its bow some bright, yellow Chinese characters. Wisps of fog shrunk back in awe, sped away to make room for this apparition. The ship wasn't even that big, Jack noticed, but still it seemed to surround and close them in from all sides, like an all-powerful machine with huge, strangulating claws that were going to squeeze the last air out of his body. Where had the ship suddenly come from? From the haze that was hanging over the water not too far away a few minutes ago?

It was almost quiet. Steve whispered some unintelligible words. Jack heard them, but they didn't register. His forehead and arms were sweaty. Albert's hands were shaking; he felt the gripes coming up in his belly and turned as white as a sheet. They were all completely bewildered. What was going to happen next? Like people condemned to death they stood looking at this apparition; a ship, a deserted ship, a ghost ship, or so it seemed, where the last judgement was going to come from.

Grim-looking, menacing, Chinese faces, without visible necks, appeared on deck of the black ship. Dressed in black uniforms and on their heads a kind of space helmet, carrying the same yellow characters as the bow of the vessel, 永恒, the short men in their high boots looked as if they had escaped from a box of Lego or Playmobil. In some of the helmets was a narrow slot and they were equipped with eye-controlled electronic visors. On their chest they had a rectangular, semi-synthetic plate, with buttons on it; probably a control panel. In total silence the men stood looking at the yacht and its four crewmembers on deck.

There was another strange noise and the four felt their boat moving sideways, as if it was being sucked against the other vessel. They could see the ship really well now, which, because of its shape and unusual colour, looked totally unconventional. It rather resembled a Stealth aircraft. There were several, mysteriously looking gantries on board, possibly weapons.

The fog lay like a ring around the two vessels.

From a turret on board the ship a kinetic arm emerged and lifted a couple of heavily armed Chinese men onto the yacht. Although Jack had regained his English composure, the others were still trembling with fear. They had to stay on deck under the supervision of a Chinese marine, who, in rather good English, asked who the owner of the yacht was and said he wanted to see his passport. Jack stepped forward, went to fetch his passport and reluctantly handed it to the marine. Jonathan, as the only other member of the crew, was also asked to get his passport.

Another marine slid below deck, almost noiselessly, probably to inspect the boat, but apart from an occasional click and a buzzing sound, they heard nothing. While Steve and Albert stood waiting in silence, transfixed with terror, Jack wondered what the guy was up to below deck. Maybe he was installing a tracking device or, in the worst case, placing an explosive.

In the meantime a number of marines, with their visors down and armed with titanium coloured weapons, kept a close watch on them. A few minutes later the man who had gone below deck came back, moving just as smoothly and noiselessly, and when his visor went up, there was a tiny, robotic smile on his face, which looked just as artificial as the smile of the man who gave them their passports back. Maybe the guy just had a tic, Jack thought.

The Lego men closed their helmets; the kinetic arm came out again, picked them up and in seconds they were back on their own ship. They had moved as swiftly and smoothly as swallows. With gestures and a green signal, a Chinese marine, possibly an officer and the only one with a beard, indicated everything was in order. All the marines disappeared, the hatches were shut and off they were. The ship literally vanished in a haze, a mist they created themselves. It was as if they had witnessed the manifestation of Guan Yu, the Taoist God of War, Jack thought.

'I don't know what to say,' said Albert, still as white as a sheet. 'Were these actual men, or robots?'

Jack laughed, but it made him think.

'You may be right,' he said. 'They were a bit weird. 'It was some sort of inspection, I assume. Let's not worry too much about it. Everything turned out right, didn't it? But that ship, incredible, how streamlined she was.'

'And those marines,' Jonathan added, 'so incredibly well disciplined. Technologically those Chinese are much more advanced than any other nation, I suppose.'

Later they spotted a vessel of the U.S. coastguard. They couldn't imagine these guys hadn't noticed or seen anything. Fortunately, they weren't stopped again; the Americans just waved to them. Jonathan suggested alerting them, but Jack said it wouldn't make any difference; it would probably delay them even more.

Still full of surprise, astonishment and maybe admiration for how fast, efficiently and also correctly the Chinese had done their job, they sailed on. It wasn't only because of the speed and sudden presence of the vessel, but the overpowering attitude of the crew, the Lego men, as well.

'What would have happened if we'd been American nationals?' Steve asked, 'Would it have made any difference?'

'No idea,' Jack said. 'I only wonder what these guys were looking for, now that the war is over. Anyway, tomorrow we're in Jamaica, guys. Let's have a drink,' he said, while he thought of what John Lennon had sung on one of his last CDs, *Life is what happens to you while you're busy making other plans*.

They sailed to Kingston, on the south coast of Jamaica and moored in the marina, at a peninsula not far from the airport, which almost stretched out into the sea.

'They'd better have called the airport Bob Marley after the internationally most famous Jamaican, instead of Norman Manley,' Jack said to the others.

'Who's Bob Marley?' Jonathan asked.

'OK,' Jack said and laughed.

Close to the marina was a disused motor racing track, where they went to have a look, but it was quite overgrown and a bit disappointing. They were all bored and longing for the next lap of the journey, the trip to the Panama Canal, 'only' about 650 miles away.

As his memory was still lousy and now that they were getting closer to the Panama Canal, Albert wanted to re-read some of his books about South America. He could recall bits of what he'd read in London, but most of the parts he had read later were like new to him. Gazing at the beautiful covers and peering at the horizon, musing on his life in London and Paris, he suddenly called out, his heart almost in his throat.

'There it is, the coast of Panama!'

Steve woke up with a start; Jonathan ran towards Albert, wanting to be closer to whatever there was in the distance.

'Take care, Jonathan,' Jack called. 'That must be Colon,' he said, when they saw the first buildings of a town appear on the horizon.

Getting closer, they saw hundreds of ramshackle houses, which didn't even deserve the name of huts. They formed a shrill contrast with the posh hotels a bit further away.

This was where their adventure, the trip to another world, would really begin. Albert thought of Ecuador, tropical beaches, the paintings of Louis Burgos Flor, freedom, while for Jack every country was a new challenge. Steve told them he was beginning to feel better, that Albert's dream had made him think about his relationship with Rosalie and he even said he was longing for the great unknown, in whatever shape or form. Jonathan could already see himself walking in the heights of the awe-inspiring Andes, following the Inca trail to Machu Picchu, meeting interesting people.

Just before the entrance to the canal they cast the anchor, so that they could embark on their new adventure first thing in the morning.

31

Roonah was riding the high waves on the hard surfboard that made her go faster and faster, the salty water splashing in her tanned face. The incredibly imposing horizon, the powerful sun that glittered over the water; the sand that was dappled with thin layers of water, reflecting with ever increasing light the images of people on the beach, who had become figurines, enveloped in an aura of morning light. These were moments of concentration she knew, the current, the direction, the power and the height of the waves, other surfers, and the beach. Paddling over the lower, unpromising waves, she was thinking of the greater depths with the bigger waves and, determined to get there, she stuck her hands deep into the water and paddled even harder.

Behind the wide, curling wave formed a valley of water; she could feel the current of the oncoming swell get stronger; she knew it would suck her to the depth under the high, fast approaching wave. She turned round, paddling as fast as she could, looked behind her and, feeling the wave lifting her and pushing her forward, she stood up on her board, in a split second, her knees bent, Kung Fu style, ready for the attack and off she was, planing on the water, turning, rising, turning, flying, a vertical dash, going faster and faster.

'Wow! Coooooooooooool!'

Seconds later she jumped off the board, felt the sand beneath her feet, struggled to the surface, pulled the board with the line around her ankle towards her, lay on it and floated on the water, exhilarated. She took a moment to enjoy the view, to look at the beach, where more surfers were getting ready.

Desmond was there too, with his white hair and black wetsuit. Because of a cold allergy he always wore a five millimetre thickwetsuit and took his time to adapt to the temperature of the water. She saw him walking with his board beside him to the deeper part, where he lay down on it, enjoying the higher waves. He was laughing and waved at her.

This was a great moment to look at the world from the ocean, she thought, to see the huts on and near the beach, the people who lived there and who were coming back to life again, the children who were running about, the warm sun, bathing everything, the high, jagged mountains, the hinterland with the vast jungle, the culture of the Incas, the fog that was hanging there now. The Amazon, the rainforest, the Indians, their ancient knowledge of plants and herbs, their wisdom. For how much longer? The Western pharmaceutical industries don't give a shit; they had rather these forests, herbs and all these people didn't exist. They're only interested in selling their often addictive and hardly effective drugs, which are never tested properly anyway, at exorbitant prices and in making ever bigger profits. Has mankind made any progress? she wondered.

She was also thinking of her dreams, which were so often prophetic and sometimes came back, or even appeared in other dreams. They were all messages, hints, she believed. Nature is perfect, she thought, but mankind is the problem. It's no longer tip-toeing, but racing towards its doom by destroying nature. And then?

All these things flashed through her head in seconds, while she was lying on her board, in the lovely morning sun. These moments were important to her; she needed them to try and determine who she was and where she stood in this world. Even when she was a girl her parents and sisters would tell her she was thinking too much, that she should spend more time leading her real life. But she couldn't help it; all sorts of thoughts just kept emerging from somewhere deep inside her head. Of course she knew a lot of thoughts were sheer noise, like some people in your life are sheer noise. They only divert you from your goal and, yes, I know, by thinking too much, all too often my mind is full of things from the past or the unknown future. But what's the point? she asked herself; you can't relive the past and the thoughts and feelings of pain and sorrow from moments that have gone by lead to nothing; they're more like quicksand and even become self-sustaining, an addiction, part of a vicious circle. They were thoughts she had to banish from her mind, unless they shone a light on the present, because she only wanted to think about things of the present and, by consciously thinking about her own life, she had already managed to break free from the straightjacket of imposed standards and values, which were often hundreds of years old and had been invented by narrow-minded hypocrites who were afraid their secure world would be dismantled, or of losing their position, their status, of becoming part of the 'common people' and, because of their arrogance, they were really only scared of losing their ego, their identity, she thought.

She turned round and looked over the ocean, the great, Pacific Ocean, the vast mass of water and, above it, a beautiful, clear blue sky with birds in it and a few odd clouds. Peace.

Mankind, man – kind, man kind? Rape, torture, war? Progress? The Third World War had only added more pain and fear to the already overflowing reservoir of misery of the collective unconscious. The last 150 years were nothing but a catalogue brimming with human failures: three world wars, the Holocaust, hundreds of local wars, many more terrorist attacks, genocide in Africa and Europe. Again and again horrific experiences are passed on to the next generation, to innocent children who have nothing whatsoever to do with what happened in the past. What about the old adage that every generation has a chance to change the world? Bollocks! What, for example, if you happen to be an underprivileged child? It all depends on where you live, she thought, and if you're Jewish, black or white, have an Indian or aboriginal background, or if you belong to an ethnic minority or not. Some kids grow up with the innate knowledge that the situation in their lives can take a dramatic turn. Somehow they know that they may have to pick up their belongings and move on.

She thought of Desmond. He wasn't Jewish, because his grandmother's mother wasn't Jewish, but even he was always vigilant, aware of his immediate surroundings and he always became angry and sad when he heard somebody had been tortured or murdered, only because he was Jewish, or different in another way. After watching a documentary on the Holocaust some time ago he was virtually inconsolable and weeks later he still had a sombre look in his eyes. She knew he was carrying a burden of pain, of old, inherited sores. She had asked him would he like to talk about it, but he said nothing and only stared, probably trying to repress the memory and pain.

The collective unconsciousness of the Irish, too, had always been suffused with sorrow and the pain of hundreds of years of oppression, killings, the *Gorta Mor*, attempts to exterminate their language and, thus, their identity. She knew it, for she could feel it herself. Why do the Irish so often sing melancholy songs and why do they drink so much? Not just because of the rain. Even here, in Ecuador, many people who should be enjoying the beautiful life of 'here and now', carry a history of pain inside and are ashamed of their own, beautiful, indigenous culture. She remembered the void, expressionless faces of some of the native people she'd seen in various places in South America. Like the Irish, they were nations who had lived through hundreds of years of oppression by aggressors, men with a different language and culture.

Would animals have a collective unconscious? she wondered. That would be horrific, as some species have been completely wiped out by mankind, while others are on the brink of extermination, because there are loonies in this world who believe animals are here only to serve mankind.

A wave woke her up. She hadn't come here to think, she suddenly realised. So many thoughts, her head was saturated and it was still so early. She had to keep moving. She changed her course and paddled to the high waves, which would chase away all these thoughts, at least as long as she could keep her balance and the swell kept coming.

Desmond looked at Roonah, who was much faster than him. She could jump on her board in one go, like she was doing now. Wow! He was glad if he could just stand up and enjoy the surf.

She often talked about her 'roots', her Ireland. He would like to go there, also because it seemed to be a great place for surfing. She had told him about some great surf spots in County Clare, 'her' part of the country, like Lahinch, a small town on the coast, not far from the famous Cliffs of Moher. It had a long, sandy beach, impressive waves and, besides, in most pubs there was traditional live music. Why were the Irish sometimes called the 'negroes of Europe'? he wondered.

Roonah kept fascinating him, although there had also been some petty skirmishes, tests of strength, like when she put the soap in the bathroom in a place which he had claimed as his own. He removed it, but she just put it back again. And sometimes she upset his system by putting things in the kitchen in the wrong place. He couldn't stand that and put them back in the right place. Perhaps it was a form of autism, she sometimes thought, but after a couple of days they would be back in the place of her choice.

'Sometimes you're so overpowering, so over-confident, Desmond. Why do you always think you're right? Why don't you simply discuss things with me?' she had asked him. 'And when I try to bring some structure into our lives, you nearly always react like I'm some sort of invader, and you're a partisan.'

He couldn't stand it if she was tough on him; he wanted to flee then, retreat into his den and escape from reality. He had been quite good at that for almost forty years, he knew, and maybe because he was a proficient escapist, untouchable, people often said he was an island in a sea of people. That's why he could walk through New York for hours on end, all by himself, taking pictures, thinking about life, asking himself why the Jewishness of his ancestors and the deaths of his great-grandfather's brothers, sisters, cousins, nieces and nephews, relatives who perished in the gas chambers of Auschwitz, Sobibor and Mauthausen kept haunting him. Who was he? he regularly asked himself. That never-ending struggle, wanting to be somebody, pretending not to need anyone else, thinking that turning away from people made him feel safe, that he always needed to be ready to pick up his suitcase and move on when the moment was there; it was so much.

An obscure shadow was watching him from behind the beach house.

The water was splashing against the surfboards. Roonah and Desmond were smiling and waving at each other. The world was theirs for a moment, with a distance between his quiet, controlled waves and her high, wild ones. Watching and predicting, lying in wait, paddling, the sudden jump, knees bent, arms stretched out for the attack, their eyes focused on the path to follow. Nothing mattered but self-control and respect for the powers of nature. Off he was, singing *'I must away now, I can no longer tarry'*, words from a beautiful Irish song, which she would sometimes sing to him with so much passion. An empty head, he thought, wouldn't that be wonderful?

32

The distance from the Atlantic side of the canal to Panama City was about fifty miles. If they switched the engine on, they could easily sail through it in a day, and from here to Ecuador it was approximately eight hundred miles. Via Baha Limon they reached the first part of the canal and right after it came a very long lock or, rather, a double complex of old and new locks, so that the larger ocean-going vessels could also use the canal, followed by a series of locks at Gatún, which lifted the boat twenty-six metres, in three stages, to the extensive waste of water of Lake Gatún. Apart from straight parts that had probably been dug, there were also stretches of the canal that consisted of lakes, often surrounded by dense woods.

They passed lots of islands, like the large Barro Colorado Island. Jonathan kept on saying he wanted to jump into the cool, inviting water and swim to one of those islands. After these lakes a long, straight section followed. On one side of the canal the land was sometimes bare and empty, while the shore on the other side was strewn with trees. In the distance there were more locks, two series of locks, actually, those of Pedro Miguel and Miraflores, which lowered them by nearly twenty-six metres. Their excitement was mounting, for they could now see the first buildings of Panama City. It was quite different from what they had seen so far. Because of its gigantic blocks of flats the city looked like a genuine modern metropolis.

With twenty-seven degrees the weather on this Monday was excellent again, but the humidity of eighty-nine percent made it very oppressive and there was no breeze to refresh them. It was so incredibly humid that it felt as if they were in a sauna. They felt like diving into the water and going for a swim. Jonathan was the first to jump overboard; he didn't care about Steve's story that jaguars sometimes swam across the canal too, from one jungle to the next. Steve had also said that, already as far back as 1928, somebody had swum the whole length of the canal and also that the Spaniards were already considering digging a canal through the isthmus in the sixteenth century. Very soon the others followed Jonathan's example to cool down their bodies. Later that day they reached Panama City, where they moored in the small marina of the Club de Yates Y Pesca to spend the night.

The Pacific Ocean, the incredibly beautiful view they had from the marina, both of the city and the ocean, the slightly nervous, bubbling atmosphere which they felt; it was almost too sensational to describe. Jack got out a bottle of champagne and four glasses, shook the bottle, unscrewed the wire to make the cork pop out with a bang and fly into the air, the foaming champagne gushing, swishing over his hand.

'Cheers, guys. Great to have you on board. Thanks for everything. Here's to a new future.'

'*Proost*, Jack,' Steve said. I'm afraid we have to thank *you* for everything you've done for us, miserable guys. *Op je gezondheid*, to your health, to our futures. Cheers.'

Quiet, transfixed with excitement, they couldn't take their eyes off the ocean, as if they were waiting for an oracle to tell them something, or for some creature to rise from the depths of its mystical waters to bring them a message or send them on a quest.

In the evening Jack told them one of many stories he had written down in a logbook. He had been to quite a few countries, mostly alone, but also with all kinds of hitch-hikers, who sometimes turned out to be very strange people, and he had found himself in lots of crazy situations too. When he had finished this sentence, he suddenly fell silent and looked at the table. The others looked at each other and at Jack, waiting for him to go on, but it remained quiet and there were tears in his eyes. This was the powerful man, their chief, who had been so supportive of each of them and now he was almost crying. Albert didn't know what to think and was deeply moved. He put his hand on Jack's shoulder. It took some time before he could say something.

'What's up, Jack?' he finally asked.

'Sorry, guys, I have to tell you a story,' he said with difficulty. 'When I was in my cabin earlier tonight, I was looking at some photos.'

He got out two photos and showed them to the others.

'This is Djamila, my youngest and only daughter. I was talking to you about some crazy situations I've been in and then I thought of this photo and it made me think of a trip to another ocean, one of sand, a desert, the Sahara. That's where I heard the name Djamila for the first time, at a very bizarre moment. It's a very unusual story and, when other people hear it, they mostly think I've made it up. Like Coleridge's Ancient Mariner I have to keep on telling this story.'

'I was in Libya for my work and one evening I was walking in the Sahara with some mates, not far from our compound. The sun was slowly going down and, apart from myself and three mates, there was nobody to be seen or heard for miles around. When we were walking past along a hollow in the dunes, I suddenly felt the hand of my mother on my right temple and I heard her voice say, 'lie down now, Jack', like she used to do when she put me to bed after reading a bedtime story. I stood looking around me in bewilderment when, once more, I felt her hand and heard her voice. I had no choice, I was remote-controlled. I got into the hollow and lay down, still feeling my mother's hand. While my three mates stood looking at me from above, laughing, there was a sudden burst of gunfire; hell broke loose. Two mates fell down, dead; they had both been shot in the head several times, while the third was crying out and writhing in agony on the ground and died a few minutes later. I was the only survivor of a gruesome attack, possibly carried out by terrorists. After the echoes had died down it was quiet again, as if nothing had happened. I was terribly scared, but knew I had to get out of the hollow. I raced back to the camp to get help. The police were alerted, but they weren't interested. A young nurse, who went with me to the place where the shooting incident had taken place, cried when she saw what had happened. 'The hand of God', was the only thing she said, when she looked at me and held my arm. The tears on the pretty, dark face, illuminated by the red glow of the setting sun, touched me so deeply, that I knew I would never be able to forget her beautiful face and name, Djamila. I decided that if ever I had a daughter, I would call her, Djamila, after this nurse. I did get a daughter and, although she was blond, I called her Djamila. She's always been a quiet, sweet girl. She lives in England and I love her, with all my heart. To me, she's the emblem of kindness. This is her photo.'

Everybody was quiet; there was nothing to say. Jack looked at each of them, his eyes making contact with their souls.

'But this is not the whole story, I'm afraid,' he said, looking at the table again. 'I had another daughter, Django. She was two years older than Djamila.

She was called after Django Reinhardt, the great jazz guitarist. This is her.' Once more he fell silent, overcome by emotions.

'Have some water,' Albert said, stroking Jack's back.

Jack nodded and took a sip.

'I'm sorry,' he said with a hoarse voice and continued his story.

'She was a witty, temperamental girl, very chaotic and rash. She sometimes had a sharp tongue. Not everybody liked this, but she was very honest. She was highly original in her thinking and creativity and I often found it difficult to follow her roving thoughts. She could be provocative and even irascible, the very opposite of Djamila. I'm sure she would have loved to sail with me to America, when she was having a difficult time. She didn't know anything about the tumour in her breast then, which ultimately proved to be fatal.'

Jack's eyes misted over.

'I wish she could have come with me on one of my trips. How we would have laughed. I always loved her so much, so very, very much, but we had to give her back, our first-born daughter.'

It was quiet once more, apart from the water splashing solemnly against the side of the boat.

A dark, sometimes hard to fathom person, Django was a bit like himself, he thought, and he remembered how her death had struck him deeply and that it had been the reason why he'd finally turned his back to England, to travel the world, with his ship, his home without a fixed mooring-place, without a destination.

He went on deck and peered over the water for a long time; his head was flooded by thoughts. His old life was behind him. Would his wandering life come to end somewhere in this part of the world?

33

Bernard sauntered along the beach, looking at the surfers. He thought about Albert and the cottage in which he'd slept. What sort of things would these gay men do? he wondered. Sex between men. He shuddered. An adult man, a boy, a father, a son, pain, shame, fear. Boys. When you're young, you do crazy things and you try everything out, of course, like in the caves, in Montreal.

He thought of his parents, his mother, who lived her life in the background of the family; his father, a manly man, who wanted everything in the house to go according to his plan. He remembered what Isabelle had told him, after she had been at his parents' home for the first time to meet them, that his father didn't just ask her things, because he was interested, but that it was more like an interrogation and if he asked Bernard's mother a question, it sounded like a command. He never wanted an answer from her.

'What are you talking about?' he had said to Isabelle, as if he felt he had to defend his father, but he knew better than that, as things weren't much different for himself. Although he liked English language and literature, his father only appreciated the grammar part, because it was helpful to write good business letters. Literature was only for wimps and it was utterly useless in everyday life. He never had the guts to tell his father he sometimes wrote poetry. Some poems he read he found quite unsettling; they made him doubt himself, especially the pessimistic ones. They had all become images, or fragments of images, in his head.

'Why did you actually go to that military academy?' Isabelle had asked him another time. 'It's so unlike you; you're much too kind-hearted. I think you could have chosen a language related study, like creative writing; you always write such beautiful sentences.'

He had never had a compliment like this before.

'It's not true,' he replied. 'I'm not kind-hearted. Nobody ever said that and I don't like literature or art. It's only for softies. Besides, I'm not good at writing at all.'

He was glad she didn't know he wrote poetry.

'But why is the academy so unlike me? I was even one of the best students there, so I don't know what you're talking about. I'm afraid you don't know me very well.'

'No, maybe not. I'm sorry. I didn't know you'd get angry. You're a bit like your father when you talk like this. And the way you're looking at me now. It frightens me.'

That infuriated him even further, but he said nothing. All he did was look at her. At that moment he felt his power over her.

'Sorry, Bernard, but I do like your mum. She's so sweet and I'm sure you take after her.'

She was right, but it still hurt him that she thought he was too weak, although she was really proud of his uniform and stripes.

He kicked out at the sand.
Wow! There's that young woman who was at the bar last night.

Sometimes his mother burst out in tears; it hurt him so much, while it didn't affect his father at all. Why did she stay with that man? 'Daddy, Daddy, come home soon…' He was disgusted.

When she'd met his father a few more times, Isabelle said she didn't like him very much.

'It's hard to find the right words, but isn't he a bit of a bully? Bernard, did you ever bully other students at school?'

'I never did.' He couldn't say he had; he knew he'd be in trouble then, while he remembered how he had deliberately intimidated other students at school, even the girls who became his lovers.

'But I never let anybody make fun of me, or fool me. I would definitely have said or done something then.'

He looked at Isabelle and knew she didn't believe him. He had always loved it when women looked at him in his uniform, worshipping him, as it were, for it made him feel superior and yes, maybe those poems of his were a sign of weakness after all and perhaps he should stop writing them. It hadn't made his mother very happy, had it? But in spite of what he said to himself, he knew these conflicting feelings were part of an on-going battle with his inner self.

Was that also the reason why he looked up to that girl? He wondered, because she didn't allow herself to be intimidated so easily, he had noticed. Isabelle was very different; she had more or less worshipped him, although he had to admit he had fallen for her beauty and wanted to conquer her. This hadn't been so easy, which had only made him even hungrier to get her, he remembered. It was a battle he had to win.

Although the sand was very hot now, he loved going through it with his bare feet, till they were red and almost burnt. The pain, the burning pain, he thought, looking at the blue ocean and the clear sky above it. There were more surfers on the water now and in the distance he saw some fishing boats.

After having had a relationship with Isabelle for a couple of months, she broke it off and let him stew in his own juice. He couldn't make head or tail of it; he didn't know whether she loved him or not. Later on she had another friend, while she still kept in touch with him. It drove him crazy, he remembered, and he even hit her once. She then called him names, told him to fuck off. She left him, but later she had still come back to him.

Afterwards he felt really bad about what he'd done and even wrote some poems for her, although he never showed them to her. But nobody would ever call him a softie with impunity. She stayed with him, but she didn't want to have sex with him for the time being. He hated her for it, for he hadn't done anything wrong, had he? And didn't he do his best to make their relationship work?

Shortly after his graduation his father had died of a heart attack, or of his own chagrin, he thought. All the energy that man had drained from him, his mother and his colleagues at work, had led to nothing; it hadn't added a single day to his life. His father, the stone statue he had always looked up to when he was a little boy, had gradually slid off his pedestal and fallen into thousands of pieces.

The Third World War had been going on for a while, when, together with a battalion of three hundred men, he, the fresh lieutenant colonel, was sent to the north west of Canada, to Prince Rupert, on Kaien Island in British

Columbia. The Canadian Ministry of Defence had received information from U.S. intelligence sources that a Chinese landing was imminent there. He remembered the scenery along the road to that part of Canada. It was so impressive; high mountains, icy lakes and snow, while its tranquillity and peace seemed to neutralise the power to think.

The second night they were there he decided to take part in a small patrol, also to let his men know he was one of them. One of the men, Joe Winkling, kept hanging around him. Joe was a quiet, shy, young man, with lank, blond hair, a delicate face and a much shorter and thinner than him, a bit feminine. He was in awe of Bernard, the colonel, and felt attracted to him.

During that patrol, half the group crossed the water to Digby Island, where Prince Rupert Airport was, while the rest stayed behind. He and Joe were in the first batch. They followed the road to the small airfield, when they saw a number of searchlights ahead of them. They didn't know where these were coming from and went off the road. The lights were getting closer. Joe and Bernard were standing close to each other on the north side of the road, among some trees and bushes, right beside a lake, while all the others had sought shelter on the south side. Joe first started shaking and suddenly grabbed him by his sleeve.

'What's up, Joe?'

There was no reply.

He tried to disengage himself, push Joe away, but it didn't work; Joe was clinging to him. In the clear light of the moon he saw a strange look in Joe's eyes. It frightened him, although nothing had really happened.

Through the cold moonshine he saw the steam coming off Joe's breath and heard him say in his ear with a trembling voice,

'I'm so scared, so terribly scared. Please, get me out of this army. They're bullying me all the time. Rescue me. Take me with you, I want to be with you.'

Bernard didn't know what to do; he felt trapped and once more tried to disengage himself from Joe, who had started stroking his face, holding onto his trousers at the same time. Bernard wanted to shout, but he couldn't. Black trees and bushes, the silent, freezing water with a thin layer of ice on top. Turning, pulling, pushing, dragging, they stood up to their knees in the lake.

'I love you,' Joe called out.

Standing in the water, with their kits on their backs they were struggling with each other, Joe to hold on to Bernard, Bernard to get rid of Joe. Bernard was scared they would fall into the ice cold water together. He managed to pull his right arm free and, accidentally, with his elbow he hit Joe's temple, very hard. Joe stood still for a second; his hands let go off Bernard. He was dizzy, lost his balance, fell backwards into the water and disappeared, his heavy kit dragging him down. Bernard tried to catch him, but it was as if he was watching a film, where the victim just slipped away, out of reach, beyond control. He didn't even realise what was going on. Suddenly Joe came back to the surface, floundering feebly, before he disappeared again, this time for good. Bernard stood there, numb and stupefied, his heavy army boots sinking into the muddy ground. Some words arose from his mouth.

Joe had vanished in the darkness of the water and the night. Minutes later Bernard heard voices and rustling sounds coming towards him through the bushes and trees behind him, felt some arms pulling him out of the water. Apparently, some soldiers had heard a noise, of someone plunging into the water.

'Where's Joe? Where's Joe, goddammit?'

Bernard couldn't say a thing; he only pointed. The words 'I love you' were still reverberating in his head and he saw the recurring image of the silent, sinking Joe before his eyes.

Joe was picked up from the water later and taken back to the camp. There was going to be an enquiry into the circumstances of the incident. Bernard was suspended. There were rumours. What had he done to Joe? Why were these two guys together? It was even said Joe's trousers were undone. Bernard was scared. He had robbed somebody of his life, someone who apparently loved him and he kept seeing images of the water and Joe's eyes in the cold moonshine. He was prescribed some pills and sent home, pending the conclusion of the inquest.

After a week he was back home with Isabelle and said he wanted to leave Canada as soon as possible and go away as far as he could, preferably to South America, to Ecuador or one of those countries over there. Isabelle sensed the seriousness of the situation and didn't ask too many questions, thank God, for ultimately he would just be a deserter if he fled the country.

Fortunately, he had put quite a bit of money in his secret savings account in the U.S. and he knew they would be able to live comfortably on it, especially in a less wealthy country. Apart from that he had inherited money and a collection of valuable watches, some Breitners, Rolexes and Chopards, from his father, some of which he had sold, so he had plenty of cash. He wanted a new life in the heat under the equator. As far as his mother was concerned, he would go and see her one day, but it was time to leave now.

Through some contacts he had, he was able to lay his hands on an old American car without any modern electronics and, together with Isabelle, he set off from Vancouver. They drove straight through the U.S. and Mexico, in the direction of South America.

However, at the border between Guatemala and El Salvador they ran into trouble. The immigration officer who checked Bernard's passport went away to talk to some colleagues. He came back with two of them. They couldn't let him through, they said. Bernard then paid them a fair sum of money, the only thing they were after, he thought, but he still didn't get his passport back. Instead, they handed him a note saying he could retrieve it at a police station in San Salvador, but it didn't say when. The trigger-happy faces of the men told him it was better not to make any trouble. It wasn't just about money, he now knew; there was something else going on. Did they know he had deserted from the Canadian Army? Although it wasn't their intention, they'd have to stay in El Salvador for a number of days now.

San Salvador, the capital, looked like a very modern metropolis. He didn't have his passport, so they planned to make the most of their stay. After browsing through a brochure at the hotel to find out what nightlife was like there, they chose to go to the NFE, or *Neuromotive Frequency Experience*. They had heard about it, but had never actually seen one. Bernard thought it looked rather like a club or a disco.

It was very quiet inside and there were several rooms, like in some discos. In one of them they saw lots of colourful light shafts, probably laser beams. Some people were moving and dancing, while others just stood there, motionless, as if they were in some kind of trance..

Before Bernard and Isabelle went into one of the rooms, a young woman put some thimble-like things over their fingertips. In it were miniscule sensors, they were told. These sensors registered several data, such as body heat, heartbeat, neuropulses, movements of the body and eyes and brain frequencies The woman explained that the NFE was based on the concept that the psychodynamics of the mind, as an electromagnetic structure, determines the nature and reality of a human's consciousness as an inter-dimensional process of energy.

Neither of them had a clue what the woman was talking about, but while Isabelle had the decency to listen to what the lady had to say, Bernard was getting impatient and turned round to see what some other people were doing.

They were told that biological systems are influenced by the terrestrial, electrically charged environment, such as electric and magnetic fields, aerion (positive and negative) concentrations and biological waves, while electromagnetic brainwaves work in frequencies that, according to the 'Schuman Resonance', are parallel to those of the electromagnetic field of the earth. According to mathematical principles a range of vibrations will multiply its own frequency many times and, in this way, harmonically raise the frequency of everybody who is within its range. Because of the presence, or the result of the creation of a higher energy body, the frequency and amplitude of other energy bodies, also of people, in the area will be raised as well. In fact, the physical body becomes another light frequency causing a human to transcend from a more material to a more refined 'light' body.

What a load of bull, Bernard thought.

'Are you sure?' he said to the lady, trying to be funny.

The woman looked at him. She was clearly annoyed, but ignored his remark and went on,

'When a human, or, in other words, energy and frequency, becomes more inter-dimensional and multidimensional, his frequencies change and his energy accelerates, causing the body to suddenly undergo a drastic, rapid change, which has to be dealt with by the nerve system. This can cause dizziness, but the process leads you to new dimensions and gives more room for the evolution of consciousness, while physically it seems as if nothing changes.'

After this introduction the lady shook hands with Isabelle, looked at Bernard, and left. The sensors on their fingertips and the receptive beams triggered music waves which were in harmony with the frequency of their bodies. Isabelle and Bernard looked at each other in amazement. It felt great and they started dancing.

Their signs of the Zodiac appeared on the wall and via earphones they received information on the universe and their existence in it was whispered into their ears, while the music went on and only changed when their own frequencies changed. This sensation called up emotions, brought them into ecstasy, and it released them from space and time. Around them three-dimensional projections appeared, a form of rapid prototyping of everything that was going on in their heads, alone and together.

It was as if they were visually manipulated, in a joint cocoon of experience. New, higher frequencies of their bodies and their inherent vibrations kept creating new images and made these visible, like in a dream. There wasn't any difference between their world of thoughts and the physical world around them. It was the highest form of adaption, in which space time, or 'hyperspace', like a gas, showed images from the past.

Isabelle found herself at the house of her grandmother, who, as a young woman began to talk to her, about her mother, Isabelle's great-grandmother, and she showed Isabelle the bedroom she used to sleep in, as it was before the house was destroyed in a fire. Then they went downstairs, to the living room. It was an old-fashioned room, where the sunlight was coming in through an open window. Isabelle saw her great-grandfather sitting in a Windsor rocking-chair, listening to a primitive tube radio, while her own mother, a three-year-old girl, was playing on the floor. The scene Isabelle saw here, with her mother, grandmother and great-grandfather, was more beautiful than any photo or film she had ever seen. She was moved and it felt so good to be with her mother and grandmother. The womb in a womb in a womb, she mused.

While Isabelle was at her grandmother's place, Bernard was taken to the Battle of Waterloo. He was standing in front of a farm, 'la Haye Sante', which lay in a valley and was used as a garrison by the Prussians. On the other side of the hill lay a farm where the French were getting ready for the battle. They were now leaving and with stamping boots they moved across the hill. It had been raining most of the night and the men had great difficulty pulling and dragging their heavy guns over the soggy ground. Bernard saw the men sweat and heard them swear, but in their faces he could read their determination. Further to the north the Duke of Wellington had had to withdraw his troops that morning, which gave these French soldiers hope and strength. They positioned their guns and started shelling the farm. In no time at all the wall surrounding the farm was full of deep holes and one of the buildings had almost been destroyed. Time and again Bernard could hear groans and heart-rending cries of pain rising from the German garrison, where the soldiers were fighting a desperate and hopeless battle.

Bernard had difficulty breathing; he felt so powerless.

It was getting late in the afternoon, the Germans were running out of ammunition and the farm was ablaze now. Men, their clothes on fire, were running about frantically, and soldiers who were trying to escape from the scene of death, became live targets, mere cannon fodder.

Bernard wanted to shout at them, to tell them where to go. Blood and limbs. It made him feel sick. Only thirty-nine of some 360 survived the attack.

It wasn't over yet. Bernard was taken to Brussels, where he was surrounded by more scenes of chaos. He saw coaches of wealthy people without horses - the horses had been requisitioned by the military - and there were men and women who lying drunk in the streets. It made Bernard nauseous. He wanted to get out, but couldn't.

A century later, it was 1916, the Great War was going on. Once again Bernard witnessed a scene of violence. Muddy roads, deep puddles, holes, trenches, British soldiers, trying to flee the scene of a poison gas attack, with lumps of fat clay on their already heavy boots, wet and dry mud on their trousers and jackets, dangling helmets on their backs, the men ploughed on. Broken, and utterly exhausted, they didn't know where they were or where they were going, or what they had to do. He saw the sleepy, absent-minded, perhaps even desperate look in their eyes, as if it no longer mattered whether they would live or die. They were young men, like Joe Winkling, with fathers, mothers, brothers and sisters at home, wet, muddy and faded photos of their loved ones in their pockets. They were boys whose egos had already been smothered and whose brains, even if they survived the war, would be mutilated for the rest of their lives. Shouting, panic. Some were too tired to put their gasmasks on in time and died a terrible death. It reminded him of a poem by Wilfred Owen

Gas! GAS! Quick, boys!—An ecstasy of fumbling
Fitting the clumsy helmets just in time,
But someone still was yelling out and stumbling
And flound'ring like a man in fire or lime.—
Dim through the misty panes and thick green light,
As under a green sea, I saw him drowning.

In all my dreams before my helpless sight,

He plunges at me, guttering, choking, drowning.
And watch the white eyes writhing in his face,
His hanging face, like a devil's sick of sin;
If you could hear, at every jolt, the blood
Come gargling from the froth-corrupted lungs,

and the lie that it's wonderful to die for your country. Then several images of Joe and the lake surfaced, Joe's floundering, his eternal face in the moonshine. It was all so real and seemed to be everywhere around him, like air and he felt terrible feelings of pain and guilt, while at the same time he realised it was good he had turned his back to the army. Isabelle could see the pictures too and she didn't know what to think of them. What had happened?

After that the frequency of their brains was changed. Isabelle and Bernard were in Tibet, looking in silent awe at the Himalayas, the breath-taking 'roof of the world'. Around them lay snow and they could smell the clean mountain air. Beside them were some yaks, which they could even touch; everything was four dimensional. A bald man in a long, white garment with a red sign on it beckoned them. Isabelle wanted to go to him, the man smiled, she was already on her way to him, but Bernard was feeling terrible due to the high altitude, and they were both getting very cold. The images began to fade; it was the end of the programme and they returned to the actual present.

Isabelle noticed there were also blind people at the NFE, who, like everybody else, could see and experience everything. Although they were visually handicapped, their nerves were still working and responded to the pulses. They could move freely, as they no longer felt any limitations. The woman took the gloves off their hands and told them that deaf people could hear every sound, including those from the past.

It was a place where the duality of matter and space, characteristic of all life forms that exist at the same time, came together; yin and yang, light and darkness, heavy and light, being one and the same, resonated with the same frequency, she said. In spite of different forms of density at the level of resonance, opposites, paradoxes in the earthly life of humans, had ceased to exist and final fusion, harmony, the essence of the Tao, had taken its place. In a cosmic ocean that generates waves and energy, and comprises, amongst other things, thoughts, emotions, feelings, love and hatred, intentions, man is absorbed in the harmony of the multidimensional unconscious.

They were exhausted after the three hour session, but it had all been so incredibly special that their daily existence seemed one of emptiness, they both thought. A taxi took them to their hotel. They were still speechless, and their train of thought was still in motion.

The cab driver broke the spell by telling them they had better not go out into the street at night; it was a dangerous place for tourists. It wasn't hard to understand why he said that, Isabelle thought. The city looked sinister; there hung an eerie, grim atmosphere, and when they got out of the car she saw some men fighting. She was gutted and wished she was back home in Vancouver.

Back in their hotel room she didn't say much, but undressed, had a shower and went to bed. Bernard was already in bed. She thought he was asleep, lying on his side, as usual, his face turned away from her, but he suddenly turned round, took her hand and kissed her, something he had not done for years. She was perplexed. Why did he do this? Was it because of something he had seen at the NFE, or maybe the harmony, the frequency? she wondered. Why, Bernard? she wanted to ask him, but he was already fast asleep. Why, Bernard, why? She was confused and couldn't sleep. In the dim light that was coming from the alarm clock, she could see his face. She got tears in her eyes; she felt so utterly lonely and sad. Why had he touched and kissed her? It kept her already weary mind busy.

She remembered reading somewhere that, as a foreigner, it was better not say anything about the political situation of El Salvador or to be critical of any domestic issues, for this was a country with a great deal of lingering pain and suffering in its collective unconsciousness. The indigenous people, Indians who were descended from the Aztecs, had disappeared and there hardly lived any black people in El Salvador either. The nation was struggling with economic, physical and psychic traumas. During the civil war of the 1980s more than 70,000 people had been killed. Right-wing death squads moved through the country, killing about 30,000 people. A number of years later a hurricane ravaged El Salvador, making tens of thousands of people homeless and at the beginning of this century the country was struck by several big earthquakes, causing even more people to lose their homes, and, on top of that, the country suffered terrible droughts, which destroyed some eighty percent of the crops. People were dying of starvation, and the whole situation led to extreme poverty and enormous social injustice.

She lay awake for a long time before she finally fell asleep.

The next day Bernard was his old self again. It was as if he had never touched her, as if it had all been a dream. In the evening he asked Isabelle to go out with him.

'I don't think I want to go out,' she said.

'Why not? If we stay in we won't be seeing anything,' he replied.

'I don't care. I don't need to see anything. I hate this place. Why don't we leave? One day we will be mugged or kidnapped.'

Bernard wasn't too worried. He was glad he'd managed to sell their small car to the brother of the hotel owner at a good price and, waiting for the moment he'd get back his passport, so that they could get on a bus and leave San Salvador, he sometimes went out alone. As a former colonel of the Canadian Army, he carefully avoided saying anything that could compromise him. However, one afternoon, when he was sitting in a bar, he made a remark about the obsolete medical care of the country, because he couldn't get any ordinary medicine for Isabelle. He also said that, in spite of the fact that the country was poor, he had seen quite a few obese people. He'd better have kept that to himself, he later realised, for although the other people at the bar seemed to be smiling at his remarks and appeared to have sympathy for his observations, he was suddenly dragged from his stool by some policemen and taken to the police station. He didn't know what was going on. He wasn't allowed to contact Isabelle and the two policemen, who were interrogating him, said if he made a donation to them, they could see to it he would be released. As an ex-colonel and control freak this made him sick and he lost his temper.

'Fucking hell, what a bloody mess this is!' he shouted, but it only made things worse and one of the two men was feeling for his truncheon.

'Where's your superior? I demand to speak to him.'

The answer was clear: '*Superior, desertor?*'

Bernard didn't say another word.

There he was, sitting helplessly, in a squalid interrogation room, at the mercy of two policemen. They knew that they could put him, a deserter, a foreigner with an American accent and money on him, under pressure. He understood what they wanted and promised to pay.

There was a knock on the door of the interrogation room; another officer, a bespectacled man in a smart, three-piece suit entered. Bernard looked up in surprise at the appearance of the man; he looked like a Nazi from one of those films he had seen. The other two cops left the room. The man looked at a paper.

'So you've fled from Canada,' he said, 'and you came here via the U.S. and Guatemala. Hmm. It also says here that there was an inquiry. A man that drowned and you fled. So you're a deserter?'

'Well, yes, I don't know.'

Bernard knew it was no use trying to deny anything. That man knew more about him than he thought.

'I know you've also been to the NFE and a couple of other places, with your wife. And now you're going out alone?

'Yes, my wife thinks it's too dangerous.'

'She may be right. Don't you know your government is looking for you? Although this country doesn't have any ties with the U.S. and Canada, you'll have to watch yourself, for there is a rumour that, apart from what has happened at that lake, you took some classified military documents with you.'

Bernard's eyes went wide open. He strongly denied the allegation.

'I know the secret services,' the man said. 'This is how they work. They hope we will extradite you. I advise you to keep a low profile and to get out of this country as soon as you can.' He also said the two policemen Bernard had spoken to would return his passport. He then shook hands with Bernard and left.

The two cops returned and accompanied Bernard to his hotel to collect the money. Fresh air, at last, he thought. He felt a lot better, although he still wasn't sure what was going to happen next. One of the policemen got a phone call and walked away, while the other cop told Bernard they could protect him and his wife for only five dollars a day. Bernard looked horrified.

'Fuck off. You're only trying to screw me. I'm leaving this fucking country as soon as I can.'

'Maybe. *Usted elige*, it's your own free will.'

'You don't even know what that means.'

'We'll see,' the cop said, elbowing Bernard in the stomach. 'Let's get you home first.'

Isabelle was standing at the window when he came back, the two cops walking beside him. She wondered what was going on. She already had the feeling she was near a nervous breakdown and this made it even worse. She felt her heart beating in her throat and started walking up and down the room nervously. This man was driving her crazy. What the hell were they doing in this country? she wondered. Why had she come with him? She took a draught of bourbon to calm down. The men were coming up the stairs. The door swung open and there they stood.

'*Buenos dias, Señora.*'

She only nodded and, without even looking at the men, she felt she was being looked at from top to toe.

Bernard took some money from her purse and gave it to the two men, who touched their hats and left the room, saying, 'If the Señor needs us, he knows where to find us'. They handed him a piece of paper with a telephone number and off they were.

Isabelle started screaming and Bernard tried to calm her down, promising her they would leave as soon as he had his passport back. She said she wanted to go back to Canada, to civilization.

'Why did we come here, for God's sake?' she asked him.

'Leave it to me', he said, 'It'll be all right.'

'I've heard that before. You and all your plans. I want to go back home! I'm fed up with you, you selfish bastard!'

'I'm afraid that's impossible, darling. There is no home to go back to. This was our choice.'

'Yours, you mean; I never chose anything at all! And don't call me 'darling', 'cos you haven't got a clue what it means.'

'Don't get so fucked up; we're going away as soon as we can. Don't tell me you believe this is what I want? You talk as if I'm here for my own fun. Stop your nagging. In Ecuador we'll get the life we want; the weather is great there, every day, and you can drink as much as you like.'

'Don't be stupid.'

'I'll go into town and find out when we can leave,' he said. 'As soon as I've arranged some transport, we're off. I know what I'm doing.'

'Why then did you have to pay those cops? Because they know you're a deserter?'

This question struck deep. He resolved not to answer it and only told her what had happened at the bar.

'Shit,' she said. 'Let's get out of here now or I'll go crazy!'

'Take it easy, I'll take care of it. Why don't you lie down for a minute? It'll do you good.'

'Pooh, how do you know what's good for me?' She snapped.

He touched her, just to calm her down.

'Take your hands off me! Get lost!' she called out.

Things took a dramatic turn. At about three in the morning, they were fast asleep, the door was kicked open and three men came in, shouting and swearing. Bernard wanted to call reception, phone the police, but it was no use, of course. Isabelle started screaming, which must have woken up everybody in the hotel and the neighbourhood, but the robbers didn't care; they knew no one would come to the rescue of these two foreigners.

'*Cierra la boca, mujer estúpida*,' one of the men said and smacked her across the face. She was dazed for a minute and when she came to herself, she realised she'd better be quiet. Bernard could do nothing to help her; he was held at knife-point.

The same guy who had hit her, put a knife on her throat, while another told Bernard to give up his watch and money. Running away didn't even cross his mind, so he took off the watch that had belonged to his father and looked at Isabelle, whose eyes were bigger and looked more frightened than ever before. The man who had put the knife on her throat moved his other hand over the upper part of her nightdress, touched her trembling body and let it slip under her nightdress to fondle her warm breasts. He invited the others to have a feel as well, but they only laughed, with their almost toothless jaws. Bernard was fuming with rage.

'Piss off, you fuckers!' he shouted.

The third guy hit him hard with his right fist. Groaning, Bernard fetched Isabelle's purse to hand the money to the men, so that he would be rid of them, but before he had opened it, it was snatched from his hands by the man who was standing at the door.

The door to their room was ajar and they could hear one or two people running up the stairs. Was it the police, who had come to their rescue? Bernard wondered. The robbers looked at each other and were unsettled for a second. What was going on? The door flew open and fire burst from a gun, followed by shouting, panic and screaming. The robber who had been standing at the door, was lying on the floor; he didn't move. The man with the knife, who was still holding Isabella as a human shield, looked about him and jumped from the window, while the third, the one who had hit Bernard and taken his watch, first hesitated what to do, but then jumped out of the window as well. More random shooting followed.

One of the two men who had come into the room saw the purse, took out all the banknotes, and said *'Gracias, Señor. Es usted muy amable.'*

It was one of the two policemen who had arrested him the day before. He gesticulated to his colleague to have the dead man carried off. He smiled at Bernard and said,

'You pay me and I help you. *Usted elige*, remember? Your own choice, your own free will. You pay dollars and I can help you leave the country, or there will be more problems for you. I am your *savior*.'

Of course it was all a set-up; those criminals had been tipped off, or asked by the police to do this, Bernard thought, and someone was sacrificed for the 'good' cause. Within an hour the dead man was carried off. The hotel proprietress peeped round the door, but disappeared quickly; she didn't want to be involved. The policeman thanked Bernard once more for his donation and, because there were plenty of dollar bills in the purse, he said they would arrange transport to Panama. Bernard became angry again, but he knew he didn't stand a chance. Maybe he should be happy they were able to get away from this corrupt, stinking hole.

'You are leaving tomorrow. A small van will collect you at eight o'clock a.m. Here's your passport. Catch. *Adios, superior, desertor,*' he said, putting the rest of the money into his pocket.

Isabelle was quiet; she knew they would finally be leaving this place. Bernard was happy he had put most of his money in a safe place. He locked the door with the chain and sat down on the sofa, beside Isabella, who had calmed down now. He stood up again, went to the window, looked outside and saw a third person standing on the kerb; it was the man from the police station, the one in the smart suit who had advised him to leave. He waved his hand at Bernard. All three got into a car and vanished in the wan light of the only working streetlamp.

34

Albert was sitting at his easel, staring at the canvas in front of him. It looked so empty with the red strokes against the white, yellowish background, but it was enough. His eyes wandered round the room, only to come back to the red strokes, which might just as well have been discoloured blood. He thought of what he had wanted to paint, but his hand had put down something else, an impression or a reflection of his mind. Since his arrival here, right at the beach, he had become more at peace with himself, he felt. It could also be due to the fever and disease he had had in Cuba that he was so calm, he thought. He still wasn't feeling quite his old self yet, although he felt stronger now, but sometimes he didn't have the mental drive, the spirit to get a grip on things. Although he had been here for a while and made a few paintings, he still hadn't taken any steps to go to Guayaquil, the town where Flor was from, which was the most important reason why he'd come to this part of the world. Sometimes he disliked himself for his inertia, his terrible laziness; he needed someone who would take the initiative and kick his lazy ass. He suddenly remembered he had promised Margarita to help her mother move a cupboard. How stupid; he had almost forgotten. Bloody memory.

The sand was nice and warm; he took his sandals off and walked to the hut where Margarita lived with her mother and two little brothers. Her father had been drowned at sea during a fishing-trip. The poor soul was good at sailing, but he had never learnt to swim and when a huge wave swept across the small vessel he was in, he was thrown overboard and swallowed up by the ruthless waves. Two mates who were with him didn't even see where he'd gone so quickly. Seven days later his body was washed ashore and only then did everybody believe he had really drowned.

When he was nearly there, the three children came running towards him, calling, '*Mami, Mami, Señor Jésus!*' All three wanted to hold his hands, so he gave one hand to the boys, while the other one was for Margarita. They bounded happily along with him and he was very pleased that the kids were so fond of him. Looking at the happy kids and thinking about painting, he thought maybe he should try and catch the expressions of those three faces on canvas.

The moment he entered the beach house where the family lived, he could feel the warmth and homeliness of the place, something he had missed for a long time and he loved the colours that had been used, red, yellow and blue. He heard a woman, probably the kids' mother, singing.

'*Buenos Días*, Alberto. *Siento mucho* to have waken you up,' the woman said, stroking her hand over his right arm.

'It's all right. I went to bed much too late.'

This woman emanated strength and love, he felt, positive energy and her children were part of it too.

There was a large cupboard that had to be moved to another room and it was just a little too heavy for the woman to do that. Albert first tilted the cupboard slightly to see if he was going to lift or push it. Six little hands were there to assist him, and six sparkling eyes, but the cupboard wouldn't yield.

'Hang on, guys,' he said, 'I will first try and lift it a little and, if that works, you can help me.'

Margarita stood there, silently, her gaze fixed at Albert's eyes. She had such a sweet little face, he thought, with the fine features of an Indian girl. With her dark peepers she looked straight through him. She had a very serious look on her face, until a smile broke through.

'Señor Jésus, you're not very happy now, are you?'

He couldn't utter a word and just stood there, frozen, forgetting the wardrobe he was holding, trying to take in what she said.

'Just wait a little longer and you will be very happy, just wait a little,' she went on.

He was dumbfounded. Where did this little child get her information from? he wondered.

Her mother, who was watching this scene, said it wasn't the first time Margarita had said unexpected things; in fact, it happened quite frequently.

'Sometimes her eyes are suddenly fixed on something or someone I can't see and they follow the movement the object or that person makes,' she explained. 'And I've also heard her say things, speak to someone none of us could see, even in different languages. I have asked what it is that she sees or does, but usually she can't even describe it herself,' she said, 'and, if she can, I don't quite understand what she means. Kuntur, my grandfather, had it too, and much stronger, but well, he was a shaman,' she said. 'I hope you won't think ill of her.'

'I certainly won't. Don't worry,' Albert replied. 'I only think it's a very unusual gift she has and it makes me curious.'

Margarita looked at him again and it was just as if their minds were somehow connected.

'You want to look at the beautiful *pinturas* of that señor, but you can also make them. Everything is near.'

He understood her at once.

'Yes, I want to see his paintings. That's why I came here.'

It was really strange that he, a grown-up man, should be having a conversation with a young girl about his happiness, his life, he thought.

'What else can you tell me, Margarita?' he asked, with some tension in his voice.

'I don't know that yet,' she answered. 'But not now.'

The next moment the child was back in the girl, the 'knowing' had left her and she was just like the other kids again.

'That's what I meant,' the mother said. 'It's just as if nothing has happened, as if she has never said a word; she can't even remember what she has said.'

'That is very special,' Albert said, pronouncing the last two words as if he was speaking French. 'But it doesn't make much difference to me that she can't tell me anything else. What she said was good enough.'

It had struck him that the girl appeared to get her information, or visions, at certain, lucid moments, and that it also disappeared as quickly as it had come. Maybe she could make contact with spirits, he thought, but he didn't say this to the mother; he didn't want to worry or scare her more than she already was.

The wardrobe was moved, with the help of all the six little hands. When it stood in its place, one of the doors fell open and a cloth fell out, a poncho. The mother laughed at it and said the poncho had belonged to the grandfather she'd just talked about, the shaman.

'*Mon Dieu!*' Albert said. 'Isn't it gorgeous? Look at those beautiful colours.' He wanted to pick it up to have a closer look.

'Take care, otherwise it can't tell me stories any more,' Margarita said. 'I sometimes hold it with my hands to hear them.'

Her mother's mouth fell open; she was dumbfounded.

'Now I get it,' she finally said. 'Whenever Margarita's near this wardrobe, she has a story to tell. It must be my grandfather telling her all these things.'

That an ordinary woman should say such things impressed him very much. In Europe people would have said she was crazy, but here, in this part of the world, the ancestors lived on and people accepted that as something very normal, he thought. In Europe, or probably in the entire modern world, people had strayed from those things, grown away from them, since everything had to be rational and completely intelligible. He remembered the dream he had had at the hospital, about the omni-conscious, which like a cloud contained the past, the present and the future at the same 'time'. The entity of this man from the past, Margarita's great-grandfather, was still present. It was moving about in the unconscious and manifested itself through this girl, the shaman's great-granddaughter, to become conscious again. This man, the continuation of a primordial human, was probably able to look from the past (the former present) into the present (the past of the future) and into the future (the new present) and, maybe via his DNA, his great-granddaughter was able to receive the frequency of this entity, so that he could manifest himself.

Wasn't it Yeats, the Irish poet, who mentioned the *Spiritus Mundi* in his poem, *The Second Coming*? Apparently, Yeats believed that every human mind was linked to a single, huge intelligence and that this intelligence saw to it that certain universal symbols appeared in individual minds. Nowadays this would be called the 'cosmic' or 'universal unconscious', Albert thought. Understanding things at ground level, without being aware of it, is not, as many people wrongly think, a *Zeitgeist*. It's not just about symbols or images that are present and can be perceived by people who are sensitive to it, but it's something much greater than that; it's part of the collective unconscious.

Today everything has come from that magical cupboard, he thought, like the spirit from Aladdin's lamp. That cupboard couldn't but go open today; it had to reveal something, he thought. It wasn't an accident or coincidence. However, the only thing Margarita had said that still puzzled him was 'everything is near'. He couldn't figure out what she meant by that.

The texture of the poncho felt very special, unlike any other fabric he knew, but maybe that was because he now knew the history of that garment and had seen what it did with the girl. It was put back, the door was closed and the wardrobe left in peace. After he had had a cup of coffee with the woman and some fresh, homemade bread, he stood up, ruffled the kids' hair, said goodbye and went back to his own place.

'*Adios, Señor Jésus. Gracias,*' they called after him.

It was quite hot outside. He saw Roonah and Desmond walking to the water, their surfboards under their arms and he thought of going surfing himself. Thinking about the events of the morning he wondered why all these unusual things were happening to him; his crazy dream, the Canadian guy on the beach, the girl and the cupboard.

35

Bernard and Isabelle couldn't sleep any more and decided to stay up and have a coffee. There wasn't much to say; they were totally knackered and could only sigh and yawn. Isabelle wanted to go back to Canada, but Bernard couldn't and wouldn't give up, although this time he knew it wasn't for them to decide where they were going; they were at the mercy of other, dark, forces and could only wait and see what would happen, if they were to arrive, alive, anywhere at all.

They started packing their suitcases and at eight o'clock a very old, tiny Fiat van stopped at the door of the hotel; it was a Fiat 600 model from the 1960s. For once the policeman had spoken the truth, when he said a small van would pick them up. This was probably the smallest van that had ever been built and the fumes coming from the exhaust could easily supply a whole village with carbon monoxide for a year, Bernard thought. He saw an old man getting out, smoking a cigarette. With all the CO_2 coming from the car it wouldn't make any difference to the man's health, Bernard thought. The man called 'Taxi!' and waited for the two to come down. The suitcases were put into the van and Isabelle got in. After that Bernard squeezed himself into the van as well. Accompanied by a lot of puffing, sighing and banging noises they left the city behind them, for an unknown destination.

In places the roads were very dusty, strewn with stones and rubble. There were lots of volcanoes, deep ravines and sometimes they drove through dark forests. There were moments when the old banger was about to give up; it groaned when the gears were changed, coughed when it had to go up a mountain, belched big plumes of black smoke every time the accelerator pedal was touched and once it was at the top of the mountain and raced down again, it was the brakes that were giving problems. It didn't affect the driver at all; he drove on happily to the next challenge, talking gibberish in some unintelligible accent.

Bernard was no longer scared they would be murdered. Why make such a long journey if the first ravine could have done the job? It was becoming terribly hot and oppressive; the temperature must have been in the mid-thirties and the humidity was very high. They were almost sweating out of the car, but at least they were free and heading south.

For hours the narrow, never-ending road wound its way through vast forests before the landscape finally changed and the woods became less dense. It grew lighter, which made the road look wider.

'We're out of El Salvador. This is Honduras and the first town is Aramecina,' the driver told them.

'Thank God,' they both said and were eagerly looking for a sign or something else that proved they really were in Honduras. In the distance they saw a town, but the paint had almost completely peeled off the sign. The only letters they could make out were an 'm', an 'e', and a 'c', but they were satisfied. This had to be Aramecina. They had made it. .

In a somewhat larger town, San Sebastián de Aramecina, they stopped and got out, but it wasn't the end of the journey yet; in some sinister-looking alley the next car was waiting for them. Once again it was an old banger, but at least it was a lot roomier than the tiny Fiat. The driver was about the same age and, he too, looked friendly and happy. The two drivers talked and laughed; they clearly enjoyed life, in spite of the shit and poverty most people lived in. Although grey, they both had a lot of hair, Isabelle noticed. Other things they had in common were far too wide trousers, half-open flies, braces, and worn-out, check shirts.

She smiled for the first time that day when she saw the men had unshaven, but sweet, innocent, little boys' phizzogs. Most of their teeth were missing and both spoke almost unintelligible Spanish. She gave the first driver a tip; she was so glad to be out of El Salvador. The man, out of immense gratitude, almost literally crept through the dust and under the paving-stones of the alley. He shook hands with Bernard and wanted to kiss Isabelle, but that wasn't what she had in mind and she tried to evade the old guy. Unfortunately, that didn't work and her nostrils were invaded by a putrid smell emanating from his mouth, a mixture of bacon, chicken, alcohol and chewing tobacco.

In the meantime the new driver had put their suitcases in his vehicle. The engine was already happily purring and, of course, emitting black, thick plumes of smoke. They got in and off they were. The next stop was going to be Nicaragua, about sixty miles down the road. They would drive along the CA-1 and CA-3, both highways, the driver told them and gave them an old map. At least they now knew where they were going. Once more they were driving through a dark forest when, all of a sudden, the driver hit the brakes. Bernard's heart was in his throat. What's going on now? he wondered. Isabelle saw there was a vast hole in the road, probably the result of a landslide. They had been lucky. Only one lane was available, but fortunately there wasn't much traffic on the road, so they were past it in minutes. Just like its coughing predecessor, the car spluttered and gasped for breath; its lungs could only just get them up the steep incline, but the views were tremendous and in the distance they could see the ocean.

Looking at the map, they saw Honduras wasn't very wide between El Salvador and Nicaragua, so it probably wouldn't take long before they were there. It was still incredibly hot and sultry, but they were slowly getting used to it. They didn't have a real conversation with the driver, as they didn't speak much Spanish and the man's English was nothing to write home about either, but because Bernard spoke French, he could follow some things the man was saying.

Being very tired, the two didn't have much to say to each other either. Isabelle just sat quietly, thinking about the NFE, still trying to understand what had really happened to her senses and how it had been possible for her to speak to her grandmother . And what about the Himalayas, the snow, the cold, the man in the white garment? Unbelievable.

Later that day they arrived in San Lorenzo, a pleasant looking town on the coast. From here it would only be another sixty miles to the Nicaraguan border. They dreaded travelling through Nicaragua, because they were afraid that the atmosphere and the political situation there would be similar to what they had experienced in El Salvador. One nightmare had been more than enough.

There wasn't much going on in San Lorenzo, although it had about 30,000 inhabitants and plenty of restaurants, mainly for tourists. Like many other places in this part of the world, San Lorenzo looked very Spanish, South European. They pulled up at a big hotel that was built on poles and took a room there, while the driver would spend the night somewhere else, maybe with friends; they didn't know. The room they took appeared to have air-conditioning, and it even worked. Isabelle lay down on the comfortable bed to relax and recover from all the events and impressions of the last few days. Within minutes she was fast asleep. Bernard sat down on an easy chair, recapitulating everything that had happened so far.

He looked at Isabelle; she reminded him of his mother and her sweet, worried face, the questions his father was always asking her and the nasty remarks he couldn't stop making, 'Why don't you do it differently? Didn't you see that? Can't you see why I was right? Can't you cancel that appointment? I don't feel like waiting any longer. I would like to have something else for dinner.' What a jerk he was.

His mum, home, Montreal, and he saw himself playing with his friends near Le Plateau Mont Royal, just outside the city, building huts under the ground with old building materials, keeping sweets, lollypops and chocolate bars in biscuit tins, taking their clothes off and walking through the 'living room', romping around on all fours, like wild bears. He remembered how smooth and white James' body was. He could never be a bear, maybe a goat or a lamb, and he also had a very little willy, which was bent like an old, rusty nail. His other friend, Sam, was much darker and a lot tougher too; he was a good and fast digger, a genuine bear, just like himself. Together they were in charge; Sam a bit more really, but Bernard did his damnedest not to show he looked up to Sam.

In that same 'living room', it was rather a cave, they would burn candles they'd brought with them from their homes, while a couple of big, old cans of hot water served as stoves. By the light of the candles they would look at pictures of naked girls, photos they'd secretively ripped out of magazines at a newsagent's and they talked about the girls from school or in the neighbourhood. They compared them to the beautiful girls in the photos, while they were holding their thin, white tall candles and moving them, so that they started dripping and, because of their panting and hot breath, the flames began to flicker, producing irregular and unpredictable patterns on the wall, while the white wax lay soft and warm on the floor.

With lustful glances on their faces they decided to try and persuade some girls to come with them to their secret cave. Wouldn't that be exciting for the girls? They could also take their clothes off and become part of the bear family. Wouldn't that be great? And, even if they didn't want to be involved, they would make them. Bernard got an erection when he remembered how they had touched each other's private parts more than once, how they had fondled each other and masturbated together, looking at the photos of the naked girls, talking about the female bears from the neighbourhood and, of course, they knew everything there was to know about girls, didn't they? Yes, but they would have to 'explore' them too.

The recollections of the underground hut were linked in the cave of his own unconsciousness with the things he had really wanted to do then, like tying up a female bear, feel her and then mate with her, as bears did, although, thinking about it, he didn't have a clue then how bears mated, like dogs, maybe?

Isabelle was light-years away. She was dreaming that she was at the NFE. Bernard was there too, together with the three robbers, that one guy, the creep with the bad odour who grabbed her. She shuddered. He now had very large, coarse, dirty hands with black, very hard, long nails. It sent shivers down her spine. With one hand he held her two breasts and started groping her, went over her belly, while holding her in a vice-like grip with his other hand. She screamed, but nobody listened. The guy smirked in triumph at the others, and at Bernard too. He then lifted her, so that they could look under her dress, while a yellowish slobber was trailing from his mouth. Bernard just stood there, sheepishly looking at her, smiling somewhat uneasily, while a terrible, rancid stench rose from the man's muzzle, where rotting teeth were patiently waiting for judgement day, the moment of final disintegration. A thick, long, scarlet tongue, with a black line in the middle, moved up and down, in and out, spattering the yellow saliva over her body and through the room. She screamed again and begged Bernard for help, but judging by the filthy look in his eyes, she knew she wasn't going to get any help from him; standing there, enjoying himself, fondling his crotch. She started shaking and uttered some unintelligible words.

Bernard looked at her. What the hell is she dreaming about? he wondered. He wasn't pleased, for, because of her screaming and shaking, he'd forgotten what he was thinking about. Not that it mattered, for he was very tired himself, too tired to lift himself out of the chair. He closed his eyes and fell asleep.

Early in the morning their driver was waiting for them. The suitcases were put in the car and after an hour they were on their way. They first drove to Choluteca and San Marcus de Colon and from there they followed the Carretera Panamericana to Nicaragua. When they got to the frontier, the driver didn't slow down; he just drove on. The man probably knew there was no border control.

The scenery was absolutely breathtaking; in the distance they could see the impressive mountains of a Grand Canyon. They looked at it in awe, quietly, until the road went into another direction and the mountains were out of sight. A little later, in a friendly looking town, Somoto, they stopped alongside the local cemetery, where another car was already waiting for them. Only now did Bernard understand the extent of the influence and connections of the police, the secret service, or whatever organisation in El Salvador; it was a complete network that stretched far across its borders. The suitcases were put in the next car, the two drivers shook hands, Bernard and Isabelle got in, and off they were again. The driver from Honduras had turned round and was already on his way back home.

Their new driver was a dashing young guy in his early thirties. He had long, black hair and a thin moustache; a real Don Juan, Isabelle thought. Somehow he reminded her of Zorro, a film hero from long ago, and the sign he always made, 'Z'. He spoke very good English. When he looked at her, she didn't know where to put her eyes; she could feel his piercing eyes looking at, and through, her dress. The man was really charming, she had to admit that, for when she got into the car, he took her suitcase from her and put it in the boot, opened the door, so that she could get in, and closed it after her. She felt like a princess. The man smelled good too; it was a scent she hadn't smelled for a long time, something by Calvin Klein, she thought, really nice. Bernard was sitting in the front, but the man kept looking at her in his rear view mirror and she noticed he was sometimes completely oblivious to what Bernard was saying to him. Maybe she would have preferred the driver to cut across Nicaragua as quickly as possible, to enjoy the warmth and, reputedly, more civilised and better atmosphere of Costa Rica, but the trip was really good. They stopped for lunch at a restaurant.

'Let me take this chair. Please, lady, sit down,' the charming man said. 'Can I get you a drink?'

The country was magnificent and he knew a lot about it. He also told them about his family and showed them some photos of his wife and kids. He must be very proud of them, she thought and was wondering where they were heading. He seemed to have read her thoughts.

'We're going to Estelí, the third biggest city in Nicaragua.'

Bernard had fallen asleep and didn't hear anything the man was saying. Isabelle was impressed by the new, modern buildings she saw wherever she looked and, like in New York and other North American cities, the streets were all straight and perpendicular to each other.

'The city was bombed very heavily during the civil war in the late 1970s, which made it look like a cemetery of building shells,' he told her. 'It became a ghost town.'

'How awful,' she said. 'It must have left a terrible imprint.' She wished she was sitting in the front, so that she would have a much better view and the driver wouldn't have to speak so loud.

'Twenty years before the civil war, the city was a refuge for cigar makers who'd fled from Cuba, which made Estelí one of the most important cigar making cities in the world.'

She didn't find it very exciting, the cigar business, but it was very kind of him that he wanted to tell her so much, she thought. By the look of it, Estelí had been rebuilt very extensively, and the vicinity of the city was very imposing as well, with woods and high mountain plateaus. The man told her proudly about the resurrection of his country that had slowly disengaged itself from a very tragic past, contrary to what most people abroad were thinking. She could see what he meant, for she felt the country was one big surprise, in a positive sense.

Long after they had left Estelí behind them, Bernard woke up again, pretending he had been awake all the time. She chuckled and saw in the rear-view mirror that the driver was smiling at her.

The next stop was at Laguna de Moyua, a big lake with wonderful views and early that evening they arrived in the capital, Managua, a city of over two million people. Again the driver told them lots of things and, like in the past thirty minutes, he kept turning his face to look at her when he was talking. She quite liked him; maybe he liked her too, she thought, but, looking at Isabelle, he only thought she reminded him of his own sweet wife, whom he missed so very much.

Fantasising about the driver, Isabelle was looking at the city. What was it called again? And the images of the driver were ousted by a film of the unreal city she was looking at; ruins, a hotchpotch of hovels for the poor, big, posh houses around it. The heavy earthquakes the man had told her about, had clearly left their mark. She was happy to see the hotel, which was close to the old city centre. The driver would also stay there for the night, but something was up with him, she thought. She had noticed he had become more and more quiet in the course of the day; he didn't appear to be at ease.

'I'm not coming with you today,' he told them the next morning. 'I miss my wife and children; I'm going back to Somoto.'

So that's what she had felt the day before, she thought.

'It's a pity you're not travelling any further,' Bernard told him.

'I would have liked to drive the beautiful lady around, and you could have slept a bit more, but I can't help it.'

Isabelle smiled. Wasn't he charming? But it didn't really matter, she thought. In fact, they had been lucky someone like him had shown them all these beautiful things and, when she thought about it, all three drivers had been very friendly, decent men. It was quite a contrast with her horrific experiences in El Salvador. She figured it was probably another seven hundred miles to Panama City from here and now that they had come so far, it shouldn't be a problem for them to find somebody who could drive them there, but, of course, there were other possibilities too. They could get a coach or buy a cheap car and drive there themselves, she thought. Bernard, however, was at a loss for a minute and asked the driver for some advice.

'You take one of those coaches. They may be quite basic, but they're the best and safest option.'

'Thanks very much,' Isabelle said. 'I can understand you want to get back to your wife and children.'

In her head she could still see the Don Juan of the first hour, who had turned out to be a faithful husband in the end. It was nice, she thought, and maybe it even moved her a little.

'Here's some money for the family. Thanks for everything,' Bernard said, giving him a tip, an unusual thing for him to do.

They shook hands and the driver kissed Isabelle on the cheek, looked at her, and immediately kissed her on the other one too. He smiled and left, waving his hand.

At twelve o'clock they were sitting in an old coach that first went into the direction of Liberia and from there to San José in Costa Rica, where they arrived nine hours later. They wanted to stay there for a few days to chill out and do nothing, apart perhaps from a visit to a museum maybe. After that they'd take a coach to Panama City, a sixteen-hour trip.

Some of the cities and the scenery had been amazing, Bernard thought, but he was tired and wanted some rest, a place where they could stay a bit longer. Isabelle, however, was only just beginning to enjoy herself. They finally seemed to be in a normal, civilised world and perhaps the journey was much nicer than the final destination, she thought, and she resolved to enjoy every minute of it. During the rest of that week they slept late and had brunch in a different restaurant every day. After that they would roam the city, which was the most relaxed place so far; the people were very friendly too; it was clear they were used to tourists, for apart from Spanish, most of them spoke English too and some even German, they heard and the food was great, wherever they went. They visited the Museo del Arte y Diseño Contemporáneo, to see modern art and the Museo de Oro Precolombino, with the most wonderful collections of gold objects, erotic statuettes and amulets from the time before Columbus set foot in America.

After four days, on a hazy afternoon, they took a coach to Panama. Early the next morning Bernard was woken up by the sunlight in his face. He put his seat up and looked out of the window. That must be Panama City, he thought, when he saw all the high-rise buildings basking in the early morning sunlight. Beautiful! It might just as well have been a Canadian city, he thought. It wouldn't be long before they'd be in Ecuador. They must be halfway now. He looked at Isabelle and smiled.

'What are you smiling at?' Isabelle asked. She had just woken up. 'Your eyes are beaming.'

She wondered what was wrong with him. The happiness in his eyes must have something to do with the city in the distance, she thought, definitely not with her.

They drove along the Panama Canal for a couple of miles and were impressed by the number of ships they saw; large container vessels on their way to Chile and Peru and sailing yachts in all models and sizes. Although it was only a canal and the land across the water was still called Panama, they both had the feeling they were at an enormous, symbolic intersection, a meeting-place of roads, water and the future.

36

For Roonah and Desmond water had a very special meaning, not only because they went swimming in it and loved to surf on it, but in water, whether it was an ocean, a sea, a river or even a bathtub, they came together. It was a kind of love-bed, a natural cradle, just like a wood, a park, or a place where they were one with nature, where the birth of life lay, the beginning of everything. And well, what's the difference really between 'bath' and 'bed', just a few letters, he thought, and in Dutch it was only one letter, he remembered someone telling him, 'bad' and 'bed'.

Desmond remembered that fine day in September, when they had sex in a wood, on the grass, among the leaves, the branches and insects. They'd been walking for some time when they reached a clearing in the wood, with beautiful lush grass. They took their clothes off to feel and be one with nature. Roonah had James Joyce's *Ulysses* in her hand. It was a crazy book, but it fascinated her tremendously and she kept reading fragments from it.

They lay down, naked, in silence, listening. *Ulysses* fell open and the wind leafed through it, looking for a suitable scene. Beside it, two piles of clothes on two pairs of shoes, to keep most of the insects away from them. Her bra, which slipped from the pile, became a bridge for the ants to walk across, freely and happily, and it made them curious to find out where this new road was leading to.

First they were lying on their backs, looking up through the open spaces between the trees at the blue sky far above them; white and black, birches, stripes, silver-white, like cigarette-paper, ultrathin, films of bark, peeling, fluttering, the smell of the grass, hands looking for and finding each other, intertwining; her navel, her *Om*, a very long, round vowel, like a female sex organ, a womb, *Om*, the primordial sound of the creation of the universe, a woman in labour, the origin of sound, mother and keeper of other sounds, all words, all languages and all mantras, the beginning of 'being', and his *phalos*, or phallus, her warm loins, vulnerable, so white in the grass, his white hair, silver wires, a hand under them, only just, muscles contracted, relaxed, grass itching, or ants, her fine round breasts, his broad back, turned, eyes met and asked questions, in silence, expressing an as yet suppressed desire, a hand on a buttock, searching, up, down, left, right, falling on *Ulysses*, a smile, her hand, his loins, his hand, her neck, her lips, kissing, eyes open and close, detection of an erection, wind through the trees, soft, leaves rustling, fall, move, silence, peace, penetration, om, phallus, om, phallus, om, phallus, omphallus, organisation, birds, twittering, togetherness, the wind, shaking, yearning, deeper, shallower, deeper, fingers, nails, feet, toes, curling, kicking, breath, shortage, intensity, flexibility, deeper, shallower, pushing, asking, around, everything, the nucleus, the summit, the condor, lava, cooled in a mountain lake of slime.

Peace.

Primordial silence, birds…

No toilet paper, no tissues. *Ulysses*, yes, the first page she could lay her hands on was torn out; the last page… and I said yes I will Yes. The page, the *pagina* for her vagina. Only one letter, in Latin, he thought.

37

The windows and doors of the hostel stood wide open. Several guests were sitting in the sun outside, having a late breakfast. Erasmus was one of them. He stood up, washed his plate and knife, dried them and decided to go to the beach to get rid of his headache. After the long journey he'd made from Iowa and New York to Ecuador, he was happy to relax. Why worry about things? He had seen and learnt so much that he was thinking of writing it all down, arrange it and publish it as a book. Of course he could also go back to university, he thought, finish his education there and do a PhD, or, alternatively, forget about the academic world altogether and use the knowledge he had gathered to do something completely different.

His thoughts were interrupted when he looked at the sea and spotted a few familiar faces on the beach. One of them was the young man who lived in one of the villas on the beach. The other one was the girl he'd seen at the bar early that morning. How long had she been in Ecuador? She was with her friend now; they were carrying their surfboards. He hadn't met the guy yet and didn't know his name; the girl just called him 'my friend'. Had he said anything stupid to her? he wondered. He couldn't remember it exactly. Oh yes. Hadn't he been trying to tell her how pretty she was and that it was a shame she was living with that old guy? Now that he thought about it, he found it a bit embarrassing, although it also made him smile. He remembered she had been a bit condescending, but at least she was honest and he liked her for it. Perhaps it had been his own fault she was so direct. That other guy at the bar, the one with that Canadian accent, he really was a fucker; the way he talked about his wife, and to him.

He looked at the young guy again, the one with the beard and the black, curly hair who lived in the largest house on the beach. He hadn't met him yet, but that was probably because the guy kept himself to himself quite a bit. The only visitors he got were a man in his sixties or so and a younger person, someone his own age. They lived a bit further away, in another, much smaller beach hut. He hadn't seen them for a while.

It was quite funny; all those foreigners who had come to live here and who somehow still needed each other's company, whatever country or part of the world they were from. They all felt they were strangers here and were longing for some sort of togetherness. But the girl's friend never came with her to Pepito's, or maybe he had when he wasn't there himself. That man must have a lot of sex-appeal or something else, he thought, maybe money. How else could such a beautiful young chick fall for someone his age? He chuckled. Maybe he was just being jealous. Perhaps the old guy was more interesting than he thought.

The young man was on his way home and saw the two surfers coming out of the water and waved at them. They probably knew him, for they waved back.

Didn't she look gorgeous with her wet, blond curls and the short, black wetsuit? he thought. She was looking at him. He felt his face turn red and got a funny feeling in his belly. He shyly put his hand up and waved at her. She waved back. Her friend also looked at him to see who she was waving at. He nodded at Erasmus, whose thoughts started wandering off, from Roonah to another girl he had recently met.

38

Albert came back home. He was still thinking about the magic cupboard and what the girl, Margarita, had said. He looked at the canvas on the easel. Yes, I'd better leave the composition as it is, he thought; adding something to it won't do any good. He started cleaning up the mess in his room and thought about the three kids and that he wanted to try and paint their faces, to do something new and make a fresh start. He saw his own reflection in the glass and decided to do another important, almost symbolic, thing; he was going to shave off the beard and moustache that had been growing on his face ever since his involuntary stay, his 'confinement', in Cuba. On Jack's yacht it had been quite practical, but now it was time for a new look; the beard had to go. He went to the bathroom and after fifteen minutes he was another man. It felt good, light and airy, but, looking at himself in the old, posh, French shaving-mirror with the golden frame, he saw something else. He still had a thin face, the legacy of his illness, he thought. It looked even thinner now without the beard and moustache.

'Does it matter? he asked himself. 'No, not a bit. So stop, Albert, flick the switch, forget about the dark ages, the past is the past; it's time to move on now.'

It worked. A fresh feeling started flowing through his body; his strength was coming back, the very opposite of what had happened to Samson, that man in the bible, he thought. He smiled at himself. Was this what the girl had meant when she was talking about happiness and said everything was near? Wasn't it also time then to take the painting, the impression of Rosalie, off the easel and start with something new, fresh, like the children's faces?

He made some coffee, had something to eat and went outside to look at the ocean from the veranda. The coffee and croissant made him think of his aunt, bless her, and her balcony. What a view, quite different from Paris. He thought of the two surfers he had seen and felt like going surfing himself.

'Shouldn't you be going to Guayaquil?' his conscience asked him. 'Didn't you come here because of Flor?' Fortunately, there was another voice that said, 'Don't worry about your mission to Guayaquil now. Carpe diem, Albert.'

He put on his swimming-trunks and went back to the beach. The sand was lovely and hot and the sky so beautiful and blue, every day again, and the people were so friendly.

He went to the guy with the dilapidated old Volkswagen van to rent a surfboard and saw the two surfers he'd waved at earlier. They were talking to the bald owner of the van. They had their own boards and wetsuits, but the old man was returning a couple of surf boots he had rented. They could speak Spanish quite well, he noticed, but he could still clearly hear where they were from. The bald man turned round to ask Albert what he was looking for, to which he said he needed a surfboard and a short wetsuit.

'The weather and the waves are absolutely mega today,' Roonah said to Albert. 'Especially over there,' pointing at the spot where the waves were long and curly.

When Albert heard that voice, from so close, he was sure he had met her before, that he knew her, but his memory was so dreadful. It really upset him and it didn't seem to be getting any better. The only things he could remember fairly well were those from before he had fallen ill, but he couldn't recall where he'd heard this girl's voice before, however deep he dug. Paris went through his head, Jargeau, London, Sylvain's studio, London again, the gallery in Bond Street, the art bookshop in Charing Cross Road. After that his thoughts drifted to the Canary Islands, boat lifters and it was always so difficult to recognise someone if you were not in the place where you met or saw that person. Her voice, it sounded a bit Irish, or English, perhaps even American, so difficult, the face; he couldn't place her, his memory, so awful. It made him so angry sometimes, like now, as he was convinced he had seen her before.

'You also live on the beach, don't you?' Desmond asked Albert.

Although Albert heard the question, he didn't hear the exact words. Desmond's voice or face didn't ring a bell, so he must have seen or met the girl in a place where she was alone, without her friend.

39

Erasmus was still gazing at Roonah and Desmond, reminiscing, not about the two people he saw there, but about all his recent experiences, like the crazy events in New York, especially those at Mrs Hopper's, the clairvoyant, who had given him all those hints and told him about the future and her saying, all of a sudden, that his father was close to him, a thing he still couldn't make much of; in fact, he couldn't understand at all. After that came the autistic man, his uncle, who kept repeating the names of all those presidents and putting right what was awry, but who was so kind, just like the woman who was looking after him. What couldn't he or wouldn't he say? That woman, Mrs Schwartzkopf, also knew something; he was quite sure of that, but, frankly, what had it all brought him?

Opium and sandalwood incense, Mrs Hopper. Only now could he remember the scents he'd smelled in her bedroom. It wasn't important, but she had shown him new ways, taken him, as it were, to Mexico, the Toltec, the Aztecs, the Mayas, to himself even. Thinking about it now, why hadn't he asked her any more questions about his father and why had she actually told him his father was close to him?

For a moment he broke away from his thoughts, looked at the beach and was surprised to see the young man was standing at the surf rental van, in his swimming-trunks, shaking hands with the girl and her friend. Seconds later the girl and the young man were holding and hugging each other and Erasmus noticed the girl's friend wasn't, or didn't want to be involved. What a funny guy he was. The young man handed the surfboard back to the bald man. How strange. After that Erasmus saw the three of them walking to the young man's beach house. The girl and the young man, no longer with a beard and moustache, he now noticed, were talking and gesticulating wildly. Sometimes they stood still and took each other by the arm, her friend following them at a distance.

40

From New York Erasmus and Jim took a bus to California. There they got a lift from a lorry-driver and so, like the Aztecs, they travelled south to Anahuac, the 'Land Between The Waters', the area in Mexico where, apart from the Aztecs, the Teotihuacan and Toltec had lived as well. The trip was breathtaking. It was very long, but the driver was friendly and very happy to have some company. He wasn't allowed to take hitch-hikers with him, but he didn't care about that. Who is going to check on me? he asked, laughing.

From L.A., via Phoenix, Arizona, it was a journey of nearly two thousand miles and it was incredibly cool, with a great variety of landscapes; deserts, mountains and plateaus. It took them several days to get to Mexico City and, unfortunately, they lost a whole day due to long delays at the border between the U.S. and Mexico. Apparently Mexican border control officers were on strike.

'You can have dinner with my family tonight and sleep at my place as well,' he said, when they were approaching Mexico City. 'I have a small casa in the *afueras* of Mexico City, but it's very easy to get to the city centre and buses and taxis are *económico*.'

Although they would have preferred to find accommodation that was a bit nearer to the city centre, they accepted his friendly invitation. When they arrived at his house, they saw he had a very beautiful daughter, called Juanita. She had long black hair, piercing eyes, a face with wide cheekbones, enchanting eye-lashes, a slightly stout, but beautiful body, wrapped in a long dress. Jim stood gaping at her when they entered the house and fell immediately under the spell of her beauty. The attraction was mutual, it seemed, by the way she looked at Jim.

Erasmus, too, thought she was incredibly beautiful, but saw how she kept glancing at Jim from where she was sitting and Jim, in turn, couldn't keep his eyes off her, so that their four eyes met, over and over again, accompanied by shy, but loving smiles. Of course her father had noticed it too; but he liked Jim, for on their way to Mexico they had often talked about lots of things together; Jim's Spanish was pretty good. Erasmus could already see it coming that he would have to travel further on his own.

The next day Jim and Erasmus went to Huastepec, near Texcoco, the old Aztec capital, about eighteen miles from Mexico City, amongst others things to visit the royal garden of Texcotzingo, which was a vast complex of steps, structures and lawns.

You don't need much imagination to see what the place must have looked like, Erasmus thought. Real awesome. I can understand that ancient civilizations and cultures had a lot more in common than is generally thought when you try to envisage the world those people lived in; how they looked upon nature, the changes of the seasons and the universe, he thought, while there were still so many other things they couldn't yet comprehend.

There were many ruins and objects dating back to the period after the Aztecs, or 'Mexica', had left Atzlan, possibly after the volcanic explosion at Sunset Crater in Arizona in 1064, but there was virtually nothing left from the time in Atzlan itself, the paradise they were driven away from in the end, so what he had read in those Greek texts in New York was very unique, as they *did* describe the time in Atzlan. He started looking for depictions of Aztec art, but unfortunately there was nothing that bore any resemblance to their Greek counterparts. What he did come across though was a depiction of a two-headed figure, which reminded him of Egyptian sphinxes.

From there they went to Teotihucan, 'the Place Where Gods Were Born', which was about thirty miles from Mexico City, as Juanita's father had told him. From far away they could see the immense complex with the gigantic, stepped pyramids on a vast plain. The funny thing was that it was just as if they weren't going to the pyramids, but as if those huge bulks of stone, which were lying there so calmly, sedately and imperturbably, eternally quietly, were coming towards them and would stealthily swallow them up.

'How can these two massive mountains be only between forty-five and eighty metres high?' Erasmus asked Jim, 'They look so much bigger with all those puny ants, people, crawling all over them and look, there are flights of steps everywhere. How were the designers of this incredibly big complex able to oversee the construction of these structures? It's unbelievable.'

Because the grass covered soil lay high against the pyramids, it seemed as if these structures had torn open the earth and pushed themselves up, an underworld striving to become an 'upperworld'. Lying there, in their callous grandeur, tired and old, crumbling away, with an eerie mix of concealed magic and a dormant aggression, they were only waiting to be roused from their slumber; they looked so fearfully imposing.

They walked to the Pyramid of the Sun along the Calzada de los Muertos, the 'Avenue of the Dead'. Alongside the road lay smaller, equally dense, thick, mini pyramids; like sheds behind big houses, or children standing safely in between their mother and father. The almost immeasurable space around them and the feeling it conveyed, the very wide avenue, everything seemed so far away, so vast, and in the distance they saw mountains that were the very image of these pyramids, or the other way round. They just stood there, gazing in awe, their mouths wide open.

'How can we ever tell anyone what we've seen here? The Pyramid of the Moon looked huge enough, but this one's colossal,' Jim said.

Because of the dark clouds surrounding it, The Pyramid of the Sun looked menacing and, like at the Pyramid of the Moon, they both felt an impenetrably thick, massive ruthlessness. Breath-taking, a way with the dead butterflies in front of them, light and airy, freely fluttering, back and forth, from flowers to stones, on the ground and back, in circles, frolicking, until they settled, blinking with their wings, taking to the air again, weightlessly.

They went back to the Pyramid of the Moon, where Jim strolled off on his own.

'I'd like to climb onto the pyramid,' he said.

'Do as you please. I haven't got a head for heights,' Erasmus said.

He saw there was an archaeological team at work and went over to have a look. He asked one of the men what they were doing. It was a new dig, he was told. The last time a team had been there was at the beginning of the century, but quite a few new techniques had been developed since that time, which made it easier to detect objects. Several artefacts that had been found were carefully carried outside. Apart from sculptures and utensils, they had also found the remains of animals and humans.

Wouldn't it be fantastic to do this work himself? he thought, especially in a place like this. Among the archaeologists who were at work there, he saw a young, Japanese woman. He was distracted for a moment, while the man went on talking.

'I'm sorry, but I don't know what the original names of these pyramids are. The names that are used today were given much later by the successors of the Toltec, the people who probably built these structures, but this pyramid is also called Tenan, which probably means "Mother" or "Protected Stone".'

'Very interesting.'

'The gods that led the Aztecs from Atzlan were Huitzilopochtli, the God of War, who also represented the sun, and his sister, Malinal Xochitl, who was the goddess of the serpents and also represented the moon.'

'So it's not so strange that these two pyramids should have been built here,' Erasmus said.

The man became very enthusiastic and couldn't stop talking.

'According to a legend, Copil, Malinal's son, took over his mother's role of representing the moon. Later, after committing treason, he was killed by Huitzilopochtli, who ordered a certain Tenoch to bury Copil's heart. Although, symbolically speaking, the Sun, also called the Eagle, had defeated the Moon, the Rabbit, the latter retained her important role of conserving the water of the Cosmos, of bringing rain and preserving the moonlight.'

With all the information he had, Erasmus wanted to have a look at the layout of the area, the place where the pyramids stood and the Avenue of the Dead. He thought of the fragment from the museum in New York that related in Greek what had happened here. It wasn't a recent fragment, but from before the Christian era, which meant that it was about the time from before the Aztecs arrived here. But even that was rather vague, as there had been several civilisations in Mexico, before, after, or at the same time. Besides, they could have influenced each other, like the ancient Egyptian and Greek civilisations. But did it really make any difference if they called one pyramid the 'Pyramid of the Sun', a male entity, and the other 'Pyramid of the Moon', a female entity, for in the end they were one and the same, weren't they? he thought. Moreover, in this case, they were symbolically connected to each other by the avenue. Mythology was full of duality anyway, he remembered. In the time of the Aztecs the symbol 'sun', for example, wasn't just a sun; they had two different suns, a male light, or 'Day' sun, and a female dark, or 'Black' sun, who, together, formed the concept of 'sun'. It reminded him of the picture of Yang and Yin and the well-known anima and animus.

In Aztec mythology there was the god Xiuhtecuhtli (often depicted with a fire serpent on his back), the 'God of Fire and Volcanoes', the personification of life after death, warmth in cold, light in darkness, while, at the same time this god was one of the nine 'Lords/Guardians of the Night', and he was considered to be the father and mother of the gods, so they all constituted nothing but duality, he concluded.

There was also a temple that had been purpose-built for the 'Feathered Serpent', whoever or whatever that was, as the god Quetzalcoatl was also a 'Feathered Serpent', and connected to the gods of the wind, to Venus, to dawn, art, knowledge and books.

So why was this feathered serpent so important? he wondered.

He walked over to the young Japanese woman. She was wearing a surgical mask and the blue coat of a doctor.

'Excuse me. Can I ask you a question?'

She took off her mask and said, in an enchanting tone, 'Sure, no problem. By the way, my name's Izumi.'

'Oh, sorry,' he said, blushing a little. 'My name's Erasmus.'

She smiled and told him she was a student at Todai, The University of Tokyo, and when he asked her about the feathered serpent, she said,

'The "Feathered Serpent" motif can be found in both Xiuhtecuhtli and Quetzalcoatl and, apart from the fear they inspired, this motif also stood for the Creator of Man and Vegetative Renewal, creation and re-creation, or regeneration; death by sacrifice and (new) life.'

'Wow. I wish I had brought a note-book,' he said.

She smiled.

'I have also seen that image of the serpent at several other archaeological digs,' she continued, 'but then as a man with a black sun sitting in a yellow sun. So you see that a lot of gods and goddesses were multi-layered, multi-functional.'

'Yes, very interesting,' Erasmus said, thinking about the duality of gods. But doesn't our own, modern, reality consist of more than one layer, too? he asked himself.

'But there's something else,' she said. 'Of course the Aztecs had a different name for Venus, the planet, than the Romans, but there are several structures here that were built in such a way that they were in line with this planet. It was the Romans, who had given the planet this name and she was both the Evening Star and the Morning Star, depending on the position of the planet with regard to the sun.'

'Isn't it strange then that there are also structures in this part of the world that are positioned in line with the same planet, whatever its name was?'

'No, not really. Everything is connected,' she said.

So many things were going through his head. It was as if he was getting more and more pieces for a jigsaw puzzle. The Romans called her Venus, the Greek Aphrodite, while she originated from Egypt or the Near East. According to a German researcher, for instance, there was a link between her and the 'serpent goddess' of Minoan culture, a goddess who stood for love, amongst other things, but still, like here in Mexico, she was depicted as a serpent. But, and that was even more interesting, he thought, the Egyptian serpent goddess Wadjet was also associated with the city the Greek knew as Aphroditopolis, the City of Aphrodite. Besides this resemblance there was once more the duality in oneness, for Aphrodite was associated with the Egyptian goddess Hathor, and according to Babylonian texts in which the goddess was mentioned, her name meant 'She who rises at dusk', that is, the personification of the Evening Star.

His head started spinning and it didn't stop. He seemed incarcerated in the world of antiquity, where various cultures, however far apart, geographically speaking, had comparable concepts or even shared some of them. The main question was, did the Greek, or the Egyptians before them, know anything about the Toltec or other civilisations, like the Mayas, in Meso-America? The text in that New York museum said that cultures from different parts of the world were definitely familiar with each other. But there were some more important questions to be asked. If these cultures were so far removed from each other in space, then what was the relevance of that and where lay the original source of their thinking?

The Japanese student looked at him, waiting patiently. He returned from his thinking and told her what was going through his mind.

'What you're saying sounds very interesting,' she said. 'What else can you tell me about Aphrodite and your theory about it all?'

He started with the Egyptian goddess Hathor, who was also called a 'primeval serpent' and with whom the Greeks associated Aphrodite. Her very name was special, for in Egyptian mythology it meant 'House of Horus', while Horus was, amongst others, the god of the sun, so a man in the house, or body, of a woman. Hathor stood for the principles of joy, feminine love and motherhood; he/she was depicted on the burial tombs of important people as the 'Mistress of the West' and welcomed the dead in the next life, while she was also the goddess of music, dance, foreign countries and fertility. There was a stone urn on which Hathor was depicted as a goddess of the sky and which showed she had a relationship with Horus, who lived in her, Erasmus told Izumi.

In another complicated relationship Hathor could be Ra's mother, daughter and wife and, at other times, also Horus' mother. All the dead, male or female, became an Osiris (so oneness), whereas the early Romans associated women with Hathor and men with Osiris, pulling them apart again, as it were. He could follow this line of Hathor, Aphrodite and Venus to Mexico and apply the comparison to civilisations in this part of the world.

'It thrills me and I want to find out more, do new research.'

'Yes, I can imagine that,' Izumi said. 'I knew some of what you told me, but I didn't know anything about the connection between Aphrodite and Hathor as goddesses of fertility, or what you told me about the early Romans and Venus. It all reminds me of the platform on the Pyramid of the Moon.'

'What platform?'

'Well, on top of that pyramid is a platform that was used to perform ceremonies in the honour of the Great Goddess of Teotihuacan, the goddess of water, fertility, the earth and creation. The sculpture at the bottom of the pyramid is dedicated to her. This goddess compares to Aphrodite/Venus, especially if you think of Venus Cloacina, a fusion of Venus and the Etruscan goddess of water, and for that reason it was important, of course, how the pyramid and the whole complex was going to be built with regard to the planet Venus, in the same way the pyramids in Egypt were also built in accordance with astronomical calculations,' she explained. 'Although there are still ignorant people around who refuse to accept that,' she said, with a seductive, somewhat secretive, smile.

'The ceremonies also entailed the sacrifice of human beings and animals, as a tribute to the goddess and to make sure the balance between life and death, light and dark would be maintained. If there was an eclipse of the sun or moon, people were scared the goddess was angry, because it meant new sacrifices had to be made, as death led to new life.'

'Yes, it sounds quite logical', he interrupted, 'because Venus, through her partner, Mars, was also connected to war and death.'

She continued by telling him that, according to the Aztecs, who came here later, Coatlicue was the goddess of earth, of life and death. She was depicted as a woman who wore a skirt or dress of snakes and a necklace that consisted of the hearts of her victims.

'In the pyramids here we have found the bodies of people who had been sacrificed and whose hearts had been removed. The heart could be taken out with knives or scalpels that were made of obsidian, a mineral that is found in volcanic areas and which is sharper than even the most modern metal scalpels. We have also found obsidian in the pyramids. The mineral was used to make eyes for the stone depictions, so that they glittered when light fell on them. According to tradition, Coatlicue's son cut off his sister's head, which was used to make the moon. He may have used obsidian.'

Erasmus was ruminating on the connection between the Pyramid of the Sun and the Pyramid of the Moon. They were linked up by the Avenue of the Dead and he thought of the sun, the earth, the moon, a trinity. One was male and two were female and, from a depiction he had seen, of a head, symbolising the moon, which had been symbolically cut off a body, the earth, Erasmus gathered several older civilisations believed the moon must originally have been an integral part of the earth.

This may have influenced the construction of this complex, he thought. This avenue could also be called the 'Avenue of Light to Darkness', from the white to the black sun or from man to woman, he thought. A symbolic journey was made from life to death, from the beginning to the end, and back again, by a goddess of fertility and new life, he reasoned in himself.

The black sun and the earth, a oneness of the female aspect, or Mexico, which meant 'Navel of the Moon', an Omphalos, the dark womb from which new life travels into the light through a shaft. To be able to move from darkness to light, from the dark inside of the pyramid via a shaft, sacrifices had to be made; and he also thought of shafts, tunnels in Egyptian pyramids and possibly here too, where the light, or sperm, from the male sun could get into the dark womb of the female earth. A new birth or rebirth, that's what it was all about, he concluded. For a moment he thought of Astarte, the Phoenician goddess of fertility, whose name meant 'womb', 'Omphalos', the goddess the Greeks accepted as Aphrodite.

'Some of the dead went to Tlaloc, a god in the underworld,' Izumi said.

She had taken her coat off, and Erasmus spotted a small, but beautifully coloured, multi-headed snake and a butterfly on her bare arm.

'You've given me so much information. I really need some time to let it all sink in. Can we meet up later?'

'No problem, but I'm very busy in the next couple of days, so next week would suit me better. What about next Friday? Everybody, the whole country, has a day off then, because it's the 'Day of the Dead'. The team is off as well, so I will have plenty of time then.'

Friday he thought, Freya, the Norse goddess of war, love, death, a feathered cloak, Day of the Dead. Coincidence?

'Yeah, great,' he said. 'Let's stay in touch. Have you got a telephone number, so that I can give you a call?'

'Sure. I'll write it down for you.'

'Thanks.'

'Here you go. Can you give me a call on Wednesday or Thursday?'

At that moment Jim came back.
'That was incredible,' he said. 'I climbed onto the pyramid. 'Great views from the top. Oh, sorry to interrupt.'

'No problem,' Erasmus said. 'We've just finished. This is Izumi. She works here. She's a student from Japan.'

'Hi, I'm Jim, nice to meet you. Yeah, it was really super up there,' he said, pointing at the pyramid. 'You know I like climbing, don't you? Remember the roof of the university?'

'Of course I do,' Erasmus said.

They went back to Juanita's house. She was already waiting for Jim, as if he'd been away for days and in the evening the three of them went out to a bar in the neighbourhood. When he saw how close these two were, Erasmus realised that his life and theirs were heading in different directions.

'I've made an appointment with that Japanese student later this week. Are you coming with me?'

'I don't think so. I'd rather stay with Juanita. You don't need me there anyway with that girl. I bet you want to chat her up.'

'It hadn't even crossed my mind,' Erasmus said, but he was blushing, so that Jim and Juanita had to laugh out loud.

'See? I was right,' Jim said.

The three spent the rest of the week together, with Juanita showing them several very interesting things in Mexico City, like the magnificent Museo de Art Moderno.

For some reason Erasmus had to think of his father. He had no idea where he'd be able to find him and the clues his uncle had given him, if they were clues at all, were no good either. The U.S. presidents entered his head again and he remembered his uncle's words, 'I have seen him as my brother, but not as a Hopper'.

What the hell did his uncle mean? he wondered. He was getting tired of the whole thing; all the random information in his head. I wish I'd never started this search, he thought, I will never find him. He may be dead and gone, so what's the point of going on?

Of course Mrs Hopper's words followed, not only what she'd said about his trip to Mexico, but also that his father was close to him. Maybe her vision was scrambled. Perhaps she saw all kinds of confusing images, which she was trying to organise, or maybe she had meant that his father was living in the recesses of his heart and that they were not, and never would be, physically close together. Now that he was here, in this extraordinary place, wasn't it better to take leave of his father, symbolically, to bury him in some way and be done with it, so that he could get on with his life?

All these things made him so restless. He wasn't getting anywhere and, maybe not accidentally, next Friday was the *Día de Muertos*, the 'Day of the Dead', although he didn't know exactly what it meant. So he asked Juanita's mother if she could tell him something about it and although he couldn't understand every word she said, he got an idea what it was about. It was on the same day as two Catholic holidays, All Saints' and All Souls' Day. The original, Aztec 'Day of the Dead' was in August and lasted for a whole month. Erasmus gathered that this celebration had probably been adapted to the holidays of the Catholic faith, which became widespread all over South and Central America in the wake of the Spanish conquests.

41

After nodding to Erasmus, who was sitting on the wall at the hostel, Desmond wondered what a young man like him was looking for in this part of the world. Erasmus, however, was much too lost in thought to notice somebody was looking at him. He was watching a film in his head that was very different from this scene on the beach. His thoughts didn't go that far back into the past and not so far away from where he now was either. He saw a restaurant, and a beautiful waitress, with wonderful, dark, sparkling eyes and a sweet smile on her face. He would love to see her again and go out with her.

42

The days after his visit to Teotihucan passed by very slowly. Erasmus went back to the old settlements at Lake Texcoco and heard from an old man there that the site had been laid out very carefully, in line with astrological events, with Venus in particular. Astonishing, he thought, but why Venus all the time? There used to be a royal palace with extraordinary gardens at the nearby hill of Texcotzingo, which was supplied with water from a smart system of channels, while it was also designed as a holy place for the god of rain, Tlaloc, whose name Izumi had already mentioned, and meant 'he who lets things grow', the old man said.

Erasmus could hardly wait for the day of his appointment, his 'date', as Jim called it, with Izumi; the hours crept by and every day seemed to last a week

On Wednesday he rang Izumi, who sounded terribly excited. She was still at work, she said.

'Oh, Erasmus. So much has happened. You've really got to see this. Your theory about mythological synchronicity. I can't explain it on the phone. Are you still coming on Friday?'

'Sure. But, wow, what you're saying. It's giving me goose pimples. I can hardly wait to see you. By the way, I don't think Jim's coming with me.'

'OK. Don't forget to put on some good boots. It might be slippery there.'

'OK.'

'Erasmus, there's something else. Have you ever heard of Ayahuasca?'

'Not really. Why?'

'Well, what I've found is amazing.'

'What is it? You sound so mysterious.'

'I can't tell you. Not now anyway. Sorry.'

'Why not?'

'My colleagues. I'll tell you later. But there's this drink, called Ayahuasca, and it helps you to see things you normally can't see. It might help you with your search into the ancient world, the past, your theory.'

'OK. But it sounds pretty weird to me, confusing.'

The ancient world, mythology, the past. He thought of his dad and became nervous.

'I'm sorry, but I can help you, Erasmus, if you want to,' Izumi went on.

'What are you talking about? Have you been drinking, or smoking funny things?'

'No, I'm fine. Don't worry. I only want to help you, share my experiences with you so that you can put your own thinking into perspective.'

'Thanks. But it still sounds like one big mystery to me. I'll think about it. See you on Friday.'

In the evening he got a text message from her:

Be sober when you get here at 9, i.e. if you want to go into another dimension of reality.

He didn't know what to make of it. Why would she want to help him? She had her colleagues, didn't she?

Jim laughed after he had read the message and said,

'She's a funny bird, Erasmus. When you come back you might be married.'

He wasn't happy at all when the weather changed the next day. The fine, mild days seemed to be over and dark clouds were hanging angrily over the city. It was getting darker and darker by the hour and the weather was so oppressive; his clothes were sticking to his humid body. When the rain finally started pouring down, it looked like dusk in the middle of the day. The usually relaxed Mexicans rushed from one side of the street to the other to seek the shelter of shops and houses.

Maybe the appointment was going to be cancelled now and he thought of what Izumi had told him over the phone or, rather, what she had not told him. It was so weird, but also so exciting and he had made up his mind not to miss this opportunity.

At last, it was Friday, the *Día de Muertos*. The whole country seemed to be having a party. Apparently people had held rituals to celebrate and honour deceased ancestors for more than 2,500 years and even before Columbus came to America, death heads were kept as trophies and exhibited during the rituals to depict death and rebirth. The streets bustled with people; a lot of them had left home early that morning to go to the cemeteries where their loved ones lay buried. They were carrying picnic hampers and took special flowers with them, orange, Mexican marigolds. There were stalls in every street where large bunches of these flowers were sold. It was just like carnival, one big party with crowds of people everywhere.

Juanita's father had already told him that, apart from flowers, people also took other *ofrendas* with them, such as the favourite food and drink of those who had passed away and that they sometimes built private altars, using death heads of sugar and marigolds, which, he said, were called *cempasúchil*, the Aztec word for 'twenty flowers'.

'Nowadays most Mexicans call this flower *Flor de Muerto*, the Flower of Death,' he said.

What a shame. A lot of old names will gradually fall into disuse, which will make it more and more difficult to find the origin of things, Erasmus thought.

'People also leave blankets and pillows at the cemetery, so that the dead can rest and in some places people spend the night at the graves of their relatives,' Juanita's father told him.

'You really know a lot about these things,' Erasmus said.

'Thanks. There are some peculiar things going on in other parts of the country,' Juanita's father went on. 'In Pátzcuaro, for example, which lies on the southern shores of Lago de Pátzcuaro, people light candles at midnight, white or yellow ones, decorate them with black paper (like the white/yellow and black sun, Erasmus thought), and sail in boats with wings attached to them, representing butterflies, to an island with a cemetery on it in the middle of the lake, to honour and celebrate the dead.'

'How extraordinary,' Erasmus said, 'a boat representing a butterfly.' He thought of the archetypal symbol of the transcendent soul, of transformation, mystical rebirth and the paradoxical meaning of marigolds, 'Herb of the Sun' and 'Flower of the Dead'.

In mainly Catholic countries, all over the world, All Saints' Day and All Souls' Day were also national holidays, with people going to cemeteries with candles and flowers, giving presents to the children, as if there is a collective unconscious telling humans that there is more than a physical life and that the spirit is a separate entity, functioning independently of the body, a bit like the autonomic nervous system, he thought.

The Greek, too, had a 'Festival of the Dead', he remembered from college. It was called *Anthesteria* , which was probably derived from ἄνθος, flower, or flower of the grape. It took place in January or February and lasted three days, a kind of carnival. During these feast days the spirits of the dead were called up to come to the land of the living and slaves could also take part in the festivities. The third day of Anthesteria was called *Chytroi*, 'Feasts of Pots', when the dead received food that no one else was allowed to taste. Funnily enough Juanita's father had told them that the people in Mexico did eat the food, because they believed that not the food itself, but the spirit of it was eaten by the souls of the dead. Although it wasn't quite the same, there still was a similarity, he thought.

The dead; deceased relatives. It set him thinking, also about his father. But what was the point? What could he do? In the end he resolved that, once he was in the pyramid, he would burn the photo, put the ash in a jar and place it somewhere in a niche. In that way he would give his father back to the dark world that now lingered in his head, but which needed to return to its own dimension or universe.

When he got to Teotihucan, Izumi was already waiting for him. They shook hands and she kissed him on the cheek. He blushed. She looked really gorgeous, he thought, and remembered with a smile what Jim had said.

'Let's go to the office first,' she said, while the first, soft drops of rain fell from the menacing, dark clouds. Inside, on the walls, was a floor plan of the pyramid, some beautiful photos and drawings. Izumi gave him a safety helmet and put a big rucksack on her back, as if she was going on an expedition.

'We are going into a tunnel my team discovered with the help of the latest muon detector. It was found behind a huge stone on the left side of the pyramid.'

'So that's what you couldn't talk about on the phone. That sounds very exciting,' Erasmus said.

'Yes, but there's a lot more.'

'What?'

She looked at his boots.

'I'm not sure if they're the right sort of boots. The ground isn't only rocky, but very wet and slippery in places as well, so you really have to watch out.'

He smiled. She sounded like an official guide. He put the helmet on and looked at his boots. He wasn't prepared for this, he knew, but he was too excited about the prospect of going into this newly discovered tunnel to care. When they arrived at the place where they would enter the pyramid, Izumi looked around to make sure nobody was watching or following them. Once a big stone had been moved aside by means of the provisional hydraulic system the team had fitted, and the entrance became visible, a musty smell, a draught, came outside.

So there had to be one or more openings in the pyramid, Erasmus thought.

They went inside, after which Izumi closed the entrance. Apart from the light emitted by Izumi's torch, it was pitch-dark at first, but after a minute or two lights went on in several places; small, glittering mirrors that had the shape of butterflies.

'What are these?'

'Mirrors, made of obsidian,' Izumi said.

'It feels as if we're entering the underworld,' Erasmus said.

It made him think of Hades, who didn't only dwell at the verge of the ocean, but also in the deepest, darkest, recesses of the earth, in places like this.

'Are we coming to one of the five rivers of death in a minute?' he asked.

'According to a translation, the Codex Rios, the underworld consisted of nine levels,' she said. 'The first level was the surface of the earth, where the entrance was, or the face of a giant toad that devoured the dead and gave access to the eight other levels. The souls of the dead dwelled in the ninth level, which was called Mictlan Opochcalocan, but the toad wasn't the only one that devoured those dead. You see, the Aztecs associated the course the black sun ran during its nightly journey through the underworld with the image of a butterfly (hence the 'butterfly boats' in Pátzcuaro, Erasmus thought), but the crazy thing is that the image of a peaceful butterfly could also be seen in the fearsome, violent, warrior goddess, Itzpapalotl, the 'Obsidian Butterfly' that devoured people during the eclipses of the sun, while for the Aztecs the underworld was an eternal resting-place for the souls.'

Erasmus was thinking of the little snake and the butterfly on Izumi's arm. What was the comparison? he wondered. Or was it just coincidence?

The ground of the tunnel they were going through was very rocky and the path was sloping downward, going deeper and deeper into the bowels of the earth. On the wall he could vaguely distinguish some murals, but it was too dark to see them properly, in spite of some light that was coming in from outside through long, thin shafts.

What would those shafts look like on the outside? he wondered, thinking of his ideas about the light from the sun. People on the pyramids should be able to see those openings or shafts, shouldn't they?

After about a hundred metres, at the end of the tunnel, they came to a small cave, a round space that looked like a waiting-room, because of the stone benches.

'This is how far we got with the team,' Izumi said. 'They didn't want to go any further; they said they had proceeded far enough that day. I couldn't believe it. "Why go back now?" I asked them. "It's still early and I feel we're very close to a subterranean chamber." But they just ignored me, maybe because I was the youngest and only a student, I don't know, and they were already on their way back. I wanted to see more, so I went back later that day, all by myself. I wasn't worried, because I was sure I could find my way back. What I discovered then was amazing; I will show you in a minute. But these guys, my colleagues, they were really strange. It was as if they wanted to keep me away from it all, and the next day I overheard them talking about objects they might find in the pyramid and the money they could get for them. With hindsight I was glad I went back on my own. I didn't even want them to come with me,' she almost hissed. 'That's why I couldn't speak freely to you on the phone. They kept watching me.'

Erasmus looked at her and saw venom in her eyes.

'So where are we going now?'

'Just follow me.'

Erasmus looked over his shoulder as if he wanted to go back to the safety of the world he felt he was leaving behind, but only a trillionth of a second later these thoughts and feelings were interrupted by an incredible, phantasmagoric scene; the butterflies on the wall that reflected the light had started moving. Was someone playing a game with him or was it a trick of the light?

'Wow! This is truly amazing, Izumi. How come those butterflies are moving now?'

'It's got to do with the light, the angle of incidence and the index of refraction and how the stones have been cut. But butterflies are supposed to move, to fly, aren't they? Take care now. We have to slip through a very narrow opening behind this stone.'

The opening was well concealed and very narrow indeed; Erasmus wondered if he could get through. They entered another tunnel, or a room maybe, he thought. It was even darker here than where they had just come from. A fine fragrance, the smell of incense, greeted them; quite different from the musty smell he had expected. They heard some dull sounds over their heads.

'What's that noise, Izumi?'

'Don't be afraid. What you hear are the footsteps of people on the pyramid.'

'OK,' he said, but he wasn't sure, for they had to be quite deep under the pyramid now.

The walls were cold and the ground was wet and slippery. They came to some stone arches, or maybe they were gates, he couldn't see them very well by the faint light that was coming from the peculiar light source Izumi was carrying.

At the eighth gate, or arch, the light, Izumi, halted. She spoke a few unintelligible, Japanese sounding words into the darkness and put her hands together, as if she was going to pray. After that she proceeded in English again.

'I suggest we sit down on those stones for a minute before we go any further. Have you eaten anything this morning?'

'No, I haven't. You told me not to eat anything, didn't you?'

He looked at the huge stones, which, like beds or couches, were lying in a semi-circle on the ground. They were at least ten feet long by three feet wide, he guessed. How did they get here? he asked himself.

Izumi took a thermos flask and two cups from her rucksack and poured something into them that looked like tea, while Erasmus sat down on one of the stones and took some sandwiches out of a carrier bag.

'Wait a minute,' she said, putting her hand on his arm, 'there's plenty of time for that later. You mustn't eat or drink anything with this drink; you really need to be sober, or everything will be messed up. Unless you don't want to try it out. It's up to you.'

'What is it then?'

'It's an ancient herbal brew from South America. Some people compare it to the hallucinogenic Ayahuasca, but it's not the same. Close your eyes when you drink it and you will see the green fields of the land of the Aztecs, feel the dark warmth of the Amazon forest, enter and explore the recesses of your mind and soul. Your third eye will open up and show you the inner and outer reaches of consciousness.'

'What the hell are you talking about?'

'Be at peace with yourself, Erasmus. It will help you find answers to questions, within you and without you, solve riddles and eradicate pains. But it can make you feel nauseous, and if you don't want to, you don't have to drink it, of course. I'm drinking some as well, but I don't want to push you. Actually, maybe it's not such a good idea after all. We should have been better prepared. Let's forget it.'

'No, it's fine,' he said, thinking it wouldn't do any harm. He had become quite curious.

'Are you absolutely sure? Do you really want to go ahead?'

'Yes. Come one. Let's do it together.'

'All right then. Here you are. Take it easy. Take some sips first; don't swallow it too quickly.'

It smelled a bit like Guinness, he thought, and the brown/reddish brew tasted a bit like cider as well, but it had a bitter and sour aftertaste. After a few sips he got a funny feeling in his head and stomach.

'It's not too bad, although I do feel slightly nauseous,' Erasmus said and slowly emptied his cup. His eyes were still closed.

Izumi stood up and spoke some more Japanese words into the darkness, before she turned round again and smiled.

'Don't worry. I'm not going away; I'm only coming back, as you will see.'

Erasmus opened his eyes and smelled the humid darkness of a forest while he saw extensive green fields and, before him, the temple with its columns, niches, a bath and a circular washing-place in the middle. The outside was in and there was Izumi, gracefully proceeding to the bath, a long robe in her hands. She put it on, sprinkled some drops of water on her forehead, kneeled and kissed a stone. She then put a diadem on her head, which was full of tiny, glittering butterflies and in the middle was a moon. She murmured a few more words, a mantra or so and slowly the room they were in became illuminated; not with normal light, for when he looked at Izumi, he saw her in contrasting colours; her Japanese skin had turned greenish, her dark hair was light now and her eyes, that is, the irises, were blue, while her pupils were white, the silver rings on her fingers had a golden glow and the torch emitted black light, strangely scintillating on the silvery wall, where he saw depictions of a black and white sun. Along the wall, in niches, stood black objects, candles, which emitted a dark blue glow and around them were statues of ancient gods and huge butterflies, all in black. Where had they come from? He hadn't seen them before and he thought of what a student at university had told him about an LSD trip. This was cool.

Izumi was wearing a mask now. She looked like a priestess in her coral red dress. Her feet were bare, although the ground was sharp, slippery and rocky. Across the mask, her dress and her body, flat, empty boats were sailing slowly on white water. When the boats were about to go round the corner, to the rear of her body, they turned over, as if they were being dragged along by the strong currents of a waterfall. The boats then metamorphosed into people with masks on their faces. They kneeled, stood up again and merged into one person, after which they disappeared, together with Izumi, into the darkness.

A few minutes later she came back and slowly removed the mask. Erasmus was dumbfounded. The face that used to be Izumi's, was no longer hers; all the fine, female features had gone and he was staring at what looked like an unknown, almost transparent entity. He wanted to shout, call for help, but not a word passed his dry throat and parched tongue. He heard the sound of a broken voice, a mix of Izumi's feminine voice and the male voice of an unknown being, but he couldn't see its lips moving.

'You and I can speak, but we do not need sound. You can hear me, and I can hear you. Fear not, for I am here to help you, to extend a liana to your spirit. Come, look at yourself, through my eye.'

Erasmus saw himself sitting, full of fear. He looked at the entity again and waited, trembling. The voice spoke again.

'I am part of the unbounded conscious, infinity, 無限大, the origin and fusion of duality, Energia. This is an ancient temple in the Pyramid of the Moon, a womb, an Omphalos, as you know, a meeting-place of the four dimensions and elements, enhanced by light. I will show you time in a handful of water.'

The being, the existence, had a staff in its hand, an image that reminded Erasmus of a picture from the Bible. It was Moses or Aaron's staff and it was coming to life. It turned into a snake and looked at him, before changing back again into the staff. The being touched a rock with it; water came pouring out and formed a pool. The staff dissolved in the green reflection of the water and became invisible. The being proceeded to the water, dipped one hand into it and sprinkled some drops on Erasmus before going back to the water, this time dipping both hands into it and while 'it' was washing its face and arms, the diadem on its head came to life; white butterflies, started moving their wings up and down, as if they were basking in the sun.

The same deflections of a light beam that made these butterflies move, revealed a series of wonderful murals, all in contrasting colours, depicting how different cultures envisaged the creation of the world and the origin of the gods. Erasmus saw a depiction of how gods were 'born' from an incredibly big, imposing tree, an ancient oak. In each successive picture the tree grew larger, while losing its leaves and twigs. Even the thick, big branches at the bottom gradually disappeared, until there remained a gigantic, virtually bare trunk with beautiful branches at the top, thicker and thinner ones, full of leaves, reaching the very sky. In the following picture the tree had split twice, crosswise, from top to bottom, leaving four quarters. One of these changed into a super god and another into a super goddess. Underneath these pictures he read the names Caelus and Terra, the Roman gods of heaven and earth and they were still connected to each other, literally, on the inside of their trunks, by long wooden threads, filaments, which hadn't been cleft, while at the top intertwining branches made it impossible to see which branches belonged to which split part of the trunk. In the next picture these two parts had been disentangled and become heaven and earth. The two remaining quarters of the tree were split a few more times to become lesser gods. Underneath one of the pictures was a name, Claudius Virgilius. How odd, he thought, a Roman name, here, in a pyramid in Mexico. I must be dreaming or hallucinating.

Next to these murals were some more wall paintings, depicting Huitzilpochtli who, after killing his half-sister, ripped her heart from her body with a blue snake and threw her body off a mountain. Hieroglyphics indicated that Huitzilpochtli stood for the sun, chasing away the stars in the morning, so that the day, or new life, could begin. The Aztecs probably followed this example by ripping the hearts from their victims and throwing their bodies off a temple that was dedicated to Huitzilpochtli. The Avenue of the Dead, Erasmus thought. The last mural depicted a hell with the Greek name Tartarus written underneath. In this underworld, or alternative hell, Erasmus remembered, dwelled sinners and gods that had been defeated, side by side.

There was no other conclusion, he thought. Different cultures were compared here by means of depictions and hieroglyphics, but how on earth was he able to read these hieroglyphics? Was he going crazy, or was he granted an insight into ancient cultures?

'What you see are merely concrete representations of abstract concepts of the conscious on their way around the globe, passing through consecutive rising and falling civilizations, through the minds of numerous thinkers and philosophers,' the voice said. 'There have been "primitive" peoples that were still highly conscious, as some impulses, connective insights, ideas of consciousness, manifested simultaneously in various civilizations around the world, whereas there have also been cultures, both primitive and more advanced ones, who have failed to become more conscious, sometimes due to the perverted minds of only a handful of powerful people, thus frustrating their own attempts to understand these concepts. They sometimes copied ideas from other cultures and civilizations without being aware of what they actually stood for.'

'But who or what are you?' Erasmus asked.

'The one who is speaking to you now is Kaito-Itsuki-no-Mikoto, which means 'exalted sea and tree'. I was a son of Izanagi-no-Mikoto and Izanami-no-Mikoto, who got the assignment from the gods to create Japan. With a spear they received from the gods, they stirred the water. By doing so they got two islands, children, but they weren't good enough and were disowned. Later they had eight more children. I was their third child, the one in between that was never talked about, that never existed. I was the temporary embodiment of a spirit, a soul, and was therefore cast out. I had no spear; I was defenceless, but at the border with the underworld of the outcasts, the doomed ones, I received Aaron's staff, the one Moses later took over from him. It was the staff that was transformed into a serpent and swallowed the serpents of the Egyptian sorcerers at the court of the Pharaoh, and became a staff again. It was later used by Moses to part the Red Sea and to get water from a rock. It's a staff that revitalises water, so me, as it were and is an antidote to evil.

'I left Japan; it was my Exodus. I roved the seas of the world and in the end I arrived here, in Mexico. While I was roaming around I came to a tunnel; it was at the border of Lake Toxcoco. The entrance was grown over with grass and thick brushwood and I only found it because of a snake that suddenly disappeared. I went into the tunnel; it seemed endless. Sometimes it went up and then sloped downward again. Here and there it was illuminated by small flies, while in other places there were long pipes, or shafts, going up to the world outside to let in the light, which was then deflected in the tunnel by obsidian. I finally came to an enormous stone, which blocked off the tunnel. I managed to remove it and arrived here, in this part of the Pyramid of the Moon. What I found was amazing: an ancient spirit, or rather a bundle of consciousness, Light, *or*, אוֹר, energy, 気, a reflection of the beings from different dimensions in multiple universes. I became one with it, merged with the infinite tree of all life; call it 同一性, *Gouitsu*, in my language, אֵין סוֹף, *Ein Sof* in Hebrew, ἕνωσις in Greek, or *Monad*, but names are useless and barely adequate.

'This is the empire, the realm, the temple, where thinking is not thinking, where the unconscious can become conscious and the conscious unconscious. I am here to lead those who wander and seek, those who have become outcasts, back to their promised land, their awareness, the Holy Grail. Some aren't strong enough and lose themselves in a cloud, in a life of amnesia, oblivion.

'I, or perhaps it should be "we", have seen many civilisations and cultures, the Chinese, the Aboriginals, the Inuit, the Mongols, the Romans, the Mayas and in the Realm of the Souls I have seen the great ones of the earth, souls with a greater consciousness and purer individuality, but also black souls, sources of destruction, Attila, Talat Pasha, Hitler, Mengele and Stalin, souls that turn around in anti-conscious circles.

'Some people who have come here, like Izumi, also became part of this infinity, charging both my soul and their own. I, the old Kaito-Itsuki, am still here, but many more souls have merged with me over the years. I can still demerge from them whenever I wish, and be an independent entity and they can return to the world and come back again if they want to, like Izumi. We are all free to develop ourselves and learn, while the conscious keeps expanding.

'You came here from the north on a mission, not to quench your mythological thirst, that was only an afterthought, but mainly to find your father. You had no patience, no belief, so you wanted to give up your father, sacrifice and forget him, erase the memories you have of him, but you cannot do that, for he is in you and with you; alive in your unconsciousness. You wanted to reach him and he wanted to come to you, but he couldn't. There's no point in burning the photo you've brought with you. The ash may float away on the stream that flows through this temple and you may think the thoughts of your father will eventually sink into oblivion and delete painful thoughts, but although you can burn a photo, you can never burn a thought. Take out the photo and look at it. Look at your father and into his mind. You can also go back to the past, if you like, for time does not know the past.'

'But I am afraid, Izumi, Gouitsu, Ein Sof, Light, or whoever you are and whatever you call yourself,' Erasmus said.

'There is no name and never be afraid of the unknown or the conscious. Of course, the great consciousness, some like to call it, or him, God, knows the mechanics of creation, has all the foreknowledge, the blueprint of time in space. Everything will happen, no matter what, and it can interfere in many things, also in human nature, but man has a choice, a creative consciousness, so don't be scared. You have your soul on loan.'

'So this great consciousness, or God, is responsible for many things, thousands of disasters and human tragedies, because it allows them to happen,' Erasmus concluded. 'Isn't that terrible?'

There was no answer.

Erasmus thought of his father; he was longing to be with him; not to forget the pain. He saw water, a huge mass of it, and sand. But also love, new, young love, fun and happiness, mountains, heat, and then he saw himself, a little Erasmus, who was playing in the garden with a ball, running, falling. There was laughter, he felt love. In his funny balloon pants he sat down at a small table, on a small chair, and started reading a book. It was a book he could still remember. His uncle, on a chair in the garden. How absurd! And his dad, smiling; a memory he should never forget. His dad at a desk, looking worried, writing letters, missing his son, a feeling of pain.

The scene was suddenly gone again. It was as if he was looking at a film from another time now and he felt sadness, his dad's sadness. Erasmus got tears in his eyes. His dad, his wonderful dad. Once more he saw some images of himself, as a little boy, and again he could feel love, but apart from happiness, fun and water, there was also this sadness and there were other images, words; he wasn't sure. Zyklon B? Gas? Watchtowers and barbed wire? Helmets and swastikas. He knew those. A baby's face, not his, the faces of two girls and a woman, rooms full of thin, shaven heads, naked people, panic and a deep, dark shadow? He didn't understand, and there were faces he didn't know, and a plane taking off and falling back again. It was a huge plane. He saw an engine come off, just as if he was watching a live broadcast. The plane rolled over and crashed into the ground. Flames everywhere. Tears. Two faces, a man, a woman and the Star of David. Love, he felt love. His dad must have loved these people. Friends, maybe. His dad, pursued, a hooded man with a Kalashnikov, an escalator, screaming silence. Suddenly he saw himself again, and again, but there was also fear and he felt an utter loneliness. His father seemed to be stuck.

'What's going on?'

'I don't know. Only you can see what you see.'

'My father; I think he's stuck in his thoughts.'

'Have you ever heard of the paralytic power of airy thought matter that liquefies? It's like a black hole in the human micro-cosmos, which is full of dark, heavy, anti-thought matter. Light, positive energy, cannot enter or escape from it. It's when there's a multiplicity of emotions that holds someone in its grip, it paralyses him or her and makes that person cry, often out of self-pity, or powerlessness. He or she can only see the world through the lens of a tear and fear. It's quite sad.'

'I see,' Erasmus said and thought of his mother's sorrow and loneliness when his father had left them. But his dad? Why also his dad?

'Now look at yourself, Erasmus, inside out, outside in. What do you see or feel?'

'What do you mean?' he asked, looking at his arms, body and legs.

'I can feel the scars of the motorcycle accident, if that's what you mean. They are itching now, playing up, hurting me.'

He loosened the belt of his trousers, opened the zip and looked at the scars.

'The scars are transparent, as if they've opened up to let something in. The blood's gone green, but I can see the skin before the scars were there, when everything was whole. The scars feel like gel; as if my fingers can slide through them into my body.'

'Scars are special, like sliding-doors to the unknown. They open and close, but never without leaving a mark. Bad things can be taken out through them, but as potential disturbers of balanced fields in human bodies, they will always need attention, will always be reminders of the unusual. They may play up like the mental scars of the past, until some form of healing, balance, is achieved.'

'I understand. I've also been lucky; I could've been killed. Maybe it wasn't my time yet.'

'No, it wasn't. Your soul has a long way to go. But beware of darkness, whose cold, dark cloud may become your shroud and catch you when you least expect it.'

'What is a soul?'

'Let me show you.'

Erasmus felt himself floating around on the water of a vast, green, warm sea. There were thousands of luminous, white bubbles, all around him. The sea turned blue, then black and it began to dawn upon him that it wasn't a sea at all, but the universe, with millions of stars, a Milky Way. He was a foetus in the warm womb of the cosmos, his own limited unconsciousness, a soul, an entity he was telepathising with, and it became clear to him that, as a human on earth, there is no soul in your body. A stem cell of the unconscious, it is somewhere in the universe, in another dimension, and constantly communicates with you via waves of a certain frequency, like interacting, wireless devices, via ports that are constantly open.

Through the images that he saw and the beautiful sounds he heard, maybe the after-sounds, the reverberation of the music that accompanied the creation of the universe, Izumi's voice was in his head:

'What you send to your soul are all the impressions and experiences you get on this earth, images, recollections, thoughts. When, for example, you see the blue sky above you, you are reminded of earlier moments, moments when you also had these experiences. Not just the memory, but also the feeling that came with it, or even images from a former earthly existence; they all come back to you.

When people die, this communication with the soul stops. The images they have seen, the things they have experienced, have been filed and can be used by the next human body, although not everyone is sensitive enough to recognise the older experiences, the data of a former human being, a previous life. It may give a 'déjà vu' or '*Aha Erlebnis*' sensation, something they cannot understand at all. When someone receives an older soul, which has all those earlier experiences stored in it, that person seems old and wise, while he or she is still young in age, but time does not know age; it is not sequential. Time is space.

The 'soul matter', their Nebula, gives prompts and lets them think about situations, but if they are no longer able to do that, or if they're stuck for good, the soul may have to leave them, for if it can't grow, it will die and its energy, its entity, will disappear forever in a void and invisibility of antimatter.'

He was trying to think, but there was so much and it was all too complicated and complex for him to take in right there and then. He could normally think deep, but his head was still in some haze and it took a long time before the vision let go of him and gave him back to himself. His inquietude was gradually dissolving and he became more at peace with himself, calmer, like the water of a river that widens the closer it gets to the sea and, like a drowned sailor, who wakes up in the Land of the Dead, he looked around him to see where he was and what was left of him. He still had a body and his being wasn't only a spirit or a soul. He had funny clothes on, with colours that were just as odd. Stupefied he was, elevating himself amidst pieces of driftwood and other, undefined objects from a thick, heavy, sucking layer of mud, after the water of a deluge had retreated, leaving an empty mass of mud behind. The sun was trying to break through the still lingering clouds, lending a cautious tone of yellow to the dispersed, cotton wool sky. The itchy feeling and transparency of the scars were ebbing away, the green blood withdrew behind the closing tissue, the black gods and the butterflies he had seen, grew white before dissolving into nothing. Once more there was a voice that spoke to him.

'The potion you have drunk has been used for thousands of years by the indigenous peoples of South America. It gives you peace and, if your mind is ready, it can help you look back into the past, many thousands of years, and even into the future. Everything is connected, One.'

Erasmus couldn't reply straightaway; it was all too much.

'I don't need to see more of the past. I have enough to think about for the time being and I don't think going back to the past will solve anything. Not now, anyway.'

'You're right; you've got to move on. Go south and you will see your father before you return here. We could have travelled together, but that time will come, maybe too soon, and then we can go wherever we like.'

It was Izumi's own voice that had spoken these words and he saw her face coming back again; the face of the nice, Japanese girl.

High above him sunlight was peeping through a small hole, functioning as a diaphragm. The contrasting colours were regaining their original hues. What had happened? Was it another world he was looking at, a dimension he wasn't part of; a void in his head? He could hear voices, questions, but he couldn't speak. And there was so much to think about, so much.

He knew the *Día de Muertos* was over, as the sun was shining through a shaft that was perpendicular to the side of the pyramid, illuminating the room we were in, but he also knew he would return there one day. How long had he been in the pyramid? he wondered. An hour, six hours, or maybe even longer?

Izumi had put her normal clothes and walking boots on again.

Why he suddenly couldn't get any air, he didn't know, but he became dizzy and got a sick feeling in his stomach; he had to throw up. A second later it came out, with one big gulp, through his mouth and nostrils. Izumi was speaking to him, but he could barely hear her.

'You'll be fine. Don't worry. I was in a trance, when you and I were communicating via our minds.'

Telepathy, my arse, he first thought, but hadn't he also spoken without using any words himself? And what about the things Izumi had said about the soul? The words were there, in his head.

He thought of what the consciousness had said. It reminded him of that equally weird Mrs Hopper and in milliseconds Mrs Hopper's words flashed through his head, *'The woman from the Land of the Rising Sun will lead you to the moon, bring you into her, show you lots of things, but your eyes won't believe what they see.'*

Once again, something Mrs Hopper had said had come true and it was no coincidence; it was too detailed for that. Mrs Hopper just knew things, saw things in a future that was present in the past. Crazy.

The nauseous feeling was coming back; more vomit was pushing upwards from his stomach and he could already feel the awful, stinking wetness, the bitter, black taste or bile, burning and biting in the back of his throat and nose. His whole head was sick and he wasn't sure if he could stand up. Izumi took a tissue from her rucksack and gave it to him. He cleaned his chin and mouth and stood up. He was a bit shaky at first.

'How's it going, Erasmus?' Izumi asked.

'Not too bad, thanks, but I need some fresh air.'

'Sure. Let's go.'

They went back to the tunnel. It didn't take long before they stood outside.

'Fresh air, the sun, at last,' Erasmus said, and smiled.

There were some people waiting, probably colleagues of Izumi's. Although Erasmus couldn't understand what they were saying to her, he could tell by their faces they weren't too pleased. How did they know she was here? Had they come back to smuggle out some objects they had stored away?

Izumi said goodbye to him and he saw she was escorted back to the office by some members of the team. She turned round, looked at him, closed her eyes and put her index finger up. One, he thought. She then entered the office and disappeared from his view. He thought about what had happened in the pyramid, and although Izumi had given him clues, told him to travel south and that he would see his father, she was an unfathomable, weird, sinister person. But there were more things that puzzled him, the murals depicting the origin of the gods, creation, cultures that were compared, the hieroglyphics he could read, and there was also the mystery of the entity. Maybe one day he would understand.

43

A butterfly with a lame wing was crawling over the Avenue of the Dead towards the Pyramid of the Feathered Serpent.

44

'Excuse me, but aren't you Alberto, the patient from the hospital in Santiago de Cuba? I was a nurse there. My name's Roonah O'Shea.'

It took a couple of minutes before it began to filter through in Albert's head.

'The Angel? Roonah? Cuba? *C'est vraiment toi?*'

'Yes, Alberto, erm sorry, Albert; yes, it's really me. Holy Mary, sweet mother of Jesus, this is amazing.'

'How wonderful. Alberto Jésus, the man with the beard. I didn't recognise you at first with your shades and without your beard,' she laughed. 'I still can't believe it.'

'Roonah, this is crazy. I knew it somehow, but it didn't register.'

'From a hospital in Cuba, to a house on the beach in Ecuador. It's almost impossible. God moves in mysterious ways.'

'Every time I saw you, it was as if I knew you,' Albert said. 'But as you know, I got a lot of problems with my memory after my illness and I still struggle sometimes. Somehow I knew your voice, but I just couldn't place it.'

'I heard some kids calling your name this morning, but I ignored it, thinking it couldn't be you. Albert, bloody hell. Sorry, excuse my French,' she said, laughing at her choice of words, 'what a coincidence. Come here, my sweet, let me hug you.'

Albert gave Roonah a perplexed look.

'You do feel skinny, though,' she went on, 'but isn't this wonderful, you and me in Ecuador? It's almost too crazy to be true. Come, let me introduce you to my friend, Desmond.'

She almost dragged him along to Desmond and introduced the two to each other.

'I know it sounds crazy, and maybe it'll make you jealous, Desmond, but Albert and I have known each other for a while. We met when I was a nurse in the Caribbean, in Cuba. I happened to be a nurse in the hospital where he was a patient.'

She gave Desmond a brief version of what had happened, the biological attack, her night duty, the reason why she'd never seen Albert by daylight and, consequently, why they'd never been able to say goodbye to each other when Albert went back to Havana.

Following Roonah and Albert in front of him, Desmond thought about the coincidence that had brought Roonah and Albert together again. But he no longer believed in coincidence; everything worked according to a preconceived plan or pattern, he thought. He and Roonah hadn't met by accident either and it had nothing to do with choice. They had to meet, because there were things they had to share; experiences, ideas, visions, life.

'Roonah, Angel of the Night. I didn't even know your real name,' Albert went on, as if he still couldn't get it. 'Nobody will believe me when I tell them this story.'

'Yeah, I think you're right. The stupid thing is, that last night, or rather this morning, when I saw you standing on the beach, I was dazzled by the light of the early morning sun and didn't recognise you. It's too crazy for words.'

'The fragrance of your perfume; I remember it now. It was Trésor, wasn't it? Things are coming back to me. I smelled it every night you were around; I was even longing for it in those dark, horrible nights. It was so lovely and it reminded me of Paris,' Albert said and looked at her. He could finally see her.

'My sweet nurse, *mon ange*, you were always so good to me. I still can't believe it.'

His angel, his beacon in the darkness of all the pain, all the desperation and shite, was standing here, right in front of him and she had opened the floodgates of his pent-up feelings. Roonah gave him another cuddle, while he, completely engulfed, stood there, just holding her hand.

'But how are you now, Albert? I need to get used to that name. I can still see you before me, with your beautiful beard, lying in that hospital bed. How poorly you were. Sometimes I thought you wouldn't make it. All I could do then was pray.'

Albert just nodded.

'What was the name of that other nurse again?' she asked. 'Oh, yes, I remember now, it was Gabriel, wasn't it? Have you ever heard from him? And what about that policeman and the taxi driver? I can't recall their names. The three of you were suddenly transported back to Havana. What happened after that?'

Typically Roonah, Desmond thought, once she gets started, she can't stop.

Albert didn't know where to begin. Roonah kept asking him new questions and he hardly got the time to answer them. He told her he had moved in with Raoul, that he had become friends with Eduardo, the policeman and how he had managed to leave Cuba and sailed to Ecuador through the Panama Canal. There was no time for the whole story, the event with the Chinese ship or the tragic deaths of Rosalie and Raoul. He would need at least a week, he thought, and what difference did it make, if he couldn't tell her everything?

'Gabriel actually asked me to come and stay with him in his flat in Santiago and later he asked me if I would like him to live with me in Havana, but I wasn't too keen on that, to be honest. He just wasn't my type. Besides, I desperately wanted to get back to Havana to find out if there was a chance for me to get out of the country as soon as possible, because Cuba was becoming like a cage to me. I felt imprisoned. But how did you get here, Roonah?'

'That's a long story too. Why don't we talk about it some other time? You're not leaving this place tomorrow, are you?'

Albert laughed.

'Yes, that's a good idea.'

Wasn't she an exceptional woman, he thought, and remembered how she had helped him overcome his doom and gloom by just being there. Once more he thought of Margarita. Was this what she meant when she said that he would just have to wait a little, that everything would be fine and that 'everything was near'?

'Albert, why did you want to go to South America?' Desmond asked him.

Albert told him about his time in London, the depressing and crazy scenes he'd witnessed there, that he was fed up with all the misery of the Third World War and the crazy people he had seen and met.

'Yes, the tragedy of mankind.'

Desmond was silent for a moment. Something seemed to worry him.

'But why Ecuador? So far away from Paris, from Europe?'

Albert explained that during his stay in London he'd happened upon a gallery where he saw some astonishing pictures by a painter from Ecuador. They had inspired him so much that he didn't only want to see more works of this artist, but also visit the country this man came from.

'But maybe you're asking yourself if I was only trying to escape from everything. But why would you want to keep hanging in misery when there's a choice? Don't we all try to escape from unpleasant situations now and then?'

'I'm not judging you. Actually, I think you're absolutely right.'

'By the way, this is my place,' Albert said, 'and now that you're here, may I invite you for a coffee or something else, or would you rather go home and take off your wetsuits first and come back later? We've got so many things to tell each other, so why not do that over a drink in the shade on my veranda?'

'Sounds good to me, Albert, thanks very much,' Desmond said.

'Yeah, great idea, but I'd like to get out of this hot wetsuit first, if you don't mind,' Roonah said.

'Not at all. See you in a bit.'

Coming back later, Desmond looked at the elegant chairs and the fine table on Albert's veranda.

'You've got style, Albert,' he said before he sat down.

'Let me give you a hand, Albert,' Roonah said.

'Yes, that's fine. Thanks.'

How strange it was to suddenly see Albert in a very different and distant country, a place that was even further away from the U.S. than Cuba, Roonah thought, and here she was, in his kitchen, while the last time she'd seen him he was lying in a strange bed, in a strange city in Cuba. She cast a glance into the living room and noticed the stylish interior, the table, the lace curtains, the tubes of paint beside the easel, a palette and the painting of Rosalie.

'That looks good. What is it?'

'A girl I knew,' he said.

'Oh, OK. Quite abstract. Who was she?' she asked, inquisitively.

He heard a touch of jealousy in her voice.

'I met her in Havana.'

'Tell me a bit more about her, if you like.'

'Well, she was special, even though, unfortunately, I didn't know her long,' he said.

'Oh.'

'By the way, could you take the tea outside? Yes, she was *very* beautiful,' he added, with a smile on his face.

'You're only kidding me,' she said and began to laugh. 'I like your house, Albert, it's lovely.'

'Thanks.'

They took the drinks to the veranda, where Desmond was sitting, gazing at a ship in the distance.

'Desmond, he's made an abstract painting of a young woman in red and yellow,' she said. 'She's absolutely amazing.'

'Well,' Albert said.

'Sorry, Albert, I was only teasing you.'

'Can I have a look at it?' Desmond asked Albert.

'Sure, no problem,' he said, but remained seated.

During the conversation that followed, Albert realised Desmond had seen a lot of the world, that he was widely read and knew the works of Kant, Descartes, Bergson, Montaigne and quite a few others, and also learned that he was specialised in abstract photography, all things that interested him very much.

'Which painter was it that inspired you so much?' Roonah suddenly interrupted.

'Louis Burgos Flor.'

'What I'm going to say will sound really bizarre, but I happen to know that painter. He lived in L.A. and that's where I'm from. He was on TV several times and his house is one of the famous landmarks of L.A. I've also been to an exhibition about his life and attended a lecture about his work. Yes, I agree he's a very good painter.'

'Terrific!' Albert said, 'I wish I could have seen it.'

He told them Flor was from the city of Guayaquil, which wasn't so far away and that he still intended to go there, but that for some reason his plans hadn't materialised yet.

At first Roonah couldn't understand why he hadn't done that yet, if he liked that painter so much, but then she realised that, after everything that had happened in his life and what he had done, he needed to get his life sorted first.

'How about going to Guayaquil together? I wouldn't mind seeing a bit more of his work, or where he came from.'

'Good idea,' Albert said, knowing it would give him that extra push to really go and do it.

Desmond saw something in Roonah's eyes he'd seen only a few times before; big sparks of enthusiasm, as if she was finally going to do something exciting in her life and why didn't she ask him to come along as well? He knew he didn't have any influence on her choices at all. Wasn't he just a control-freak after all, as his own brother had once called him? He hated the idea, but maybe that was only because somewhere, deep in his heart, he knew his brother was right.

Roonah and Albert were talking enthusiastically about their plans to go to Guayaquil together. They could probably make it in a day, but they didn't have to; they had all the time of the world.

'Albert, did you know that Flor even changed utensils and pieces of furniture, such as chairs, tables and cupboards into objects of art? That man was extremely creative and completely captivated by art.'

Albert didn't know this and found it fascinating to hear; it made him all the more curious. They decided to fix a date for their trip right away.

'Sorry to interrupt, or were you guys finished?' Desmond asked.

'*Je suis vraiment désolé*,' Albert said, realising they hadn't only excluded Desmond from their conversation, but from their plan of going to Guayaquil as well.

'Never mind,' Desmond said. 'But could I have a look at your paintings, please?'

'Oh sorry. I had forgotten all about it. Well, they're not that special,' Albert answered, still feeling slightly embarrassed. 'Please come inside.'

Looking around him, Desmond got the feeling he had arrived on a romantic film set, the whole place had been furnished so stylishly. It reminded him a little of *Chatterton's Death*, a painting he had seen at the Tate Gallery in London, years ago; there was something tragic about the place, he thought and, somehow, it made him think of Oscar Wilde and the atmosphere in that strange book of his, *The Picture of Dorian Gray*, but the room was definitely beautiful; perhaps delicate was a better word.

Albert put the canvas back onto the easel, where the light that fell on the painting through the white, lacy, net curtains that were hanging around the bed, gave it the exact lighting it deserved. Desmond was struck by the splendid simplicity of the composition and how the red brushstrokes faded into the white background. Or was it a palish yellow? He wasn't sure, but that only enhanced its beauty.

'Wonderful, Albert. I really like it. The red, the white, the composition.'

'Thanks. 'Would you like to see some more?'

'Sure,' Desmond said.

Albert took the painting off the easel and put another one in its place.

'Wow. This one's very good too, Albert. I like your style.'

'*Merci*, I'm still trying out different things, like using as few colours as possible, a kind of minimalism. It's the feeling these colours give me. They're very powerful, I think, but having said that, I must say I would also like to try my hand at black and white.'

'I see,' Desmond said, when another painting caught his eye. 'That blue one, over there. It's beautiful.'

'Thanks, but it's not finished yet.'

'It's great as it is. I can see now what you mean by powerful. Wow.'

Albert didn't know what to say. Desmond just smiled. They went back to the veranda, sat down and had another drink.

Roonah was quiet; she was thinking about her parents and siblings. She wanted to go home and be alone. Desmond saw her thinking.

'Shall we go home?' he asked her.

'Yes, that's fine.'

'I'm sorry to see you go. You can always come back later, if you like,' Albert said to them.

'Thanks a million, Albert. We'll see.'

45

Erasmus came back from the pyramid in the evening and told Jim what had happened.

'What are you going to do now, Erasmus?'

'Funny you should ask. I've been thinking about it on my way here. I'm afraid the time has come for me to move on; I have to go south. There are so many unanswered questions in my head now. My dad, the past. I'm sorry. How I'm going to get there, I don't know yet, but there's a solution for everything.'

'Yes, I understand,' Jim replied. 'As I said earlier, I'm very happy here with Juanita and her great parents. Of course there's my father in New York, but now it's my turn to start something new and, if I want to, I can always go back to New York, but, as you've seen, Mexico City is also an exciting place, with a long history. I want to seize this new opportunity in my life with both hands, and hold on to it, Erasmus. I'm afraid I'm not coming with you, but if you're looking for transport, why don't you ask Juanita's father? He knows a lot of people.'

46

Bernard and Isabelle stayed at a reasonably posh hotel in Panama City. Like in Costa Rica they felt they had finally come back to the Western world, to civilisation. With its huge buildings, numerous hotels and wide streets, Panama City looked more like a north American city than a Central American one. However, there were also many sad-looking houses and slums. Their hotel was in a beautiful old part of the city with lots of great architectural buildings.

Panama exceeded Bernard's wildest expectations. In the evening they went for walks in the vicinity of the hotel and enjoyed the relaxed atmosphere. They went to a couple of bars and when they stood peering over the water of the Pacific, Bernard even put his arm round Isabelle's waist, although it was rather from force of habit than out of love.

'What do you think of this?' he asked her.

'What do you mean by "this"? Your arm?'

'Well, what do you think?' He wanted to add 'stupid' but managed to bite his tongue. 'Panama, of course. How does it compare to Montreal or Vancouver?'

'I don't know,' she replied.

It was the end of their conversation, he knew. She had had quite a few drinks in the bar they were coming from and found it hard to stand on her legs, which was something that had always annoyed him. He also knew what would happen next; she would start slurring her words and repeating things. How he had always hated that. He would pretend not to hear her then, but she usually didn't notice that, being stuck in her own, small world. Still he sometimes felt sorry for her. She couldn't help it either, could she? It was her background that had made her so miserable.

If they hadn't already planned to go to Ecuador, he would have liked to stay in Panama a bit longer, if it had been a little cheaper, but somehow he didn't feel quite at ease, since Panama had been under the influence of the U.S. for many decades and, if they wanted to, the Canadian authorities could easily track him down here as well.

Isabelle stood staring over the water with a hazy look, ruminating, unaware of what Bernard was saying. Vancouver, what a wonderful city it was. Although it was always busy, with about four million inhabitants, the atmosphere was super. It was; a happy melting pot of many different cultures. The immediate vicinity, with its fabulous scenery, was an oasis and had always given her a sense of peace. Vancouver was a godsend, for Montreal had been Bernard's city, not hers, she thought, and the people she'd met there were friends, or friends of friends, of Bernard's. She was more or less Bernard's appendix then. She remembered going to her 'friends' one day to seek help and support, because Bernard was acting strangely; he had beaten her and she recalled what one of those friends, that bloody Sheila, had said.

'Perhaps you see it the wrong way. He can't be all that bad.'

Isabelle could still hear the irritating intonation with which she'd said it, the bloody bitch.

'What do you mean by me seeing it the wrong way? Can't you see for yourself what he has done? Look at these bruises!'

'But what did you do to upset him?' another ignorant 'friend' had asked.

'I didn't upset him at all. He just started beating me, the bastard. But I can clearly see you don't understand. Sorry to have bothered you, with your indoctrinated minds and your wonderful, boring lives.'

'This is drunk talk, Isabelle. Why don't you sober up?'

'Me sober up? You're the ones that binge at nearly every party and you're nothing but a sad bunch of playmates for your army husbands. I only came to you because I thought we were friends, but all you can do is nag, nag, nag.'

'Why don't you piss off, Isabelle, you're draining our energy,' one of them, the woman who was past her sell-by date, said, the foul smell of stale wine coming from her red-lipped mouth.

Things with Bernard got worse and one day she had enough of it and left him. She met somebody else, the very opposite of Bernard, a very nice guy, who did everything to please her, but it was so terribly boring. She just couldn't go on with it.

How Bernard had changed since that party where they'd met. He was a bit arrogant then, it was true, in his fine uniform, but it also made him cool, macho, attractive, with his short, black hair and beautiful cheekbones, the funny snub-nose, green eyes and broad shoulders. He really did his best to conquer her, but once they were living together, it was as if the spoils were safe, and sometimes he was so unreasonable that she was really scared of him, especially if he didn't get what he wanted. She remembered the night he had forced her to have sex with him, taking her from behind, when she was tired out and just wanted to go to sleep. She had told her new friends in Vancouver what had happened.

'You're crazy, Isabelle. Don't ever put up with such behaviour. It can only get worse. Throw him out of the house, or move out yourself.'

'But I can't. I love him so much.'

'Don't, Isabelle. Forget him. Get out of there.'

She never talked about it again. It was her own problem, wasn't it? She thought about their sex life and how he always wanted to do crazy things. He had tied her up a couple of times, against her will, and one night he had even cuffed her hands and feet when she was fast asleep, saying it would improve their sex life. Maybe for him, she thought, but it scared her if he wanted to subdue her and she remembered the evening he pretended to be a bear. He had lit some candles and told her she was his and that he wouldn't release her, that however hard she would scream nobody could hear outside their cave. Of course she knew people would be able to hear her outside, but that was not the point; it was rather that he said these nasty things with a very serious, sometimes menacing look. There were also times when he wanted her to give him a blowjob. The mere idea. It had made her shudder.

'You're just an old-fashioned bitch,' he told her.

She didn't reply then; only asked herself if perhaps she was.

'You're a-sexual and you always drink too much!' he went on.

'Have you ever asked yourself why? Could it be because of you?' she wanted to ask him, but it was no use, she knew, and said nothing.

She smiled when she thought of the moment when he told her they were moving to Vancouver, because he had been transferred. How happy she was. Bernard didn't care much; he could probably live anywhere and he had no qualms about leaving behind his lonely mother, who was so fond of him. The problem was, and she knew it sounded crazy, that although he could be very peculiar, to put it mildly, he still had an undefinable attraction for her, maybe also because he had this mysterious sensitivity that he was so good at hiding from everybody.

Still looking at the water, she thought of their ocean view apartment in Vancouver. She loved it, and they both liked the city, where eco thinking came natural. In no time at all she had her own circle of friends. It felt like paradise until, all of a sudden, the place turned into a nightmare. The Third World War. It had finally reached Vancouver. One night in November, she remembered it well, she had first felt tremendous shockwaves, and after that the city was shelled from the sea for a short spell of time, maybe for only ten minutes. Vancouver and its inhabitants suffered great hardships and loss of lives, for it was mainly the west coasts of both Canada and the U.S. that were hit. Where they lived, close to the sea-front, was the worst place to be. She tried to phone Bernard, the emergency services and some friends, but everything electronic had stopped working. It was mayhem and there were many hundreds of casualties near where they lived. Isabelle was lucky to be alive.

After the attack it was completely quiet. Everybody was holding their breath. The city was in total darkness. It was terribly frightening and she was all alone, as Bernard was on a military mission in the north of the country. She spent the rest of the night with the neighbours who had also survived the attack. Apart from a broken window, their apartment was OK.

Unexpectedly, Bernard came home the next day. He had a gloomy, uncanny look in his eyes. It scared her; she'd never seen him like this, and although he hardly spoke a word, it was obvious that he was deeply worried. She didn't know what to say or do and he didn't even ask her how she was, but went straight to the bathroom. After a couple of minutes he came out again and said,

'We're leaving. We gotta go. All the chaos. Nothing's working. I'm fed up. We're going to South America; great weather and much cheaper than here.'

'South America? Are you crazy?' she asked, incredulously. She had many other questions, but she noticed he was very short-tempered.

'Start packing tonight,' he snapped. 'We're leaving the day after tomorrow.'

'What about your mother?'

'She can look after herself. If she likes, she can come later.'

She was disconcerted, speechless.

Leaving the room, he added, laconically. 'Oh, before I forget, I have left the army.'

This was another shock. Bernard leaving the army; that was impossible. There had to be something else behind all that, she thought, but even now, here in Panama, she still didn't know what it was, and she wasn't going to ask him. He might get angry. He'd have to tell her himself.

Bernard had created only more chaos. She hardly had any time to do what she needed to do, like saying goodbye to her friends and she didn't know what she could take with her or how they were going to travel. Because of the nature of the war she knew flying was out of the question and most cars were out of order, just like all trains and buses. In the end she packed two large suitcases. They had to leave a lot behind, but as they had rented a furnished apartment, they didn't have to worry about the furniture.

They weren't the only ones to leave the city that day; there were men, women and children everywhere, carrying bags and boxes; some were pushing wheelbarrows. These were scenes she only knew from documentaries about the 1800s or early 1900s and the Second World War. Most people went to relations who lived further away from the coast. It was a weird, frightening atmosphere and Vancouver had changed from a refuge into a place of refugees. There was smoke rising from many areas in the city. Nobody knew who was going where, so it was quite easy for Bernard and Isabelle to vanish into thin air.

'Shall we go back to the hotel?' Bernard asked, interrupting her reminiscences.

'Yes,' she replied. There were tears in her tired eyes.

Back in her room, Isabelle went straight to bed. Bernard had stayed downstairs in the lobby to talk to the receptionist.

'Do you know anyone who could help us get to Ecuador?'

The man scratched his head.

'I might do, but everything is different today and it's all getting more and more difficult. Besides, nothing comes cheap any more.'

Bernard sighed.

The man looked at Bernard, waiting for the next move, as if they were playing a game of chess. Bernard didn't look at the man; he knew the game that was being played. Neither did he say anything. He wanted the man to come forward with a proposal.

'I will ask my contact what possibilities there are,' the man said.

'Great. I look forward to hearing from you very soon.'

He winked at the man and went upstairs. It was dark in the room. He brushed his teeth and got into bed, still thinking about how they could get to Ecuador. Isabelle was already fast asleep, snoring a little, and from her open mouth came the smell of wine and cigarettes. When it reached Bernard's nostrils, he forgot what he was thinking about. Grumbling, he turned over and finally fell asleep, an angry frown on his face.

The next morning the sun was shining into their room through a chink in the yellow curtains. Isabelle got out of bed, drew the curtains wide open to let the light come in. Bernard looked confused around him; for a second he couldn't remember where he was.

'Can't you close the bloody curtains? I'm asleep,' he called.

'It's already past eleven. Look at the fine weather,' she said, teasingly. 'Panama is not such a bad place. Can't we stay here for a while?'

'We'll stay here for a few more days, but after that I hope we can move on.'

The receptionist wasn't going to be back at the hotel until that afternoon, so he needed to be patient and, besides, it wasn't certain if the guy would be able to tell him anything. His mind was already busy again and it was no use trying to get some more sleep. He didn't even get the chance, for Isabelle threw a damp towel at him from the bathroom. It landed on his head and some muffled noises that sounded like curses arose from under the towel, but although he didn't want to, he had to laugh. He was surprised; he didn't know Isabelle like that. She had never done a thing like this before and he liked it.

What was up with Bernard? Isabelle asked herself. He was more relaxed and seemed to be enjoying simple things. Like last night, she thought, when they were out walking and she had pointed at some tiny pink window shutters and told him to look at how some living rooms were illuminated and decorated. He liked it, whereas he normally never had time or patience for things like that. And there were a couple of other things that surprised her, like when he said he liked the sweet fragrance that was coming from some big, yellow flowers in a garden, and the sound of the angelus bells that were ringing all over the old city, when they stood looking at the beautiful sky over the rooftops and the warm, fast-fading colours of the setting sun on the facades of the old houses. And later there was the restaurant where she had let him try some of her food and asked him if he could taste what ingredients had been used for the sauce. He was very nice to her.

He threw the towel back at Isabelle, who caught it, laughing, and he thought she looked even happier than when they were still in Vancouver. It was a good thing she was far away from her stupid friends now, he thought. They had done the right thing.

Isabelle sat down at the dressing-table and furtively looked at Bernard in the mirror. It made her think of the old days, when she had met Bernard and was trying to discover what life was about. By moving into his place she had thought everything would fall into place, but perhaps she had given him too much room and he, being the man he was (a friend of hers, a psychologist, had even called him a 'usurper') had clutched it with two hands, without even thinking about it. It was just one of many things he took for granted. Now that she thought about it, looking out of the window over Panama City, Bernard sometimes was a bit like her own father, who could also be quite bossy and moody. But, to be fair to her dad, that was only when he was getting these prostate problems, and after the successful operation he was the loveliest man in the world again. She smiled. She had always looked up to her dad, like she had looked up to Bernard, when he was an ambitious young man and she desperately wanted to be part of his interesting life. Perhaps too desperately, she thought. She had made his ambition hers in order to be somebody. She had always supported him and was very proud when he became a colonel and she remembered the party that followed, how those women looked at him, the handsome colonel, and at her too, his wife.

She had never believed that friend, the psychologist, who had called him a 'usurper'.

'You're talking rubbish,' she had said. 'There's another side to him that you know nothing about. He's very sensitive, you know. He also loves and writes poetry.'

'How do you know? Did he tell you that?'

'No, he didn't. But I know he does.'

'You see? That's what I mean. I think he sees his love of poetry as a sign of weakness, a soft spot he carefully needs to hide from other people behind a mask of toughness. He's too scared to show that side, afraid it will detract from his tough personality and make him vulnerable.'

Isabelle looked at Bernard again. He was brushing some dandruff off his dark blue blazer. Would she ever get to know him?

After breakfast they went for a walk along the promenade, the Ciclovia Cinta Costera and the marina, to have a coffee at the yacht club. It was very busy there and they heard people talking about the countries they had just come from. There was a kind of excitement, a positive tension in the air, which felt very good.

Coincidence doesn't exist, a German scholar once said, but if they had gone to the other side of the marina, to the jetty near the long, narrow pier and looked over the bay, the ocean and the city, they would have seen Albert, Jack, Jonathan and Steve, drinking champagne, but of course they didn't know them.

From the yacht club they walked to the historical part of the city, the Casco Viejo, which dated from the seventeenth century. It looked imposing with a big wall at the waterfront, built to protect the city from pirates in the old days. There were also several churches, some cosy squares and lots of other interesting sights. Why move on? she wondered. Why not stay here, in Panama City? She liked it. They walked to the Bridge of the Americas to watch the ships sailing up the Panama Canal and the ones that were going to the Pacific.

After dinner they went back to the hotel to hear if there was any news, but the receptionist wasn't in. He had a day-off, but when Bernard saw him the following day, the man still didn't know anything, although he had tried hard, he said. It was a clever move, the chess game was still on. It took another couple of days before he came up with some information, but only because Bernard had threatened to go to a cheaper hotel.

'I have two options for you and your lady,' he said. 'You can either sail or fly to Ecuador. There's a freighter leaving in a week, but I can probably also get you on a small plane that's going to Ecuador in a week or two. The six hundred mile flight shouldn't take more than three hours, I assume.'

'Sounds good. The plane I mean, but how much is it going to cost me?'

The man bent forward, looking aside, as if he was going to tell Bernard the biggest secret in the world, and whispered in his ear how much it was going to cost.

'Are you serious?' Bernard asked indignantly. 'You're kidding me. That's absurd. Is that the best you can do?'

He was shocked and wondered how big the man's share of the profit was.

'I'm afraid so. It's very difficult. I'm sure you know what it's like these days; all the planes are grounded.'

'Yes, I do, but surely you can do better than that?'

'I don't know. I can give my contact a call, but I don't expect the price to be negotiable. Hang on, I'll give him a call now,' he said and went away.

After a couple of minutes the man came back, frowning.

'You're a lucky man,' he said. 'I managed to get almost a hundred dollars off the price, but my contact wasn't very pleased.'

Isabelle knew he hadn't called anyone, for on her way back from the restroom, she had seen the man, a notepad in his hands, making some hasty calculations.

It was Bernard's turn. He moved his ivory tower to a strategic position and said,

'Well, we're not here to please your friend, are we? It's still too much.'

He took some money from his wallet and put it on the counter, saying, 'This is all I'm going to pay.'

The receptionist relented and wanted to take the money, but Bernard quickly put his hand on it.

'Not yet. I first want to know for sure everything's fine, but don't worry, I'll pay you some money up front.'

'I'm sorry, but it doesn't work like that. You'll have to pay me fifty percent, or there's no plane for you. It's a risky business; the plane will have to leave in secret, without permission from the authorities. It's a very dangerous mission,' he said, talking under his breath, looking around cautiously to make it more mysterious.

It made Bernard feel uncomfortable; he didn't know if the money would ever reach the right people, but he had no choice and paid the deposit. The man greedily took the money and made a phone-call in his office. A few minutes later he was called back; they were to leave in two days. It sounded like music to Bernard's ears, but, once more, things didn't go smoothly, for the two days became four and the four became eight. After another couple of days, a lot of hassle and many phone-calls, he was told it could take as many as sixteen days before they could leave.

A few days later a note was pushed under the door of their room. The moment Bernard saw it he immediately pulled the door open, but of course there was nobody there and the receptionist was off that day. He turned round the paper and read what was on it, 'You are being watched'.

As if struck by lightning, he was paralysed with fear, while many words and images flashed through his head. Who? What? Why? Where's that plane? What's going on? Where's my money gone? How can we get away from here? There's no one I can talk to or rely on.

Since his only contact, the receptionist, wasn't in that day, he finally realised there was no other option but tell Isabelle why he had wanted to leave Canada. He wouldn't tell her about the note yet; he didn't want to scare her.

'Isabelle, I need to tell you something, but I don't know how to begin. It wasn't my fault. Shit, how can I tell you? You see, I had some problems with one of my soldiers when I went on this mission to British Columbia. Anyway, it became a rather nasty affair and my superiors sent me home. There was going to be an inquiry, but, pending the outcome, I decided to get out of Canada, but, of course, it was an act of desertion. The other thing is, there's a rumour I took some classified documents with me. It's not true, but it's their way of getting me extradited. They just want to nail me.'

'What will happen if they extradite you? Can we go back and live in Canada then?'

'If they catch me, they…' He tried to go on, but faltered.

'Come on, Bernard. Take it easy. Have some water. Here you are.'

'Isabelle, if they catch me,' he stammered on, 'I will be court-martialled for desertion, or, possibly, treason. They may shoot me.' He sighed and was quiet for a moment. 'The world has changed, Isabelle, for the worse,' he finally said.

She had never heard him stammer before, but she also knew he still had not told her everything. He took her in his arms and looked into her eyes. She couldn't believe this was happening and kissed him. He let her, but had second thoughts and turned away from her. He had humiliated himself, he thought; he was a complete shit.

At first he didn't want to go out into the street any more, but he couldn't imprison himself in his hotel room, so when they went out later that day, he looked around him as inconspicuously as possible. Were they being followed? he kept asking himself. Did he see any suspicious faces? Who would be waiting for them in their hotel room?

Overnight, Panama City had turned into a different place for him. His instinct and military training kicked in; he no longer went to the bars they had been to before and he avoided walking the same streets twice; he had to be unpredictable. Of course, he had also thought of the possibility that the receptionist might have pushed the letter under the door himself, but the man would probably never admit that. Maybe he should talk to him privately or, rather, grab him by the throat and squeeze the truth out of him. The days dragged on, while he felt a prisoner in a free country, a place that had reminded him of the U.S., but it had all been sham.

One afternoon, they were nearly back at the hotel, Bernard saw a couple of men in uniform standing at the entrance of the hotel. They were probably waiting for them. His heart stood almost still and he had difficulty breathing. Between his teeth he said to Isabelle, who hadn't seen the men yet, 'I've forgotten my wallet in the restaurant; I need to go back.'

Because she knew how important money was to him, she didn't doubt his words for a second. On their way to the restaurant he 'discovered' his wallet was in another pocket. Back at the hotel he saw the men were gone. He wanted to go to his room, but the receptionist called him.

'A few minutes ago there were some men here who urgently wanted to speak to you. Two of them were plain-clothed policemen, detectives, who said they were looking for a Canadian colonel, a *desertor*.'

'Is there any chance at all of leaving earlier? We've been waiting for a long time and I still haven't heard anything.'

The receptionist immediately rang up his contact.

'You have to act now; it's urgent,' he said and put down the phone. A minute later they called him back and said it was OK and some other things Bernard couldn't hear.

'You're leaving tomorrow, at five a.m., but unfortunately it's going to cost a bit more, they say.'

Bernard looked a bit glum, but nodded it was OK. He had no choice.

The next day, at half five in the morning, a car stood waiting for them in front of the hotel. They drove off at high speed and half an hour later they arrived at an airfield that looked like an upgraded meadow. A large barn went open and a small, sputtering plane came rolling outside. They got out of the car and no sooner had their suitcases been unloaded than the car drove off, as fast as it could. Isabelle and Bernard just looked at each other.

47

Jack stood on deck, looking at the water. All the miles he'd sailed, he thought, all the things he'd seen and now he was here, sailing along the west coast of America, something he'd dreamt of, but had never thought it would really happen. Wasn't it great? Albert and Steve were laughing; Jonathan had probably told them one of the many jokes he knew. Jack smiled when he looked at Jonathan, the young, sometimes reckless, bouncing ball. He was a bit different from the others. Not because he wasn't a pleasant person, on the contrary, he was always very friendly and spontaneous and everybody loved him, but now and then he could be quite rash, impulsive.

Panama lay behind them now and the next destination, Colombia, wasn't too far away. Its name called up some ambivalent images, as this apparently wonderful country also had a long history of violence, because of internecine fights between drug cartels, the mostly fruitless attempts of the authorities to restore order and the devastation caused by death squads. If you had a choice, you probably wouldn't go to Colombia, but how can you have an opinion if you haven't been there? With mixed feelings they were heading for Buenaventura, a port which lay approximately half-way to their final destination, Ecuador. It would take them two or three days to get there, he had calculated, and possibly another two or three to reach Ecuador. For the time being it was going to be the last leg of their sailing trip, for him the longest journey he had ever made, but he was looking forward to it.

From the moment they were sailing along the coast of Colombia, everybody was deeply impressed by the beauty of this exotic country. Albert, who had had another close look at the books he had bought in Charing Cross Road, said that every year a large number of whales came to this part of the world for the mating season, just like many hundreds of turtles, although their numbers were gradually declining. Looking at the ocean, he thought it was perfect for surfing and if it wasn't for the never-ending battle between drug trafficking cartels, paramilitary organisations and the authorities, this place would be a true paradise. What a pity that this mysterious country, with its white, tropical beaches, palm trees, mangroves, azure seas, woods, rivers and mountains, was shrouded in such a dark, negative haze.

Jack would have liked to sail past Malpelo Island, a high, volcanic rock about three hundred miles off the coast of Colombia, although it was nothing else but a deserted island with only a navy post, different species of shark and where all sorts of other marine animals could be spotted. Unfortunately, it wasn't really on their course.

Early in the afternoon they arrived at the mouth of the river on which Buenaventura lay. There were woods and islands on either side. A little later the first buildings of the town and its harbour came into view. They couldn't see much though, as it was pouring with rain. Apparently, Buenaventura was the wettest place on earth with an average precipitation of seven thousand millimetres per year, Albert said. It was like they were entering another world, after all the wonderful views they'd had of the country earlier that day. They saw pile dwellings, shabby huts of the poor, like a separate village in the water and the moment they sailed into the harbour they regretted coming here, to this godforsaken corner of the world. Ahead of them they saw one big, dark grey dump of large container vessels, coasters, old harbour cranes, which were too tired to raise their wet, rusty heads, broken, burnt-out cars, filth, old sheds and other decrepit storage places. The whole scene exuded an atmosphere of sadness, desolation, pain and poverty. The rain was running from rusty, hollow-sounding, corrugated iron roofs, over planks, pieces of concrete, grass, tanks, tubs, rails or steel bars, onto the ground, where men in wet oilskins were busy putting a large sheet of polythene over objects that weren't supposed to get wet. It was a useless endeavour, for while they were straightening out the sheet, sharp or pointed objects tore it in several places. They then put stones, boards and bricks on top of it to 'protect' the objects underneath against the ruthless, incessantly pouring rain. Rust, water, rusty water, soaked earth, strangely coloured mud, yellow, worn-out oilskins, white helmets, dark, sad faces; it was all a reflection of the realisation that this was all life had to offer the people here. They heard some men on a Chinese freight vessel shouting orders, in English.

'Hey, you, stinking Colombians, get off your lazy arses. Have you never learnt to work? This whole place sucks, and you too.'

Further away, on the other side of the quay, lay some more Chinese ships. Those guys knew very well where to sell and buy their goods.

Wherever they looked, they could see big tree leaves, broken pallets, wood, brown rusty oil barrels, large pieces of polystyrene packaging, plastic bags and sacks floating on the water; it was one big, sad cesspool. The water in the harbour looked and smelled like fresh vomit, thrown up by creeks and several rivulets, like the Duadualito, whose names sounded so beautiful, but the contrast with their appearance couldn't be more striking.

They had sailed too far, simply because they couldn't believe the first pier they saw was the one where they were supposed to moor; it looked far too grimy to be a marina, they thought. Unfortunately there was no other option.

Jack didn't want to leave his yacht alone; he was too scared his yacht would be gone when they returned. Steve and Albert weren't sure either if they wanted to go ashore, but Jonathan had no problem with it; he went ashore and asked some hooded guys he saw on the quay if it was all right for them to be there with their boat. With their ravine-like, wrinkled faces and dark eyes they just stared at him, as if he was an alien, and said nothing, pretending not to understand him, although he spoke good Spanish. A bit further down the quay he saw a few dark-skinned boys, probably of African descent, and asked them the same question. They were quite friendly, but didn't have a clue and said it was probably all right; they'd seen yachts there before. He went back and told the others what he'd heard. They all stayed on board and decided to leave the following day.

Apart from Jonathan they could hardly sleep a wink that night, lying in bed, their ears pricked up, almost waiting for the first suspicious noises, like footsteps on deck, or a boat touching their yacht. But they wouldn't have been able to hear much, for it was pouring with rain all night. The thought that nobody would want to come out in weather like this put them at ease and they finally fell asleep.

Jack woke up early, because the sun shone right in his face. He got out of bed and went on deck. Albert was already sitting there; he had seen the sun shining through one of the portholes and wanted to see what this drab place looked like in the sun. It didn't look too bad now and the people who passed by nodded kindly at him. Jonathan also appeared on deck and said he would go and try to get some fresh food. When he came back after fifteen minutes, he saw policemen, or army people, all over Jack's yacht, but it wasn't as bad as it looked; all they wanted to do was check the passports, look around below deck and find out why they were there.

'I'm not surprised that this town, where the jet set used to come in the previous century, should have become the centre of the cocaine trade in Colombia,' a dockworker, who was standing nearby, told him. 'Maybe there's a link between the two,' he said, laughing. 'I've seen quite a few strange things going on here. This whole cocaine trade is the main reason why this town has so often been the scene of brutal violence. It's true that things have improved a great deal,' he said, 'but the police still keep an eye on all vessels, especially European ones.'

Jonathan went on board, they had breakfast and then weighed the anchor. The next stop was definitely going to be Ecuador. It didn't matter whether it would take them two days to get there, or more.

They sailed down the river back to the ocean where they continued their journey southward, happy to be away from the stifling atmosphere of Buenaventura, although it had been another unusual experience. They stayed quite close to the coast to be able to see the wonderful beaches and forests. Later that day, when they had a look at the map, they saw an island that didn't look too big, and decided to go there. It was called Isla Gorgona and beyond it lay a smaller rock formation, Isla Gorgonilla. Apart from this and some other, even smaller rocks, tiny islands probably, which lay further south, they couldn't discover much else on the map.

When they got closer to the island, they saw the place looked deserted; they couldn't detect any sign of life. They cast the anchor on the west coast of the island, lowered the rubber boat and rowed to the shore. Steve didn't want to come with them and stayed on board. Approaching the green shore, all three became more and more enthusiastic when they saw the beautiful emptiness of the place. Albert got the feeling he was an explorer and could imagine a bunch of savage people, spears in their hands, shouting aggressively, would come running onto the beach.

'Wow, isn't this a cool place?' Jonathan said. 'Doesn't the blue water look inviting? Come on, let's go for a swim.'

He was already taking off his clothes.

'Don't!' Jack called. 'These waters are infested with sharks.'

Jonathan thought of the great white sharks off the coast of South Africa and how surfers and swimmers were regularly mauled there. He quickly put his clothes back on again.

'I don't think I feel like diving here,' he said.

They got out of the boat and pulled it onto the deserted beach, which looked incredibly peaceful and quiet. Somehow they still found this a bit weird, maybe even frightening, for why would no one want to live on such a beautiful island, which was so close to the mainland? Of course, there was plenty of space in Colombia itself, so why would one hide on an island? But what about the ever-present tourists?

Standing on the beach, Jack put his thumb up to Steve to let him know everything was all right. After that the three went further ashore and saw a number of huts among the trees. They were on their guard, watched out and listened. They arrived at the huts and saw they were probably used for tourist accommodation. Jonathan walked round the huts and disappeared into the dense wood beyond them. All of a sudden he let out a terrible cry. Albert and Jack called out to him, but he only screamed. When they got to him, he was lying on the ground, holding his leg, writhing in agony.

'What's happened?' Jack asked.

Jonathan didn't reply and his eyes, which he sometimes opened, were rolling in his head.

'What's going on?' Jack almost shouted.

'*Mon Dieu*,' Albert called, 'what can we do?'

'I don't know. But this doesn't look good at all.'

They weren't the only ones who had heard Jonathan's cries, for two men had arrived, both armed with guns. They had a look at Jonathan's leg and started shouting things in Spanish. Jack couldn't follow them and wondered where the two had suddenly come from, but Albert understood what they said and realised the situation was very serious.

'They think Jonathan's been bitten by a venomous snake. They're very worried.'

The man who was trying to help Jonathan told them in English they were conservation officers. They'd seen their yacht and were on their way to the beach to warn them. The other man was on the phone to their post to tell them what had happened. Within minutes a Land Rover was on the scene.

Jonathan got an injection, but his eyes remained closed and he was saying incoherent things, about South Africa and his mother. Albert, thinking of his own time in Cuba, felt really sorry for Jonathan. The loneliness, an island, so far away from home. Jonathan was put on a stretcher and driven off.

On their way to the post the men told Jack and Albert some snakes on the island were extremely venomous and that no one was allowed to come to the island without permission. Even if they did have permission, they weren't allowed to roam the island on their own, unless they were accompanied by a guide. In fact, they could only walk from the hut where they stayed to the beach and back again, and never without boots or wellies on.

'But there are always people who ignore the rules and some will be bitten by a poisonous snake, sometimes with fatal consequences,' one of them said. Jack and Albert looked at the ground.

Jack had already wondered where the name of the island, Isla Gorgona, came from; he first couldn't figure it out, but because of what the men had told him, he knew what it meant. It came from Gorgon, or *Gorgos*, the Greek word for 'awful' and he thought of the myth of Medusa. She was one of three sisters, called the Gorgons, whose hair had been made from live snakes, if he remembered well.

Rosalie's death flashed through his head, the pain and sorrow they had felt. He thought of what Albert had been through in Cuba, of the incident with the Chinese vessel, and the policemen and soldiers who had 'raided' his yacht this very morning. It was getting to him. What was going to happen next?

When they got to the post, they heard Jonathan was in a critical condition. There was blood running from his mouth and nose; he was in a coma and all they could do was pray for him. The man who was treating Jonathan said he had tried to contact a doctor on the mainland, but he couldn't get through to him.

'Not many people die of snakebites these days, that is, by the sort of snake that bit this young man,' he said, 'but there are victims who get sepsis, which can go together with the dysfunction of important organs, such as the heart, brain, kidneys, lungs and liver. The patient goes into a coma or shock, when the blood pressure drops too quickly.'

He had another look at Jonathan.

'Your friend is very unlucky. I've given him an antidote and tried out other things as well, but nothing seems to work. I don't know why. Holy Mary, I wish I could help him,' the man said desperately, crossing himself. There were tears in his eyes.

Crying, with his head in his hands, Albert was sitting beside Jack, thinking of the shit he'd experienced in Cuba. It was all coming back to him. He felt sick and dejected. He remembered seeing the likeable Raoul deteriorate and die, just when there was a glimmer of hope and, after that, the devastation of Raoul's family. He also recalled the sad faces of many Cubans who had lost loved ones and, like Jack, he thought of Rosalie, the beautiful young woman in her red dress, standing by the yellow painting. He was the last person to see her alive and they hadn't heard any news about her disappearance since they'd left Havana.

Jack couldn't say a word. Through his tears he was trying to read a leaflet which was lying on the table in the waiting-room. It said that in the previous century the island was used as a penal colony for criminals, who had committed violent crimes or serious sexual offences. It was impossible to escape from the island; it was the same as committing suicide, as the island abounded with venomous snakes and the waters around it were full of sharks, waiting patiently for a prey. Trying to cheer up Albert, he said,

'Look at this. It's an article about that man Rogers, the later governor of the Bahamas who dealt with piracy there. It says here the man stayed on this island after attacking some Spanish galleons and he was also the person who inspired Daniel Defoe to write *Robinson Crusoe*, the book I loved when I had to read it for school and which probably aroused my interest in sailing.'

But Albert didn't care and he couldn't quite remember it anyway, because of his terrible memory. Why don't you shut up, he wanted to say to Jack, but he remained silent, knowing Jack was only trying to help him.

Steve was waiting in vain for the rubber boat to return, but it remained empty and there was no sign of Albert, Jack or Jonathan at all. He was getting worried and wondered what was going on, while all he could do was wait, look, wait, walk round, eat, quickly look at the boat again, wait, become more and more worried, scratch his head, go for a pee, stay on deck for fear of missing something, wait and peer at the shore. He couldn't leave the boat, even if he wanted to; there was no rubber boat and he wasn't too keen on sharks.

It was as if Albert had read Steve's mind.

'Shouldn't we let Steve know what's going on?'

'Yes, you're right. I hadn't thought of that,' Jack said. He told the men about it and asked them what they could do.

'I'll go back with you, so that you can tell him what's happened. Maybe he'd like to come here too. And don't worry about your yacht; it's quite safe where it is,' one of them reassured him.

'Thanks very much,' Jack said.

They went to the rubber boat together. Jack got in, picked up Steve and told him the bad news.

'If you want to you, can stay here for the night,' the man who was treating Jonathan told Albert. 'All the huts are empty because of the crisis.'

'I think we shall all want to stay with our friend, but thanks anyway.'

Jonathan's condition, however, was rapidly deteriorating. He didn't respond to anything. There was nothing they could do.

Steve became very emotional; the tragedy reminded him of what had happened to Rosalie. He shut himself off again and prayed; something he hadn't done for years.

They spent the whole night at Jonathan's bedside, while the man who was treating Jonathan was nervously walking up and down. He kept trying to make contact with the doctor on the mainland, but to no avail. Early in the morning the kind-hearted Jonathan, who was so eager to go to Ecuador and Peru to meet people of African descent, the lovely and lively young man, who took such an interest in everything and everybody, passed away. They'd only known him for a very short time and already they had to take leave of him.

Albert took Jonathan's hands in his and it was just as if Jonathan's muscles contracted for a last farewell handshake. It frightened Albert a little, but then he thought of the dream vision he had had in hospital, which seemed to have been etched in his memory. Jonathan's soul had been alone for some time and now his energy had flowed back to the great being, existence, *das Dasein* and the consciousness of the universe. He hoped Jonathan would rise and shine as a black star in the galaxy; a kind of anti-matter, part of the duality and balance of unity, the yin of the yin and yang. He kissed the soft, dark hand of this beautiful young man, Jonathan, the boy God had given and had now taken back again. Once again he had lost somebody who was close to him.

'*Merdre! Merdre!* When will this bloody misery stop?' he called out. He thought of his mother, of Rosalie and the tender Sylvain he still missed so much, especially now, during this lonely search for himself. Who could ever have thought he would go to Paris after losing his mother, to London, Spain, Central America and South America, that he would make a journey through the jungle of his heart and head, led by dreams, experiences and shades? He closed his eyes.

Touching Jonathan's arm, Jack said, 'Thank you for coming into my life.'

Another young person, someone who could have been his son, and with whom he'd sailed many, many miles, from one world into another, had sailed away. There was a kind of callousness inside himself, but also a huge feeling of anger and frustration, and it was fermenting, growing, becoming denser, building up like an enormous thunderstorm, like red-hot magma pushing itself up through a volcano. He could no longer restrain himself; he began to swear out loud and it went on for minutes. The others were petrified; they'd never seen or heard him like this before. It took some time before he calmed down.

'I'm very sorry, guys, for letting myself go like this, but it hurts so much. Maybe this is what life is about. You have to learn, but you stumble and fall; you can't accept the pain of fate, its ruthlessness, and you explode. I'm sorry.'

Steve said nothing and went outside.

It was decided to bury Jonathan's body on the island. There was no other way. Jack helped the conservation wardens dig a grave, while Albert was sitting on a chair, staring at the jungle.

'I want to go back to the boat,' Steve said.

Albert looked at him.

'I think you'd better stay for the funeral ceremony, so that you can take leave of Jonathan in a proper way, something you haven't been able to do with Rosalie. It will help you come to terms with his death, so that you can close another chapter in your own life,' he said.

They didn't have any contact addresses or telephone numbers of Jonathan's family, so the only thing they could do was try and inform his former employer on the Bahamas about what had happened. It was no use postponing the funeral.

The doctor finally arrived from the mainland, but all he could do was establish the cause of death. The man looked at Jonathan's body, shook his head in pity and sighed

The next day a coffin arrived. The rain was pouring down. One of the men said Gorgona had its own cloud, which was always shedding water. They spent another night on the island and had long talks with the men, who told them that, because of the rain, they always had fresh drinking water and, since the penal colony was dismantled and only people who had permission could come to the island, they worked hard to make the ecosystem work well.

'Has nobody ever managed to escape from the island?' Steve asked.

'As far as I know that has happened only once,' one of the wardens said. 'There was a prisoner who had built a raft to outsmart the sharks and he succeeded in sailing to the mainland on the right current, having studied them for a long time. Some years later, however, he was captured in Ecuador where he had abused and murdered a young girl. He was executed, I believe. It is said this island was probably even worse than the notorious Alcatraz off the coast of San Francisco. Would you like to see a bit more of the island? I can show you some beautiful places.'

They got into the Land Rover and went to the place where the penal colony had been, but the greater part was overgrown with plants and trees.

It was still raining on the day of the funeral, although the heavy clouds were hanging higher in the sky and sometimes they could see blue patches. Because Jonathan was a Christian, Jack, as captain of the ship, would conduct the funeral service and read from the bible. When they were standing at the wet grave, with the coffin on two beams, the sky cleared and the sun came peeping through the slowly disappearing clouds, its rays falling on the wet foliage, making pearls of the raindrops and crystal sticks of the water trickling from the leaves. Here and there birds began to sing cautiously and the last, fat drops of water were falling from the trees onto the grass around them. After Jack had read from the bible, the two men lowered the coffin, covered it with some soil, crossed themselves and took a few steps back. Jack, Albert and Steve remained standing at the grave, Jonathan beneath them.

'Don't lose heart, you two,' Jack said to Steve and Albert, 'every cloud has a silver lining.' He threw a spade of sand on the coffin and spoke a few words. Albert followed his example, but Steve averted his eyes and face from the scene. The men filled up the grave and said they would later come back to put a wooden cross with Jonathan's name on it.

In the afternoon the three shook hands with the men and thanked them for their help before they were taken back to the rubber boat. Three men had set foot on this island together and three men were leaving now and still a soul was left behind. As had happened so often before in the course of history, this discovery trip too was overshadowed by death.

The horror, the horror, the horror.

The anchor was weighed and the boat sailed away in silence.

48

Erasmus was strolling through Mexico City. He'd just had breakfast with Juanita's family and didn't mind being alone. In fact, he was happy to plot his own course, think about what he wanted to do and how to do it. He decided to go back to the Palacio de Bellas Artes, the building that had so much impressed him earlier and he didn't want to travel any further without having seen what was inside. The museum, both on the outside and the inside, surpassed his expectations. The exterior of the building was constructed in Art Nouveau style while the interior surprised him with its Art Deco design.

Isn't this fantastic? What a beautiful combination, he said to himself. He loved this style. He had already seen a few beautiful Art Deco style buildings in New York, like the Chrysler Building and the Empire State Building.

In a brochure he read that when the museum was being constructed, the workers found a sacrificial Aztec altar in the shape of the Plumed Serpent Since the building was finished, it had sunk four metres into the soft soil, which, apparently, was nothing compared to some parts of the city that had sunk more than nine metres into the soil due to, amongst others, over extraction of groundwater where the former Lake Texcoco used to be.

There were breathtaking murals to be seen inside and some fine depictions in Art Deco style of serpents' heads on the window arches. The world of antiquity and modernity came together here, he thought. Once more he saw a depiction of the god Tlaloc, while in the crystal roof of the centre he saw another link to Greek mythology, a depiction of Apollo and his muses.

But it was enough for the time being and he wanted to move on. He thought of what the being had said to him about his mythological thirst. It was true. It was his dad he wanted; the rest was diversion. After his visit to the museum he went to the modern part of the city with its huge skyscrapers, which had the most sensational shapes. From there his trip went along the Avenida Cuauhtémoc to Colonia Roma, a district from the beginning of the twentieth century, where he came across all kinds of European architectural styles and at the Plaza de Rio de Janeiro he saw an enchanting, castle-like building, with a rather dubious name, La Casa de las Brujas, 'The House of the Witches', which had a beautiful Art Deco entrance.

While he was walking around, he thought of Juanita and Jim, but it was time to leave this spectacular city, and Mexico, behind in the coming week,, to travel further south. He thought of what Mrs Hopper and Izumi had told him, but he also had to make a decision about what Juanita's father had said to him that, if he liked, the man could arrange a long lift for him. These lorry drivers were incredible. Not only did they know their way about very well, but they also knew lots of people and it wouldn't only be the very cheapest, but also the safest way to travel. The only drawback was that he had no idea how long it would take before he'd reach South America. But did that really matter? He had all the time of the world and all the things he did and the people that he met were building blocks of experience.

'Just do it, Erasmus,' he said to himself.

In the course of the afternoon he went back to Juanita's house and talked with her father about the trip.

'I've heard of a *camionero* who's going to Guatemala and, if you like, you can get a lift to the port of San José on the Pacific Coast, a distance of nearly nine hundred miles and I'm quite sure that man can easily find another *camionero* there, who can take you further south,' Juanita's father told him.

'Let's go for it,' Erasmus said, without thinking any longer.

'OK. We can go and see him on Wednesday. He's at home then.'

The lorry-driver turned out to be a short, unshaven man with a big smile and, rolled-up trousers and a shabby shirt. Although the man didn't speak much English, he was very kind. But why should the man speak English? Erasmus thought. It was about time he learned some Spanish himself, especially now that he knew he was going to stay away much longer than he'd first thought.

He spent a few more days with Jim and Juanita and at the end of the week, on Sunday morning, he packed his rucksack and said goodbye to Jim and his new family.

'Let's get going, Erasmo,' Enrique said, with a big, warm, practically toothless smile.

He had a lot of food and drinks on board of the ancient lorry, with the compliments of his wife, so that they wouldn't starve to death. They left Mexico City via the south east side and very soon they were driving south through very high, imposing mountains. The trip would take two days, Enrique told him.

He didn't have much to say about the scenery, but that was no problem, for the views from the cabin were magnificent. Enrique said he wasn't from Mexico City, but from a town somewhere in the south, called Arriaga, more than five hundred miles away, where they would stop and stay the night with a sister of his.

There was plenty of time for Erasmus to take in the wonderful scenery. He just couldn't get enough of it. Now and then the sun shone brightly in his eyes, which was very tiring, so that he fell asleep a couple of times. They made some stops to eat and drink something from the elaborate supplies 'mother' had given them, after which Enrique would take a nap. He closed his eyes for half an hour, started snoring immediately and sometimes even talked in his sleep. After the first stop Erasmus decided to follow Enrique's example by taking a nap as well. Enrique didn't need an alarm clock; even when he was fast asleep, snoring heavily, or talking, he suddenly woke up, blinked his eyes, started the engine and drove on, as if he hadn't done anything else.

The toll booths on the motorway were all out of order, so they could push on without delay. Before turning left onto the Mexico 190, when they were just under a hundred miles away from their destination, they had a terrific view of the Pacific. It was absolutely stunning what he saw; the dark red, brown, black and sometimes even golden colours of the mountains in front of him. It became even better when they got closer to Arriaga; jagged mountains with unbelievable colours projected themselves on the left, while on the right he got some terrific views of the ocean. He was so glad he had decided to accept this lift. It was no use taking pictures, it was simply impossible to catch what he saw.

Now and then Enrique muttered something, but because of the false air flowing past his battered teeth, it was mostly impossible to understand anything of what the man said. Sometimes Enrique smiled when he was talking, pressing his dark, small, happy eyes together. Erasmus didn't understand what he was saying, but nodded and smiled politely. One thing was for sure, Enrique was a terribly kind person.

When they got to the outskirts of Arriaga, Enrique pulled up and parked his big lorry on a wide road. From there they walked to his sister's house. Funnily enough she lived in a district called Hollywood, but in spite of the name the houses looked very modest. The welcome, however, couldn't have been warmer; Enrique's sister, her husband and their five children were standing outside, waiting for *Tio* Enrique and Erasmus; wine and tacos appeared on the table, while Enrique and his sister were chatting away about all kinds of everything. How great, he thought, these people, their hospitality. He had never experienced anything like this before.

The kids couldn't stop talking to Erasmo, but he understood only very little of it, which the kids, in turn, couldn't understand. They had no idea that apart from Spanish or Nahuatl there were other languages. When he said something in English, they looked at him strangely and began to laugh. The two eldest boys asked him to come and play football with them and very soon he was the focal point of all the kids in the neighbourhood. For the first time he hardly felt his scars when he was playing football, which surprised him. Did it have anything to do with what Mrs Hopper had done, or maybe Izumi? But that had only been a hallucination, hadn't it? He touched his scars, but the skin didn't even feel tight. He could kick a ball without even thinking about it. Wasn't it incredible?

After the game they went back inside to have dinner, which was a party in itself. It was a long time ago he'd felt so happy and laughed so much, he thought, especially with the kids and every time he learned a few more words of Spanish, while he also taught the kids some English words.

'Please, come and see our *recámara*, please,' they said, taking his hands, dragging him to their room.

Apparently they wanted him to put them to bed. Somebody needed him, wanted him. Why? It was so wonderful.

A couple of hours later, after a few more glasses of wine, everybody went to bed. He got the cosy, happy room of the two eldest boys, with a ramshackle bunk bed, while they went to sleep in their parents' bedroom and so he had two beds to himself. He had a good look around him and felt happy. Who could ever have thought that, one day, he would sleep in a creaky old bunk bed in the house of a Mexican family, somewhere in the south west of Mexico?

He realised how happy a man could be if he went back to the basics, an unpretentious home, no car, with laughing, uncomplicated kids who knew nothing about all sorts of technical, electronic gadgets, such as mobiles, ports, you name it; who had real boyfriends and girlfriends to play with, talk to and learn things from. They didn't need to collect as many virtual friends as possible via the so-called social media, with useless, meaningless passers-by in their lives. This was happiness, sheer happiness. Maybe in vain he hoped these kids would stay the way they were at that moment.

What the connection was, he didn't know, but he suddenly thought of his Uncle P.J. in New York, who, it appeared, wanted to share so many things with him, maybe wanted to tell him things, but who was so confined to his own, straight world. He thought of the photo of his father and only at that moment did he ask himself if his father looked like his uncle. How bizarre, that it had taken him so long to think of it. He was longing to find his dad, wherever and whoever he was; like these kids he wanted to feel what it was like to be with a father. These thoughts led him back to Mrs Hopper, to Izumi and the voice that had told him not to burn the photo. Mrs Hopper had said to him that his father was close to him. Maybe she didn't mean this literally, but he now knew his dad was close to him, deep in his heart, in his genes and hadn't he seen in the pyramid that his father was thinking of him too?

He fell asleep on the lower bunk bed, with a smile on his face and blankets that were much too small. It was as if he had become a child again.

The next morning he was woken up by the excited voices of the children.

'Is he still here?' he heard them ask their parents and Enrique.

'Hush.'

'Will we see him before we go to school? Please, Mummy, can we wake him up, please?'

The house was rather noisy, so he couldn't get back to sleep. The sun was shining through little holes in the curtain, projecting dozens of little suns on the wall, the bed and the chair. How wonderful, he thought and he wanted to stay in bed, stay here, with this happy family in Arriaga, but there wasn't much time to think about these things, he found out, for the kids were impatiently knocking on his door.

'*Puedo entrar, Erasmo?*'

Before he had time to answer they had already opened the door and sat down on his bed. After that they climbed onto the top bed and kept on nattering, until their father called them to come downstairs for breakfast. Off they were, running and singing. Erasmus got up, washed and dressed. When he came downstairs, everybody was already sitting at the table.

'*Ven y siéntate junto a mí*,' one of the boys called.

He had an idea what the boy meant and sat down on the rickety chair between the two boys, which they'd kept free for him. They were beaming at him; they were so happy. Once again a survival packet of food and drinks was made for Enrique and himself. How hospitable these people were, he thought again, it was unbelievable.

'Can you take us to *escuela*, *por favor*? the kids asked him, but Enrique was ready to go, so he couldn't go with them. The kids' mouths were more or less wiped clean with the wet corner of a towel, teeth were brushed and their hair combed. They gave Erasmo a cuddle, shook hands; with tomato sauce and all, kissed him goodbye and off they were to school, laughing happily.

He hadn't even had time to think about the trip of that day, but now that it was quiet, he looked at Enrique's old road atlas. The next part of the great adventure, the journey to Guatemala was, almost literally, at his doorstep. Before they went back to the lorry, they said goodbye. Enrique's sister gave Erasmus a big hug.

'You come back whenever you like,' she said, 'you're always welcome. We love you and the children love you too. Adios, Erasmo.'

Christ, he thought, with tears in his eyes, this is the happiest moment of my life. He didn't know what to say; he just shook their hands and kissed Enrique's sister.

Half an hour later they were on their way for the next leg of just over three hundred miles. It was about 180 miles from Arriaga to the border. They'd only just left the town, when they got a great view of the mountains; on the left was the volcanic mountain range of Tacaná, Tajumulco, Quetzaltenango and San Pedro, which stretched into Guatemala and on the right he saw more mountains, lagoons and the ocean. Stupefying! He also spotted some weird circles and mountain terraces, too many actually, to have a really good look at.

Early that afternoon they reached Ciudad Hidalgo and the river that formed the natural boundary between the two countries. After that more volcanoes, rivers and forests followed. They made some stops to smell the clean, fresh air, to listen to the silence and feel the surroundings. Enrique enjoyed it as much as Erasmus did and was happy the young man loved 'his' part of the world so much. At the big city of Esquintla, a place not too far to the south of Guatemala City, they took a right turn and drove towards the ocean and Port de San José, their, well, at least Enrique's, final destination.

The end of the journey was approaching fast; Erasmus could already see the harbour, where a number of ships were lying, waiting to be loaded or unloaded. Beyond the harbour was the ocean, the Pacific. Wouldn't it be cool to travel further south by ship? he thought. Enrique parked the lorry at the terminal of a trans-shipment company. The goods in his lorry would probably be loaded into a ship.

'Could you find out if there are any ships sailing to South America?' Erasmus asked Enrique.

'*No hay problema*,' Enrique said. The friendly man was only too happy to help Erasmo. He went straight into the office at the terminal and came back after fifteen minutes with an even bigger smile on his face.

'Well?'

'There are *dos barcos* in the *puerto* that are leaving *en estos dias*. The *barco por ahí* is going to Ecuador and *el otro* to Peru.'

It was very hard to follow what Enrique said, but the names of the countries were clear enough.

'Do you really want to go *muy lejos*? Isn't this part of America *suficientemente linda*?' Enrique asked him. 'If you like I can also ask another *camionero* for a lift.'

Erasmus was about to open his mouth and say something, but Enrique was already gone again. A few minutes later he came back and said,

'There are at least three *camiones* going south, one to Costa Rica and two to Nicaragua.'

That sounded very attractive too and he would definitely see a lot of those countries. At the same time he realised he hadn't come here to visit all sorts of countries; he just wanted to find his father, although he had no idea where to look for him. Maybe he was somewhere in Mexico, or even in Arriaga, in a street round the corner of the street where he had slept. Then Mrs Hopper would definitely have been quite right that they were close to each other. He smiled. He tried to reason out his options, but at a certain moment he was fed up. He couldn't make up his mind, for there wasn't much to reason. It was all about the hackneyed old word 'if', 'If he did this, or if he did that', or 'But if he first…'. It was completely useless. It seemed an even harder decision than the one he had to take in Mexico a few days back. There was only one option; he had to follow his heart, his intuition.

'Something purer than that doesn't exist', Mrs Hopper had said, because his thinking was constantly influenced by data and things he had been taught. Besides, thinking drives you crazy, and if there was one thing you should beware of, it was emotions, he had learnt. Wasn't that also what Izumi had told him about the black holes, anti-thought matter, the paralytic power of emotions? It was true, he thought, remembering his negative thoughts and feelings about his dad when his mother was so sad. Unlike intuition, emotions have nothing to do with purity or objectivity, although it seems they do. His heart told him only one thing now: go to Ecuador.

He couldn't explain what it was, but there was something peculiar about the ship that was going to Ecuador. Maybe he was ignoring his intuition now, but he thought he shouldn't always allow himself to be put off by something he wasn't familiar with, or by negativity or fear. What he was feeling now, wasn't that also some form of intuition? he reasoned within himself. He didn't want to dwell upon it too long. Whatever it was, he had made up his mind, he was going to Ecuador, full stop.

Together with Enrique he went to the office at the terminal to get more information about the ship and make the booking. Because Enrique was beaming with positivity, everything was arranged in no time at all and it was going to cost him next to nothing. What seemingly unimportant lorry drivers can do, he thought. It's incredible. He owed him so much and found it extremely difficult to say goodbye to this special, little man, who hadn't only taken him through a spectacular part of Meso-America, but had given him so much more by going to his sister's family in Arriaga. How lovely they were. If only the world was full of these people, he sighed.

Later that day, when the lorry had been unloaded, the two took leave of each other. It was quite emotional. He pressed the little man against his chest and thanked him several times. There was a connection with Enrique, he could feel it.

Erasmus' words of farewell didn't leave Enrique unmoved either; he had sensed Erasmo's loneliness, his search for something he couldn't express. He also felt he had been a sort of father to him. His little happy eyes didn't squeeze out the sun this time, but the moisture of rising tears. He liked this nice young man, this lonely Erasmo, who, he thought, was still only a child, looking for something important.

'*Vamos a tomar una cerveza*, have a beer?' Enrique asked.

'Have we got enough time for that?'

'Yes, *no hay problema*. It's OK.'

They went to a truckers' café and had a drink. Erasmus wrote down Enrique's address, for he wanted to look up this man again one day. Enrique also gave him his sister's address and repeated what she had said, that Erasmo was always welcome there too, since all of them, the kids included, liked and loved him. Erasmus didn't know what to say; he wasn't used to hearing such sweet words about himself. It was as if he had become part of a new family, he thought.

Several pallets of goods were loaded into Enrique's lorry, so that it didn't have to go back empty. On his way home he was going to spend the night with his sister's family again. That wasn't only much cosier, but it also meant he wouldn't have to sleep in the cabin of his lorry somewhere along the road, which he didn't like very much. Erasmus waved goodbye when Enrique left the terminal.

He walked to what, with a little imagination, could be called a hill. He went to the top and there he stood, all alone, without feeling lonely. In fact, he thought it was a very good moment to realise how far he had come, standing here on a hillock at the coast of Guatemala with the sun going down over the Pacific. His thoughts wandered in images around the world of his past, the parental home with his father and mother, but there was an image he'd never seen before, because he could even see his father's face. Or was it a watered down version of the photo he had in his rucksack? He wanted to hold on to this image, store it in his memory. There were also images of the university, of Jim who had climbed onto the roof, followed by the terrifying moment of the motorcycle accident when he was sliding over the surface of the road and then there was New York and Jim, Mrs Hopper with her music scents and the bed scene, his autistic uncle, Izumi and the scene in the temple, the happy family in Arriaga, Enrique and the lorry.

For one reason or another he remembered a song text by the Beatles, apparently a very famous band from the previous century. It was called *The Fool On The Hill* and was about someone who was all alone on a hill. He never seemed to speak to anyone and perhaps that was why nobody wanted to know him. From the hill he was watching the sunset and saw the world spin round in his head.

Erasmus returned to the image he had just seen of his mother and father. He was probably only two then, or maybe even younger, but images are never really lost, as the voice in the temple had said and also what a man, called Freud, had said in this old book, which was about images that are stored in a part of your pre-consciousness, about repression, censorship, resurfacing images, and images will probably never become conscious again. But wasn't it possible, he wondered, that the picture had found him, instead of the other way round?

The image he saw of his father now was one where his father wasn't wearing glasses. He looked like another father, a shadow father, from earlier in his life and it matched the music, the Beatles. That was why he was suddenly thinking of *The Fool On The Hill*, the music he had heard before, and which he was still listening to later. For him it was a kind of 'primordial' music, linked to an original image of his father and for that reason he had looked it up on the Internet many years ago, and listened to it. He felt the search for an unknown area of his life had already started then and the hill he stood on had triggered his thoughts. He knew Ecuador was the place he had to go to, if ever he wanted to find his father and the image he saw of his father might one day help him recognise his father, he thought.

It was a special, tender moment for Erasmus, because he had always thought the photo in his rucksack was the only image he would ever see of his father. He realised there might be lots of other pictures hidden away in the dark cellars of his, sometimes inaccessible, recollections. That day, because of an association with an image or thought, he was allowed to take a look in one of the cellars and find, somewhere in a corner, under a thick layer of dust, a couple of pictures. He picked them up and, under the poor light of a lamp shaded by cobwebs, he scrutinised them, but he could only distinguish some vague forms. One picture in particular struck him, for he saw something that fascinated, touched him and he took it with him to his studio. There, under a special lamp, he could see a bit more, but still not enough, so, very carefully, he removed the dust and most of the dirt. Now he was better able to see the forms, but they still remained a bit vague. Like a painter who wants to restore and old painting, he took a solvent to remove the old, grimy, layer of varnish. It turned out to be a revelation, for now he couldn't only see the forms he had seen before, but they were much clearer too, and there were also new forms and images that were invisible before.

Maybe this was the reason why he'd selected this very picture. Excited about what had happened, he went back, this time to another cellar, selected a picture and repeated the process, but the result was disappointing, as the composition wasn't quite right. Something was missing. He knew what it was. He fetched his paint and added something to the picture, let the paint dry, varnished the picture again and looked at it once more. Now he was satisfied. For months the painting remained on the easel and every time he looked at it, it made him smile. After some time, still contented, he put it back into the cellar, where the dust was lying in wait, ready to hover around it once again. He went back to his studio and forgot the picture. One day the altered, unreliable image of his father would also fade away.

49

Through a small door Isabelle and Bernard got into the plane and sat down on some seats in the back, right behind the pilot. They couldn't see his face. Only when Bernard had to pay the rest of the money, did the pilot turn round and did they see the pilot wasn't a 'he' but a 'she'.

'Are we on the right plane?' he asked.

Isabelle smiled when she saw the pilot was a woman.

The woman took the money, put it away and taxied to the start of what was supposed to be a runway. It looked more like an old road with grass and other plants growing through big cracks in the concrete. It was just as well Bernard couldn't see what was ahead of them, otherwise he would have doubted if they were able to take off safely.

The pilot, who was so calm at first, suddenly became nervous. Bernard felt uneasy; he was scared his suspicions about a female pilot were coming true, but the cause was of a very different nature. On their way to the runway, the pilot had seen a car appear in the distance; a police car with blue, flashing lights. The two didn't see it, but when the pilot said,

'They are probably looking for a Canadian colonel,' the penny dropped at once. They looked outside through the tiny window and spotted the fast approaching police car. Bernard probably thought he was driving a car, for he pushed his right foot as hard as he could on the floor of the plane to make it go faster and take off more quickly.

The pilot kept her head cool, while the plane quickly gathered speed, now and then jumping on the broken concrete when, all of a sudden, they were off the ground and climbing fast into the palish blue sky. They made a sharp left turn and flew away from the miniature field, the dwindling police car with the two puny plainclothes policemen, the shrinking barn, the high-rise buildings, the bay, the ocean. After that, the still low-hanging, dazzling sun deprived them of this view, as if it had never existed. Gone they were; as free as birds in an infinite sky with some straggling clouds, the sun on the left and an endless, blue-green waste of water with white foam heads on the right.

Isabelle looked down at the earth beneath, where, through the clouds, she could see the Pacific and the magnificent coast of Colombia. What a different world this was, she thought, so different from what she could ever have imagined. Bernard was sitting with his eyes closed, rolling with the movement of the plane, hanging in his seat. He reminded her of a soft, warm, vintage Camembert cheese. Now and then a little snore escaped from his mouth or nose, which the pilot couldn't hear because of the drone of the engine. The woman spoke good English and she sometimes exchanged a few words with Isabelle, keeping her eyes on the dials and on what was going on outside.

'What actually made you want to fly?' Isabelle asked the pilot.

With her rather deep voice the woman said, 'Well, that's a long story. I mean, I need to tell you something else first. I have always been proud of Latin America and of all the people who live there, whether they come from Argentina, Chile, Venezuela, Mexico, Paraguay, Honduras or any other Latin American country. To me it is one great Hispanic America and the people who live there are all connected, for although they may still speak their own Indian language, Nahuatl, or Spanish, even though it is the language of the conqueror, is their lingua franca and unites them. Don't think this is my theory. It comes from my hero, Che Guevara.'

'I didn't know that. How interesting.'

'I am from Peru,' she said, 'and my grandfather, who is in his late nineties now, actually saw Che Guevara, the man who had always been his inspiration. Isn't that extraordinary? Well, my grandfather told me so much about this man that I started reading everything he wrote and I also watched this film, *The Motorcycle Diaries,* which is about Che's trip through America. It's astonishing. He was such a great man and I am lucky to have grown up in a good family with leftish sympathies, like Che.'

'I can imagine that, although I don't know much about Che Guevara.'

'My father was a lecturer at the University of Lima and my mother was a teacher of English and Spanish at a secondary school, so I had a good education and managed to find an interesting job. With the money I earned, I was able to realise the dream of my childhood, get a flying certificate. It has literally given me wings and I have always enjoyed doing exciting, challenging things, like the flight we're making now.'

She then told Isabelle that during the past few weeks she'd been in Panama, partly for her work, but also for another reason, which she didn't want to talk about. By word of mouth she had been asked to help two people, a Canadian colonel and his wife, get out of Panama as quickly as possible and take them to Ecuador.

'I assume you, or your husband, haven't got a clue why you were suddenly pursued, but that's exactly how these things go. You see, Panama, like many other American countries, is still a puppet of the U.S. administration and, if I can contribute a little to subversive activities aimed at reducing the influence of the U.S., I am more than happy to do so. Of course I know my back is being watched and that I lead a risky life, but well, either you have principles or you don't, and if you don't try anything, nothing will happen and your life will be pretty uneventful and meaningless.'

'You're absolutely right,' Isabelle said, thinking of her own life.

Che Guevara's fight wasn't the only example she gave, but also the resistance against dictatorships, armies that ruled the roost, like in Argentina, where, in the past, so many opponents of the military junta had simply disappeared and in Chile, where a democratically elected president was assassinated by the military.

'Fortunately, there have been pop musicians who have stood up for South America, not only by helping to preserve the Amazon rainforest, but also by drawing attention to the people who have gone "missing" during the years of the junta. With their fame and songs they have been able to reach many different age-groups and thus created a greater awareness, both politically and environmentally, hoping people take action.'

She then sang part of a song by Sting. It was called *Cueca Solo, They Dance Alone,* and was about the people that had gone missing during the dictatorship of General Pinochet in Chile. She sang the moving story of mothers who were dancing with their loved ones, their invisible sons and dead husbands, who had all disappeared. They were dancing, alone.

Isabelle was moved.

'What a beautiful song.'

She noticed this woman was very well informed, for after what she'd said about America, she mentioned the struggle for independence of the Basques in Spain and of the I.R.A. for a united Ireland. She even knew the names of the main political activists in those countries, like Gerry Adams.

'Did you know that British politicians from the last century, like Margaret Thatcher and John Major lied to their own people, the men and women who had elected them, about the sincerity and integrity of the Irish cause, the Peace Process and that they put a lot pressure on other politicians, even the President of the U.S., Bill Clinton, not to give visa or even talk to the Irish leaders of the resistance about a solution? Or how the media colluded with these politicians. It's almost too sickening to talk about. They were just filthy politicians, like many after them, such as George W. Bush and Tony Blair, that guy with the eyes of a fox. They were very good at misleading their own people and the world. And they left a legacy of global shit behind.'

Her voice sounded fanatical and if Isabelle could have seen her eyes, she would have seen fire, passion, indignation, anger and disgust.

After that it was quiet for a while.

*

On the beach below them stood a man, with long, grey hair, looking at the ocean, the blue sky, the small plane. Right beside him was a large colony of ants, whose members carried on with their work, imperturbably, while the plane whizzed past. The man shook his head and stepped aside.

*

Why are we flying so low over the water? Isabelle wondered, while she was quietly enjoying the sometimes breath-taking views. She remembered how she used to sit at the window in the back of her father's car, peering outside, over the rolling, vast, savannah-like landscape when they went to see her grandmother and grandfather, who lived a few hundred miles away from them. Her mother usually stayed at home. Her father always wanted her to sit in the back, for her own safety.

There she was, sitting all by herself on that lovely-smelling, very wide, empty back seat. She thought of her sweet grandma, who originally came from Poland, her funny Granddad, who could play music by Bach, Mozart and Chopin on the piano with his eyes closed. He was so easy-going. The car moved up and down when they went through deep potholes in the country road. On the way to their grandparents she sometimes took her father's long hair in her little hands to make curls, or she held him by his earlobes. On the way back she mostly fell asleep. She would never forget those images.

*

La Persistència de la Memòria in *À la Recherche du Temps Perdu*, whereby the time in the plane wasn't the same as on the ground. Time hanging, lost time, with the watch going past its sell-by time, so that it started melting, smelling and growing, all soft like a cheese. Decay of time. Only a timeless, sometimes involuntary, memory was left behind, a tragedy pursuing mankind.

*

She looked at Bernard who occasionally opened his eyes to make them think he wasn't really asleep, but at other moments the sound of his snoring was louder than the drone of the plane's engine. Isabelle and the pilot looked at each other and laughed. It wasn't the laugh, but the expression on the pilot's face that reminded Isabelle of her grandmother.

The pilot didn't ask Isabelle why they were in Panama or what they were going to do in Ecuador. She would have liked to ask Bernard some questions about his role in the Canadian Army, or the army itself. The only thing she knew was that Bernard had deserted the army, which was enough for the moment. She could always ask him about it later. She was enjoying this trip; every time she flew in her plane, over or along *her* countries, she was in her element. Cool-headed though she was, she had still felt the tension when the car with the policemen arrived at the air strip, but she was all right now.

Hopefully her plane wouldn't be spotted on the radar of the Colombian Air Force, but then again, she didn't really care. The thought of freedom and illegality made her feel good, gave her adrenalin. She grinned. It wouldn't be long now before they'd reach their destination. It was a pity she didn't have an adventure like this every week. The very word reminded her of the film she had just mentioned to Isabelle, the great adventure in the 1950s when two men, Ernesto Guevara and Alberto Granado, rode on their ramshackle motorbike, the *Pondarosa II*, a British Norton, through Argentina, Chile and Peru, how it had influenced and probably transformed their lives and vision, and how Che had become a hero of international allure, but was captured and murdered with the help of the C.I.A. in the end, and how both historians and politicians had succeeded in playing down and suppressing the greatness of his human side.

'Watch out!' Isabelle suddenly screamed. 'A plane, and it's very close to us. Oh God. No! Please.'

Bernard woke up with a shock.

'Where?'

'There, on the right.'

The pilot looked around her in terror, realising what was going on and she knew the military plane wouldn't be alone; there had to be one or two more planes, probably behind them.

In a flash Bernard looked to the left, for he knew about their tactics.

'There, on the left, a few hundred metres behind us, another plane! It looks just as obsolete as the one on the right,' he called out.

The pilot realised her plan to fly low above the water to avoid radar detection hadn't worked.

They all knew what the scenario was going to be like. They would either be shot down or forced to follow the plane and land on a military airfield, where they would be arrested. The pilot's head was working overtime, thinking of the military airfields she knew. She had an idea which one it was going to be.

'I don't think they'll shoot us down. They could have done that right away, above the water, if they had wanted to.'

At the same time she had to be very quick to see what options there were.

'I know a few fields where I've landed before. They're not far from the airfield where I think they want us to land.'

She knew she had to pretend to be very submissive or they would never land at all. The plane beside them indicated clearly where they had to go. She followed the instructions and in the distance she could already see the airfield where they were going to land.

'I think they want us to land first, or maybe one of those planes will land first and we will have to land on the parallel runway, unless the one behind us makes another turn before landing. Look, the airfield's right in front of us now.'

While she was looking at the dials, she made radio contact with some people she knew on the ground. Bernard and Isabelle couldn't make head or tail of what she said, it sounded like a coded language.

'Listen,' she said, when she had hung up, 'I will let them think I'm going to land, but at the very last moment I will pull up again and fly to this field I know. It won't take long to get there. The coast of Colombia has no surprises for me. Hold tight now, wish me luck. Here we go.'

Bernard wasn't scared, but Isabelle was terrified; she had only just managed to overcome and suppress all the shite they'd had in El Salvador and now there was another nightmare. She had heard so often that, when a plane almost touches the ground, it is very difficult to take off again without crashing. If this was true, she didn't know, but even if they survived this, and landed safely on the ground, she could imagine being interrogated, over and over again, without being allowed to eat or drink anything, until she was broken. Ultimately they would be locked up in some obscure, squalid, South American prison and they would never get out alive.

'Please, let me die,' she whimpered and started crying. 'I've had enough of it all. All those disgusting men; they're just animals.'

'What are you talking about?' Bernard asked her.

She didn't reply. She was just sitting there, her eyes closed, tears rolling down her face, wishing she was sitting safely in the back of her father's car, and she saw her parents before her, her childhood, her school, her girlfriends, Montreal and Vancouver, as if she was reliving her past in the eye of imminent death.

They were now heading for the runway, where she didn't want to land; she would rather crash and die, be shot or explode. She grabbed the railing next to her seat, for she knew the end was near, when, all of a sudden, she got a very strange feeling in her stomach; they were going up again, climbing into the sky. Only a fraction of a second ago had she seen some soldiers along the runway, waiting for her. They were becoming bigger and bigger, but they had vanished now.

What the pilot did was incredible. She made a right turn, followed by a sharp left and another right, as if she had turned the plane into an acrobat, so flexible it was, so agile. Seconds later they made a deep dive and flew very, very low. Another dive followed. That narrow strip, that meadow, was that where they were going to land? she wondered. Surely not?! It was nothing but a bumpy stretch of grass.

'We've made it! I've shaken them off,' the pilot called out.

'Phenomenal! Terrific!' Bernard shouted.

'Thanks. We've been very lucky. The planes were very old,' she said, with a trembling voice.

Moments later they touched the ground and immediately went up again, bouncing back into the air, making a hop, skip and jump landing, but although the pilot was still very nervous, she had everything under control, Isabelle noticed.

'The moment we've come to a standstill near those trees, get out and go for that overgrown shed on the right there,' the pilot instructed them.

She pulled up.

'Go! Now! Quick!' she shouted.

'Hurry, hurry, hurry, Bernard. Get out!' Isabelle cried. 'Oh my god.'

Chaos in her head, door, luggage, seat belt, run, so much to think about.

The pilot turned off the engine, looked at the sky and listened. It was quiet. She knew they were safe, for the moment anyway. She was convinced the planes would come back. They had to be quick.

'Leave your luggage!' she called to them.

The little, light doors flew open. Isabelle and Bernard ran to the shed. Beside it stood a nervous-looking man in a raincoat, wildly gesticulating that they should follow him. Isabelle looked over her shoulder and saw two men who were busy camouflaging the small plane with netting and branches from trees. She stopped thinking and ran faster than she'd ever done before.

50

On her way back home Roonah was still thinking about her meeting with Albert. Why was she actually going back home, when there was something to celebrate? she asked herself. She didn't have any obligations. She was free and had just met someone she hadn't seen since her time in Cuba. Was it the thought of her parents or a reflection of Albert's loneliness or the impact of the war? Sometimes she couldn't understand herself. Yes, sometimes she just wanted to be on her own, remain in her own world, especially when there were so many things to think about. For a long time she had thought she had to be friends with everybody and that she had to be with the crowd, so as not to miss things, or being missed herself. As far as that was concerned, Desmond was a lot more easy-going. If there was something he didn't want to do, he just didn't do it; he didn't have to be everywhere and with everyone.

She took a book by Virginia Woolf from the cupboard and sat down, but the book remained closed; she could feel the content. Her world. She loved being here, in Ecuador, but sometimes she missed the mist, not just a fog, no, but drizzly, wet mists, like she remembered them from Ireland. Occasionally she even missed the melancholy atmosphere of a village or a town, not a city like L.A., but a European one, although New York was an exception, that city was so European, for somehow it was in her genes, especially when something emotional happened, like meeting Albert, that she found herself in a melancholy mood, as if she was longing for her background, that special piece of herself that could bring oneness and, because of her upbringing and education, it didn't have to be Ireland, it could also be England, and in her head she heard some beautiful lines from the poem, *To Autumn*, and she could see the images that belonged to it, to this ode, which the Romantic poet John Keats had dedicated to that beautiful (perhaps even the most beautiful) season, and which made the sensitive strings of her most inner violin vibrate.

Season of mists and mellow fruitfulness,
Close bosom-friend of the maturing sun;
Conspiring with him how to load and bless
With fruit the vines that round the thatch-eves run;
To bend with apples the moss'd cottage-trees,
And fill all fruit with ripeness to the core;
To swell the gourd, and plump the hazel shells
With a sweet kernel; to set budding more,
And still more, later flowers for the bees,
Until they think warm days will never cease,
For summer has o'er-brimm'd their clammy cells.

This scene, she felt, was so European; no, quintessentially English, and for her this was a piece of DNA she had probably inherited from an English ancestor and something her emotions and feelings were sometimes so much longing, no, yearning for, and she felt these were the very images, the very feelings she couldn't share with anyone, for they were hers; they were part of her innermost self, and she could hear the bees hum, no, dance to the rhythm of the words, while the soft sounds of the rhyming words reinforced the image of warmth and juicy fruits, the slow, stretched out vowels that emphasised the sound of the silence, no, the peace of autumn, and she could see Desmond, with his white hair, as the ripening sun in his own autumn, among laden apple trees, thinking that the warm days would never end; it was because of the energy he had and he was so sensitive, maybe because he had Jewish blood, and despite the warmth of the Indian summer in Keats' poem, her feelings floated with the evanescent clouds whose thin, translucent edges glowed in the low-hanging evening sun of autumn to shade into the white of wintry days and right away she could feel the chilliness, no, the cold and the extensive, vast, desolation, the total physical and mental solitude in the opening scene of *Jane Eyre*, when Jane, sitting behind the bare glass, in the cold window frame of the frigid house of her departed uncle and icy, no, frozen aunt was reading her book, Bewick's *History of British Birds*; Keats' intense autumn had been replaced by a cold winter with sombre clouds, shedding intrusive rain, with Jane identifying herself with the bird, which, at rarefied heights in the ice-cold areas of Norway, Lapland, Siberia, Nova Zembla, Iceland, Greenland and the extreme Arctic region, lived a lonesome and chilly life on deserted rocks, promontories and vast ice fields, and her comparing these images of deathly white areas, where extreme cold is concentrated, to something 'shadowy', like half-understood notions that vaguely float through the head of a child, but in a strange way still make an impression and give meaning to other images, like the rock that stays upright in the waves, the broken boat that has stranded on a deserted beach, the thin, vague, shivery, silvery moon, peering at a sinking ship through beams of clouds, thus concentrating her intense loneliness in a comma in the middle of a sentence, a sad, silent feeling of utter abandonment which made Roonah long for a text from the book in front of her, in which she found a 'warmer', cosier wintry scene, one which, again, was probably so very English, so typically London: *How beautiful a London street is then, with its islands of light, and its long groves of darkness, and on one side of it perhaps some tree-sprinkled, grass-grown space where night is folding herself to sleep naturally and, as one passes the iron railing, one hears those little cracklings and stirrings of leaf and twig which seem to suppose the silence of fields all round them, an owl hooting, and far away the rattle of a train in the valley,* images contrasting nature and industry, light and dark and she could see the posh streets of Bloomsbury before her, walking there with Desmond, Blooms' Bury, bury Blooms, bury Bloom, bury Paddy Dignam, bury the dead, The Dead, the aunts, Gabriel, Gretta, Michael Fury, Bury, snow, loneliness, tears, death, the snow in western Ireland, Galway, Clare, beautiful white snowscapes, peace, peat, bleak, black, the black front doors with their golden letter boxes and doorknobs, reflections of a rich past, the hard, ice-cold, iron gates, softened by the snow, which didn't only lie on top of the iron gates, but on everything, and here was a hot Ecuador and that was a cold, wintry London, Europe and Roonah immersed herself in *Street Haunting*, while asking herself in another stream of thoughts what she was looking for herself, where she was heading, only to be semi-swallowed and dragged along by the text she was reading and remembering this bust of Virginia Woolf's in the small, lovely park, Tavistock Square, where Gandhi was sitting so humbly in the middle and she felt warmth and respect for Virginia Woolf, a woman in a man's world, looking for her own sexual orientation and her place in a dramatically changing world; married to a Jewish man and still being accused of anti-Semitism, psychically damaged by the Great War and her filthy half-brothers, so that, in the end, she put on her coat, filled its pockets with stones and walked into a river to leave this drowning world drowning, taking her ablution, like Ophelia, as one incapable of her own distress, to be blessed before her descent into Hades; and in her grave rain'd many a tear; running their course, welling up in Roonah's eyes, watery, distorted; his hair as white as snow, behind his ears the colour of flax.

Desmond went to Roonah and kissed her dewy eyes.

'Your head's so full, my dear, so full, too full now I should say. Hundreds of images of the war and many thousands more of words and sounds,' he whispered.

He took the hand that touched her moist cheeks, felt the thin fingertips and Claddagh ring, but let her hand go again, for he knew she wanted to stay in her own world a bit longer. He fell silent, put on Vivaldi's *Four Seasons* and sat down to have a look at a series of photos he'd taken in New York, L.A. and San Francisco, all details of mainly modernist and post-modernist buildings. He scrutinised them, asking himself if, after the days of Art Nouveau and Art Deco, the search for new architectural styles had come to an end. That's what it looked like anyway, but, actually, even these weren't pure architectural styles, but omnipresent, general trends in art, he thought. After the Second World War houses, churches and public buildings became more and more minimalistic, plainer, constructed with a lot of cheap building materials, like concrete and steel and they looked more down-to-earth. Not until much later did they experiment with daring designs and glass, absorbing and reflecting, interacting with the immediate environment, nature and other structures, which could all complement each other's beauty or detract from it. The most important thing about art after the 1960s was that artists would no longer be caught in one style, he thought, that they were looking for freedom, for new limits, and for architectural styles that were liked mainly by themselves and a few other people; it was an escape from mass design, or anything else that was dictated from above and which had to be followed by everybody, uncritically and dogmatically.

Although he loved architectural art photography and walking the streets of big cities, he wished he could paint. He remembered that rainy Saturday in September, London, the River Thames, The Tate Modern, how he felt dwarfed by that huge industrial building and, looking at the works of Turner, Dali, Monet, Miró and many others, he remembered being drawn into their paintings, sucked into their compositions, absorbed and dissolved by their landscapes, seascapes, flowerscapes, colourscapes, everyscapes, questionscapes and nothingscapes; how he was becoming part of their art, like a passive pixel in a photograph.

A shadow was looking back at him from behind the rock in *The Mountain Lake*.

In spite of the wonderful surroundings and the excellent climate in this part of the world he was troubled by a sense of dissatisfaction. Although he was looking for peace and quiet, he also loved action, a thing he couldn't get rid of. It didn't mean he needed to go to that bar on the beach every night, for he would only meet the same people there and most of them were sad, miserable bastards, longing for their past lives. No, that was a waste of time, even though he had plenty of that now. He would rather read books like the ones he had recently read, *Quartier Perdu* and *Le Médianoche Amoureux*, with that brilliant short story, *Les Amants Taciturnes,* or articles on scientific discoveries, especially in the field of ecology.

This feeling of being dissatisfied sometimes manifested itself in anger and he knew he was sometimes truculent and grumpy to Roonah, while there was no reason for it. What's my problem? he asked himself. He didn't know, but there was definitely something gnawing at him.

'Desmond, shall we go back to Albert?'
'That's fine by me, but I thought you wanted to stay at home.'
'Well, you know how fickle I am.'

51

Isabelle and Bernard ran towards the barn and the still wildly gesticulating man. The moment they got to him he made for a path that went into the woods. They followed and knew they had to keep running, because it wouldn't be long before a search party would come after them. Perhaps it was already under way. Panting, blood rushing, flying. Isabelle heard a plane flying very low over her head. With infrared they'd be able to see the plane among the trees and them running through the woods, but the planes were outdated, flashed through her head; they might be lucky again, she thought. Where the luggage was or went, she didn't care. Wherever they ran, thin and thick tree roots were sticking out from the sandy, sometimes muddy soil. If they weren't careful, they might trip over them and fall headlong onto the ground. They were so hot, due to the high humidity, their fear and the exertion. Isabelle saw Bernard was lagging behind, while the man in front of them could only just stay ahead of the two women. After a couple of hundred metres the path became much wider. They saw an open Jeep-like vehicle; it seemed to be waiting for them. Oh my god, Isabelle thought, it's over.

'That Jeep, over there,' the pilot called. 'Get into it.'

They jumped in and off they were. Still panting heavily they looked down, at their feet, their clothing. They looked behind them, their hearts pounding. The man who'd run in front of them was sitting at the wheel and had no time to recover in his far too hot, plasticky raincoat. He was short of breath and perspiring terribly, as if he had run a marathon. He tried to take his coat off behind the wheel, but it didn't work and it only made him perspire even more. His face was red-hot; he looked very uncomfortable and Isabelle saw he didn't keep his eyes on the path. Fortunately, he decided to give up his senseless attempts to get the coat off, but he was so hot that, after a few minutes, he started pulling on the other sleeve. The pilot helped him, but still it didn't work. He took his seat belt off to have more freedom, but even that didn't help. A tree, a bend, branches on the ground; the car flew up, as if it had been launched; trees were turning. The blue sky was no longer above them; three wheels turned round freely, while only one of the rear wheels was in touch with the ground.

*

The ants worked on quietly. The grey-haired man walked through the water with bare feet, looking at the turtles.

*

The man in the raincoat was thrown out of the car, while in the distance, behind them, another car came driving towards them at high speed. No one seemed to notice it. The pilot, who had seized the steering-wheel, was too busy trying to get the car under control, while Bernard and Isabelle were dazed, but happy to be alive. Their heads were a tangle of impressions, images, words, sounds, memories, circles, planes, cars, the sky. The pilot managed to bring the car to a standstill, while the other car pulled up right behind them. Two men jumped out. They turned out to be the guys who had taken their luggage off the plane. They went to the man in the raincoat, who was lying on the ground, badly injured. Carefully, they put him into their car.

'I'll drive in front,' the driver said to the pilot.

Quickly they went on their way through the jungle again. How someone could find the way here was a mystery, Isabelle thought, but the pilot knew exactly where they were. They weren't afraid the military would chase them by car; they were more scared of being spotted or attacked from the air, so they resolved to change their course, taking different roads than ones they had planned.

There were several camps in the jungle, where they would probably be safe, but the pilot didn't want to endanger other people's lives, if she could help it. They had to get to Ecuador as quickly as possible.

'Where are we going? What's happening? Are you sure we're going in the right direction?' Bernard asked.

'We're OK.' the pilot answered. 'Are you scared?'

He didn't reply.

Isabelle, who had hoped her life would be over only an hour ago, was sitting next to the pilot.

'Don't worry, Bernard,' she said. 'We'll get there.'

'Where?'

The car in front kept changing direction at the very last moment, so that the pilot sometimes had only just enough time to get round the corner. Apart from a brilliant pilot she was an excellent driver as well. How could she do this dangerous work for the money Bernard had paid? Isabelle wondered, knowing how stingy Bernard was. This woman was a lifesaver, an idealist, no doubt about that, she thought.

The terrain began to change slowly and there were more clearings in the jungle.

'I hope we're not far from the border,' Bernard said.

'What border?' the pilot asked.

'I don't know. A border.'

After a few hours they arrived at a settlement. They got out of the car and were immediately surrounded by a large group of Indians.

They've all got Inca faces, Isabelle thought.

Their car was driven away by a woman and hidden in the jungle, while the injured body of their first driver was carefully taken out of the other car and placed in a hut.

'How is he?' Isabelle asked the pilot.

'Not too good, I'm afraid.'

Isabelle and Bernard stood looking around them; there wasn't much else they could do. They saw how their pilot was embraced and kissed. It was as if they were watching a play, as invisible spectators.

No one is taking any notice of us, Isabelle thought, but that wasn't true, for many eyes were directed at them, from various sides, without them being aware of it.

'It looks as if we're in a time warp, back at the NFE, watching a scene in the past,' Bernard said.

'Yes, you're right. We might just as well have gone back in time to the fifteenth or sixteenth century,' Isabelle answered.

But that too was an optical illusion, for they hadn't seen what was inside the huts, which were only mock-ups. There were people living in them, but many more things were going on inside as well. Somebody came up to them and led them to a veranda. The roof was made of a material Bernard had never seen before; it looked ultramodern, although from the air it probably looked like a primitive dwelling, as it was covered with leaves.

'What kind of material is it?' Bernard asked.

'*No comprendo*,' was all he got.

Maybe I'd better not ask any questions at all, he thought.

'Do you think we're safe here, Isabelle?'

Isabelle wasn't listening to him and she didn't care what material the roofs were made of. She was looking at the men and women.

'Look at those faces, Bernard. Aren't they beautiful? Although they express a certain sadness, resignation, there's also something mysterious about them; they match the environment they're in.'

'What do you mean? Where do you think we're going?' he asked.

They were offered a refreshing drink.

'*Gracias*. Lovely. *Fantastico*,' Isabelle said to the woman who gave it to her, hoping the woman would understand her.

'What's it made from?' she asked, pointing at the drink.

The woman only smiled. Nobody spoke English or even Spanish here, it seemed. The pilot helped her out by asking the old woman who'd given them the drink.

'Apparently, it's made from several plants in this region, but there's no translation for its name,' the pilot said.

More and more people came to them and they all smiled very friendly. Isabelle smiled back and, quite unexpectedly, she received a very beautiful garment, a poncho, from a younger, very beautiful woman.

'Thank you very much. *Gracias*.' Isabelle said.

Bernard had already noticed this woman was pretty. He looked at her from top to toe and smiled and winked at her. The rest didn't much interest him.

Aren't all men the same? the pilot thought. They look tough, strong, cool and sometimes even intelligent, but when there's a beautiful woman around they are reduced to a dick. For a long time people have been saying we are moving towards a more spiritual era, but when I look at Bernard, I'm not so sure.

'We have to move on,' she told them. 'I want to get to Ecuador today.'

'That's all very well, but I have paid for a plane ticket, not a trip in a car,' Bernard said.

'Today's your lucky day. It isn't going to be a car ride.'

'What then?' he asked, frightened.

'We'll first go on foot and after that by car, perhaps. If we're lucky,' said the pilot, whose name they still didn't know.

'Can't we stay here for the night?' Bernard asked.

'That's not a very good idea, as you well know,' she said, 'with the military looking for us. We'd better get out of here as soon as possible. We mustn't endanger the lives of these people.'

'I still wonder why they should be looking for us,' he said.

'I was hoping you could tell me that, colonel,' she answered.

'I really have no idea.'

'Why don't you just tell the truth. Even I know that you deserted the army and there's a rumour you also took some classified documents with you.'

Bernard couldn't utter a word. He now realised that a lot of people knew more about him than he thought. He confessed he had taken advantage of the chaos in Canada to leave the country, in spite of the inquiry that was going on against him, but that he had never taken any documents with him.

'I believe you, but it's a shame, really. I wish you had, but, to be honest, I think things have only got worse and more complicated, as they must be mad you outsmarted them in Panama City and they probably know by now you got away with the help of our organisation, with me in particular. Whatever you do now, you can't make up for that any more. Just get out of here as soon as you can and go to Ecuador. That's probably the best place to go now. At least, I hope so. One thing's for sure, you can't go back to Canada.'

Bernard began to look even more scared than he already did. This pilot was a lot more resolute and vigorous than him. The tables were turned; a woman was setting out a course for him, the macho ex-army man and all he could do was follow.

Isabelle didn't say much; she felt there was nothing to add. She was happy that at last things were becoming clear and she took pleasure in the fact that Bernard's ego was gradually dissolving due to this powerful, impressive woman.

They got a rucksack to put most of their stuff in and they had to change clothes as well. What they couldn't take with them, they had to leave behind. The rucksack made Bernard think of that night at the lake near Prince Rupert, and of Joe, or, actually, Joe's face.

They were quite lucky with the pilot, Isabelle thought, for that woman could also have said it was nothing to do with her, that they should sort out their own problems. In fact, she could easily have handed them over to the military, but fortunately it was a woman with a mission, someone who had her own principles and who didn't shy from danger, she thought, and remembered the determination she had seen when they were making this sham landing on the military airfield and it hadn't stopped there; this woman was prepared to pull them through all this misery and lead them to safety, while taking the safety of other people, like in this settlement, into consideration as well.

After getting a number of instructions, they left. Isabelle could never have imagined that when they left their hotel in Panama City this morning, they would be going on a hiking-tour into the bush that very afternoon, with a rucksack and special clothes.

'It's about fifty miles over the road from here to the frontier. I don't know exactly how far it is through the jungle,' the pilot said.

Bernard made a quick mental calculation and knew they couldn't do more than two or three miles per hour, so it was going to be quite a walk.

'What about food or sleep?' he asked, thinking about the practical things he never had to worry about in the army. He was now one of the ordinary foot-soldiers and he still didn't realise he had to be grateful to the pilot.

'I don't know.'

Isabelle, however, had a lot faith in the pilot and felt much more secure and comfortable than before. The death-wish she had had when they were approaching the military airfield that morning had disappeared altogether and had been replaced by something else, the hope that this adventure wouldn't be over too soon. Mentally she was ready for it, especially when she had put the other clothes on, the walking boots and rucksack on her back. She felt she'd undergone a metamorphosis. This was another aspect of herself and she wanted to hold on to it.

The pilot knew precisely how long the walk would take, but didn't say anything about it; she wanted to see who the stronger of the two was, Isabelle or Bernard, and she didn't feel like putting all her cards on the table in advance, also for security reasons. Besides, it was another good adventure.

The terrain was hardly passable; first they had to climb quite a long distance up a mountain; they could barely see the winding path they had to follow and now and then they had to stop to get their breath back. When they were nearly at the top, they could see the ocean in the distance, dark clouds hanging over it. The path then went along the edge of a gaping abyss; in the depth below them a ravine opened its welcoming, treacherous arms.

Walking along the ridge, the path took them steep down the mountain, back into the jungle. The humidity must be very high, Isabelle thought, for it was just as if she was continuously standing under a shower; the rucksack stuck to her back like a large, warm, clammy hand and, because of the high altitude, breathing was very hard. The soil, the plants, the leaves, everything was wet. The rucksack became heavier and heavier, hotter and more humid; beads of perspiration were running down her forehead, cheeks and neck; time and again she had to squeeze the sweat off her eyelids and eyelashes, but the growing drops just continued their journey down her body, along her neck over her back and her breasts, gathering momentum, and like small, underground streams, they flowed under her clothes and into her boots. All these drops of perspiration began to itch so badly that it was as if there were hundreds of tiny creepy crawlies swarming under her clothes. Perhaps there were.

Very considerately Bernard gave her a hand when they had to climb over fallen tree trunks or branches. Sometimes there were long spells of silence. They were thinking about the most diverse subjects, the events of that morning, Canada, Joe's eyes, the easy journey through the U.S., the army, the trip through Meso-America, the ocean, the countries and islands on the other side, Japan, China, the Philippines, the Third World War, a fight for independence, escaping from violent mercenaries of some drugs cartel, friends.

The pilot told them they had to keep drinking. There was water and they still had some juice the woman had given them, but the result was only more perspiration, more heat and clammier clothes. Isabelle's feet were soaked, with all the sweat in her boots, and sometimes the air pressed heavily on her chest. It was a very unpleasant, stifling feeling and everything she held in her hands first became humid, then wet. They also ate bits from the food they'd been given at the settlement.

She noticed that Bernard had stopped talking about the money he had to pay for the flight; he'd resigned himself to the situation, she supposed. She didn't care about money and didn't even know how much he had on him. It sounded quite old-fashioned, she realised, a woman who didn't know how much her partner had paid and how much something cost, but it wasn't her fault, she thought. Every step she took made her feel stronger, more herself maybe, she thought. It was very heavy for her right knee joint, the one that had given her a lot of problems when she was playing squash, but she was hard on herself; she had to go on and wanted to enjoy every view, every bit of the jungle, in spite of the wet warmth that was hanging on and around her like a wet blanket. She could hear herself breathe and pant when they went uphill again. Beside her, but usually behind her, she could hear Bernard plodding on. He wasn't used to this sort of thing either, she thought, and apart from the short-lived mission in Northwest Canada, he hadn't done any exercise over the last few years, but she did what she could and giving up didn't even cross her mind; she was determined to get to Ecuador, or wherever. The pilot was her example, an icon even, someone who was soaking her off Bernard's small world and making her look at it critically. Since Bernard, as far as his genuine, deep feelings were concerned, was reserved and therefore inaccessible, she didn't really know what was behind that mask of his. She remembered one day, when she was vacuuming his study, she had accidentally found a poem, one he had written himself. He denied it was his, but she recognised his handwriting, for he had written it with a fountain pen. The moment she asked if it was his, he blushed and looked embarrassed. She was surprised, because she had seen another Bernard, a sensitive, gentle person. But it didn't change anything for her, for she was definitely not going to be allowed to see that side of his, ever.

This walk wasn't only good for herself, but also for him, she thought, because they had to sweat it out, come to terms with themselves, push back their limits. More steep slopes, dense jungle, silence, sighing, moaning, complaining and sweating followed. They'd covered about seven or eight miles and the end wasn't in sight yet. Big, fat raindrops began to fall upon the large leaves of trees and plants. Shortly after that the clouds burst and heavy rain started pouring down from the sky. At first it felt like a gratifying shower, but the oppressive heat just lingered on. It became darker and darker, as if the night was already setting in. The heat pressed on Bernard's head and throat; his perspiration was diluted and washed away by rainwater. He noticed the soil was soggier and muddier than before and they had to beware of venomous snakes, the pilot said. It was very slippery and every step he took could send him sliding down the path, the mountain, into the deep, greedy gorge. The worn-out boots were hurting him; they didn't fit well and he could clearly see Isabelle was beginning to show signs of weariness too. By trying to spare her painful knee, the other one started hurting as well, but she didn't complain.

The pilot tried to encourage them and told Isabelle, who was walking beside her, about some funny incidents she'd experienced to keep their spirits up. Ten metres behind them Bernard followed, trudging through the mud. She was beginning to see who the stronger of the two was.

The two women weren't surprised when they suddenly heard a cry. They looked back and saw Bernard sliding headlong through the mud. After a few metres he picked himself up, making all sorts of funny movements with his arms and legs to keep his balance, but his feet kept sliding from under his bottom. He tried to hold on to some thick branches, but it was in vain; he turned round and slid down the muddy slope on his belly and chest. Everything that had stayed mud free, was wet and filthy now. He swore, complained, shouted abuse, which made the pilot and Isabelle burst into uncontrollable fits of laughter. Bernard became angrier and angrier; more cursing and swearing followed.

'I'm fed up. I want to get out of here,' he called.

'Don't we all?' the pilot said. 'But go ahead, no one is stopping you. Have fun. Say hello to all your friends, if you have any.'

Isabelle started laughing again.

'Stop it, you stupid cow!' Bernard shouted.

The pilot got furious and stood up for Isabelle.

'If you can't treat a woman with more respect, you're nothing but a simple, pathetic asshole!'

Saliva flew from her mouth as she spoke these words.

'This is none of your business, interfering bitch. I have paid for this trip. You should have more respect for *me*!'

'What a terrible, presumptuous jerk you are. You're a coward, a pig-headed egocentric, macho dictator. You're not even worthy of the dust of this land. I know a lot of men and women here, in South America, who have been stripped by their governments of everything they had, but they have more balls and decency than you, fattened up bastard, deserter. Damn you. I have risked my own life for you today, twice. Who do you think you are, pathetic creep?'

Her eyes flashed fire; she could have killed him, she felt, this fucker, with his easy life, but she controlled herself. She wasn't going to allow herself to be dragged down his spiral of negativity. He wasn't worth it, and images from the past popped into her mind's eye, of people who'd been tortured, mutilated and murdered, for nothing.

'You're not even worth a single thought. A mountain, a little mud, a little water and, floundering in it, a sad sucker, feeling very sorry for himself.'

Isabelle didn't laugh now. The pilot's face spoke volumes.

Bernard became quiet. Something inside told him he didn't have the right to say the things he'd said. They still knew nothing of her; she shielded everything with great care, her name, who she was, what organisations she belonged to, her work, her contacts, and he knew she wasn't bluffing; everything about her was genuine and true. It felt as if she'd pierced the hardwood shell of his coconut and had arrived at the soft lining and the milk in the centre. Like an eagle she'd plunged from the sky, pounced on her prey and ripped it open. He felt shit, embarrassed, and was ashamed of himself.

'I'm very sorry,' was all he could say when he extended his hand to her.

Isabelle was baffled; she didn't know him like this.

The pilot took his hand, accepted his apologies and finally introduced herself.

'My name's Aquilegia, like the flower.'

'That's a nice name,' he said. 'But what made you a revolutionary?'

'I'm sorry, but I have to protect myself and that's why I can't tell you much about my life and what I've done, but I can tell you this. I've seen so much misery and injustice that I've lost faith in politics and all politicians.'

She gave them some examples, and the more she told them, also about her parents and Che Guevara, the more Bernard began to understand and respect her. It made him think about the western ideologies he had been brought up with and, especially, indoctrinated by. There was water running down his loins and mud all over his clothes. He hated it, but in the end a smile appeared on his face and he even had to laugh at himself.

Half an hour later and soaking wet they reached a major road. There was no car to be seen or heard and because of the rainwater the road looked rather like a river, but at least it had stopped raining. It even seemed to feel fresher, but that was only short-lived. There was one thing they could be sure of, whatever happened, they couldn't get any wetter. They followed the road for some miles until they heard a car.

'Move away from the road. Now!' Aquilegia shouted.

They immediately hid in the dense forest. In spite of the wet road surface, the car, an old American one, drove past at high speed and disappeared round a bend. They re-emerged from the wood. A few minutes later they heard another car approaching. Rush hour in the jungle? They wanted to hide behind some bushes along the road again, but before the car reached them, Aquilegia had recognised it and stepped onto the road to stop it. When it had come to a standstill, she opened the doors. They got in and the car drove off. Apparently, they were at the exact spot where she'd told the driver of the car to pick them up.

Isabelle could understand some words of the conversation that followed and told Bernard. She heard that the man, who had been thrown out of the car that morning, had survived the accident. An Indian doctor had operated on him and given him some herbs. He was no longer in a critical condition. Aquilegia thought it was funny that it was Isabelle who had picked up some words in a, for her, unknown language. After a thirty minute drive they arrived at another settlement, where they were going to spend the night. The border wasn't too far away any more. At last they could have a bath now and put on some clean clothes, Bernard hoped. They had some great food, which was made from ingredients they had never heard of. Bernard began to feel guilty.

'How much do I owe you?' he asked Aquilegia.

She started laughing.

'Nothing. It's very kind of you to ask, but it's all included in the price, even the mud,' she replied, and laughed.

That evening they sat in a village hall, in a large circle, with all sorts of people. They couldn't follow what was said, but Aquilegia translated it for them and explained there were shamans, healers and other sagacious men and women, who had come together to discuss not only diseases and their treatments, but also politics, ideology and the environment. One of them, a man in his late twenties, with big, bulging eyes and an enormous moustache, had some very interesting things to say about out-of-body experiences during sleep. He told a story about a woman who lived in Quito. When she was asleep she saw herself going outside through a window she always left open and flying all over the city, where she met other spirits. Her greatest fear was that somebody would close the window, so that she wouldn't be able to get back into her own body.

'But there was no need for her to be scared,' he said, 'for a spirit does not know windows, walls, doors or anything concrete for that matter. Such an experience is a way of reaching your "primordial I".'

They would have liked to stay there for a couple of weeks; it was all so interesting, in spite of the language barrier, but, actually, they had already embarked on a new journey, maybe the most interesting one so far.

At night Isabelle heard the strangest and most hair-raising noises, animal noises she'd never heard before in her life, while in the part of Canada where she came from there were plenty of wild animals. She had heard mosquitoes buzzing around, but these sounds were different. Were these birds, foxes, jaguars, weasels, a condor maybe, or even bears? she wondered. The sounds echoed on the trees in the jungle and were amplified, or so it sounded. Now and then she lay trembling in her plain bed, very close to a snoring Bernard, and hoped it would become light very soon. The darkness was deeper than she had ever seen before, blacker than black, and everything felt so warm, sultry and sweaty. With open eyes she stared into the thick blackness of the night and every time she heard a strange, screaming sound that tore through her tympanum, she sat up straight, switched on a torch and looked into two white, open, equally frightened eyes. The sounds came from different directions, and sometimes they seemed to come from the corner of their own hut. Maybe it was only her imagination, because they had heard stories about spirits from the jungle and of departed ancestors coming into the house at night. With a pounding heart she lay listening, while all sorts of thoughts began to surface, and memories of what had happened during that day with Aquilegia, and she wondered if that woman's influence on Bernard would be a lasting one, for he was so peculiar and could be so fickle. After a couple of hours her tired mind finally shut down.

When they got up in the morning they were the only ones who had slept badly, as the others were used to sounds from the jungle.

'Have you got time to look at the animals?' one of the people there asked them.

'I'm sorry, but I want to press ahead. We need to be out of the country as soon as possible. I can't take any more risks,' Aquilegia replied.

They took leave from the whole group of kind-hearted, warm, intelligent people they had met in such a short time. They no longer needed the walking boots, the rucksacks and the other clothing. In fact, they had never needed the rucksack. Only if something had gone badly wrong, would they have had to spend the night in the open, Aquilegia said. They had been very lucky, they realised. Not a word was said about their pursuers. Either Aquilegia didn't want to say anything about them or there really was no news. They would never know.

Once more Isabelle received a garment from one of the women, a skirt this time. She realised it wasn't just a gift. She guessed giving an article of clothing had a symbolic meaning; the people accepted her as one of their own. She took the skirt with gratitude, and although her handing in the 'survival outfit' she had worn the previous day had something dramatic, as if she had to return to her 'old' world, getting the skirt was very endearing. After all, it was a present from one woman to another. She would have liked to put it on at once, but there was no time; Aquilegia was already waiting for them in the car. It was such a pity and again she got the feeling that she would have to come back here one day.

Funny Bernard shouldn't have received anything, she thought, but she didn't realise that, without his being aware of it, Bernard had received a different present, something that was just as meaningful and symbolic as the dress and the poncho that Isabelle had received. He had received an insight, learnt a lot from the walking tour, the night with the shamans and the others, the confrontation with the pilot and, especially, with himself, although Aquilegia asked herself how long that would last. She knew him a little better now and realised it would take a lot of time and effort for him to stay on this road to self-knowledge and to discover and show who he really was, for wasn't it much easier to hide behind a mask of toughness?

52

Albert stood looking at the coast. There it lay, at the edge of the blue ocean, the country he had wanted to travel to: Ecuador, at last! Wasn't it foolish really, to travel half the world, defy dangerous currents, high waves, lots of other perils and even death, just for a dream you want to pursue, or to make an abstract picture in your head, coloured by prejudice, come true? He chuckled. Man is a funny thing, he thought, but if you haven't got a drive or an urge, nothing will happen in your life and if you want to make your dream come true, you've got to go for it.

Jack was thinking of Jonathan; how the young man would have loved to stand here with them, and he thought of Spain and how he had met Albert.

'It's your fault, Albert,' Jack said. 'Your enthusiasm and perseverance were so terribly contagious that I just had to come to this part of the world. I could have opted to run around in the same circle, sail to all the ports I already knew, but that wouldn't have added much to my life. I should be grateful to you, I suppose,' he said, laughing, patting Albert on his shoulder. 'Just look at that. Isn't it beautiful? Who knows what happens to us in Ecuador. Maybe I'll meet a beautiful Latina,' he said, 'and what about you, Albert, wouldn't you like to meet a gorgeous, tanned Latino?' he asked, smiling.

'I don't know,' Albert replied, thinking of Sylvain, 'but God moves in mysterious ways.'

'Perhaps a plain hut near a jetty with a panoramic view of the ocean will be enough to keep me happy for the rest of my life. Who knows?'

'You're right. Let's take things as they come, but maybe we should first find a place where we can moor.'

They were fast approaching the shore and all three felt the excitement of their 'provisional', final destination. The very name of the port that lay smiling at them, right ahead, sounded very promising, Esmeraldas.

53

Still standing on the hill near the harbour, Erasmus stood looking over the ocean once more and heard the ship was leaving within an hour. He saw a freight ship that had arrived from Europe that afternoon and its cargo was now being unloaded. Something very big and red was slowly emerging from the bowels of the ship; a London double decker bus. Incredible! He only knew it from pictures and thought even its name, '*Routemaster*', was special. They were old, reliable buses, 'masters of the road', which never seemed to wear out and always brought you safely to your destination. The bus was hoisted from the hold with thick cables that were suspended from a crane. It was pretty dark, but he could still see that one of the cables hadn't been secured properly. He ran to the ship, calling, shouting, waving his arms at the crane driver, who couldn't see very well what he was doing after the wine he'd been drinking over lunch that afternoon. Some dockworkers, who heard Erasmus shouting and saw him pointing at the cable, warned the crane driver, just in time. The bus was slowly lowered back into the hold, secured and then hoisted out again.

On the quay stood an elderly couple, probably the owners of the double decker, watching how the bus was being unloaded. Only at the last moment, when they heard Erasmus shouting, had they noticed what was going on. They came up to him and said, 'We don't know what to say. Without you we wouldn't have been able to go to South America. Thanks ever so much.'

Seeing Erasmus with his rucksack, they asked him where he was going. He told them about his plans.

'Would you like to come with us? We're going in the same direction. You're welcome on board our bus. After Central America we're planning to visit countries such as Colombia, Ecuador, Peru, Bolivia, Chile, Argentina and finally Patagonia, where we're going to look up some relatives, who moved there from Wales some years ago. Apparently, the people in Patagonia speak Welsh too.'

Erasmus needed time to think about this proposal, but there was no time, because his ship was ready to depart. Once more he thought of *The Fool On The Hill*, maybe because of this bus, which could be the start of his own *Magical Mystery Tour*. What a terribly difficult choice this was, with the trip being completely free, even his food was included, but the big question he asked himself was, 'Do I want to be so long on my way to South America and stay with people I don't even know?'

'Why don't you come in and have a look?' the couple asked him.

There were several bedrooms and lots of memorabilia from earlier travels.

'This looks really cool and cosy,' he said.

'There's plenty of room; you'll have a bedroom of your own and, as we said, it won't cost you anything.'

It was so difficult to make a choice, but maybe I will never get to my destination in this way, he thought, what or wherever that is. He thought of the long trip he'd have to make through several countries in Central America, followed by a long journey through Colombia. No, he didn't want this. If fate had it, he would meet these people again in Ecuador and, if he liked, he could always travel further south with them then, but no, not now. He wanted to get to Ecuador as soon as possible and there was more, a gut feeling he couldn't explain that was pushing him into this direction.

Like a condor he had to set a course, follow a straight a line, retain an overall picture, keep things under control and let go of the earth. He had read somewhere that when you go over land, you get stuck, you get attached to the land and other earthly things, whereas the sea will take you to your destination without any feelings attached to it. Maybe a sailor thought differently about this, but for him it meant he had to decline this alluring invitation and put his fate into the hands of the waves that had no origin, no earthing and no goal.

'Thank you for your kind offer, but I'm going by ship. Sorry.'

'I understand, but you will be able to see many different countries and cultures, you won't have to cook and you won't be alone; there's always somebody to talk to, while you also have the privacy of your room,' the woman said, deploying all her charms.

She reminded him of Izumi and the strange things that happened in the Pyramid of the Moon. He was afraid history might repeat itself.

'Maybe we'll meet in Ecuador,' he said. 'And then we shall see'. They thanked him once more. The man shook hands with him, and the woman gave him a cuddle (which he thought was very un-English). He then stepped back, went to the ship, walked up the gangway, and waved at them. A minute later he stood on the upper deck, looking at the double decker bus that was driving past the customs to leave the harbour compound. The thought of the opportunities he might have let slip through his fingers, flashed through his head, but it was no use thinking about it; he'd made his choice. He looked at the stars that were gradually beginning to take their place in the sky. The hawsers were cast off and the ship, unattached now and free, sailed away.

The last lights of the dark, black ship were slowly swallowed up by a deep darkness. Only very far away, where the sky and the horizon came together, could the last orange-red particles of the setting sun be seen.

54

Aquilegia took all sorts of narrow roads and lanes, without the help of a map or satnav, as if she used them every day. As much as she was at home in the sky, she knew her way on the ground, having driven here so many times. Nearly every road and junction called up a story, memories of people, or complicated, perilous situations. Sometimes she had helped resistance fighters get away from Colombia and at other times they were men, women and children who were trying to escape from the terror and violence of the drug cartels. To her these were all challenges, struggles for justice and although some people, especially men, would make fun of her, saying that, being a woman, she wasn't hard enough, they had swallowed those words or taken them back once they were on their way. She had more balls than the average man, she knew, and where they pulled out, she kept her head cool and only became fiercer and more fanatical. She had to laugh at herself now, thinking about these things.

'What are you laughing at?' Isabelle asked.

'I was thinking of a funny incident some years ago. There was this big, arrogant man with a huge ego and he couldn't stand it that he had to listen to me. He was calling me all sorts of names, not to my face, but I heard him talking about me to his mates. One morning, when we had to make a long walk through the jungle, I had taken the belt out of his big trousers and when I said he had to hurry, because we really had to go, he just stood there with his big mouth, holding up his pants with his hands.'

Isabelle laughed.

'That's how vulnerable you are with your big ego,' I said to him, 'if you haven't got a belt you can't even move and you're a sitting duck.

'The guy didn't know what to say. I showed him the belt and said that all I had to take from him to finish him off was his belt. His mates laughed at him and he never said anything unpleasant about me again.'

Isabelle and Aquilegia looked at each other and knew they could have been friends. Isabelle admired Aquilegia's decisiveness and thought she looked very cool in her fighting gear and boots, sexy even, with her slender figure and long, dark, curly hair and her overalls showing the fine contours of her body. She looked at the striking face again and yes, she saw it again, it showed determination, perseverance.

The admiration was mutual; every time Aquilegia looked at Isabelle, she saw a fine woman, a sensitive person, who had perhaps lost herself in this confusing world, someone who had had a lousy time and still had, maybe every day, having to stand up against a man who constantly wanted to boss her around and who sometimes even humiliated her. She felt sorry for her, although she thought every person had to stand up for herself or himself, while she realised this was a gigantic, and sometimes impossible, task for some people.

Bernard noticed the two ladies got on well with each other. It made him a bit jealous, for he was the one who always wanted attention and he wasn't getting any now, sitting in the back of the car as well and he felt like a little boy who was being taken to school and who wasn't expected to say too much. It was as if this woman protected Isabelle from him and, yes, he had to admit it; even one of his mates had made it very clear to him he was a control freak. The guy also told him he had only 'taken' Isabelle, because he knew instinctively he could boss her about, that he had unerringly detected Isabelle's weaknesses and made derogatory remarks about them. They were weak points he was going to put right.

'I bet you keep telling her what she does wrong, how she can do it better. That's how she's lost herself. She no longer knows who she is and that's why she watches so many TV series, so that she can identify with other people, without realising they're all virtual people and that, once the programme's over, she's all by herself again, with her bottle of booze,' his mate had said. 'But, Bernard, it's your fault. You project your own weaknesses on her. You could also try and stimulate her.'

Here in the jungle, too, he had come to realise he wasn't as tough as he thought he was. For all his military training he wouldn't even be able to survive here; he was entirely dependent on the pilot, for whom this jungle didn't have any secrets. She had even helped the people to pick the right, strategic places for camps and settlements, like the place they were now coming from.

It wouldn't be more than an hour before they'd reach the frontier, Aquilegia said. The scenery didn't change much, apart from the fact that the jungle was less dense; there were more and more open spaces, so that they could see the blue sky.

Both Isabelle and Bernard felt a weight being gradually lifted from their shoulders. There were no more countries to traverse, no more secret flights, walking tours through the bush, or policemen who had to be bribed. The end of their long and wearisome journey to Ecuador was finally in sight and they were looking forward to a new future. Where they'd be going in Ecuador, they didn't know yet, but Bernard would prefer to be in a place near the coast, away from the larger towns and cities, which would also be cheaper, he guessed. They were surprised to hear they had already crossed the border and that the narrow road they were on now led to Quito.

She's got guts, Bernard thought, this fascinating, good-looking woman, but she's probably one of those man-hating lesbians. She's gotta be. What a shame.

Isabelle sat silently thinking; it was a pity the end of their adventure was drawing near. It was even worse she'd have to say goodbye to Aquilegia. She would have liked to spend a few more weeks with her, go back with her to the two settlements where she had received the garments. She wouldn't mind it if life was a little less complicated. What she dreaded most of all perhaps, was being stuck with Bernard again, but at the same time she thought he was special and she had the feeling there were still so many unexplored regions in him, areas he closed off for all the world. Wherever she looked, she saw the beautiful landscape of her new future.

Sitting on the rear seat, Bernard was very quiet, like a child in the back of the coach, enjoying his school trip. Had he fallen asleep again? For a moment he wanted to forget all the weird incidents of 'his' trip. Here he was, at last, in the promised land, Ecuador!

55

Erasmus heard he didn't have a cabin of his own on board the ship; he'd have to share one with a member of the crew. For a second he thought of the double decker bus and the friendly people he would most probably never meet again. They were now driving southward, somewhere in the darkness, away from his life. He went into the cabin and saw the man, his cabin mate, with whom he had to share it. He seemed a quiet enough man who, everything going well, wouldn't trouble him. He put out his hand to introduce himself, but the man stayed where he was, sitting on his berth, and completely ignored Erasmus and the hand held out to him. What a jerk, Erasmus thought, and decided to make his bed and unpack his rucksack.

The man kept a close eye on Erasmus and followed every movement he made, observing him from top to toe, thinking Erasmus was a bit, he didn't know, a bit feminine maybe, but not quite, and noticed the young man had the beginnings of a paunch and therefore concluded he came from a wealthy family, which made him think of the poor, desperate family he himself grew up in and how he had had to look after himself from a very early age, sometimes by begging or stealing.

Erasmus didn't know the man normally had this cabin to himself and therefore saw him as an intruder, but, somehow, he felt the man was watching him while he was unpacking his rucksack and, instinctively, as if he sensed some danger, he turned round to find out if his feeling was right. I'm not going to be intimidated by this guy, he thought and looked the man straight in the face, but he couldn't detect a single trace of emotion or feeling; the man didn't even move a muscle, his very eyes were expressionless.

The man knew he was good at that; nobody could ever see what he thought or felt, if he didn't want them to, but in his heart he felt hatred, nothing but deep hatred and profound contempt for everything and everyone he didn't like, and for every person who had had more luck in his life than him. He was embittered, hard, callous, and most men on board were scared of him and he knew it, exploited it. With his almost jet black eyes he stared back at Erasmus' exploring eyes, wanted to make him feel and realise that the negative charge of the silence, and everything in it, belonged to him and the fact that Erasmus kept looking at him, only fanned the fire of his hatred and contempt. What right did this young fucker have to be staring at him like that? he thought.

Erasmus didn't care and, almost provokingly relaxed, went on unpacking his things. He was vigilant though, and listened to every move the man made. In the end the latter stood up and left the cabin, enveloped in the dark cloud of his own negativity. Erasmus thought about the situation and supposed the man was terribly frustrated. He actually felt like going to bed, but it was still early and he couldn't sleep anyway if that man, whose name he didn't know, decided to come back unexpectedly. Still he undressed and lay down on his bed; he'd make a tour of the ship the next day. Lying there quietly, thinking about all the impressions of the day, he could hear music and singing coming in through an open porthole. It sounded good, so he got off his bed, got dressed and went to have a look.

On the deck above him somebody was playing the guitar and singing some songs. Now and then several others joined in for the chorus. On the floor, beside them, stood a large range of alcoholic drinks. When the men saw him they turned quiet.

What's going on? he wondered and got a funny feeling. He wasn't welcome here, that was clear, but he didn't care. He said hello to the men and smiled at them. After some hesitation they started talking and singing again and one of them even offered him a drink, holding out a dirty, old mug to him. Erasmus didn't want to be unfriendly and took it from the man, who filled it, probably with whisky or vodka, he thought. What weird people, what a strange atmosphere. Could he trust these guys? he wondered. He put the mug to his mouth and smelled the strong drink. Was it blue spirit mixed with whisky? Seeing the guys empty their mugs in one draught and wanting to be second to none, he did the same. It was like he was on fire; he coughed and gasped for breath, while they were laughing at him. Among the men he spotted the clumsy shape of his cabin mate with his hostile, contemptuous look. The man's nasty eyes told him he was going to get him.

Wouldn't it have been more sensible if I had accepted the lift from the people in the double decker? he wondered. He shuddered when he looked at the man again. He was scared, incredibly scared and had a terribly negative feeling, something he had never had before. It was as if the man's two dirty hands were going to rip out his heart or throttle him.

His mug was being re-filled and held in front of him, but a voice in his head told him not to take it; he was the only one who would decide what he'd do or not and so he pushed the mug away. For a second the men didn't know what to do. His cabin mate stood up and came slowly walking towards him. Everybody fell completely silent and looked on, with bated breath, while the seedy, yellow light from the spotlights on the bow and the corpse-coloured glow from the squalid, insect covered neon tubes fell on their tanned, marked, frightened, battered mouths.

'*Más fuerte, más fuerte!*' the man shouted at the men, because they didn't sing loud enough. In his head he could see how he was going to humiliate that little prick, squeeze the air out of his fat, rich body till there was nothing left.

'Is that the best you can do?' he asked the men. 'You have to sing *más fuerte*. If you don't I'll beat your brains out! *Más fuerte! Más fuerte!*'

The men were scared and 'sang' as loud as they could, so that the music and the singing began to sound like the deafening screams of birds that had gone mad. Erasmus held his hands to his ears to shut out the noise, but it didn't help. The voices, the sounds. Was he at a funfair? He heard the sharp, metallic noise of large iron sheets clattering on each other; one great cacophony of noises and his throat was still on fire.

Had he gone to hell after all?

'Izumi, help me!' he shouted at the top of his voice.

All of a sudden he looked into the terrifying eyes of his cabin mate, which brought him back to his senses. Instinctively he knew the man wanted to grab him, but he wasn't going to let him.

'I'll kill you,' the man said.

Before Erasmus realised what was going on, the man had got hold of his waistband and was looking around him, arrogantly, triumphantly, and into the frightened eyes of the other men, feeling almighty, until he felt a terrible, heavy, sharp pain in his groin. He wailed, cursed and swore. A shockwave went through the men, the singing faltered, the guitar strings, cautious and frightened, were still vibrating, more and more softly, until their infinitesimal sounds had died down and the men's voices had fallen silent.

The man began to curse again and wanted to have another go at Erasmus, but he lost his balance when Erasmus took hold of his fist and twisted it. A new Erasmus had arisen; something he'd never felt before went through him, an enormous drive, something invincible, a huge wave of adrenalin. He was almost beside himself with rage; had extracted himself from a feeling of fear that had always lived in him. Nothing could stop him. He thumped the man until the latter collapsed and toppled over, still swearing, his knees pulled up, deeply humiliated.

Erasmus came out of his high and realised he had been very lucky to kick the man in the groin at the right moment and he saw relief and a kind of adoration in the eyes of the men around him, as if he had liberated them. It looked as if they wanted to cheer, but were held back by fear, until softly, and still hesitatingly, two or three men began to clap their hands.

Several officers came running from upstairs.

'What's going on here? What's happened?'

'That young lad over there. He's knocked down the big *bastardo*,' one of the men said.

The keel of Erasmus' status as a hero was laid; the officers were smiling.

'Incredible,' one of them said. 'I don't think I would have dared to attack him. Are you all right?'

Another officer offered him a different, much better, private cabin with a shower.

In the meantime his cabin mate had been picked up by some others. He tried to put up a struggle, but fell down again and was carried off, still cursing. He was locked up for the duration of the rest of the journey and was to be handed over to the police in Ecuador.

Erasmus couldn't sleep, got in and out of bed, sat down on a chair at the table and went back to bed again, only to get out later. The whole night all sorts of images passed through his head and he remembered the eerie, yellow light, where he could see the gigantic hatred in the eyes of that man. Why that hatred? What had he done to him? he wondered. How is it that people so often behave like animals? Envy, poverty, neglect? Or was he only imagining things and didn't he know anything about life? Yes, of course he had hit the man too, but that never was his choice; it was just self-defence. But being bullied at school, tormented every day, till nothing is left of you and you're always scared of other people, of life, and you can't move on, you stop eating, you become anorexic and you don't want to get any better and you waste away? What about that? Having parents who care is so important then. But why then did my father never try to find me? Didn't he want me any more?

He thought of Izumi's words, that his father did want to see him, but wasn't allowed to. By whom? His mother? He shouldn't have listened to her and just looked me up. He could have if he'd wanted to.

'Stop it,' he said to himself, aloud. 'Don't think like this or you will once more fall into the self-pity trap. That time is past. There are millions of people who are much worse off than you.'

It was true. He thought of his uncle, who, though autistic, was still happy in his own environment, his own reality, his own world, with the presidents of America, Kennedy, Johnson, Nixon, Ford, Reagan and Carter. He had remembered a few names and the peanuts too. It made him smile. What a crazy world it was. But still, in the end, we, the people of this world, separately pre-programmed, growing stem cells, might all be connected through one human consciousness.

His thoughts travelled on, roaming along the Milky Way through the universe, with millions of stars and black holes, the big bang. Why does everybody always look at the stars and not at the infinity of that black, wonderful space? Is it the purpose of my DNA, my existence, my $ύπαρξη$, that my own experiences, my own journey through life, my own pain and happiness link up with the strings, the one-dimensional objects, the DNA of the universe and become part of what mankind will ultimately carry with him in the, perhaps infinite, black holes of the unconscious and, hopefully, learn from it? When he had travelled this far on his cosmic journey, he finally fell asleep.

The next morning he was broken and felt a bit nauseous. He was sitting on his bed, head bent down, when there was a knock on the door. It was one of the officers with a big breakfast in his hands. Erasmus unlocked the door, opened it and let the man in. The smell of toast and eggs pervaded the cabin. His nauseous feeling was suddenly gone. He was being spoiled.

'Good morning. How are you?' the man asked.

'Not too bad, thanks, just a headache. That's all.'

'The man that attacked you apparently had a criminal record. We didn't know that, otherwise we wouldn't have employed him, but another crew member told us.'

Erasmus thought about himself and could hardly believe what he'd done that night. It made him feel good; he had overcome himself and he was convinced it wouldn't have happened if he had got on the double decker bus with people who would have looked after him and he remembered the strange feeling he had in his belly the previous day, when he had to make the difficult decision about how he would go on. His intuition had been right; there was something funny about the ship, but he was glad he hadn't allowed himself to be put off; he had made the right decision and he thought of what the voice in the temple had said about the omniscience of the great consciousness and free will, and had told him not to be afraid of the unknown.

He ate his almost cold breakfast and thought it was time to explore the rest of the ship and enjoy the views. Only when he walked to the door did he realise why it was so light inside his cabin; two big windows were letting in the sunlight. He pushed against the heavy teakwood door, which didn't want him to leave the cabin; it wanted to close itself with a big, strong spring the moment he had opened it. In the far distance he saw land. Was it Panama or Colombia? He had no idea. He would ask one of the crew members, but what an enormous breathing and thinking space this immense mass of water gave him, the extensive blue sky, the soft roll of the ship on the grey blue waves, countries in the distance with tropical forests and animals.

The next day he looked breathlessly at a large number of dolphins that were cutting all sort of capers, as if they wanted to attract his attention. What great animals, he thought, just like the sharks that were also found in these waters. Unfortunately, he didn't see any. He was hoping to see some humpbacks that came to mate here this time of the year.

The country in the distance appeared to be Costa Rica, a name with such a beautiful sound to it, calling up images of bananas and pineapples. Isn't it funny, he thought, how the names of countries call up associations? He had all the time of the world, so he fetched a deckchair, got himself a beer and sat down. Isn't life great? he thought.

'Two more days to Ecuador,' somebody told him.

That wouldn't be a problem with such a fine cabin, the unparalleled sea-view from it and the rays of the rising sun that were welcoming him to another new day.

Because of his 'talks' with Enrique and his contacts with the Spanish speaking crew he'd learnt a few more words and expressions, although it sometimes was very hard to understand them, but they all did their best to involve him in their music and singing. After all, he had delivered them from a big lump of nastiness. He still couldn't quite understand how he had managed to tackle that guy, but it felt good all the same, as if he was floating on a cloud.

He smiled. 'Cloud', he thought and the word called up pictures of New York and Mrs Hopper, the cloud of music and scent. How wonderful it would have been if they'd really been related, he and Mrs Hopper, his 'clairvoy-aunt'. He could have asked her loads of other questions then, he thought, but she hadn't disappeared from the world; he knew where she lived and that he was always welcome at her place, so, in a way she was a kind of aunt. How funny.

His uncle was a funny man too, he thought, but it was a pity they didn't have a click, that there weren't any warm feelings, not even a real 'uncle' feeling, if there was such a thing. In fact he had more of an 'aunt' feeling with Mrs Hopper. Great too, that there were still a few Hoppers in New York, he thought, for it wasn't a very common name. Maybe Uncle P.J. was a lot smarter than he thought. What have I missed of what he said? he wondered and tried to reconstruct their conversation with the presidents, the peanuts, but he couldn't figure it out. What was the link with his question about his father or the Hoppers? Am I stupid, or was there something my uncle *did* know, but couldn't or wouldn't tell me? He kept on thinking.

This stream of thoughts continued right into the next day. He was sure; what his uncle had said, had to be hints. But what did he mean to tell him? Whatever, I have to write down my experiences and the things I remember, now that they're all still fresh in my memory, he thought, or I will lose those as well.

Quite a different thought, something no one on board would be able to understand, he could hardly comprehend himself, was that he was thinking of paying a visit to the man he'd knocked down, but since nobody could vouch for his safety, they wouldn't let him. But why did he want to do that? To try and understand why that guy had such strong feelings of violence and hatred? Or to bring the hidden secrets from the dark, deep catacombs of his feelings into the light? Perhaps it was his wish, his desire to help that man, for he couldn't stand unsolved matters and thought of the angry, heavy negativity that was cooped up, somewhere deep down in the ship, and couldn't get out of it, while here, on deck, the sun was shining and there was nothing but positivity, but of course he could understand that they couldn't release this psychopath among the crew and, of course, he wasn't a psychiatrist.

He remembered reading or hearing somewhere that everything, and every person you meet, is also 'you'. He found that very strange, very alarming even, for it meant that this guy, with all his hatred inside, was also part of himself, for, as some people said, the people you meet are more than just a reflection of yourself; they *are* yourself. So what did this mean for himself and the hatred he felt? He remembered the terrible situation at home and how he hated his father for what he'd done to his mother and the moment he realised that his father was leaving her, when he saw her despair, her helplessness. As a child you don't want to see your mother suffer; it had hurt so much and he knew his father was to blame. That man was bad, he hated him, maybe as much as this man hated him, while he didn't know anything about what was really going on between his mother and father, but still he hated his father, only out of emotion and his own unhappiness. His father was a scapegoat, the target of his own pain, the pain he got from his mother; just like he himself embodied all that was despicable in the eyes of that man below.

Maybe that was why he wanted to find his father, see who he really was, without the hatred, the painful hatred that blinded everything. If that man down there could forgive him, see who he was, he could see himself, because that heavy hatred, those black sunbeams, which came from the deepest, jet-black shafts in the coalmine of his lowest consciousness, made him blind and could never bring the cause of his own pain up and into the light. The guy had been swallowed up by a black hole, where no consciousness existed, but only anti-consciousness. Erasmus realised the first thing he had to do was to enlighten himself, go back to the basis, the womb, the navel, his 'omphalos'. What heavy reflections, he thought, here, on the silent mirror of a vast ocean.

On the fourth day the coastline of Ecuador came into view. It was only a couple of hours' sailing to Guayaquil, the port where the ship was heading.

Ecuador, at last, he thought, and they were getting closer to it by the minute. It made him think of delicious food that you have ordered at a restaurant. You can already smell it, but you have to wait till the waiter brings it to your table. Ecuador, food, an alluring smell, excitement.

56

Isabelle woke up a few times that night and noticed that Bernard hadn't come back from Pepito's yet, but well, if that was his choice, so be it, she thought. She had more space for herself in bed, while he probably thought she was worried because he wasn't back yet. She woke up again; the sun was already shining brightly. What time was it, nine, ten or maybe even eleven o'clock? She could hear him coming home, trying to enter the living room as quietly as possible and she could just see him through the open bedroom door. Looking at him, his ruffled hair and creased clothes, she knew he had slept in them. He had been drinking a lot as well, she guessed. She laughed to herself and thought what a fool he really was, but that laugh was also for his helplessness, something he didn't realise himself. He was a little, sweet boy, she thought, and she knew that, in spite of that big mouth and his selfishness, he was begging for attention and love. However, because of his very attitude, he was pushing everything and everybody away from him. She got out of bed and went up to him, took the hem of his shirt that was hanging from his trousers and put it right. He even let her; it was unbelievable, she thought.

'How was Pepito's?' she asked. 'Where have you been? Your clothes are a mess and there's sand coming from your trousers. Where have you been doing with yourself? Come here a minute,' she said and stroked his hair.

Something touched him deep inside. He looked a bit nervous, uncertain of himself, disconcerted, but he didn't resist; he felt something he had missed for a long, long time. For all his adventures and his experiences with women, the brave Canadian ex-colonel was a little confused. This time he hadn't asked for attention, but got it all the same.

'Yes, it was a bit late and I fell asleep on the beach, when someone, a gay guy called Albert, from Paris or so, saw I was a mess. He asked me to come with him to his house. Probably had to drag me. I couldn't stand on my legs. I dropped on his bed and fell asleep, until I woke up this morning and came home. Had a little too much, I suppose. There were some other friendly people at the bar, a girl from the U.S. with an Irish accent, a very nice young woman she was, and a young guy from Iowa. He was quite drunk and seemed to fancy that girl. I don't even know their names. Did they give me their names? I don't think so. Can't remember. It doesn't matter. That young man from Iowa was a bit peculiar; I couldn't figure him out; can't remember why he's here and that girl, a young woman really, wants to start a new life here, I believe, with an older friend. Maybe you've seen him around; long, grey hair, well, white rather. Don't know where he's from, the lucky bastard. But that girl, I don't know; there's something about her, in spite of her coolness. And that gay guy I was talking about; you should see him, he really walks like a poof.'

Bernard laughed, but Isabelle didn't think it was funny.

'But he's OK. I think you'll like him. Maybe you should meet him and also the other two, that Irish/American girl and that guy from Iowa; he didn't say much though; he really is a bit strange, I think, or stupid.'

'Perhaps he was only shy,' Isabelle said, overwhelmed by Bernard's waterfall of words, 'and if someone, like this Albert, is a friendly person, what does it matter if he's gay? Why are you always so quick to judge others? I can also think of stupid things I've said or done, but does that mean I'm stupid? We all do things for a reason, or because of who or what we are, so what's the point of judging other people?'

'Hmm. Maybe you're right,' Bernard replied, while he was still thinking about what she had just said. He looked at her and thought of the experiences they had shared at the NFE in Sal Salvador, that it was possible to be one, to agree, to enjoy the same things, and although this moment was maybe only a shade of the resonance or echo of that experience, it had happened all the same, so apparently there was more between her and himself than he had thought.

'Sometimes you're so old-fashioned in your thinking, so staid in your ways,' she said.

'Thanks. That'll do for today,' he replied. 'Why don't you come with me to Pepito's then, or why don't we pop in at Albert's place to see if he's at home, so that you can meet him yourself? I'm sure you'll like him; women.'

He smiled, but she didn't like it.

'Stop it, Bernard. That's not very nice. Leave him be.'

Bernard then told her what had happened that night, the bits that he couldn't remember, but Albert had told him, and also that Albert had offered him some breakfast.

'What a nice man. I should really like to meet him, and I'd love to hear his version of how he rescued you,' Isabelle said, teasingly.

'You'd like that, wouldn't you?' Bernard said, slightly irritated. 'But, yes, OK, maybe we could walk his way later, after lunch maybe, or have you got any other plans?'

'Me, other plans, here?'

Later that day they walked to Albert's house, but when they were nearly there, they noticed he already had some visitors and decided to go to the village nearby. Albert saw them and called out.

'Why don't you come in and have a drink with us?'

'Yes, fine. Thanks,' Bernard said and introduced Isabelle to Albert.

'Nice to meet you, Albert, and thanks for saving Bernard's life last night,' Isabelle said.

Albert laughed, looking into her eyes, picking up the subtle undertones of her words. Bernard introduced himself to Roonah and Desmond, who had just come back. Albert told Bernard and Isabelle how he and Roonah had met some time ago in Cuba and that she'd nursed him when he was very ill in a hospital in Santiago de Cuba.

'What were you doing in Cuba?' Isabelle asked.

'I was a volunteer there, a nurse, and before I went to Cuba I worked on the west coast of the U.S.'

Bernard was impressed and wondered whether it was because of her sensuality or her powerful personality that he felt attracted to her. He didn't know, but at the same time her penetrating look and almost arrogant attitude unnerved him. Seeing Isabelle was talking with Albert and Desmond, he thought it was a good moment to direct his arrows at Roonah. He tried to make contact with her, but she didn't respond and shifted her gaze to the others. Bernard didn't get the message though and tried to keep her away from the others by asking her some more questions and saying irrelevant things.

What a fucking, annoying asshole, Roonah thought. I know what his sort wants. I feel sorry for his wife.

More questions, more rubbish.

'I'm sorry,' she said, 'but I need to speak to Albert. Excuse me.' She got up from her chair and disappeared before he could reply.

Albert went inside to put a record on and get some drinks for his guests. Roonah followed him to the open kitchen, while Desmond and Isabelle were busy talking.

'Albert, can I give you a hand?'

'Hi, Roonah, come in. Great to have you here. I bet you wanted to get away from Bernard.'

'I did indeed. Jesus. What a guy.'

'Well, he's not too bad, actually.'

'Maybe you're right. But how are things with you? I already asked you this morning, but…'

'Well, sometimes I feel tired and there are still some holes in my memory, if that's what you mean.'

'Yes, that too, but how's life treating you here, in Ecuador? I'm sure it's very different from Paris.'

'Absolutely, yes. I'm all right, but there are still some issues.'

'What's up then, if you don't mind my asking. Is there anything I can do to help you?'

'I don't know, but sometimes I feel so depressed and I wonder why that is. Of course I can think of some causes; the war, my mother's death, losing my friend, the things that happened in Cuba and after that. It's, how shall I put it, too much sometimes.'

'I never asked you before, but what about your father. How is he?'

'He died shortly after my mother.'

'Oh, I'm sorry.'

'No problem.'

'But it seems his death didn't affect me as much as my mother's.'

'Well, yes. Apparently for a son, but also for a daughter, for that matter, the death of a mother is one of the most traumatic experiences in life. Maybe you miss your father too, but because of the impact of your mother's death, his death seems less painful, or perhaps it makes you think there wasn't much love lost between you. But what about that friend that you lost?'

'Well, he didn't die, actually. I broke off our relationship. It was Sylvain, remember? I probably told you about him.'

Albert's eyes moistened when he said this.

Roonah took him by his arm and shoulder and gave him a hug.

'You're still the night nurse,' he said with a faint smile.

Looking around her in the room, she sensed what Desmond had already felt that morning. In spite of the elegant interior there was something tragic about the place.

'You can always come and see me, if you want to,' she said. 'Any time of the day or night, and I can always pop in for a talk, if you like.'

'Thanks, Roonah, that's very kind of you. We'll see how it goes. You're really wonderful.'

'No worries, and perhaps we can also set a date for our trip to Guayaquil, if only to get away from it all.'

'Yeah, good idea,' Albert said, although he felt she was a bit too pushing.

They put the glasses on a tray and rejoined the others. Bernard was still sitting all by himself and looked at Albert, who gave him a wink, which made him think of Joe and what Joe had said to him and, for the very first time in his life, he wondered if, for whatever reason, men felt attracted to him. He shuddered and was confused.

Isabelle got her drink and asked Albert if he could tell her about his journey from Paris to America.

'*Pas de problème*, but of course I can't tell you everything now,' he said, 'there's so much.'

He told her a short version of what had happened, without saying anything about Rosalie and Jonathan's deaths. They were painful memories and he still had this feeling of guilt and, besides, it would only make his story sensational, which was the last thing he wanted, and he thought of Steve, who could still be so sad sometimes. There she was, Rosalie, an impression of her, on the easel near Roonah, the painting, the restaurant in Havana, red, yellow, black, a palette, a semi-transparent décor of his consciousness.

Isabelle was much impressed by his story.

'What a perseverance. Unbelievable,' she said.

'Thanks,' he said, timidly.

She looked at him, his tender face. She liked him; he was so sweet and attentive.

Desmond was becoming a bit restless; he stood up and walked up and down the room, as if he was looking for something. Outside he saw Erasmus, standing on the beach. What, for heaven's sake, was that young man doing here all day? he wondered. Although he couldn't see what Erasmus was looking at, their eyes met halfway, near a shadow, just outside Albert's cottage, above the hot, dry sand of no-man's-land.

The moment Albert had finished his story, Bernard pounced on Roonah again, asking her when she was going to Pepito's again. She shrugged her shoulders and said she didn't feel like going there regularly.

What a creep, she thought, with his own wife sitting just a few metres away.

57

All three were fascinated by what they saw, the Playa de las Palmas, a sandy beach that gradually changed into a rocky coast with lots of plants, shrubs and trees, just like on the mountains in the distance and along the river in front of them. They had now arrived at the entrance to the harbour. The commercial port itself wasn't so impressive, like most other ports, in fact. They didn't want to moor in a big port, but this place felt good, they thought. If they wanted to go to a big city, like Quito, they could be there in a couple of hours. However, when they got closer, they also saw an oil refinery.

'This is not what we want, I think; this could be any stupid port anywhere in the world,' Jack said. 'Let's get out of here. Who has given this terrible place such a beautiful name?'

Steve and Albert agreed with him. They turned round and sailed a little further south, where they found a pleasant little town, not only with a small marina, but also with fine sandy beaches and some huge rocks. This felt so much better. They sailed up the river and moored at one of the jetties.

Where they suddenly came from, Jack didn't know, but within minutes of their arrival half a dozen kids stood at his boat, chuckling and smiling, curious to find out where these people had come from. They were pushing each other, probably to encourage one of them, the bravest, to ask if they could run an errand for them. They looked so cute, so sweet, with their little Indian faces and beautiful brown eyes. It doesn't matter where you are, Jack thought, all kids are the same. He asked them if they could get him some bottles of water. He gave them money and within fifteen minutes they were back, with the bottles and some change, which Jack said they could keep. It was great to see the big smiles that appeared on their sweet, mischievous faces. This had made their day, of course, and he remembered, when he was a kid, running errands for his aunt in Folkestone, how he had felt just as happy and rich, when she gave him some money for sweets or his piggybank.

'I'm glad we didn't moor in the other port,' Steve said. 'This place feels much more like a proper homecoming,' he added, with a happy smile on his face.

Albert didn't say very much; he was looking at the houses, the water, the people, taking it all in at ease, as if he was drinking a fine, red wine. The first sip had tasted so good that he wanted to enjoy every drop of it, as long as possible. A feeling of peace came over him, an inner contentment he hadn't had for a long time. This is just great, he thought. There was no need to say anything and, to express what he now felt, would take time. His head was a bit like muddy water; sand and other particles first had to sink to the bottom and settle there, before the water was clear. One thing was certain, though; he was in Ecuador, at last! It's a strange thing, he thought, having been on my way for such a long time and in a minute I will be standing on its soil. He couldn't think any further than this, and neither did he have to, he thought. That was a thing for the future. Without saying a single word, he smiled at Jack.

They disembarked and set foot on solid ground, a very special feeling. In spite of all the hours they'd spent together, nattering, singing, eating, they didn't have a clear picture of what they'd do now; there were only some vague plans. They went into the village and had a drink and a meal in a local bar. They passed by a shop where they sold all kinds of stuff. Albert went inside and asked the people if they knew of a house or bungalow that was to be let, preferably near the beach. He was referred to the local estate agent who appeared to have several cottages on offer.

'You're not the first person to ask this question,' the man said in perfect English, 'for this very morning I heard from a colleague in Quito that he had also had some enquiries from people who were searching for something similar, but yes, I do have a few cottages, or beach villas, as they call them, on offer. They're all very close to the beach, as the name suggests, or even on it. They belong to a travel organisation that wants to dispose of them, money problems, I've been told. They're very nice cottages and I can offer them to you at a very special price.'

'That sounds good,' Albert said.

'If you've got some time tomorrow, we could go and have a look at them,' the man went on. 'How many would you be looking for, one, two, or perhaps three?'

'We haven't thought about that yet,' Jack said. 'Let's first go and see what they're like. Tomorrow's fine.'

'All right. Would eleven o'clock suit you? It's a fair drive to the village where they are.'

'Perfect,' Albert said. 'No problem. See you tomorrow at eleven.'

'Thank you. See you tomorrow, gentlemen.'

58

Erasmus could hardly wait to go ashore, although they hadn't arrived at the port yet. Gradually the coast became less rocky and didn't rise as high above the water as before; there were sandy beaches and he saw the first houses and villages, Playas, El Arenal, Data de Villamil, Data de Posorja and there was also a river with a densely wooded island in it, which according to one of the crew was called Isla Puna. They would sail around it, then go up the wide River Guayas, where they would see even more islands, before finally mooring in Guayaquil. They sailed into the busy port; there were people all over the place, running around like ants. Voices, cars, liveliness, Ecuador! The time to say goodbye was approaching fast now.

At the quay a police van stood waiting to take the man, who'd been incarcerated downstairs, to the local police station. The gangway was hoisted into place and four policemen came on board. No one was allowed to go ashore yet and nearly all the crew members were standing on deck, curious to find out what was going to happen next. After about twenty minutes the four policemen came back, together with the man, who was handcuffed to one of the officers. It became very quiet on board, until someone at the top deck shouted some words of abuse. After that more men started shouting at the man.

Erasmus stood there, with mixed feelings, looking at the scene. On the one hand he was happy the man was being carried off, but on the other hand he took pity on the man, who didn't care to look back at the ship or at the men who were shouting at him. However, at the very last moment, when he was about to be pushed into the van, he looked back, staring right into Erasmus' eyes and, once again, there was the visible, almost tangible hatred. The van was started and drove off, absorbed by the noise and the busy traffic of Guayaquil.

Like a soft breeze that blew over the ship, a sense of relief took possession of the men on deck. Most of the crew went ashore, but not before saying goodbye to Erasmus. The story of how he had brought down his opponent was to become more and more exciting and spectacular during its tour of the bars and restaurants of Guayaquil and the reputation of that 'American', 'that Yankee Boy' would grow by the day.

Some members of the crew who stayed on board, came to take leave of him and thanked him. It made him feel a bit awkward. With a smile on his face and the rucksack on his back he went ashore. Here he was, in Ecuador. He had managed to do it, with a few trucks, a ship and very friendly, hospitable people. He hadn't thought much yet about what he was going to do in Guayaquil, but he needed to find a hostel or a cheap hotel and, after another couple of days, he'd make up his mind what he was going to do next.

He had been told that he'd better take a taxi to a hostel or a hotel, as the slightly better and cheaper hotels weren't so close to the harbour. A taxi driver found him a good place not far from the Parque Centenario, close to the city centre. The hostel looked fine and, because of its location, it was easy to get to places. What had really surprised him on his way to the hostel, were all the tall buildings. Somehow, he had never expected to see any in Ecuador. Although Guayaquil was quite a big city, he wanted to stay there for a week or two and take his time to explore it.

But there was something else, a feeling he hadn't had before. It was as if the search for his father was really beginning now; somehow, his father seemed to be closer than ever. Let Mrs Hopper be my guide, he said to himself and laughed when he remembered the peculiar, special woman, who had actually given him the push he needed.

His curiosity took him into the streets, made him explore the vicinity of the hostel. In a brochure he read about a few places which were really worth seeing and the guy at the reception desk also gave him a few tips and told him buses and metro trains were the cheapest way to travel, but Erasmus said he wanted to foot it all, if possible. Maybe he had inherited that from his unknown father, for he remembered his mum telling him, when he was shopping with her in Des Moines a long time ago, 'You walk just as fast as your father', or 'Yes, your father also wanted to go everywhere on foot. It always tired me out; he would never stop for a break'.

The atmosphere here was very different from Mexico City, the last city he'd been to. He missed the openness, whatever that was and somehow it felt a bit more oppressive here. He first went to the Parque Centenario to have a look at some monuments, which were said to depict patriotism and freedom. He was curious, because during his stay in New York he'd seen the Statue of Liberty from the free ferry to Staten Island. Freedom, he mused, the most important thing in life, in his life anyway, and it was something he would keep chasing, forever. He would never want to have an office job; he would rather do some research or work on an archaeological project, like Izumi. Although the area around it looked a bit dingy, the park itself wasn't too bad. He sat down on a bench in the shade, enjoying the warmth of the sun, the people walking about and the children playing on the grass. Once again, he was in a completely different world. Wasn't it great?

He definitely wanted to go to Las Peñas, because the guy at the hostel had told him that it was an area with a good feel. In a narrow street, not far from Las Peñas, he spotted an esoteric bookshop and went inside. Browsing around the place, he found a beautifully illustrated book on Mayan mythology. It wasn't the only book that attracted his attention; there were dozens of titles that looked alluring. He couldn't resist buying this book and, before he had reached Las Peñas, he found himself sitting on the stone window sill of an old house, rummaging through the book, forgetting where he was in this world; his journey just went on. This was what he wanted, he thought, searching for links between European, mainly Greek, and Pan-American civilisations and cultures.

Still semi-immersed in the world of mythology, he strolled through Las Peñas and, probably because he was looking at everything through rose-tinted glasses, he loved the area with its old, timber houses and cobbled streets. He felt like hanging around a bit longer and started looking for a restaurant to have something to eat. There was plenty of choice, so he just went into the first place that took his fancy and sat down in the corner near a window.

'What food can you recommend?' he asked the waiter.

'Ah, Señor, you must try our *encebollado*. It's a very nice stew, with boiled cassava, red onions and spices,' the man replied, 'It is really *delicioso*.'

'OK, I'll give it a try. Thanks.'

The part of the restaurant he was in was full of colourful paintings, which only intensified his fantasy world even further. He felt quite at home here, started reading and no longer noticed what was going on around him, children calling each other, men and women laughing, toasting and talking.

From another dimension a waitress with beautiful, brown eyes came to his table to serve the *encebollado*.

'Thank you,' he said, looking at her and the *encebollado*, but his eyes didn't really register the actual world around him and he went straight back to the words and images in the book.

The girl looked at him and wondered what he was reading. She couldn't quite understand the title, although the bright colours and golden letters on the cover appealed to her. He was quite good-looking with his straight nose, his dark blue eyes with the beautiful, absent-minded look, his narrow cheekbones, and although he wasn't very muscular, she thought he was gorgeous, and certainly different from the regular customers. Where was he from with his dark blue eyes and pale skin? The U.S., or Europe, maybe? He fascinated her, but what book was he reading? She just couldn't keep her eyes off him and whenever there was a reason to be at or near his table, she was there.

Only much later, when he laid down his book for a while, did he notice her presence. She immediately smiled at him and, although he looked a bit shy and wondered if that smile was meant for him, he smiled back at her, and, before he could even blink an eye, she was at his table.

'That was very good,' he said.

'Thank you. Would you like a dessert?'

'Yes, please. What would you recommend?'

'*Espumillas*. It's a guava meringue cream dessert, made with fruit pulp, guava or guayaba, egg whites and sugar.'

'Wow. Sounds delicious.'

'I'll get you a big *porción*. You're very nice,' she quickly added, and darted to the kitchen, leaving Erasmus behind in bewilderment.

Where the hell had she suddenly come from? he wondered, looking at the closed book in front of him. She came back with an extra-large dessert, looking at him with a sweet smile and sparkling eyes.

'*Muchas gracias*,' he said, blushing, a grin on his lovely face. Not until this moment did he see how pretty she really was; her deep, beautiful eyes intrigued him. He was speechless.

'It's all right,' she said with a sexy accent. 'Where are you from?'

'I'm from Iowa, the United States,' he replied and wanted to tell her about the countries he'd travelled through to get to Ecuador, but, unfortunately, more and more customers came into the restaurant and she couldn't be with him all the time. She came back to his table as much as she could to listen to what he had to say.

'I've also been to Mexico City and…' but she was already off again.

'Sorry I have to go all the time, but I live here, in Guayaquil, in the city centre, not far from here,' she said, and away she was once more.

How frustrating, Erasmus thought. It was no use. In the end he reluctantly asked for the bill and saw she'd given him a discount.

'Here's a telephone number you can reach me on, if you want to,' she said.

'I haven't got a number,' he said, 'I'm sorry, but I will be back. Promise.'

There was no time for more words of goodbye and when he left he realised he had missed a large part of the evening and this wonderful girl. For at least a couple of hours he'd been journeying in his book. Not that he regretted having read parts of it, but it was a shame he hadn't noticed the waitress any earlier. He thanked the people at the restaurant, gave one more wink to the waitress and went back to the hostel.

In the end he stayed in Guayaquil for a week and came back to the restaurant with the beautiful waitress a couple of times, but, unfortunately, she was never there. At least he had her number. On most days he got up early to explore the city and wander around it for hours. The lay-out of the place, because of its division into squares, like that of most cities in the U.S., was very clear. Around noon, by lunchtime, he could be found in the vicinity of the Malecón Simón Bolivar, a wide street at the riverfront, where he would get some food from one of many takeaways and eat it, sitting on a bench among the trees, looking over the water, but he didn't want to stay much longer, for apart from some nice areas, he didn't much like the city. A girl he met at the hostel told him about a cheap, pleasant hostel in a seaside village.

He could always come back to Guayaquil, if he wanted to, he thought, and it was probably a better starting-point for a trip to find his father than just a village somewhere in the middle of nowhere.

His mother wanted to send him some extra money, but it was still very difficult because of on-going problems with the Internet. There was only one thing to do, he thought, find a job, which immediately reminded him of the restaurant where that beautiful girl worked. Perhaps she could help him. How old was she? he wondered. Somewhere in her early twenties? She looked really attractive with her long, straight hair, or were there waves in it? He wasn't sure now, the brown-yellow dress and her almost slender body. To be able to describe her nose or the shoes she was wearing, he'd have to see her again. Maybe women notice these things earlier than men, he thought, for men usually look at other things first.

On the last day of his stay in Guayaquil he went back to the restaurant once more to see if she was in, but he was told she wouldn't be in till the evening.

'Could you please give her my regards?' he asked a waiter, 'and tell her I'll be back?'

In the afternoon he got on a bus to the small seaside town. He was already looking forward to the hostel by the sea. The trip took more than four hours, for the overcrowded bus went very slowly and stopped in every village. Going up a mountain, he heard all sorts of scary noises and when they went down, it was the brakes that were screeching like hell, as if the linings had gone. Maybe he was the only one who heard all the frightening sounds, for everybody just went on shouting to each other, that's what it sounded like anyway. There were men, women and children all over the place, on top and next to each other, smelling from their armpits and others parts of their bodies. It wasn't very likely they had a shower every day, not even every week, maybe, and sometimes he thought he could discern a certain tragedy in their eyes, as if the light in them had been extinguished a long time ago. Maybe it just seemed that way or, since he was foreigner, probably a wealthy North American in their eyes, they only looked at him like that. Moreover, the bus was far from comfortable and seemed to fall to pieces whenever they went through a big pothole. It was shaking so heavily then that all the armpits and other smelly body parts were thrown together and the smells went all over the bus.

The scenery, the mountainscapes they were passing through were unparalleled, and when they arrived at the village, he saw a terrific sandy beach with lots of palm trees and a dozen or so beach huts. Situated a bit higher, on a dune, was the hostel where he would be staying for the time being. Wow! Didn't that look good?

59

'What was Havana like and how did you manage to get out of Cuba? I've been told it's quite difficult to get in and out,' Isabelle asked Albert.

He was quiet for a moment, thinking about this cloud full of memories, some of them still very vague. Sometimes it was the memory of just one word or a single image, which like an arrow pierced the membrane of his thoughts and triggered his coherent thinking, while others remained dormant for a long time and then slowly died away. Some memories made him smile before they disappeared again, but many of them wreaked havoc, created chaos, inflicted pain and didn't go away. Did he want to remember everything? Did he have a choice?

He told them he liked Havana, but that it was overshadowed by his own illness, the tragedies of Raoul and Eduardo´s families, Rosalie's death, how he had met Jack again and managed to leave Cuba with the help of Eduardo's cousin.

Roonah saw the sudden pain in his face when he mentioned the girl's name. He probably found it very difficult to talk about her death.

When he had finished his story, Desmond left the room to go to the toilet. Bernard also got up from his chair and went to the corner of the veranda to look at the beach and the ocean, while Roonah and Isabelle were still sitting with Albert, in silence, impressed by his story.

'Albert, this young woman who died, did you meet her in Havana or was she already with you on that Chilean ship?' Roonah asked cautiously.

It was quiet for a long time.

'No, I got to know her later on.'

His eyes became moist. Roonah's questions, this whole incident with Rosalie. She seemed such a nice person, even though he had only known her for such a short time. When Roonah asked him again, he finally told them what had happened, how Rosalie had taken him into confidence and made him a kind of accomplice.

'I still feel so terribly stupid, naive and guilty; I should have told her friend, Steve, right away. It was *impardonnable*.'

Isabelle thought of her conversation with Bernard that morning.

'Albert, you shouldn't judge yourself so harshly; it's no good at all. You thought you were doing the right thing. Some things just happen.'

'She's right, Albert,' Roonah said, 'and, besides, you were not responsible for her life. Either she was fed up with her boyfriend, or she was looking for an adventure. I mean, why else would a woman want to go and see a complete stranger in Havana, a city she's never been to before? To see some paintings? Don't make me laugh. It's not your fault at all, Albert; it was what she wanted to do and there was nothing you could have done to prevent it.'

He told them what the police discovered at the man's apartment and in the car that had been found in the water.

'Here you are. I think she knew what was going on, but it was too late to pull out,' Roonah added. 'Don't take everything personally and, as I said, she wasn't your responsibility.'

'Maybe you're right,' Albert said, 'I hadn't looked at it from that point of view. But it's so sad.'

'Of course it is,' Roonah said, 'but don't keep blaming yourself.'

He was quiet for a moment. She was right, he thought, and he was glad she had asked him about Rosalie's death. She certainly didn't beat about the bush with her direct questions, and he thought of the hospital where she had helped him get over things that troubled his mind, sometimes by just holding his hand, praying for him, being with him.

'By the way, would you like another drink? I'm so sorry. I am neglecting you,' he said.

He felt better, relieved, now that the story was off his chest.

On the beach, walking about rather aimlessly, looking dreamily at the diorama that was Albert's house with Desmond, Roonah, Bernard, Isabelle and Albert, Erasmus was at a loose end. His eyes wandered off and peered over the ocean and he wondered if he'd ever be able to find his father by hiding in a hostel, somewhere in a village on the coast of Ecuador. Wasn't the whole thing just a useless undertaking?

He couldn't see that the two women sat talking to Albert and that even Desmond and Bernard were having a conversation, but what he did see was Desmond's white hair, while Bernard was sitting with his back towards him. His thoughts, however, weren't quite with these people; they were with the beautiful waitress. Maybe, in the end, she was the reason why he had come here, he thought. She was his present and his future, not his father.

He walked to the water, enjoying the warmth of the loose sand under his feet. It felt really good; it energised him. The blue ocean, the unlimited mass of water, beckoned him, and he responded to its lure, for like in New York he wanted to feel the ultimate, elusive essence of this freedom. He was busy extricating himself from the ties that held him back, the thoughts of his father and mother. Like a turtle on the Galapagos Islands that has just come out of its egg, he swiftly moved across the beach to the breakers now, a perilous route to a new, uncertain future.

Through the open door Albert saw Erasmus. He felt sorry for him. Why he had that feeling, he didn't know, but maybe there was something about the young man that he recognised, a mirror reflecting himself. He went outside and called him.

'Hello! *Pardon*! Excuse me!'

Erasmus couldn't hear him, as the noise of the wind that was blowing from the sea and the thundering violence of the crashing waves drowned Albert's words. Erasmus was back at sea and on his way to Guayaquil again.

60

Quito looked very impressive, Bernard and Isabelle thought, although they'd only just arrived there. It was a vibrant place, a lively, open, modern city with a well-preserved old city centre. Not just this city, but also the country, which was politically stable, reminded them of Canada and Montreal. Ecuador and Quito exuded something different, something much more positive than most Meso-American countries and cities they had passed through lately. What also struck them was the rectangular shape of the city, and although it was high up in the mountains, it still lay in a valley. All around the city were mountains, volcanoes actually, and they could see snow lying on some of them. They were told that only two years earlier a big plume of smoke from one of these volcanoes, the Guagua Pichincha, had covered the city with a one foot layer of ash and it had frightened the living daylights out of the population, because of the threat of a huge eruption.

Although the attraction of this city was enormous, Bernard didn't want to stay there for more than a couple of days, as it was more expensive here than in the country. He would prefer to go house-hunting first and hopefully find a cottage in a smaller town, not too far away from the beach. In the window of an estate agent's they saw an attractive beach house at a reasonable price; it was a few hundred kilometres away from Quito and used to be rented out as a holiday villa by a travel organisation that had gone into receivership. It looked really good and even had a very small swimming-pool. Both Bernard and Isabelle were quite excited, went into the office and made an appointment for a viewing the very next day. They'd take the bus and although the journey would take about four hours, they didn't mind.

The journey turned out to be a horrible experience, as the bus was overcrowded. All the passengers sat huddled together, like animals in transit on their way to the slaughterhouse. For only a little more money they could have travelled on a deluxe bus, Isabelle thought, but well, Bernard and money. They were sitting together on the top deck of the bus and at times they caught their breath, flying down a mountain and the driver making dead scary overtaking manoeuvres. It reminded Isabelle of the experience in Honduras or Nicaragua, she couldn't remember exactly which of the two it was, where a large part of the road had been swept away due to subsidence. How scared she was then and she thought of the unshaven taxi driver who had tried to kiss her, while Bernard just stood there, looking at them, laughing.

The gearbox was having a very difficult time too, judging by the crunching sound emerging from it when the driver was trying to change gears as they went up a mountain, but the scenery around them was magnificent and she was so much looking forward to this romantic house on the beach.

Bernard kept dozing off, but just before falling into a deep sleep he saw all sorts of pictures from the past, thousands of miles away, far removed in distance and time. Sitting in the cinema of his sleep he could see himself and his friend Sam climbing trees, digging pits, luring female bears. When the bus was shaking heavily, his eyes went open and he couldn't figure out how these daylight images, inside or outside the bus, fitted into his dream. He heard voices, but they too sounded more like hazy, incoherent, unintelligible words or sounds, coming from a different world which had nothing to do with Sam's voice, so he dozed off again and drifted off to the deep currents of his own ocean.

The bus was stopped twice by the police. Nobody knew why, but in spite of the stench that came from the toilet that was overflowing, and the broken door in front of it, so that you could see who was sitting there, no one was allowed out of the bus to go for a pee behind a bush or a tree or to find a proper toilet. After three and a half hours they reached the coastal town where they were to have a look at the beach hut. A representative of the estate agent in Quito was already waiting for them. It appeared that not just one, but almost a dozen of these villas were up for sale, so there was plenty of choice and no rush to buy the first property on offer. However, the one they had seen in the window in Quito turned out to be their favourite and it was very attractively priced, so Bernard didn't need much time to think about it. There were more people who had come to have a look at the cottages. For the first time they saw Roonah and Desmond, thinking it was a father and his daughter.

61

Albert enjoyed entertaining all these people. When their glasses had been replenished he went to the kitchen to prepare some snacks and sandwiches. The last time some people had come to his place was when he was living in Camberwell, he thought, or was it when Sylvain had come to his aunt's place? Thinking about her, he wondered how she was doing, that sweet, old darling who had always been so understanding. If only she could see him here. Maybe one day. Entertaining people gave him a purpose, he felt; it made him feel good. When he was alone he often started brooding on things without being able to talk about them to other people, so there were never any answers to his questions and he often got stuck in his sombre thoughts which sometimes drove him crazy, made him very sad, even suicidal. But would anybody notice or care if he died? Life would go on as usual, with or without him. More than once he thought about the words of Macbeth, in a play he had seen in London. They had made a big impression, and wasn't it funny that he could still remember those words, while he had forgotten so many other things?

Out, out, brief candle!
Life's but a walking shadow, a poor player
That struts and frets his hour upon the stage
And then is heard no more: it is a tale
Told by an idiot, full of sound and fury,
Signifying nothing.

When he came back to his guests, they were all talking to each other, here, in his house, and he thought of the positive things that Isabelle and Roonah had said to him, answers to questions. Wouldn't it also be nice to introduce Jack and Steve to these people? Jack would get on very well with Desmond, he thought.

'By the way, how did you manage to get here?' he asked Isabelle.

'That's quite a story, too.'

She told him how they'd driven to Guatemala, about Bernard's passport trouble and their journey in the taxis, but also about the beautiful things they had seen, the friendly people they had met and the taxi driver who kept staring at her dress and bosom.

Isn't she sweet? Albert thought, so honest and open-hearted. She isn't even aware of it herself.

While she was telling him what had happened, Bernard kept interrupting her to 'improve' on her story. It was terribly irritating, while the guy had been so affable, even romantic, that very morning, Albert thought. Was he trying to prove something? When Isabelle got to the bit about Panama, Bernard even took the story over from her.

'Can't you just let me finish my story?' she said.

She would never have dared to speak to Bernard like this before, but she felt encouraged by the people around her, Albert, Roonah and especially Desmond, who made it clear he wanted to hear her version and not Bernard's.

'Go on, Isabelle,' he said, glaring at Bernard in such a way that the latter immediately shut his mouth.

Isabelle told them about Panama City and what a great place it was, especially the older districts and the area near the marina where they had gone for a drink.

'Sorry to interrupt you,' Albert said. 'But do you mean that marina at the what's its name boulevard, something with Costera?'

'Yes, why?' Isabelle asked, surprised. 'Do you know the place?'

'It's the marina where we moored our yacht when we had come through the Panama Canal. When were you there? Wouldn't it be a coincidence if we were there at the same time?'

Isabelle tried to recall when it was, but she couldn't remember the date.

'It was on the first Monday in November,' Bernard said.

Albert couldn't believe his ears. He fetched his little notebook from the bedroom and saw they were there the very day Bernard had mentioned.

'*Incroyable*! Imagine us having met there. It's almost too crazy to think about. *N'est-ce pas merveilleux?*' he said and gave Isabelle a kiss. 'Let's celebrate and drink to this. Anyone for red wine?'

Isabelle continued her story by telling them about the flight in the small Cessna plane from Panama to Colombia, the hiking-tour through the jungle and the trip by car to Ecuador.

'That lady even risked her own life for us,' she said.

'How impressive,' Desmond said.

'Yes, it was,' Isabelle said, standing up. 'In fact, my respect for this woman grew by the hour'.

She realised how much she had learned from Aquilegia, especially about herself and she couldn't stop talking about the people in the settlement where they had stayed the night and how friendly they were, the symbolic presents she had received and how it had given her a different outlook on all sorts of things. She went on by saying that Che Guevara was a source of inspiration for the pilot.

'This hero of hers wasn't just a terrorist who was reviled by the media of the Western world for dozens of years, but a man of principles, someone who was willing to sacrifice everything for the good cause of 'his' Hispanic-American people, the sick, the poor, the Indians, all the oppressed peoples, even those in Africa, a great man, only to be murdered in Bolivia with the help of the C.I.A.'

They all fell silent. It was as if the pilot herself was standing there, speaking to them. Roonah saw power and passion in Isabelle's eyes, while Bernard was just sitting there, feeling a bit awkward.

'Isn't it disgusting how we are always fooled by our governments and the so called free press?' Isabelle asked them, looking into their eyes.

They just nodded and Albert thought of the discussion he and his brother had had about the French Government, and realised there was so much more beauty hidden in Isabelle than she showed, or was allowed to show by Bernard. Being a little tipsy after the glasses of wine he had had, he took her veined hands in his, let his fingers run over the inside, which he thought felt like those of a young woman, full of energy and strength.

'Sorry to interrupt you, but you're always welcome here, in my house. Please go on with your story,' he said.

Her sad-looking eyes began to sparkle, like dull gems that were being polished and were slowly regaining their former gloss.

'Thank you, Albert, you're so kind.'

She felt beautiful in the deepest sense of the word.

'It's OK. Are you never pursued in your dreams by all the things you've experienced?' he asked her.

'Well, sometimes fragments and faces from those experiences just turn up in my dreams, although those images are usually completely unconnected to the rest of the dream. It's just as if those wandering, lost images are searching for holes to pop through, which reminds me of the NFE in San Salvador. Sorry, I was just thinking aloud. You may not know what an NFE is,' she said.

The others didn't have a clue what she was talking about, so she first explained to them what the NFE was and how, according to her, seemingly random images emerge from the mind and, probably as a result of certain vibrations, which the simulations at the NFE showed, they can bring about a concatenation of those images, a dream.

'Astonishing,' Desmond said. 'It sounds quite logical, but please tell us a bit more about the NFE. I've never heard of it.'

She told them what she had seen there and also that she had had some very unusual dreams since then. Bernard looked at her in surprise; he knew nothing of such dreams of hers, while it made Albert think of the strange dream he'd had when he was in hospital.

'Would you like to tell us such a dream?' he asked her.

'Yes, sure.'

'I was dreaming I was walking somewhere in a jungle, like the one in Colombia, although I had the dream before we went there. I was surrounded by moist trees and a lot of green plants, bushes and huge leaves, which were brightly illuminated by the rays of the sun. In front of me lay an ancient city, maybe an Inca town. It was disengaging itself from the earth, rising from it, as if it had to erect itself and get started again, powered by a big wheel of energy. I could see the wheel turning; it was huge. Every time a large area of ground went open, and tore itself loose from the earth, almost like a hippopotamus elevating itself from the water. It was a truly vast area with grass and trees on it, from under which the next part of the city emerged. It looked like a birth and it gave off a very pleasant, warm energy. In a flash I saw a large stone circle, probably Stonehenge, of which I had once seen a photo. Two white horses were standing in the inner circle, but there were also people busy doing things, working, and I saw a man walking around with two metal 'L' shaped hooks in his hands; dowsing rods, I think, which were moving violently. This same man later entered the old Inca city via a luminous line, where he was regaled with beautiful food by the inhabitants, who probably knew him. In the meantime the whole Stonehenge scene faded under the earth.'

'What a remarkable dream,' Albert said. It seemed to connect with his own dream about the conscious and the unconscious.

'Your dream reminds me of our holiday in England,' Desmond said, 'when Roonah and I visited Glastonbury and the stone circles of Avebury and Stonehenge. Have you heard of the theory of the ley-lines that run along the earth? Apparently, ancient monuments all over the world, possibly Inca cities and settlements too, maybe even undiscovered ones in the jungle of the Amazon forest, are connected by these lines, by energy. And I'm convinced there are a lot of places where that ancient, never-dying, primordial energy is present. There's still so much left to be discovered.'

Isabelle agreed with him and added that some of the images she had seen hadn't only given her a look into the past, but had even literally taken her back to it, while others seemed to belong to the present.

'Don't you all think there's something unusual going on here? I mean, we haven't come here from various corners of the world for nothing. There's got to be a reason, a purpose; something is connecting us,' Roonah said.

Everybody was quiet for a moment.

'You may be right there,' Bernard said.

Desmond suddenly trembled. Behind Bernard, in the corner of the room, he saw the back of a dark shadow.

62

After a good night's sleep in the harbour of the pretty seaside town, Albert, Jack and Steve got ready to go and have a look at the cottages. At eleven o'clock sharp they stood at the door of the estate agent's. It was still closed, but after a few minutes they heard a car hooting. The estate agent got out to let them get into the car. It was a very long drive to the cottages, but it was a super trip; rugged mountainscapes alternated with breathtaking ocean-views. After two hours they could see the village they were heading for.

The man hadn't said a word too much, Jack thought. He was impressed, and noticed Albert looked relieved and satisfied, but would their journey really come to an end here? He couldn't believe it would, after spending so many days, nights and miles together, after all the incredible things they had been through, the countries they had seen, the happiness and sadness they had shared, the dreams, ideas and beliefs they had talked about. It just couldn't. He still wondered what Albert was hoping to find in Ecuador. Was it really all about the work of that painter? Was that the reason why he had to make that enormous journey, or was it an escape? They'd often talked about it, but Jack still didn't know exactly what moved him. He had always had the idea that Albert was secretly hoping, or had a premonition maybe, that somehow, somewhere, he would meet the love of his life again. It wouldn't surprise me if it really happened, Jack thought.

Looking at Steve, who was sitting quietly, gazing around him, ruminating, thinking of his Rosalie, Jack wondered what he was going to do in Ecuador; his plans always sounded so vague, as if he was waiting for other people to take the initiative. But, more importantly, he also wondered how was he going to spend his own days. He didn't know yet, so maybe it wasn't such a bad idea if he and Steve rented something together for the time being, until, perhaps, Steve would like to join him on another trip.

They pulled up near a hostel, where they parked the car and walked to the villas, which looked more like houses than cottages, although there were also some smaller ones, which could be called beach huts, because they were made of wood. The estate agent told them they used to belong to the travel organisation he had already mentioned, but as it had gone into receivership, or was bankrupt by now, he didn't know, they desperately needed to dispose of them.

When Albert heard the price and thought of the rent he had paid for his apartment in Camberwell, he couldn't believe his ears; these were giveaway prices.

'What if I buy two cottages, so that we have a bit more space?' he asked Jack and Steve. 'They're dirt cheap.'

'Thanks, Albert, but I can look after myself. I don't want to live off you,' Jack said.

'Don't worry about that. I can always sell them again. I've lived on your boat for a long time and, besides, you still have your mooring fees to pay.'

Steve walked up to the estate agent and asked,

'What's your best price if we buy two cottages instead of one?'

Albert looked a bit embarrassed, but didn't say anything.

'I'll see what I can do for you. Hang on,' the man said and went to his car to make a phone call. He came back with a smile and told them the cheaper of the two would be half-price, if they bought them right there and then.

That very same day Albert became the proud owner of two cottages, a bigger and a slightly smaller one. Steve said he would be happy to live in the smaller of the two. It was big enough for him and Jack, if Jack wanted to move in with him, and it contained everything they needed, beds, chairs, everything. They both looked at Jack, who finally relented. Both villas were in a beautiful location, on a superb, white, sandy beach with palm trees. There was also a bar nearby and one or two shops.

Albert was very happy with this new place of his own. Although there was some furniture inside, he could already see how he was going to furnish the place with things of his own. On their way to the cottages on the beach they had passed through a small town. It looked quite attractive, and as he was thinking of buying an easel, paint, a roll of canvas and other bits and pieces, he went back the following day. He found most of what he needed and in a bric-a-brac place he discovered some stylish French chairs, together with an old-fashioned turntable and even came across some French vinyl records by Francoise Hardy and Johnny Hallyday, music he had heard at his grandparents'. He picked them up and smiled.

Within a couple of weeks the cottage was transformed from a straightforward holiday villa into an artistic, warm place.

One afternoon he sat down at his easel and looked around him, with a grave, but peaceful look on his face and started painting.

63

Erasmus stood with his legs in the water of the ocean and turned round to face the land, wondering what he was going to do. If he did nothing, he'd run out of money fairly soon. He had to get himself a job, but would anybody here in Ecuador be waiting for someone from Iowa, whose Spanish was lousy and who had hardly any work experience? he wondered. Probably not, he thought, so hadn't he better go back to the U.S. then and pick up his old life there? But then he thought of his father and some other reasons why he shouldn't do that, although he also knew he wouldn't lose his face if he went back to the U.S., for it was his life and it was nobody else's business, but if he wanted to stay here, he needed to earn some money, also because he wanted to live in a proper house or an apartment, as the hostel was only a temporary solution. He would like to rent one of those wooden huts on the beach, if they weren't too expensive.

While the waves were splashing against his calves, he was with his head in the clouds, for this whole place, the beach with its palm trees, the sun, the temperature, the relaxed lifestyle and the good food was a paradise on earth, and everything was very affordable. But he wanted to exercise more, for when he looked at those tanned, muscular men in their white shirts on the beach, and then visualised himself in front of the mirror, he wasn't very happy. He really had to do something about it; his paunch had to go and the muscles of his arms could do with a bit more training too, just like his legs, which he had neglected a bit after the physiotherapy he had had after the accident. He was going to visit the second-hand shop that afternoon and get himself some exercise springs.

Another thought struck him. Why hadn't he thought of it before? How stupid. The answer to where he should start his search for his father was staring him in the face. There were quite a few foreigners, also from the U.S., living here, so this was the place where he could begin, simply by knocking on doors and asking the people in the houses on the beach and the village, he thought, and there had to be lots more places like this one, and it wouldn't cost him anything.

Those people who were at Pepito's yesterday were still at that young guy's place, he noticed, but forgot about them the moment he thought of the waitress in Guayaquil; she was so beautiful. He missed her and her pretty face, and he wanted a bit more happiness in his life. Maybe he should go back to Guayaquil that week to see her.

He laughed at himself, for how well did he really know her and what was he longing for? Love, attention, a beautiful body, sex? Yes, probably all these things, if he was honest with himself. It was a long trip by bus to Guayaquil, but well, he didn't have a job yet and he had nothing else to do. Maybe he could stay the night there too and take this girl out. When he came back here after that he would start his search. Problem solved.

64

Desmond was engaged in a lively conversation, but it was only when Isabelle started telling her dream that Desmond really became interested in what was being said, Albert noticed. Apparently he was someone who only wanted to communicate with others if he liked the content of the conversation and if he didn't, he lost interest and retreated into his own world. He appeared to like what Isabelle was telling him now because he kept asking her questions and told her a bit more about the ley-lines and other interesting things he knew much about.

Bernard clearly wasn't Desmond's type, Albert noticed. He then thought about himself again and wondered if he wasn't a bit like Desmond. He liked a good conversation too and wasn't much interested in superficial stuff or shallow people either. He looked at Desmond again. There was something odd about that man. He wasn't sure, of course, but was Desmond a little bit autistic maybe? But what did it matter and wasn't it wonderful how Roonah and Desmond, in spite of their age gap, had found each other? They were a nice couple, he thought.

'Shall I make some more snacks? " Roonah asked him, but he didn't hear her.

Never mind, she thought, I'll just make some. She went to the kitchen and came back with a plate, asking him if he liked a cheese empanada.

He looked at her in surprise.

'Oh, I'm sorry,' he said. 'I'm terrible.'

'Don't worry. My pleasure. Have a cheese empanada.'

'Thanks. Mmm. That's really delicious.'

'Have you thought about our plan to go to Guayaquil?' she asked him.

He smiled at her.

'You don't let the grass grow under your feet, do you?'

At least she tried to get things organised, he thought, which he wasn't very good at and he thought of the hospital, where she came to see him whenever she could and he remembered all those terrible long nights when he was longing for her, his angel, his light in the darkness, to appear at his bedside.

He could already see it before him how they would all go by bus to Guayaquil, with Desmond sitting next to Isabelle, and he himself sitting two seats behind these two, hoping Roonah would come and sit beside him. Bernard, unfortunately, was the last person to get on the bus, because some locals had jumped the queue. He found a seat in the rear of the bus, next to a big woman with large shopping bags and two children on her lap, speaking some unintelligible words to him.

Albert chuckled.

'But, Roonah, why don't we ask the others to come along with us? I'm sure it'll be great fun.'

They all pricked up their ears when he said this and, apart from Desmond, responded immediately. Perhaps they could get something organised that very same week, Isabelle said. It was as if they were going on a school trip, that's how excited they all were.

'OK. All right then,' Roonah replied.

She wasn't very pleased, but she had no choice. She would rather have gone to Guayaquil with Albert and, possibly, Desmond.

Desmond wasn't keen on organised trips with groups of people at all, but he was thinking of the photos he might take and he didn't mind Isabelle's company; in fact, she was quite charming. It was a pity Bernard couldn't stay at home.

A smile appeared on Bernard's face when he thought he would probably see some good-looking girls and women, and he thought of the beauties he had seen in Panama City and also in Costa Rica. He only hoped he wouldn't have to sit next to that boring Desmond.

Sitting in a corner, Isabelle was quietly looking at the others. She liked Albert and Desmond, while Roonah somehow reminded her of Aquilegia and her own grandmother, two women with attitude. Bernard didn't say a word, she noticed. Could he finally listen to other people?

65

Later that week Erasmus was sitting in the bus to Guayaquil and the lovely waitress, who was becoming increasingly more beautiful in his daydreams. He had all sorts of plans in his head; he wanted to find out if there were any jobs around, and maybe if there was some accommodation for rent as well and of course he would go back to Las Peñas and the restaurant. He had managed to get hold of some exercise springs and every morning he looked at himself in the mirror, hoping he had gained some muscle mass. If only he could have waited for another couple of weeks, he would have had a lot more muscles to show, he thought, but he really needed to find a job.

He looked at the beautiful scenery around him; it reminded him of his wonderful trip in the lorry through Mexico and Guatemala. A few hours later he saw the outskirts of Guayaquil. He got out at the terminal and walked to the restaurant. The closer he got the faster his heart started beating.

There she was, the beautiful waitress. She was even prettier than in his many daydreams of the past week, or was it weeks? She came up to him right away. A badge on her dress said she was called Dolores. He looked at her face and blushed. He guessed he probably looked like the rear fog light of a car himself.

'Hi, how are you? So good to see you again,' he said to her, rather shyly.

'I'm good. Thanks. Happy to see you too. I thought you'd never come back.'

'I did come back a few times, but you were never here.'

'I know. I'm sorry. If I had known when you were coming back, I could have arranged something with my work, but you could also have called me.'

'I know, but I still haven't got a port.'

'Why don't you get one of those old phones then? They always work.'

'Yeah, I might do. Anyway, shall we go out this afternoon?'

'I'll have to ask my boss. Hang on.'

It wasn't very busy yet, so her boss didn't have a problem with it.

'Could you work all day tomorrow then?' he asked her kindly, 'for, as you know, the restaurant's always very busy at weekends.'

'Yes. That's fine.'

They went to the Santa Ana hill, from where they had a phenomenal view of the whole city.

'This is where the city actually began,' she told him. 'I don't much like the rest of the city. It's a dingy, stinking old place,' she added. 'Santa Ana happens to be one of the few attractive parts of the city.'

In the evening they went out for dinner and a dance. The hundreds of lights, reflected by the mirrors of the disco ball, looked like stars in the night sky. While Erasmus was looking at them, thinking of the twinkling in Dolores's eyes, she kissed him. He was on fire. He couldn't believe what was happening to him. Was this his happiness, at last? He remembered Jim and Juanita, their happiness, and now his time seemed to have arrived. He wanted to cuddle, kiss her, make love to her, she was so beautiful. He took her hands, kissed them, saw the lights in her eyes while his were closed, went with his fingers through her lovely hair, smelled her perfume, touched her ears, kissed her nose, lips and chin, while she was stroking his arms softly, holding his elbows, whispering words of love in his ears, and in the corner of his eyes, tiny, crystal tears appeared, of love and sadness, things from home, this honest warmth, her beating heart under his hand, her breasts, her cautious kisses.

They went back to the restaurant to ask if Erasmus could stay the night in one of the hotel rooms. That wasn't a problem at all, which was great, because they'd be able to see each other at the hotel the next day then when she was coming back for work. Erasmus was very happy, but it was so hard to say this in Spanish, so it became a mix of Spanish and English.

She smiled at him.

'You don't have to explain everything.'

'I know, and I can't, but you're so, so spontaneous, and you dance so beautifully.'

'Thank you, Erasmus. You're very sweet. I love you.'

'*Yo amo te*, Dolores' he replied.

She laughed.

'Not bad, Erasmus. Very nice. We would normally say '*te amo*', but I know what you mean.'

Here she stood, right in front of him, with her funny red glasses, his girl, his Dolores.

'Am I dreaming? Is that really you, Dolores?'

She laughed.

'I'm afraid I have to go home,' she whispered to him. 'It's already late and my parents will be waiting for me, but don't worry, I love you and I will see you in the morning.'

'Yes, sure,' he said, although he wanted her to stay with him, lie next to him, all night, every night, forever.

They said goodbye; she got into a taxi and left. He went to bed and looked at the clear night sky through an open window.

That one star, he thought.

The next day, it was still quite early, the sun illuminated a large part of his room. The bright light woke him up and his head was inundated by everything Dolores. He looked around and for a sec he didn't know where he was. The sounds of the city, voices, rattling objects, cars, invaded his room. He went to the window and looked into the brand new day, the blue sky, white, blue, yellow and red houses with shutters all over the place. This scene reminded him of some pictures he had seen, but he couldn't remember where he'd seen them. He concentrated on this thought and suddenly he knew; they were photos of a long time ago, pictures that were triggered by what he now saw. He got goose bumps in the nape of his neck and on his arms, for they were photos he'd seen when his father was still at home. He could see his dad before him; they were holiday snaps his father had taken. How great, he thought and he felt a joy inside, an inner happiness, and the day became even brighter. He tried to conjure up some more images, as he had tried to do before, when he boarded the ship in Guatemala, hoping to see more of his dad, but it was so hard, a bit like when you've struck gold and you try to follow the vein of gold and all its branches. There was one thing he knew for sure: his dad was close to him and next week he would start his search.

While he got dressed a cloud drifted past and concealed the sun. He went downstairs, had breakfast and went into town. Perhaps he could find that esoteric bookshop again, the one where he'd bought the interesting mythology book the other day. It was already quite busy in the street. It smelled of cars, and the bright, optimistic start of the day slowly dissolved in a hazy cloud of exhaust fumes.

What he hadn't noticed the last time he was here were the beggars and the kids in rags, as if they only came out of their hiding-places at the weekend. He was surprised.

By twelve o'clock he was back at the restaurant. There she was, Dolores. He saw her coming, no hovering towards him, in a bright blue dress with yellow adornments, looking absolutely stunning. He could feel her loveliness before she had reached him. She stretched out her hands, put them around his neck and kissed him, her silken skin touching his pale face.

'You're magic, Dolores.'

'Thank you. You too, and I love your wonderful eyes,' she said. 'Let me kiss them.'

'Is that all you love about me?'

'There's nothing about you I don't love, you sweet *idiota*.'

He put his arms around her waist and felt her warmth flowing through his body.

Although it was still early, there were already quite a few people at the restaurant, so she had plenty to do and, unfortunately, not much time for Erasmus, but he was happy to see her wink and smile at him now and then.

'You're gorgeous, Dolores, I love you,' he said whenever she was near him. 'I'm jealous of all the people here, especially the men, who can see you all day and every day.'

Somewhere else in the city centre an old, bright red London double decker bus attracted a lot of attention when it was driving down the street. Here and there a fat, black plume of smoke rose up, mingling with the exhaust fumes from other vehicles. Behind the bus was a hearse with an empty coffin inside, but because of the red double decker bus, nobody took any notice.

66

At the bus terminal, not far from the airport, sighing and puffing, an old bus came to a standstill. The door opened with a squeak and the passengers came pouring out. With stiff limbs they walked off, droves of smaller Ecuadorians and five tall, white people, who had agreed to go from the terminal to the city centre together. Desmond was carrying his photo gear and had decided to wander around the place on his own, Albert and Roonah were going on their 'Flor mission', while Bernard and Isabelle wanted to see the sights. They would meet up later on in a restaurant to have dinner together. The bus driver had given them an address of a place where, according to him, the food was really good.

Roonah and Albert strolled through the city, from one gallery to the next, visited a museum and found Flor's birthplace. They couldn't find any works of his though, but when they got to Las Peñas, and entered a rather inconspicuous gallery, Albert spotted a small painting of the artist.

'Look at this, Roonah, a real Flor!' His voice trembled. 'It's almost too good to be true. I've got to have this. Just look at these colours, the bright red, the yellow, the green, the blue, the composition. *C'est magnifique, fantastique.*'

He spoke to the owner and within minutes the work changed hands.

'Super, Albert. Well done. Congratulations. I'm really happy for you,' Roonah said and kissed him on both cheeks. 'Let me treat you to a drink. I'm quite tired of all the walking and window-shopping. Let's chill out somewhere, my treat.'

The owner of the gallery knew a good wine bar very close by and when they walked past a restaurant and Albert looked inside, he thought he glimpsed the young man he had seen on the beach a few days earlier, the one he'd called and tried to invite for a drink. No, it was impossible, his common sense told him, so he walked on, but after a few paces, he halted.

'Hang on, Roonah. I might be wrong, but I think I saw that guy from the beach, that young man who lives at the hostel, sitting in the restaurant we just walked past.'

She didn't register everything he said, she was so tired.

Mais je ne suis pas fou, bien sûr? he asked himself.

'Roonah, shall we walk back? This is almost too crazy to be true.'

'What? Sorry. Yes, fine,' she replied, but she didn't really know what he was talking about.

She wanted to sit down somewhere and thought it had something to do with the wine bar. She followed him inside, to the table where Erasmus was sitting.

Erasmus couldn't believe his eyes when he saw them.

Albert held out his hand to Erasmus.

'Hello, I'm Albert. Pleased to meet you. This is Roonah, but I believe you've already met.

'How are you?' Roonah asked him.

'Hi, I'm Erasmus. I'm fine, thanks.' He chuckled and said, 'Yes, I've seen her before, but I didn't know her name, but now I do. Nice to meet you, Roonah.'

Erasmus. What a strange name, Roonah thought.

'Is it all right if we sit down?' Albert asked.

'Sure. Grab a chair. I'm just sitting here by myself.'

They sat down, ordered some wine and started talking about Guayaquil, the village where they lived and the cottages on the beach.

Roonah couldn't take her eyes off Erasmus; she liked this version of him much better than the nameless guy she'd met at Pepito's. He had had a bit too much to drink then, of course, but he also looked so much better now, fitter or stronger, happier maybe, and she remembered what he'd said to her at the bar that night. There was something familiar about his face, but she couldn't place it. Now that she thought of it, she'd had that same thought at Pepito's as well. She felt it was almost screaming at her and she thought of the hospitals where she had worked, but she couldn't figure out where she might have seen him.

While they were talking, Erasmus kept looking away from him and Roonah, Albert noticed. It wasn't long before he saw why, for when the waitress came to their table, Erasmus was completely absorbed by her appearance.

What a pretty girl, Roonah thought, the moment she saw her. She looked at Erasmus and saw how he looked at the girl. Am I being jealous? she wondered.

Albert looked at the clock and saw it was time to go to the restaurant, where they'd arranged to meet up with the others. Besides, they still needed to book a table. He asked for the bill and showed the waitress the piece of paper with the name of the restaurant on it.

'Do you know this place?'

She began to smile and said, 'I certainly do. It's just a few doors away. My boss owns it. It is a restaurant only. Here we have a bar as well, but that's because this place is also a hotel.'

'*Gracias*,' Albert said and asked Roonah to come with him.

'If you've got time to spare you may like to join us later,' Albert said to Erasmus and the girl. Oh, and before I forget, you're always welcome in my place on the beach. Just pop in.'

'Thanks very much, Albert, we definitely will, if Dolores can get some time off. Nice meeting you anyway and enjoy your meal. See you.'

'Thanks,' Albert and Roonah said. 'Nice meeting you too. Take care.'

'Don't worry, I'm fine,' Erasmus said, with a happy smile.

'He's a nice guy, isn't he?' Albert said when they were outside. 'And she is lovely too, but isn't it incredible to meet him, here, in Guayaquil? Talking about coincidence.'

'Yes. Remember what I said at your place? There's something funny going on here; some sort of strange, extraneous power is connecting us. Call it Irish superstition, but I'm convinced of it.'

They walked on, still talking about what had happened and didn't see the restaurant, walked back again and found it. They went inside and Albert asked if they had a table for five. That wasn't a problem, so they sat down and waited for the others. It was still quite early, but at least they had managed to get a good table.

Roonah didn't know what it was, but she suddenly felt a certain tension coming up in Albert. She had a good look at him when he ordered a bottle of red wine, but saw nothing unusual. The bottle arrived, they raised their glasses and toasted to their health and a new future.

Only seconds later the world stood still. Albert turned white, red, or red and white at the same time; he almost choked on his wine and his mouth fell open.

'Are you all right, Albert?' She took his hand. 'What's the matter?'

But Albert didn't say a thing; he couldn't utter a single syllable and only stared, frozen in time. She didn't know what was going on, but when she followed his eyes to the door, it became clear. There he stood, a very handsome man with wonderful, dark, curly hair in a white tuxedo; an archangel. She knew it could be only one person, Sylvain. What a hunk, she thought. Albert was very beautiful, but this; sweet Mother of Jesus.

In a split second little Margarita's words flashed through Albert's head: 'Just wait a little and you will be very happy. Everything is near.'

Sylvain had spotted Albert too and stared at him, transfixed. Albert stood up and went to Sylvain. Looking at the table, Sylvain thought that Roonah was Albert's lover, but within milliseconds it was clear to him she wasn't; Albert's heart was still wide open for him. They embraced each other passionately, whispering sweet words to each other.

Roonah couldn't hear them; she just sat there, smiling.

'This is Sylvain,' Albert said with the greatest smile on earth. 'Sylvain, this is Roonah, my other angel.'

'*Enchanté*,' Sylvain said, 'delighted to meet you,' and kissed her on her hand, leaving a waft of lovely-smelling eau de toilette behind.

With a very strong French accent he told them how and why he'd come to Ecuador. He'd gone to Milan for his work and, when he came back after a few weeks and was told Albert had enquired after him, he had gone straight to Albert's aunt, where he heard the story about Flor and Ecuador. He had been able to find a ship that sailed from Marseille to Guayaquil and, after that, he could only hope to find Albert there one day.

About half an hour later, Desmond, Isabelle and Bernard turned up and were introduced to Sylvain. Isabelle looked at Albert and saw a changed man, the incarnation of happiness itself. And there was Sylvain. What a beautiful guy; one of God's most successful creations, she thought. Bernard, however, didn't know what to think. Two men.

Everyone around Sylvain and Albert, even people at other tables, were caught up in the maelstrom of their love.

Sylvain joined them for dinner and they all toasted to the future of these two lovers.

'You look a bit thin, Albert. What's happened to you?' Sylvain asked.

Albert told him some of what had happened in Cuba and how he'd met Roonah, who told Sylvain her side of the story.

'There's one very important person missing here, Sylvain; the man who probably saved my sanity, Jack Weekley. Maybe I wouldn't have been here without him. You really have to meet him; he's been absolutely wonderful. But look what I've found, a picture by Flor. Isn't it fantastic?'

67

A big, dirty man entered the restaurant and went to the bar to have a drink. Around him hung a huge cloud of negativity, which immediately spread through the restaurant and the bar like the smell of dung. Erasmus, who was sitting quietly on a stool, hadn't seen him yet; he was looking at Dolores, who finally had time to come and sit with him. He did notice it had become quiet, but he didn't know why and he was far too happy to be with Dolores to be aware of anything else, until an immensely thick shadow appeared next to him, absorbing nearly all the light in its immediate vicinity. He looked sideways and saw the huge, dark mass. It felt as if he was being throttled. He couldn't get any air and turned deadly pale. There stood the man he had had the fight with on the ship from Guatemala to Ecuador. He'd never expected to see him again, but the guy had apparently been released from police custody. His eyes inspired fear and radiated terror, while they were scanning the place like searchlights, until they found and locked themselves on Erasmus, next to him, while his nose picked up the smell of Erasmus' cold sweat and fear. Like on the ship, Erasmus saw that huge, never abating hatred, that unbridled lust for power and death in the man's eyes. Erasmus, Dolores, and anyone who could see it, shuddered. Erasmus was scared and felt responsible for Dolores' safety, but, sitting on a stool and the man standing beside him, he realised he was in very vulnerable position. The sleazebag started shouting some unintelligible words at Erasmus; his time for revenge had come and before Erasmus had time to stretch out his hands and defend himself, he felt a huge blow, the malicious hardness of metal on his head, the deafening noise of a skull that cracked. It was as if his brains were squashed, split into two and as if his head was moving all over the place.

The beast glanced at his brass knuckles and smiled at them.

Erasmus wanted to hit back, but his arms only dangled for a second or two, like loose yarns of wool, blown apart by a soft breeze. He collapsed, fell onto the floor and passed out.

The man first looked contemptuously at the blood stains on his clothes, then grinned, the terrible smell of an open sewer emanating from his foul mouth.

'Please help me! Please help my Erasmo! Somebody help us, please!' Dolores screamed, cried and called, but nobody stirred.

'Oh God, please help me.'

Total silence.

The monster glared at the almost motionless, bleeding body of Erasmus, spat at it and emptied his glass.

68

Sylvain got up from his chair and gave something to the waiter. A little later the music of Francoise Hardy sounded through the restaurant. It was *Pourtant tu m'aimes*, one of Albert's favourites. Sylvain looked at Albert, changed the lyrics of the song here and there, and sang along with the chorus, ending with *'Et je ne veux vivre sans toi.'* Albert laughed. The words, they were so true.

Other people at the restaurant joined in the singing and drinking, completely unaware of what was going on in the bar-restaurant only a few doors away.

69

Erasmus was still lying on the floor, Dolores bent over him, crying and shaking. He was breathing very heavily, then very quietly and irregularly. He didn't respond to anything from outside, not even when Dolores called, said or cried his name. One of the waiters called the emergency services, but after he had done that, his faculties failed him; he stood there, nailed to the ground, completely bewildered, perplexed, scared, as the filthy, half drunken man was still there, muttering more threatening words, once more spitting at Erasmus' body.

After the first shock effect had ebbed away, some guests stood up, very cautiously. They were inquisitive, scared and quiet; they wanted to pay their bill and get out as soon as they could, but none of them did anything to help Erasmus or get that man. He was wiping his foul mouth on a tablecloth and was just about to leave the place when the police arrived, followed by frightened ambulance staff. The man didn't surrender easily; he put up a fight and hit one of the policemen. They had to use a Taser to immobilise him, while another cop pulled his gun, but he put it back when he saw his colleagues had overpowered the man, who was handcuffed and taken away.

Meanwhile the paramedics were giving first aid to Erasmus, trying to help him in any way they could, but the expression on their faces didn't bode much good. He was put on a stretcher and taken to the ambulance, which then sped off to the hospital.

70

In the other restaurant the tables had been moved to one side; people were dancing and everybody was having a great time. Some guests had seen blue flashing lights, but as they were used to them, they ignored them and went on eating, drinking and singing. After Francoise Hardy some more French 'golden oldies' followed. Albert was singing *Pour moi la vie va commencer* as loud as he could and even people who had only come in for a meal, stayed for the music and the fun, while Sylvain kept giving away rounds of drinks.

The waiters, however, had heard what had happened at the other restaurant and were told that there were some people in their restaurant, probably Americans, who knew the victim, but they didn't feel like interrupting the good atmosphere and, of course, putting their tips at stake. The headwaiter, however, felt it was his duty to inform them; he went to Desmond and Isabelle and told them what he knew, but they had no idea at all what he was talking about and sent him to the table where Roonah and Bernard were sitting, but Bernard raised his shoulders; he wasn't interested and didn't even listen to the man. Why did the fucker interrupt his conversation with Roonah? Roonah couldn't hear what the man was saying to Bernard, because the music was quite loud. The waiter gave up; he didn't want to bother Albert and Sylvain. Besides, they were French, not American.

Isabelle was slowly sinking away into her own, quiet, hazy world and became less and less communicative, while Desmond was still thinking about what the waiter had said, but he couldn't make head or tail of it and, apart from Isabelle, who was almost asleep now, and Roonah, who was looking bored, probably because Bernard was bothering her with his tiresome talk, all he could see around him were happy people, Albert and Sylvain, dancing the night away. Desmond felt for Roonah, but he didn't feel like joining in their conversation; he was very tired himself and wouldn't mind going to bed, but the waiter's question wouldn't go away, so he decided to ask the man what it was all about and was told somebody had been beaten up in the other restaurant and that there were probably some people here who knew him. Being ill at ease, Desmond went over to the other restaurant, but since Dolores had gone to the hospital with Erasmus, no one could help him and, besides, they didn't know anything about the young man; he had only been there once or twice. Desmond switched off; he didn't know anybody who had been to Guayaquil, so he went back to the restaurant where the party was still in full swing and tried to ban the thoughts from his mind. The hotel wasn't too far away and he could really do with some sleep after this eventful day, but he wanted to wait till the rest were ready to go.

Hanging in a chair, her mouth slightly open, Isabelle was fast asleep. Desmond got up from his chair, went to Roonah, and asked,

'Shall we go back to the hotel?'

'Yes, I'll be with you in a sec,' she replied.

She was glad to be delivered from Bernard, got up, went to say goodnight to Albert and Sylvain and left with Desmond.

On their way to the hotel Desmond thought he saw someone disappear into an alley.

'What's that, Roonah? A man?'

'It's nothing, Desmond. Just a shadow.'

Bernard looked at Isabelle.

'Why couldn't you keep yourself under control?' he asked, angrily, although he knew he wasn't going to get an answer. He hated it when other people could see she had drunk too much.

'Could you call a taxi, please?' he asked one of the waiters.

71

At the hospital Erasmus was diagnosed with serious brain damage; he was in a coma and the outlook was very gloomy. The doctors were nervously talking to each other. Would they have to go on trying to save his life, or stop the treatment? In Erasmus' head, however, the world didn't stand still; it was a tangle of thoughts and pictures, images of his mother, his father, a new image where his father looked like that man who lived on the beach, the one with the white hair, and images of P.J., a smiling Mrs Hopper, a beautiful Dolores, Izumi, the temple, a shaft of light, a tunnel, outside.

'There's nothing we can do any more.'

He shouted, without words, without a voice, without a moving mouth. Silence tiptoed on to the rhythm of the second hand. He felt a hand on his face, the hand of a woman? Is it you? Nothing moved. Or is it your hand, Daddy? A picture, a head, without a beard and glasses, a name change, Roonah's friend, President Carter, turned around, around, around. The fool, the moon, the sun, around.

Mrs Hopper drew the curtains	His folded hands opened
Jimmy flew away	A butterfly flew away
The moon	To the pyramid
Darkness	Omphalos
Izumi	Om
Um	ॐ

CdlM

72

The next morning Desmond, Roonah, Bernard and Isabelle were sitting at the terminal, waiting for a bus to take them back to the village on the coast. Their faces looked like wrung-out towels, the result of a hangover, lack of sleep and weariness. Hardly a word was spoken. The air-conditioning wasn't working, so it was hot and all kinds of insects were buzzing around their heads.

'Can you get me something to drink, please?' Isabelle asked.

Bernard was gazing out of a dirty window, pretending not to hear her. It became quiet again, apart from the filthy, buzzing noise of some big, fat flies.

'Yes, isn't the weather beautiful?' he finally said.

'I forgot to tell you, Desmond, but Albert and I met that young guy who's staying at the hostel near us,' Roonah said. 'Do you know who I mean?'

But Desmond wasn't listening; his hands were feverishly feeling for his wallet and his head was thinking about the papers inside.

'What's up, Desmond? Are you all right? You look so pale.'

'I can't find my wallet. Have you seen it anywhere? Is it in your purse?'

'No, it isn't. Didn't you put it in your photo bag?'

'Shit, Roonah, I'm lost without it. My driving-licence, my passport; all my important papers are in it.'

He stood up and once more went through all his pockets.

'Where did I last need it?' he asked himself aloud.

All of sudden, through shrill, ear-piercing loudspeakers, the voice of a woman made an announcement, first in Spanish, then in English,

'A wallet has been found at the information desk. Could the owner, Señor Desmond J. Carter, please come and collect it?'

After reading out the name, the woman closed the wallet again. A photo of a boy fell out. Like a leaf from a tree it feathered to the floor, where it lay still, face down. Some letters had been scribbled on the back, but the name, Erasmus, had become almost illegible; so many times had some sensitive fingers felt the photo.

73

After a long and sleepy journey they came back home. Isabelle and Bernard fell on their bed and slept within minutes. Roonah went to bed too, but Desmond's head was too full. He stayed outside and sat down on the beach, in front of the cottage, the sun in his face, his white hair waving in the soft wind, which felt its whistling way through the white stubbles on his weary chin and cheeks.

Rest in unrest unrest in rest fatigued full of tired melancholy should he change his name back no the fear of persecution always from the רחם rechem his shtetl the tireless endless ocean the infinite sky so divine unlimited in time and space nature does not know time or distance she just is life what can death add to it or six million deaths **yes six fucking million** the day in Dachau the gate the watchtowers the courtyard executions torture barracks beyond it in the corner across the living water gas chambers ovens fire extinguished death ashes couldn't breathe countless souls around his neck so heavy so many too many to whom could he pray to a god who had allowed this to happen Auschwitz two young girls Sobibor a baby boy Bergen Belsen Anne the Shoah an almost paradoxical presence in a failing all encompassing framework of space time and the conscious a shadow dancing with history turning in gyres following running forward sometimes lagging behind a black painting too abstract for mankind to comprehend

> A time within a time
> A frame within a frame
> A pain within a pain
>
> A time without a frame
> A pain without a pain
> A frame without a time

When will we ever learn? he wondered, with cracking, crying brains. A Third World War or any other war senseless useless violence greed and sacrifice when will it ever stop Abraham who was told to sacrifice his one and only child why why why everything who for the quest of life in death. No no full stop death

>Sense less
>A god?
>Less sense
>Less meaning
>A god?
>Meaningless

>Tears in his eyes.
>The sea, the skies
>A watercolour
>Many colours
>Flowing
>Floating
>On water
>Turning
>Turner
>Is God
>Lord?
>My sweet Lord
>Here comes the sun
>Someone's sun
>Someone's son

Sunrise doesn't last all morning
All things must pass away.

The shadow of history finally rose to meet him.
מנא מנא תקל